AIM for the Mayor

Other Books by Gary L. Stuart

The Ethical Trial Lawyer (Arizona State Bar, 1994)
Ethical Litigation (LexisNexis Publishing, 1998)
The Gallup 14 (University of New Mexico Press, 2000)
Miranda: The Story of America's Right to Remain Silent
(University of Arizona Press, 2004)
CONFESS! (University of Arizona Press, 2009)

AIM for the Mayor

Echoes from Wounded Knee

A Novel

Gary L. Stuart

Xlibris Corporation
International Plaza II
Philadelphia, PA, 19113.

Stuart, Gary L., 1939—
AIM for the Mayor—Echoes from Wounded Knee: a novel / Gary L. Stuart—1st Ed.

1. American Indian Movement—New Mexico—History—Fiction
2. Gallup (NM)—History—Fiction
3. Politics—New Mexico—History—Fiction

Library of Congress Control Number: 2008905316
ISBN: Hardcover   978-1-4363-5095-2
          Softcover   978-1-4363-5096-9

This is a novel, and includes fictional characters and fictional scenes, it also includes true
scenes, actual living characters, real names, events, and locales. This is the second in a
series of novels about true events in Gallup New Mexico.

This book was printed in the United States of America.

50146

AUTHOR'S NOTE

On February 27, 1973, the American Indian Movement seized Wounded Knee, a tiny village on the Pine Ridge Indian Reservation in South Dakota, and held it against the will of local, state, and federal forces for seventy-one days. Two days later, March 1, 1973, two young Navajo men seized the mayor of Gallup, New Mexico, marched him through downtown Gallup at gunpoint, and held him against the will of local and state forces for several hours. That much is literally true.

But there is also an emotional truth about what happened. This historical novel is a creative account of the connecting threads between the American Indian Movement, its takeover of Wounded Knee, and the abduction and shoot-out in Stearns Sporting Goods in downtown Gallup. The driving force that laid siege to Wounded Knee and the lesser-known, but just as important, political abduction and gunfight in Gallup welled up from the same melting pot of frustration, indignation, and demand for respect by Indian peoples all over America. The connections between the two tragedies, one national and the other local, is my story based on my research, personal interviews, and imagination. It is a novel, not a narrative history.

There are persons alive who took part in the events described in this book. It is possible, therefore, that some may be mistaken for, or with, the fictional characters who tell the story. But all fictional characters, and their attitudes, belong to me; I made them up. Many of the events in this book are a matter of history and public record. The backstory uses fictional scenes to set this historical novel in context. I used real names, places, and dates to document each historical event as accurately as possible.

The chapter headings are traditional Navajo taboos, which, unlike white-eyes taboos, carry specific penalties for disobeying the ancient wisdom of the people. Most of these taboos were in general use at the time of the events depicted in this book. They were collected at the all-Navajo high school at Fort Wingate, New Mexico, in 1966. Ernest Bulow, the high school teacher who supervised the student project, first published these taboos in his seminal work *Navajo Taboos* (Southwesterner Books, Gallup, New Mexico, 1982). I sincerely appreciate his generous permission to reprint some of them in this book.

CHAPTER ONE

"Don't Throw Rocks at a Whirlwind—It Will Chase You"

Clay Ramsey lifted the battered tin box out of the bottom right-hand drawer of his writing desk. He turned on the desk lamp to compensate for the lack of light in the room because it was a sparse, late-winter day in Spokane, Washington. Shivering a bit, although not from the cold, Clay removed the string-bound packet of yellowed envelopes and the dog-eared, rubber-banded highway map from South Dakota.

Setting the maps aside, Clay turned to the packet of letters, freed them of their string binding, and studied the packet as though there could possibly be something new, even after more than a hundred such examinations. Each envelope bore his name; his adopted city of Spokane, Washington; and Mildred Clark's plainly scribed name, all in blue pencil. The earliest one, postmarked in 1969, showed its twenty-five years of age, yellowed and brittle, not at all like the hands that held it. The newest, if you can call an eleven-year-old letter new, was the only one with a return address. The rest, all in her firm hand, bore no witness to place or time. All of them linked her name to his by a thin blue line, drawn with little arrow points. Pushing his breath out between nearly closed lips, Clay thought his life was as tattered and flat as the letters. He stifled the oncoming rush of self-pity that he always felt when he faced Millie's little blue line and her carefully spaced arrow points. Clay rubbed the thin folds on the letters with his forefinger and then set them aside.

Voices, memories, images of people lost in time, just like me. Gingerly retying the string, Clay replaced the letters and put the map back into its protective tin coffin. His mind wandered back to 1973. Whose story was this anyhow?

Maybe it isn't mine to tell, but by god, it ought to be. *Hell, who can tell it better than me.*

~~~

They came in with a gust of northwest New Mexico wind, a still winter wind, even though it was the first day of March. Nineteen seventy-four looked to be another dry year. The wind pushed bits of sand and dry grasses through the door of the Gallup city hall, which doubled as the McKinley County Courthouse. Two young Indians, herding a ghost white Anglo, made their way up the concrete steps on the east side of the building. The Indians, bony and anxious looking, wore Levi's jackets over flannel shirts, horsehair belts, last year's jeans, and beat-down boots. From a distance, they looked like brothers. Both were dark skinned and wore their black hair long. They had bloodred bandanas tied across their foreheads. Their captive, Delbert Rudy, fair skinned and frizzy haired, looking confused and dazed, stumbled his way up the steps. He didn't look like a captive, but he was.

Two middle-aged women, city employees working the front desk—busying themselves with voter forms, ordinance hearing schedules, and such—were caught midshuffle by the rude wind. As they recreated piles and files, looking askance at the first man, Larry Casuse removed his gun from Rudy's ribs, stuck it in his hip pocket, and asked, "Where's the mayor's office?" Robert Nakaidinae, the second young Indian, quickly shoved an orange-sized homemade bomb in his Levi's jacket and said nothing.

Delbert Rudy, the hapless driver of the car Casuse and Nakaidinae had highjacked two hours earlier in Albuquerque, tried desperately to make eye contact with the women. When that failed, he shoved his hands in the pockets of his cargo pants and stared at the floor.

"He's back there, at the end of the hall," said one of the women, not bothering to look up, ignoring the rawboned Indians in bloodred headbands and their disheveled Anglo prisoner.

Unlike Rudy, who shivered uncontrollably, Casuse and Nakaidinae seemed oblivious to the cold wind. Their jaws were set. Rudy's was slack. Their backs were straight, his was bent, and they marched purposefully while Rudy hesitated. Rudy was obviously not from any of the several Indian reservations surrounding Gallup. Although they had never met, Rudy and Casuse were fellow students at the University of New Mexico in Albuquerque. Their only connection was Rudy's car and Casuse's mission.

Except for the gun and the little ceramic homemade bomb, Indians and Anglos walking together was a common sight in Gallup, the self-proclaimed Indian Capital of the World. Both women ignored the consternation on the Anglo's face and the determined but not quite cocky stride of the two Indians. Likewise, the Indians paid no heed to the women.

Catlike, the two young warriors rolled on the balls of their feet toward the rear of the building. As they approached the door marked "Office of the Mayor, Emmett E. Garcia," Casuse saw a young black-tie-wearing Hispanic man at the outer desk.

"Is the mayor in?" he asked.

"He's busy right now."

Casuse clipped, "Well, is he in or not?"

Looking officially irritated, Black Tie said, "Yes, but as I said, he's busy." The clerk made the mistake of turning his back on Larry Wayne Casuse.

Casuse headed for the office door, flinging his response over his shoulder, "Well, he's gonna be busy here for a long time." Reaching behind his back, Casuse pulled his gun and twisted the door handle. He lunged as if making his way through a downpour, almost ten feet inside before anyone looked up. Nakaidinae took his cue, removed the bomb from his jacket, and tracked his leader.

Delbert Rudy, taking his eyes off the floor for the first time since they entered the building, sensed freedom. He had been with Casuse and Nakaidinae for nearly four hours. He barreled back and out of the anteroom, ran down the hall, out the east door, through the parking lot, and straight across the street into the Gallup Insurance Agency. Safely inside, he pleaded for a telephone and called the police. He managed to give the dispatcher a disjointed description of what had happened to him. He screamed that two men kidnapped him in Albuquerque and were now in the mayor's office with gun and a bomb.

Emmett C. Garcia, Frankie to his friends, sat behind the biggest desk in town. Two longtime city staffers, Paris Derizotis and Red Abeyta, sat on the other side of the desk. Derizotis—more commonly known around town as Pete, an excitable Greek with a distinct accent—was Gallup's coordinator for Alcoholism and Drug Abuse Control. Today's meeting with the mayor, about alcoholism among Gallup's large Indian population, was one at the top of the mayor's priority list and a subject that haunted Casuse. Pete recognized Casuse from meetings they had attended at the Gallup Indian Center. The topic was always one of two things, either the Indian drinking problem in

Gallup or the claim that the famous Gallup Indian Ceremonial was unfair and insensitive to the tribes.

Larry Casuse graduated from Gallup High School in 1971, the same year Frank Garcia was sworn in as Gallup's first full-time mayor. Their paths had crossed at public meetings on alcohol abuse and Indian rights issues, but neither could really claim to know the other. Garcia's initial indifference at the intrusion evaporated in the heat of Casuse's hostility.

Almost casually, Pete said, "You can't come in here, Larry, we're having a meeting."

"Let him in, let him in," interrupted Garcia, glancing up from the report on the desk in front of him and only vaguely recognizing Casuse's face. Pete rose to intercept the men. Casuse pointed his chrome-plated .32 and rasped, "Stand back or I shoot you. Freeze right there."

Everyone did. Casuse squinted at Red Abeyta, the third man in the meeting and the only one he had never seen before. Abeyta was a chronic city staffer who didn't need to be told to "freeze." He held on as if he was in the dentist's chair.

Garcia sucked in air as he remembered the phone call he took a half hour ago. The man said he was a reporter and asked if he could drop in. He wanted the mayor's comments on yesterday's ominous seizing of eleven hostages by Indian militants at Wounded Knee, a tiny hamlet in South Dakota. Garcia connected the voice on the phone with the voice of the man with the gun. *Oh god, could that happen here?*

Garcia was transfixed by the gun in Casuse's hand. "Larry, don't do it. Larry, don't do it," the mayor choked. Trying hard to concentrate but still looking like he was in charge, the mayor sank back into his oversized leather chair.

Casuse lumbered to Garcia's side of the desk. No one else moved. No one spoke. The mayor flinched involuntarily as Casuse gently laid the muzzle of his pearl-handled pistol on Garcia's chest. In a silent taunt, he traced an invisible line up Garcia's chest to his forehead as though he were measuring the path of a bullet with the tip of his barrel. "You, you," snapped Casuse, each word a bullet, a message in itself.

Me? Do you know me?

"I told you I'd get you," Casuse said. He stood still, letting his words sink in. Time stopped. Casuse jumped into Garcia's space and jammed his gun into the mayor's heaving chest.

Struggling to overcome the cold fear that knifed through his chest, Garcia racked his brain to place the man with the gun. *I remember now, that is what you said. You were there in Santa Fe last month at my Senate confirmation hearing. It's you. You hollered at me and embarrassed me in front of the governor. You spit at me when I was sworn in as a regent of the University of New Mexico. But then, you only pointed your finger at me. Now you've got a gun. It's shiny. It looks like a detective's gun, the kind they strap to their ankles on TV. That's a real gun, isn't it?*

Garcia could only mumble, "You, you are him, aren't you? You called me a *false person*. I never did anything to you."

"I will kill you, False Person," Casuse whispered, his anger checked by a vague resignation. He focused through wire rim glasses badly in need of a handkerchief. They softened the glint from the black-tumbled look in his eyes. His dilated pupils loomed large at this close distance to Garcia's face. The little wire frames held small oval-shaped lenses that seemed to contradict the bloodred bandana tied around his forehead. One signaled war while the other seemed to imply peace.

Garcia tensed, pitched out of his chair, and grabbed Casuse's gun hand. *I can force his Saturday night special to the floor.* But he couldn't. Casuse's lithe strength won out. He broke free from a distance of less than three feet, aimed the gun point-blank at the mayor's chest, and pulled the trigger.

Click. *Oh god, I don't want to die.* Click. *What's that mean? Is he out of bullets? Shit, where is everybody?* Then a third click. Casuse grimaced, pulled the hammer back, and tried to fire again. Garcia inhaled. Air plunged down into his hollow chest cavity. He could feel his teeth grating dry against the inside of his mouth. Wonder clouded his eyes, but the tremor in his arms and the flaccid feel in his knees sent a shiver of truth through him. *I'm still alive. How long, god, how long do I have?*

Then, as though remembering a B-grade gangster movie, Casuse used his left hand to rack back the loading mechanism and ram a shell from the cartridge clip up into the firing chamber. That split second gave Garcia the time, and the courage, to try again.

He lunged at Casuse. Casuse stood his ground, trying to fend off Garcia with his left elbow. Garcia grabbed the lower edge of Casuse's Levi's jacket with one hand and fumbled for the man's gun with the other. The second struggle lasted a full minute and initially seemed to turn for the mayor. *I've got you now, you bastard. You stop, damn you, you stop!*

Then the light went away, and he could feel the heat of Casuse's breath. The back of his arms seemed rubberized as he and Casuse slid across the shiny glass desktop, their bodies plastered against one another, arms entwined, feet and legs flailing askew.

Some of the papers and desk accessories flew off like piñon needles. *Remember that little black bear shaking the piñon tree up at McGaffey Park? The piñon needles flew everywhere. That time I was in Dad's truck. Now the bear is in my office.*

There were no blows, just desperate clutches, as both tried to control and push away the little gun at the same time. Casuse's gun finally spat fire. Red and Pete thought the mayor was hit, but it was a clean miss. The shiny glass top exploded as the .32-caliber bullet whirled its way down through it into the walnut top and on down into the paper-filled top drawer.

Inside those drawers, the little bullet punctuated a pile of reports chronicling Garcia's efforts at resolving the Indian alcohol abuse problem. One more drawer down, and the bullet would have hit the papers detailing the growing mess with the federal Urban Renewal project in Gallup. Those political problems took a great deal of Gallup's energy in 1972 and '73, but the life-and-death struggle over control of the pearl-handled gun bore little witness to good intentions.

Their locked arms disengaged as Casuse pushed free, savoring the upper hand. The mayor's white-starched shirt wasn't just a sartorial contrast to Casuse's Levi's jacket. The image of his white shirt over the reflective glass of his desk was one of implied political power. The contrasting image of dark blue denim and a bright red bandanna thrashing about on that same desk spoke to a violent shift of power.

The small muzzle flash and the crack of the .32 had a numbing effect on everyone in the room, except Nakaidinae. Just as Casuse's shot blew a hole in the mayor's desk, Nakaidinae decided he needed a cigarette.

Speaking for the first time, he muttered softly, "I have a bomb. Get it? I have a bomb. I am going to blow this place up." He sounded tentative although the blank expression on his face made him impossible to gauge. Derizotis, never a hand-to-hand-combat man, had no clue about guns or bombs. Nevertheless, he sensed Nakaidinae's distraction as the Indian fumbled a cigarette out of a crumpled package.

Maybe Pete will take his little bomb away.

Pete's nerve flared when Nakaidinae tried to light the cigarette with his free hand. His Zippo flickered as his high-pitched voice worked for authority,

"Stand back, I am going to blow—I have a bomb, I am going to blow the place up."

Maybe he's just run out of courage.

Pete grabbed at the small avocado-shaped pot. The Scotch tape around the short fuse at the top was slick with sweat. The odorous mix of sweat and gunpowder conveyed a sense of doom.

"Man, don't do it," Pete said as he and Nakaidinae battled for possession of the little pot. In Gallup, handcrafted Indian pots became treasures, at least in the hands of the right potter. But Nakaidinae was no potter, and Pete was not a collector. While misguided in hindsight, Pete focused on keeping Nakaidinae's hands apart so he couldn't light the fuse. Rather than trying to take the bomb away, he just pushed Nakaidinae toward the door, and they stumbled through it and out into the small anteroom.

Black Tie was gone, but just then, two other men rushed into the outer office. Chief of Police Manual Gonzales and City Manager Paul McCollum were stunned by the sight of two men with bared teeth, banging against one another for possession of a small bomb.

"Help! Help!" shouted Pete. Red Abeyta had yet to move. He froze just like he was told, but now he could see that no one was looking at him. He scrambled out the door.

Any sane person would have, but what about me?

Agonizing moments felt like minutes and caused Garcia's face to hurt as he shifted his attention between Casuse's contorted face and the gun he kept waving in his right hand. But for just that one instant, Garcia and Casuse were alone in the office. The mayor knew he was not going to talk his way out of this. His election as mayor and his appointment to the University of New Mexico Board of Regents had been based on his apparent sincerity, his solid policy positions, and a natural charisma. As though reading Garcia's thoughts, Casuse recovered both his gun and his composure.

Casuse's voice evidenced a deadly calm. "Get down on your knees."

Garcia bent to the floor. Casuse repeated his mantra, "You are a *false person* and no good to our people. Now it's your turn."

Inexplicably, instead of shooting Garcia, he reached behind his back and pulled a pair of army surplus handcuffs from his belt. Then he handcuffed Garcia, police style, with his hands behind him. The sweat on Garcia's face dripped down onto cracked lips and into his mouth. He licked his lips and tasted salt. Casuse jerked him from his knees to a standing position. The metal cuffs chafed. *A small price to pay for a few more minutes of life.*

Chief Gonzales and Paul McCollum ran from the small anteroom through the double doors into the mayor's office. They nearly collided with Abeyta on his way out and were just in time to see Nakaidinae wrench control of the homemade ceramic bomb from Pete.

Chief Gonzales pulled a black .357 Magnum from the holster on the black Sam Browne belt he had worn for more than twenty years. Ignoring Nakaidinae for the moment, he moved about six feet from the doorjamb to a spot directly confronting Casuse. Gonzales almost banged into Casuse but stopped, nose to nose, with the muzzle of Casuse's gun. Gonzales could smell the gunpowder on the tip of the barrel. His ears still rang slightly as the crackle of the little .32 faded.

Casuse spun to his right and pressed the gun barrel against the nape of the mayor's neck. The chief's black .357 Magnum revolver was a stark contrast to Casuse's shiny little .32 pearl-handled semiautomatic. Taking no apparent notice of the big uniformed man with the gold stars on his lapel, Casuse, slowly drawing in his breath, said to the back of the mayor's head, "Let's go, you're going with us."

Casuse pushed Garcia a foot or two toward the door where Chief Gonzales, with the hammer now up on his .357, both hands in ready-fire position, aimed at Casuse's chest. Casuse seemed surprised to face a bigger gun barrel, and Gonzales tried to make a point of ignoring the pearl-handled automatic.

Damn, damn, if one shoots, the other kills me. Oblivious to the irony, Garcia said, "Don't do anything rash."

Casuse looked away from Garcia and talked to the wall behind Gallup's chief lawman. "Put down your gun. Give it to me."

Chief Gonzales blinked, made a quick decision, and lowered, but held fast, to his gun. They glared at one another.

Was one about to sing his death song? The mayor again implored Casuse not to "do anything rash" and begged the chief to "do what he wants."

"I'll be damned if I will. No one gets my gun. Larry, this is no way to settle anything," Gonzales screamed at Casuse.

"Give it to me right now."

"I'm not going to give it to you."

"You give it to me, or you've got a dead mayor."

Nakaidinae elbowed his way back into the room, now free of Pete's hold and clamping both hands around his little bomb. Sensing the change in battle strength, Casuse said, "Give *us* your gun."

Perhaps out of the same sense, Chief Gonzales conceded, "I'll give it to you, but I'm going to empty it first."

"Don't you dare," Casuse warned.

Gonzales slowly looked Casuse over, smiled, and took the dare. He flipped the chamber open on his .357 Magnum with one hand and, with all the authority he could muster, dumped the bullets out onto the mayor's turquoise-colored carpet. Then, with a one-handed snap, he closed the chamber and handed the gun, butt first, to Nakaidinae.

At first Nakaidinae seemed confused. Should he take the gun or hold on to his little bomb? Without really deciding, he took the gun, pocketed the bomb, and said, "Gimme that big belt too." Chief Gonzales, without a pause or a change in his smile, unbuckled the large chrome buckle and handed the heavy belt, holster, leather ammo loops, and shoulder strap to Nakaidinae.

Casuse nudged Garcia toward the hallway with his gun tucked into the nape of the mayor's neck. Chief Gonzales and Paul McCollum stood aside and watched as Casuse pushed Garcia through the double doors and out into the antechamber. Nakaidinae tagged along as though he were an arms carrier, bringing up the rear with his bomb, the chief's gun, and the chief's ammunition belt.

They marched down the hallway to the small porch on the east end of the building. Casuse reached around, manhandled the door, and pushed Garcia down the steps and into the wind. Mayor Garcia asked, "What do you intend to do with me?"

"We're gonna march you around the state 'cause you're a *false person.*"

"Are you going to kill me?"

"That's my intention."

CHAPTER TWO

"Don't Spit on a Spiderweb—You Won't Be Able to Breathe Right"

Virgil Bahe was born in 1971, two years before Casuse and Nakaidinae abducted Mayor Garcia. Like Casuse, Virgil was born on the sprawling Navajo reservation near Chinle, Arizona. His mother, Mary, who didn't talk much, and his aunt, Millie, who did, raised him. His father, Charles Bahe, was a traditional Navajo, happy to let the women in the clan raise the children. He raised a little hell and a lot of laughs for both clans. When his father married, he had to marry someone outside his clan; that way, the blood would be strong and produce healthy children. But Charles Bahe also knew he could create a better economic reality for his family off the reservation, or the Rez as nearly everyone called it. That's why, eventually, Charles left the Rez for better work, and better pay, down in Glendale, Arizona.

The big move was twenty-five years ago. Virgil's mom, dad, two younger brothers, and three dogs went to Glendale, which turned out to be next door to Phoenix. Aunt Millie stayed behind but went to California the following year. Virgil was seven when his aunt told him his life was going to change. "You're moving down to a big city, Virgie Straight Nose." That's what she called him, Virgie Straight Nose.

Even then, Virgil's angular face, high cheekbones, and sharply formed nose set him apart from other Navajo boys on the reservation. He was taller than his friends and his many cousins. But he had the same musky skin tint, mysteriously dark eyes, and coal black hair. While his nose was his distinguishing feature, his hair was pure Navajo, shiny even when dry and straight as a soldier's back.

"But why? What's wrong with living here? Are you coming?" Virgil asked his aunt.

She looked down and was quiet for a while. "No, your parents need to get better work. Remember when you were little and I left the reservation and went to California to go to school?"

"No."

"Well, I did. But I always came back every summer. That's what you'll do too. You'll come back every summer, and we can have our fun. And everyone else will be here. They will always be here. You, your mom, and I can visit every summer. I promise."

"What's *visit* mean?"

"Well, you know when we go to Ganado or to Window Rock and we see people in our clan and we have a *sing* with them? White-eyes call that a visit. Don't worry, little one, I will visit you down there in Glendale, and when you come home to the Rez the summer, I'll be here, just like always. This will always be your home. This is where 'the people' are."

"You mean the Diné, don't you?"

"Yes, our people, the Diné, have lived here for thousands of years. That's why I come back to Chinle every summer. My clan is here." She frowned at Virgil and asked, "You know your clan, don't you?"

"Yes, I was born *to* the Whitewater clan and born *for* the Old Canyon clan."

"Well, those clans will always be here. I come to visit them, and now you will too. You will like it down there in Glendale. I've been there. I know. They have a better school there."

So Virgil's family moved. It was a better school. They went back to the reservation every summer, but Virgil didn't always see his aunt up there. At the time, he was too young to understand, but his folks and the rest of the clan quit talking about her.

Virgil wondered why his mother looked down at the floor the first time he asked if his aunt would be in Chinle when they went there for the summer. "No," was both her answer and her explanation.

When they got to Glendale and he and his brothers went to a white school, he asked his mom if it was like the one in California where his aunt went. "No," she said again and left the room. So he quit asking.

Everyone had an answer for the move though. It was always work and school, work and school. He thought they were the same thing. His father explained, "Virgil, all of us can be better if we leave the Rez for a while. I can get work that pays more money, and your mother will be better too, once she is over her *yíinííł.*"

"*Yíinííł?* Why is she sad?"

"Because her sister is going away again, and now we are leaving too. She loves the Rez. So does your aunt. But sometimes we have to go away to make things better."

Ten years later, Virgil went to Arizona State University in Tempe, and three years after that, his little brother enrolled. Their older brother went to work up north somewhere. So far, Virgil was the only one to actually graduate from college, but he knew his older brother would too, someday. He said he wanted to be a lawyer, but Virgil had his doubts. Actually, Virgil's aunt graduated too, but he did not know that for a long time because they quit talking about her.

Now Virgil was back on the Rez just as they said he'd be. He had visited Chinle every summer. But now, living in Window Rock, the capital of the Navajo Nation, things were different. After all, he was a man now, an *ashkii.*

Virgil worked in the Navajo Tribal Office of Tourism and thought his job was interesting, most of the time. Virgil's culture, everyone in Window Rock called it "the Navajo way," fascinated the white-eyes. When Virgil and his brothers were kids in Chinle, they called tourists and the store people in Gallup white-eyes. Their mom and her sister said that was not proper. They told them to speak Navajo, call them *bilagáana.*

Part of Virgil's job was to write things about the Rez and the Diné. They made signs, brochures, and posters so the tribe could turn the *bilagáana* tourist's fascination into good old American cash. Navajo alchemy, he called it.

The Navajo tribe hired him because he was the only Navajo that applied for the job and the only one who had a college degree in marketing. Virgil's motive was simpler; he took the job because he wanted to come home.

Navajos are loosely organized around clans. Each Navajo belongs *to* the clan of his mother, but is *born for* his father's clan. Clan membership is important to Navajos because it clarifies relatives. Virgil's job means he has to tell tourists the long version, the one the tribe wants everyone in the tourism office to use. "Clans are best described as sentimental links, which bind together Navajos who are not biologically related. They need not have grown up in the same locality and may indeed have never seen each other. This sentimental bond gives rise to occasional economic and other reciprocities. Sometimes clansmen who accidentally discover each other at a large gathering will exchange gifts. A Navajo will always go out of his way to do a favor or show preference for a clan relative even if the individual in question has not been previously known."

Virgil read over the long version, his first day on the job. He thought it would interest some white-eyes even though it took too long to say. He preferred to give tourists who came into the information office his own version. "Clans are like Irish families. They stick together through drink and thin." He made up that little joke, knowing it wasn't all that funny. Navajos, at least some of them, drank too much and were too thin. You could say the same about Hispanics, Anglos, and almost everyone else who lived on the Rez.

He learned about the reservation and its clans from the ground up. And he knew it had been the subject of an intense study for over a hundred years. Scholars estimate there are about sixty Navajo clans. Most had been carefully cataloged by anthropologists from Ivy League schools and historians from the West Coast. Their academic view of the cultural and historical role of Navajo clans was predicated on its importance to social control. Virgil accepted the academic notion but didn't see much in Window Rock that was either "social" or "controllable."

The modern reality on the Navajo reservation was that the "chapter house" controlled most everything. A chapter house is like the civic plaza in Santa Fe or a Starbucks in Albuquerque. Everybody shows up and argues about everything; and then, although nothing is accomplished, everybody feels better.

Years ago, all clansmen were jointly responsible for the crimes and debts of each clan member. That made it everybody's business to prevent other clan members from committing crimes. If a member of your clan stole some sheep or a rug, you might have to pay for it. Some smart-ass down at ASU told Virgil it sounded like communism, Navajo style. Maybe he was right.

Virgil's last name is fairly common; there are many Bahes on the Rez. They named him Virgil because his mother and aunt said it stood for being smart in an ancient culture. He looked it up when he first got to ASU. He was not a poet, that's for sure. He could write, but poetry complicated life whereas prose explained it. He guessed his aunt and mother didn't actually read Virgil; otherwise, they would've named him James.

Virgil spoke Navajo as a first tongue although his tongue was a bit thick. Occasionally, the words curled up inside his mouth instead of sliding out. That's because his family only spoke Navajo in their home in Glendale. There were no other Navajos in the neighborhood, and Virgil was the only Navajo speaker in his school. By the time he went to ASU, it felt a little like a lost language. His dad told him his "tone" was okay, but he didn't always get the delicacy of the language of the Diné.

The Navajo Tourism Office in Window Rock had a little infomercial on the twenty-first-century reality of the Navajo language. Off-the-Rez Navajos like Virgil had some difficulty with Navajo because many of them lost the tone once they left the Rez. Navajo is a subgroup of the Athapascan branch of the Nadene language family. Linguistic research confirmed the Nadene-speaking people arrived in the Four Corners region about three thousand years ago.

Virgil took great delight in explaining the nuance and subtlety of the language to visitors of the Rez. While the entire Navajo vocabulary consists of only a few hundred words, there are over thirty ways to say *wind*.

Like Chinese, Navajo is a tonal language. The pitch of the voice distinguishes the meaning of a word. American tourists in Europe only think they face a language barrier. Virgil had one too, right there in Window Rock, the capital of Navajo speakers. Only in Virgil's case, the barrier was elusive and harder to touch. It is like trying to feel the sound of a bird early in the morning. It sounds soft, but soft is also a feeling. The Navajo tongue is felt as well as heard by native speakers. His off-the-Rez tone made him just a little bit different from his cousins and childhood friends who were born and who stayed on the reservation.

Virgil's beyond-the-Rez world made him part of a new breed of educated Navajos. Many of them were returning to the Rez to work and learn more about their ancestry and culture. Most of them returned alone. Virgil returned to the Rez with a *bilagáana* girlfriend. He told her he worked in a salt mine. Life, on or off the Rez, needs sugar as well as salt. April Ryan was definitely sugar but tended to complicate Virgil's search for a more simple life.

~ ~ ~

"April, it's me. Are you there? Pick up. What's the deal, you hiding behind your so-called job again? Been calling all day and . . ."

April fiddled with the key in the front door lock as she heard her phone ring. She tripped over the doorjamb and couldn't make it inside before her new answering machine kicked in, and she heard Vigil's familiar clipped tones.

Grabbing the phone, she interrupted, "Virg, wait, I'm here but just barely. Let me get my bag off my shoulder. God, books weigh a ton. So you've been calling me all day. Really? What's up? Things on the Rez slowing down? But wait. Don't answer that. I've got a lot to tell you first. I spent the day at the library, and I can definitely see the light at the end of my outline. I'm nearly through with the research for this story I'm writing about the sand dunes and the red rocks. I think it will sell, god, I hope so. I'm tired of editing everybody else's stories."

"April, are you sure that light isn't a porcupine's eyes? They shine in the dark, you know. We didn't have any porcupines down at ASU, but up here, well, they'll stick you pretty bad at the end of the tunnel. Maybe that's what you are seeing downwind in the tunnel."

"Where do you get that stuff? Porcupine's eyes that glow in the dark? Besides, don't kid around so much. It doesn't become you. My work and this story about those beautiful red rocks and the mysterious sand dunes just east of here should really interest you, even more than me."

"Why?"

"'Cause you're a Native American. You are supposed to relish your heritage. Right?"

"Right, but part of it is pure politics, and that's where the Indian, or Native American if you prefer, gets the short stick. If your point is that the stick is a little longer because so many tribes have gambling casinos, I'll go along. However, the Navajo do not gamble, at least on our own reservation. That's another story. Hey, I'm happy about you getting on with your story. When do you quit outlining and start writing?"

"Soon, very soon. I have enough in the outline to get a good first draft. And the new stuff I found today is icing. What's up with you?"

"Well, for starters I want to know if you have the book bag off your shoulder yet," Virgil said, hearing April's breathing return to normal. "You must have because now you're unloading your mind. Could you take another breath and maybe say hello? how are you? You know, social stuff. It makes the world a civilized place."

And so they talked until well after midnight.

Virgil bumped into April eleven months earlier in the Memorial Union at Arizona State University. She was in the food line, and he spilled his tray on her. "Lovely," he said.

She took one look at him and agreed. Of course, she didn't tell him so, not then anyway. Virgil was getting his BS degree in marketing. April was trying to find a job after spending five years as an English major. A bachelor's degree in English doesn't mean much in the job market. Marketing, on the other hand, is something every business needs.

Because Virgil found a marketing job in the Navajo Nation, April followed him, at least as far as Gallup. She went to work as a copy editor for Red Rocks Publishing and rented a small apartment in Gallup, twenty-five miles from Window Rock.

April spent her day off working on her story at the Octavia Fellin Public Library. She'd barely scribbled the last note on her outline when she heard, "Closing time, miss." The librarian-looking person seemed irritated because April didn't scoot out the door so she could too. Instead, April lugged three books from the reference table on Indian culture and "the Navajo way" up to the checkout desk.

April's apartment in downtown Gallup was modest to the point of being meager. Looking at her duplex from the street, the stacked apartments ran horizontally alongside one another like the pueblos the "ancient ones" built centuries ago in Chaco Canyon. Those early pueblos were built for small people. At five foot five, April fit just fine. Virgil, at six foot three, made it crowded.

The bathroom mirror reflected April's reality. *I'm plain*, she thought, *damn it, just plain.* Her skin had that well-scrubbed Irish look, and her eyes were a pale shade of blue. As she studied her face in the foggy mirror, she smiled at Virgil's nickname for the generous room he called the "masterful bath." For some reason, the kitchen was smaller than the bathroom; Virgil labeled it her "minor kitchen."

April braided her long chestnut-colored hair as her mother's words came back to her, "Honey, attractive is better than pretty." Some guy, of the one-date variety, had described her as attractive; and she took it as an insult. She thought again, as she did too often, about what her mother said and came to the same conclusion she always did; it was only marginally better than the comment made by the jerk himself. She loved her mother and knew she meant well. But *attractive* was not pretty.

She finished the single braid and flipped it behind her. It made her feel like a kid again. She teased her flyaway tendrils and adjusted her undershirt over her "bone thin" chest. That's another thing. What is *bone thin*? Virgil came up with that one. When she pressed him, he backed off and said something like, "Well, it confirms you're a vegetarian."

Just what does a vegetarian look like? Slim for sure. But bone thin? Is that what passes for a compliment out on the Rez these days?

As usual, her makeup *was* limited to colorless lip gloss. Not counting, of course, the moisturizer she'd already used. It smelled unsullied. April asked her mom once what she meant. *Unsullied* means *not* like perfume. After all, April was a writer or, at least, wanted to be. She was definitely not a shopping queen. And she lived in Gallup.

Most things in Gallup are unsullied. It's a place where ancient Indian culture surrounds but doesn't always blend with Hispanic and Anglo families who are firmly in control of the economy and the politics in northwestern New Mexico.

April hoped to write creative nonfiction. Half the people she met in town said, "What's that?" The other half didn't bother to ask. Like most small towns, Gallup had storytellers who wrote fiction and reporters who wrote nonfiction. How could a story be creative nonfiction?

Her most striking feature was her accidental fondness for freckles. Growing up Irish and in Phoenix and having spent too many hours in the sun had given her an Appaloosa look. "Freckle-face" was a childhood burden although her face, even then, was angular, not round or childlike. She stuffed her undershirt into her jeans, completing what her mother called her "uniform." *Fair comment*, she thought even though her mother did not offer it as a compliment. Virgil, seeing her in a dress the first time, said, "You carry yourself well," as though *that* was a compliment. Her wry retort at the time made her feelings clear. "Bone thin and carrying herself well is hardly what a woman wants to hear."

On the upside, April knew a good part of her attractiveness, at least to Virgil, was her posture. That's something else she could thank her mother for; she never slumped. Her uniform outfit included an ASU Sun Devils sweatshirt and heavy winter boots. They were, of course, new Western boots. Virgil took her into an old-time boot shop five months ago when she first got to Gallup.

As always, she finished off her daily dressing regimen with the sanded light blue glass pendant, which dangled from a beaded leather thong. Despite Virgil's persistent questioning, not to mention almost everyone else she met in Gallup, April kept the significance of the necklace to herself.

The pendant always felt cool to her touch. She thought she could make it change from light to dark blue. Her mother's brother, Uncle Clay, gave it to her on her thirteenth birthday.

"But the why, Uncle Clay," she asked after opening the box, "why does it change color?"

"Because you're holding it, little girl, and the warmth of your blood makes it change."

"I'm not a little girl. I'm thirteen, remember?"

"And so you are. Actually, that's why I picked this for your present. This is an old Indian stone from the Pacific Northwest. It's given to young women when they come of age. It tells them that their future is in their hands because if they hold it just right, it will change, just like the future."

"But why does it get darker, Uncle Clay? Does that mean a dark future or what?"

"No, not darker necessarily. It will get deeper and more complicated. That's what happens when you get a little older. Life gets complicated. Just remember, you can control your life just as you can control the color in the pendant. Hold on to it, and life will change. Let it dangle, or sit in a drawer, and life will probably be the same. It's your choice, April."

CHAPTER THREE

"Don't Stare at the Moon—It Will Follow You"

Where have all the warriors gone? The question rang like a song that would not leave Clay Ramsey's head. He was the founding, managing, and *only* editor at the magazine known for thirty years as the *American Warrior*. However, he was not the boss, not anymore. Americana West Publications, parent company of the *American Warrior*, had cut staff, including all of the other editors, over the last decade. Boss or not, if Clay Ramsey didn't know where they'd gone, who did?

Clay's desk matched his face. Both were cluttered and bore the telltale signs of too much use and not enough renewing oil. The desktop's red oak mirrored Clay's typically Irish ruddy complexion, just as the gray green of his eyes complemented the scattered olive-colored file folders. His red hair, sand-colored by time, matched the unruly mounds of notes in the folders labeled with the comings and goings of America's warriors.

The late-afternoon phone call from the accountant-promoted-to-CEO at the home office in Denver lasted about an hour; but the fiscal problem, the main reason for the call, began ten years ago.

"But, Warren, you have to listen to me," Clay pleaded. "The *American Warrior* led the charge, defining and advancing the causes of all of America's warriors from the sixties to the nineties. Now the problem's different."

"How so?" Warren Suttcliff asked as politely as he could.

"Because the nineties were not good years for warriors. Politicians did well. The new economy and the Internet thrived, but not the warriors. The thirty-year struggle for Indian civil rights and tribal sovereignty produced warriors who made a difference and, sometimes, a splash. Damn it all, Warren, you know I wrote and edited full-length features about all of them."

"Yes, you did, Clay. You made some of them famous and some of them mad. You even inadvertently caused the capture of one or two when they broke the law. Hell, I remember you outed one or two, accidently, to the FBI. But telling the truth about those old warriors is not relevant anymore."

"Not relevant? They fought the right fight for the right reason. Why isn't that still relevant?"

"Clay, I didn't call to argue with you. I know you religiously refused to write about drugstore cowboys or wannabe warriors who fought just for the hell of it. With you at the helm, we refused to publish stories about the egomaniacs that fought for the wrong reason. Nevertheless, you know I never quite agreed with you that the wrong reason was always something intensely personal."

"Warren, I believe that those who fought for personal causes were inconsistent with the greater cause, the greater glory. To use your word, their personal causes were 'irrelevant.' But my point is that I killed every single story about someone who fought for martyrdom or money."

"You did. You always believed in causes, even lost ones. You covered every lost cause in the last thirty years because all of them sang to you. Occasionally you missed the melody, but you always got the percussion. The deep throbbing, the clang of the cymbal, and the ear-piercing sound of 'charge' gave passion to your editing and substance to our magazine. But those days are over, Clay."

"Why are they over? Those stories were 'big breath tales.' They chronicled things like respect for common people, treating the earth as though it belonged to everyone, and making things safe for everyone's grandchildren. Those ideas are still relevant, aren't they?"

"Sure. Nevertheless, life comes full circle. Now we have new issues and new young people, on and off reservations. We just can't keep bleeding the coffers dry to publish what no one really wants to read anymore."

Clay knew he was talking to the past. "All right, Warren, have it your way." He hung up and leaned back in his chair.

I was their salvation. Now those same warriors will be mine. It's my turn to pick a fight. I will save what I built. The boys back in Denver at the home office will have to toe the line. The long-gone warriors needed my editorial voice to make their case to the American public. Now I need their drumbeats to save my life. It's that simple.

How could he stir the dead? Fuming at reality was not enough.

You illiterate bean counter, how dare you ask me that? How dare you even imply that my American Warriors are relics and that your readership doesn't care about them anymore? The readers are out there. You ought to be glad some full-blooded Sioux isn't sighting his carbine on you at this very moment.

Clay lowered his chest and sighed aloud.

They are gone. Only a few of us remember the beat of the drums and long to hear them again. Those brave men and women are not relics. They are just not in the news anymore. They're still out there—gray headed, potbellied, and at peace, that's all true. But they still believe.

And Clay Ramsey believed in them. The black phone on his desk took on the shape of his boss—dark, silent about the future, and politically correct. He stared at the Mute button, wishing his boss had one.

What do you believe in besides money? Would you fight for money? No, sir, I don't believe you have a fight in you. You are not a warrior. Those guys would have left you back in camp, with the dogs and the yearlings.

Clay believed he could save himself. It came to him just today, literally within minutes of slamming down the phone. The phone call gave him the "official" word that the current issue of the *American Warrior* would be a phase-out issue.

Maybe he couldn't save his magazine or its legacy, but he could cut himself out of both. For three decades, he had been so intertwined with the *American Warrior* that the man couldn't be sucked out of the editor. He wasn't a yolk to be separated from its white with the shell still intact.

Am I the yolk or the white? She asked me that as we looked at Alcatraz Island that cold October morning in 1969. Why do I think of her so much now that even saying her name is painful? God, how stupid I was. It's Millie, damn it, Millie. Why the question, and why no answer? Was I that afraid of you, or was it your vision that dwarfed mine? Alcatraz and Wounded Knee. They were shrouded in equal measures of glory and defeat. What defeated us, Millie? Can you tell me that?

Clay moved his spiral notebook from side to side on the desk with his tooth-marked number 2 blue pencil. The lined-out, eraser-worn lines on the yellow page glared up at him.

Where have all the warriors gone? Can an editor write, or is he doomed to edit the work of real writers? Can he write a historical novel? One that will beat the old drums so loudly that the next generation of warriors will hear them. So clear that the last generation will read it, stand up, and whoop again? That's what my book, my life-saving book, will do.

Clay's memory of America's warriors was the linchpin of his life. The back-at-camp bosses in the home office showed little interest in supporting his novel. He believed they owed him that, at the very least.

"You're an editor, not a novelist," Warren said condescendingly. That truism was hardly the point. They ignored his effort at diplomacy when he suggested that management could at least take his proposition to the board. The board of directors would never see his concept.

Novels, they think, are for the masses. The new mission statement of Americana West Publications is creative nonfiction. The bastards are probably planning a series of coffee-table books. Where have all the flowers gone?

Clay's fuming relented just long enough to recall something Custer said 125 years ago, "It's time to dismount and fight on foot." So he dialed information and asked for April Ryan's number in Gallup, New Mexico.

To hell with 'em, they can stay in camp. I'll beat this drum all alone. Alone, with a little help from my niece.

~~~

April Ryan's third interrupting phone call of the day made her already-frustrating day a bit more so. "Yes," she said, with an uncharacteristic rasp to her voice.

"April, is that you?"

With her hand over her forehead and her teeth clenched, she quickly atoned, "I'm sorry. I didn't mean to bark at whoever you are. This is April, and I'm glad you called, whoever you are."

"It's me, Uncle Clay. So, Ms. April Know-it-all from ASU, what's the matter? Is the Indian Capital of the World getting to you?"

"Oh, Uncle Clay. Finally, someone calls to talk instead of trying to sell something. Is something wrong? Is it Mom? Oh god, what is . . . ?"

"No! Wait, April, nothing's wrong. And before you decide I'm not trying to sell you something, maybe you'd best hear what I'm selling. Your mom is fine, far as I know anyway. Why did you think my sister would have me call you if something was wrong anyhow? I mean, she is my little sister, but she thinks I'm a book nerd who would forget to call you even if she did ask me to."

"Oh, that's great. And I'm really sorry about answering that way. Don't tell Mom, okay? So, how are things in Washington? Believe it or not, it's probably warmer up there than it is down here in Gallup. Man oh man, do they ever have some kind of winter here. It's probably only a few degrees above zero, and it's almost 10:00 a.m. here—what is it there, are you an hour earlier or what?"

"It's just shy of nine here and going on thirty-five degrees. So let me tell you why I called, and then we can catch up on your foray into Indian country and the perils of working for a small publishing company. How would you like to do a little digging into a story for me? It shouldn't take too much time. I'm going to write my first full-length novel."

"Are you serious—really, really serious? Of course I will, I mean, I would—you know what I mean. What's the story, and how can I help? Why me? Is it about Gallup or what? I'm so glad you're going to do a novel. Will I be named in the book as your investigator, and will you thank me at the end, and all that stuff?"

"April, April, you haven't changed in the year since I've seen you. Still playing hopscotch and jumping from squares to circles, aren't you? I said I need your help to dig into a story, and maybe, only *maybe*, you could find out what happened in a political abduction case in Gallup about thirty years ago. Authors, especially novelists, are always looking for help. And yes, I will acknowledge you in the book although that assumes it ever gets published. We're a long way away from that day."

"How long?"

"Beats me. But it might take two or three months to dig out the facts, then a year to write the book, then another two after that before it gets into the printing and publishing cue."

"Man, I might be dead by then. And that assumes I ever get out of Gallup alive. What do you want me to do?"

"I want you to do some library research for me. I'll pay you for it. Mind you, I said *pay*. There will be no advance against royalties. Those belong to me, got it?"

"Okay, whatever you say. Call it what you want, but I'm going to list it as 'chief investigator' on my resume. What's the story, and why me? Don't they have the Internet in Spokane?"

"Sure they do. But that's actually the point. You are in Gallup, and the story I need some digging on is a Gallup story. Have you heard, since you've been on parole there, about a big deal back in 1973 when Indian militants abducted the mayor? The mayor's name was Garcia, a Hispanic, I presume, and the young Navajo's name was Casuse, Larry Casuse."

"Nope. Never heard a word. I've only been here for a few months, and I wasn't even born in 1973, so maybe everyone here keeps secrets from people

---

31

as young or as new as me. What happened? Why was the guy, the mayor I mean, abducted? You mean like for ransom or what?"

"Well, to tell you the truth, the motives seem clear, maybe a little too clear. In 1984, almost eleven years after the abduction occurred, a New York feature writer named Calvin Trillin included the Gallup story in a book he wrote about killings and murders and such. In fact, that's the title of his book, *Killings.* The Gallup story was just one chapter. I'm pretty sure Trillin got the facts correct, but there may be more to the story than he saw at the time."

"Why did it take eleven years to write the book?"

"Well, I think Trillin might have written a short piece about the Gallup abduction in the *New Yorker* a few years before 1984."

"Gosh, it must have been a big story if it was in the *New Yorker.*"

Clay smiled to himself, feeling good that his twenty-one-year-old niece, reared in the West, recognized how much it took to get published in the *New Yorker.* As they chatted on about the research, he began to feel that he'd made the right choice, for the wrong reason. April was there, on the ground in Gallup; but maybe, just maybe, she had the kind of imagination and spunk that could not only do basic research but also do some content editing down the line.

"To tell you the truth, the big story I would like to write is *not* the Gallup abduction story. However, it may be an important piece of the puzzle. The bigger story is about the American Indian rights movement, which fired up in the late sixties and then died out in the seventies. Do you remember Wounded Knee?"

"Sure, I majored in English lit, Uncle Clay, remember? I cried when I read the book. All of us did even though it was required reading at ASU. We all more or less buried our own hearts when we read the story. And I was working on a project with an Apache girl, and she and I talked a lot about it and . . ."

"Sorry, April. Wrong century. You're talking about Dee Brown's bestseller on the massacre of women and children at Wounded Knee in the 1880s by the U.S. Army. The one I'm talking about is the siege at Wounded Knee by a militant Indian group called the American Indian Movement, or AIM for short. That happened almost a hundred years later, 1973 to be exact, at the same location as the original massacre. By 1973, Wounded Knee was a little hamlet in South Dakota, part of the Pine Ridge Sioux reservation.

"Uncle Clay, I have to be honest, it came up in class, but that's all I remember about it. What was it about? I mean, why did it happen?"

"It's complicated, but the militant group that seized the village, and held eleven people hostage, were Sioux who wanted a return to the old days, the days of self-government—the Indians called it *tiospaye*, that is, government by traditional chiefs, headmen, and respected spiritual leaders. There was an elected government at the time, but many saw it as a puppet of the BIA, a much despised part of the Sioux tribe, even though all of them were at least half-blood Sioux."

"And, tell me again, what was AIM?"

"I know quite a bit about the American Indian Movement, make that AIM. It was formed just a few years earlier and not that far away, in Minneapolis, in 1968, by two Chippewa Indians, Dennis Banks and Clyde Bellecourt. They grew very fast. They claimed to have over three hundred thousand members by 1972, all over the country. Russell Means, a central figure in AIM, was a member of the Oglala Sioux tribe even though he was raised in California. They were an enigma to many because while they did many constructive things, they did everything in a violent and disruptive way. The siege at Wounded Knee was not constructive, but it met many of AIM's political goals, principally to bring the plight of all reservation Indians to the national spotlight."

"Yes, but what did they actually do at Wounded Knee?"

"It started with a funeral of a man named Black Elk in the nearby town of Manderson, South Dakota, who was a distinguished elder and medicine man. His death and the presence of U.S. Marshals energized about 150 AIM members, all armed to the teeth, to form a caravan and drive to Wounded Knee, just a few miles southeast. They took over the tiny town at gunpoint and occupied a trading post, the museum, and a few houses. They took eleven people hostage, one of whom was a Jesuit priest at the church, which they also occupied. Within a few hours, more than a hundred FBI agents, BIA police, and armed U.S. Marshals surround the small area, setting up roadblocks on the four roads that came together in the center of Wounded Knee. Both sides fired shots, a few minor injuries occurred, and the stage for what turned out to be a seventy-one-day siege was set. But that is somewhat beside the point I am interested in for my book. What I am wondering now is whether AIM's siege of Wounded Knee is somehow connected to what happened in Gallup. That's what I want you to research for me."

"Oh, right. I knew that. Our English lit prof mentioned the seventies thing in relation to the original event when we were reading the *Bury My*

Heart book. What do you mean connected? Were you there, smoking a peace pipe or maybe something else? It was the seventies, wasn't it?"

As soon as she said it, April regretted it. Her uncle Clay was something of a family hero because he was a man of letters, and funny besides. Even though he sounded awfully serious in this call, April bit her tongue and made a quick promise to mind her manners. So it came as no surprise that Clay responded the way he did.

"Now don't smart-mouth me this soon, young woman. Your mother taught you that, didn't she? I'm the boss on this job."

"Right. This is business. But in Gallup, everyone's a smart mouth. Now about the American Indian movements . . ."

"Singular, April. It was the American Indian Movement. Russell Means wrote a long book about the movement in 1995 and centered his book on what happened at Wounded Knee. In fact, it was his book that got me started on my project, and that led me to Trillin's book where I learned about the Gallup abduction story. But unfortunately, Means doesn't mention Gallup in his book, other than in passing, and he doesn't connect the siege at Wounded Knee to the abduction in Gallup."

"So what's the connection then? I mean, if he doesn't think so, why do you?"

"The timing, for one thing. The siege at Wounded Knee began on February 27, 1973. Two days later, on March 1, these two young Indians abducted Gallup's mayor, marched him through the streets at gunpoint, and then barricaded themselves in a gun shop. The abduction ended in a gun battle with the police. That is exactly what happened at Wounded Knee, which was 915 miles away. Militant members of different tribes demanded respect by taking hostages and fighting gun battles with the police. Maybe they aren't directly connected; but they involve the same kind of people, the same issues, and the same result in the same week. Maybe what happened in Gallup was a pure coincidence. But then again, maybe it wasn't. That, among other things, is what I want you to dig into."

"Were the Indians in Gallup part of the American Indian Movement?"

"That's part of the investigation. AIM was a nationwide movement involving lots of Indians. My guess is that we'll find that AIM was pretty active down there in New Mexico, but I'm not sure. The two Indians involved were Navajo, and Gallup is the trading center of the Navajo reservation. But the University of New Mexico was also involved somehow. In those days, local Indian rights activists went by a variety of names. AIM was really a movement, not just a group. It seemed to have broad membership although there were no dues, meetings, or secret handshakes. I'm just not sure. I expect that the Gallup group and the Wounded Knee group had similar gripes, similar goals and that both used violence to state their case. They wanted recognition and respect. And they weren't afraid to hurt innocent people to get it. Taking over public buildings, taking hostages, and making demands were the name of the game in the seventies. You were too young to remember any of that."

"No, Uncle Clay, I don't remember that, but I was alive then, and I can read now. I'll get up to speed, you'll see. Where do you want me to start?"

"Start where all historical researchers start, at the public library. They do have one there, don't they?"

"Yes, the Octavia Fellin Public Library. Ms. Fellin is a very well-known historian. I'll start there. What did you say the date was?"

"The siege at Wounded Knee began on a Tuesday, February 27. The abduction in Gallup was two days later, Thursday, March 1. Why don't you e-mail me with your reactions and give me a list of what you find. See if they have a newspaper morgue file at the library, that's often a good source. And run a check through their computer for political stuff back in the seventies and biographies on anyone you find who is connected to the story. A word of caution, don't start with the Trillin book—it's quite judgmental. You can read it later. I'd rather you just get the raw facts for now, and then we'll work out a plan. The Gallup investigation is only the first start. And, April, make your e-mails brief. If you have lots to say, do it in a separate document, and then just attach it to the e-mail of the day."

Clay and April caught one another up on family doings and then rang off to tackle their assigned tasks. Clay spent the rest of the day indexing and making notes on *Where White Men Fear to Tread: The Autobiography of Russell Means.* As he flipped back and forth through the grandiose text, he lingered on the title and its vaguely ominous warning about white men fearing. Fearing what?

I'm white. If there is a connection between Gallup and Wounded Knee, am I the right man to write about it? Do I have a right to write about this, or should I too "fear to tread"? Is this a book I can write? Do I have enough Indian in me? I've never manned a barricade.

Clay wrote about militant movements but was never part of one. His was an intellectual affinity, not an emotional one.

April had no such doubts. She spent the rest of the evening in the library, digging through the Gallup File, two large metal filing cabinets containing an alphabetically sorted group of disconnected facts about Gallup. This was a researcher's dream. There were five full drawers in each cabinet crammed with Octavia Fellin's entire collection of bits and pieces of Gallup history, gossip, and stories. This "file" contained firsthand as well as less reliable source material that spanned a fifty-year period. April combed through manila folders until, almost at closing time, she found one marked "Mayor's Abduction File." She read, made notes, read some more, and leaned back in her chair. She closed her eyes and tried to compose the essence of the e-mail she'd send to Clay. Maybe there was a connection. Maybe the Gallup abduction was not merely coincidental to Wounded Knee.

~ ~ ~

"I'd like to see the file and the transcripts in an old criminal case if I can, please?" April said to the small dark-eyed woman on the other side of the counter in the office of the district court clerk. Once inside this wonderful 1938 three-story adobe building, April could feel the soothing that comes from hand-painted adobe murals on the walls and Saltillo tile floors. She was on the second floor, one floor above the mayor's office.

"How old is the case? Do you have the docket number?"

"No, sorry, no number, but I do have the date. This is a case that happened in March of 1973. The mayor was kidnapped, his name was Emmett Garcia and . . ."

"Oh, you mean Frankie. Frankie Garcia. I knew him from way back. He was a good man. I wonder whatever happened to him. But the case wouldn't be in his name 'cuz he was the victim. You need the defendant's name. I forget what name that was."

"I have that, it's right here in my notes. Let's see, it was Nah-kay-din-ee. That's spelled N-A-K-A-I-D-I-N-A-E. But I'm not sure I'm pronouncing it right."

"You're not. Pronouncing it right, I mean. Think of it as two words, first is 'nah-kay,' that means Mexican, then 'diné,' meaning Navajo or the people. So that name means Mexican-Navajo. Loosely translated, it means Mexican Indian. I remember the name, but not the defendant. What happened in the case? I forget what finally happened. It was probably a long time between the crime and whatever he got. And that's why I forgot."

"Thanks for the help on the pronunciation. Actually, I don't really know what happened yet, that's why I need the file."

"Well, I can look it up for you, but I probably can't get the grand jury transcript now. Maybe it was not even transcribed, but the docket entry file will show that. I'll be back in a minute."

It wasn't a minute; it never was in Gallup. Thirty minutes later, the clerk returned with a microfiche roll of film and a brief instruction sheet on how to use the reader and print copies, as needed, at ten cents a shot. How hard was that to find, April thought, as she threaded the filmstrip onto the reader and looked at the heading on the first page, "Criminal Cases, McKinley County, 11th Judicial District Court: Case No. 3851. *The State of New Mexico vs. Robert Nakaidinae.* Offense: 3rd and 4th Degree Felony, Judge Donnelly." The case name, the felony charge, and the name of the judge were all written in longhand as was the rest of the form.

The first file entry, dated March 5, 1973, said, "Filed entry of appearance—Joan Friedland."

April remembered Clay's instruction to record all names and dutifully started her "cast of characters" list with Joan Friedland. She added Judge Donnelly, Robert Nakaidinae, and two other judges, Zinn and Musgrove. They had apparently disqualified themselves in the case at some earlier point in time. She wondered what caused their disqualification.

The first three pages of the file, which the clerk called a "docket sheet," contained handwritten entries from March 5, 1973, to November 29, 1973. The last entry unceremoniously noted, "Issuance & File Penitentiary Commitment." Altogether, there were fifty-nine entries, none of which told her much of anything about the case. The docket sheet implied that justice in New Mexico was swift but vague back in 1973. The rest of the file consisted of various motions and rulings. Louis E. DePauli and Joseph L. Rich were the prosecutors. The clerk had told her that Judge DePauli had recently retired and that Judge Rich was now upstairs, in Judge DePauli's old courtroom no doubt. Apparently, prosecutors became judges as a matter of routine in New Mexico.

The grand jury handed up a six-count indictment on March 9, 1973, signed by the jury foreman, Adolph A. Barraza. Joan Friedland, Nakaidine's lawyer, filed a motion to have the indictment quashed because the foreman was the only person who signed it. She argued that New Mexico law required the entire grand jury to review the indictment after the prosecutor drew it up. She lost. Nakaidinae's trial, initially scheduled to begin in Gallup on July 23, 1973, was moved to Albuquerque and reset for October 9, 1973. April wondered why the trial was moved from Gallup. Scrolling a little farther down into the microfiche, she discovered that the prosecutor wanted a change of venue "because of public excitement or local prejudice in Gallup." He wanted the case moved to Aztec, New Mexico, but the judge moved it to Albuquerque. There was no explanation about why a local prosecutor thought he could not get a fair trial in his hometown while the out-of-town defense lawyer thought Gallup was just fine.

Friedland was discharged not long after the trial date was initially set. A new lawyer, Thomas E. Horn, from Albuquerque, replaced her as defense counsel. Horn wanted the trial moved back to Gallup, which might explain why Nakaidinae changed lawyers. Apparently, everybody from out of town liked Gallup, but no one in Gallup wanted the trial there. Judge Donnelly denied his motion. The jury trial started in Albuquerque on October 9, 1973; but according to the file in Gallup, no verdict was rendered. The file was silent about the length of the trial, the result, or any other information about it. April realized that when the case was transferred, so was the file.

The next docket entry, November 29, 1973, somewhat casually mentioned that Judge Donnelly discharged Nakaidinae's bail bond and sentenced him. To what and for what, she wondered. April asked the clerk about the ambiguities and gaps in the docket entries. "I dunno. Maybe because they transferred the case over to Albuquerque, there is more stuff over there. You could go upstairs and ask Judge Rich, he was at the trial, you know."

"Thanks, I will check with the clerk's office over there. How can I get a copy of the grand jury transcript? That is a public record now, isn't it?"

"Sure, once the case is done, we can give anyone a copy. I'll get them to print one out, and you can pick it up in the morning if you want it."

April got the 129-page transcript the next day. It contained the sworn testimony of eleven witnesses. She spent the rest of the night writing up a short summary of what happened after Mayor Garcia was marched out of his office by Casuse and Nakaidinae and down the street toward Route 66 in the heart of Gallup. As she read over her draft, she could almost feel the mayor's terror and the Indians' anger.

CHAPTER FOUR

"Don't Tell a Person to Go to Hell—It Might Happen"

March 1, 1973

Stearns Sporting Goods, Gallup, New Mexico

Garcia, still limping slightly from a three-week-old sprained left knee, stumbled across the parking lot from city hall to Second Street. Casuse, pressing his .32 directly into the nape of Garcia's neck, could almost feel the push from the small crowd behind him and made it clear he was done talking. But Garcia, who always talked, tried to understand what was happening with an incoherent series of *why* and "what did I ever do to you" questions.

"Don't talk," Casuse said to Garcia. "I've heard enough of what you have to say."

It was just as well that the mayor had to shut up. Fear coated his throat as though he'd sucked in a spiderweb. As Casuse and Nakaidinae marched Garcia, north on Second Street, in the direction of the railroad tracks and Gallup's famous stretch of Route 66, the private march turned into a public spectacle. The crowd instantly appeared from hastily parked cars, suddenly opened shop doors, and quickly evacuated offices. The mayor, looking unprotected in his shirtsleeves, felt the fear of death and the sense of disgrace that Casuse wanted. The city attorney, Bill Head, fifteen feet behind but walking in the middle of the street, would later say that Garcia looked like a man being walked to his own hanging. The crowd seemed to double every half block.

Casuse constantly swung his gaze from Garcia's neck to the crowded sidewalks and back to the official entourage of police, lawyers, and city officials, who had been witness to his first attempt to kill the mayor in his office. Now they were to bear witness to his humiliation and possible death. He relished the attention, the feeling of power, and the certain knowledge that now, finally, he was doing something—no more talk, lots more action. He'd gone from speechmaker to gunman in a matter of minutes. Nakaidinae had gone from senseless follower to bomb thrower but didn't seem to realize what was happening any more than the gawkers on the sidewalk did.

Some shop owners had the good sense to stay inside, but as soon as the troop passed, they were on their telephones. In minutes, a good part of Gallup knew of the abduction and feared the worst. Garcia's terror, Casuse's anger, and Nakaidinae's shuffling were intensely monitored by Chief Gonzales. His smooth face seemed calm, and his lock-tight jaw seemed ready even though his Sam Browne belt, loaded with ammo, and his .357 Magnum were draped over Nakaidinae's shoulders like battleground booty. Everyone who knew Chief Gonzales could see in his face that familiar dogged focus he could bring to bear on lawbreakers in Gallup—Indian, Hispanic, or Anglo; he played no favorites. He was marching behind them, with his chest and chin pushed out, in a half crouch like a linebacker, waiting for the ball carrier, teeth gritted, ready to bust someone. That, along with the gun Casuse held to the back of the mayor's neck, made it clear that this was not some macabre joke.

Garcia's face, now completely drained of color but flush with fear, was painful to watch. The first reaction by onlookers was a blend of amazement and curiosity—women held their hands up to their mouths, men tightened their jaws and motioned to one another. Although indefinable, the contrast between Garcia's obvious terror, Casuse's indifference, and Nakaidinae's mounting nervousness spread like an infection through the crowd. Marching to an 1880s lynching could have been no less somber. Of course, everyone in a town of eleven thousand knew the mayor on sight, but not everyone knew the chief of police. And almost no one knew Larry Casuse or his ghost partner, Robert Nakaidinae. But today, their focus was riveted on the man with the gun. Casuse, warming to the attention, stuck out his chest, held his head high, stiffened his gun hand, and began to swagger. His dark eyes darted back from Nakaidinae to Garcia's neck and back over his shoulder to Chief Gonzales, trailing anxiously ten yards to the rear.

Without uttering a sound, Casuse demanded that everyone on the street look at him. Everyone did, not knowing why Casuse picked Garcia, or Gallup, to vent his terrible rage. The crowd began to inhale deeply, think the worst, and follow along like sheep to the edge of a cliff.

The men paused, moved on, and then headed north to the intersection of Second Street and Route 66. There Casuse ordered Garcia to turn east toward Stearns Sporting Goods, a few doors down, on the north side of the street. As they did, Garcia saw Ivan Stearns, the store's owner, walking ahead of them, with his back to them, east on the sidewalk some fifty or sixty feet in front. Stearns had just locked the front door of his store, intending to take his afternoon coffee break at the café four doors up the street. His back was to the growing but silent parade. Accordingly, Stearns was blithely unaware that his store—which held Gallup's oldest and largest supply of rifles, shotguns, handguns, and ammunition—was about to become a theater of war although some later called it a theater of the absurd.

This was Gallup's busiest street, bounded on the north by the Santa Fe railroad tracks and on the south by dozens of bars, Indian traders, boot shops, and the tourist traps that Gallup had become famous for. As the bizarre troop rounded the corner, crowd in tow, the traffic continued blithely by, unaware of the drama about to unfold. Chief Gonzales, City Manager Paul McCollum, Pete Derizotis, City Attorney Bill Head, and various other officials and less-than officials followed as though in tow by the two Indians and their captive. Other city employees, like Bob Noe, witnessed the abduction but chose to stay in their offices, no doubt to make sure the city was still open to business no matter what that "crazy" Casuse demanded. But the buzzing phone lines all over town carried the message of a gathering storm. Almost everyone who got a call got the message—some Indians have captured the mayor, and it looks like they are going to kill him.

Gallup had experienced a strikingly similar scene in 1935 when Sheriff Carmichael and two striking coal miners died just two blocks away. The 1935 parade down the same street also involved lawmen, lawbreakers, and a hostage. Some in the crowd wondered if history was about to repeat itself.

The city officials in tow on the street and the private citizens following on the opposing sidewalks were not following at what the police tactical manual called for as a safe and prudent distance. On the contrary, the city officials and the mushrooming crowd inched even closer on the heels of the obviously angry man with the gun, the closed-mouth boy with the bomb, and Garcia. For his part, Garcia, while looking petrified, nonetheless managed to maintain a dignified if not confident stride.

———

At first, the gathering townspeople were intrigued and then moved collectively to mass consternation. Everyone in town had read the story in that morning's *Gallup Independent* about AIM's takeover and capture of town officials and storekeepers in the little hamlet of Wounded Knee, South Dakota. Now, right before their eyes, they were witness to the same thing here in Gallup. For one day, at least, Gallup would occupy the media; and the Navajo, not the Sioux, would be on camera and lit up like a prairie sky over a brush fire. As unbelievable as it might have sounded the day before, the terror of the townspeople in Wounded Knee was overcoming Gallup. But they thought, *Our Indians are peaceful, aren't they? These are Navajos, aren't they? They don't look anything like those wild-eyed Sioux who call themselves warriors. These are just boys, aren't they?*

Traffic in both directions slowed but didn't stop. Horns blared, police tensed, and everyone gawked at what was either a death march or a bad joke, depending on how serious you thought the problem was. Some noticed the mayor's slight limp and remembered that he'd only been off his crutches for a few days. His injuries from an automobile accident in Arizona a month before seemed of little consequence now.

The fifty-five-foot walk from the street corner to Stearns Sporting Goods took less than two minutes. Stearns had a large plate glass window next to a single-pane plate glass door. Casuse told Nakaidinae to go in first. Nakaidinae tried and said, "It's locked." Had he had his choice, Nakaidinae would have just walked away.

"Break the glass," Casuse ordered.

Nakaidinae did exactly what he was ordered to do. He used Chief Gonzales's unloaded .357 Magnum as a sledge on the doorjamb. The noise of breaking glass alarmed the crowd. Until now, there had been no sound from the three in front. Given the mayor's precarious position, no one did anything. Now was not the time for something foolish. Within seconds, the three men were inside the store. Casuse secured the door from the inside with the oversized black steel slide bolt. Shattered glass covered the floor just inside the door. As they made their way through it, the sound of crunched glass sobered an already anxious bunch of cops on the outside. Casuse and Nakaidinae felt secure, which might have been more than a little bit foolish because everyone out on the street could see them plainly through the eight-foot-square plate glass window. The fact that he could be seen by his friends *outside* was of little solace to Garcia although Casuse likely hoped that his comrades-in-arms could see that he was taking action and in charge.

The police hastily set up a barricade on the sidewalk. Cops, merchants, customers, bystanders, and their families quickly gathered on the lee side of the makeshift barrier of yellow tape and borrowed garbage cans. In small worried groups, they began the inevitable wait for the abductors to make their demands. Speculation spread like high-grade oil over and through the crowd. Rumors about motivation and political causes ran the gamut from the release of political prisoners to respect for Mother Earth and God only knows what they want.

Ten minutes after the now silent standoff began, the busy downtown traffic still flowed by Stearns Sporting Goods on Gallup's Route 66. Nobody, including the police, even thought about stopping the audiotape recording of the events "live and on the scene" by Ken Leopold. He was about to become the most famous radio journalist at KGAK, Gallup's most popular news and country-western music station. And much to its surprise, KGAK was also about to become a real voice in America's Red Power movement.

Immediately after Casuse barricaded himself inside, Leopold started taping "live" interviews with people on the street. Pete Derizotis, the first to be interviewed thirty feet from the plate glass window, regaled the radio audience with a quirky rendition of the drama inside the mayor's office, which preceded this "awful thing." He told everyone within KGAK's hundred-mile wattage area about the struggle in the mayor's office, his effort to take Nakaidinae's little clay bomb away from him, and how Casuse tried to kill the mayor with his little silver gun. City Manager Paul McCollum spoke in a calm, collected voice, recalling Casuse's almost-comic effort to shoot the mayor without racking a round into the chamber of his semiautomatic pistol. McCollum also explained in some detail how Casuse forced Chief Gonzales to give up his gun by threatening to kill the mayor, just before the staged march from city hall down Second Street to Stearns Sporting Goods. Several other bystanders offered their speculation about what might happen, long before anything actually happened. Leopold's dramatic recording would win him, and KGAK, a Pulitzer Prize in 1973.

Like most small towns, Gallup had a vibrant grapevine. Word spread faster than a spiderweb in a dark barn. Nakaidinae was not from Gallup, but Casuse and Garcia were members of large families. Within minutes, members of both families arrived at the scene and waited, side by side, to see which of their loved ones would emerge. They did not talk to one another; and Leopold, although he tried hard, could not get anyone from either side to speak into his microphone.

Police families also raced to the scene. The Gallup Indian Community Center, two blocks away, emptied; and scores of Indians, some activist and others just curious, waited in silence. Every shop owner, for two square blocks, closed up and headed for Stearns. There, mostly silent, they waited; before it was done, almost everyone in town who had a telephone, a radio, or a police scanner was tuned in. The burgeoning crowd had no one to cheer, much to fear, and almost no rational explanation other than the vague drumbeats from Wounded Knee, South Dakota, 915 miles away. The families hoped for the best but feared the worst. For the first time in their lives, they knew the feeling of helplessness that comes with watching tragedy unfold, all the while knowing that nothing they can do now will alter the outcome. All the talking, negotiating, planning, and funding was, for now, not enough, at least it was not enough for Larry Casuse—he wanted action and attention; and he had captured both.

Captain Cordova and Lieutenant Swoboda of the New Mexico State Police joined their local police counterparts. McKinley County Sheriff's deputies arrived as did most elected public officials. Notwithstanding the arrival of the state police, everyone knew Manual Gonzales was in charge. He stationed himself, armed with a rifle and a radio, alongside the brick wall, three feet from the partially shattered plate glass door into Stearns Sporting Goods.

Farther up the street, Ivan Stearns and his friend Ed Lente alerted to what had just happened behind them, turned, and helplessly watched as two angry young Navajos seized Ivan's prized gun collection. There was little to do except wait. Just over one hundred civilians shuffled and strained for better views and more rumors. Irrespective of position or interest, all of them waited to see what Casuse would do with the man he publicly called a *false person*.

As Casuse and Nakaidinae continued to move around in plain view inside the store, the crowd started feeling Gallup's cold March wind. Police gripped their weapons with both hands, aimed, and waited for the command to fire or holster their weapons. They knew they could shoot to defend themselves, but short of that, the decision to open fire belonged exclusively to Chief Gonzales.

A few in the crowd, perhaps lulled by the quiet from inside Stearns, started to hum and speculate in whispered tones about the imponderables surrounding access by two obviously outraged young Indians to hundreds of guns and thousands of rounds of ammunition. There was a gnawing suspicion that Casuse and Nakaidinae were mirror images of the front-page pictures of those *other* Indians, the ones back at Wounded Knee. Someone said the

"Sioux warriors" on the front page of the *Albuquerque Journal* that morning were not "Navajo boys." Last night's dramatic images of desolate Wounded Knee, overshadowed by hovering attack helicopters, fearsome-looking APCs, and hundreds of newsmen and cameras. By comparison, the Gallup abduction and forced march down the street, while scary, was bloodless, so far.

The crowd murmured that those in Wounded Knee must have a lot more to gripe about than did Gallup's "own" Indians. They talked about what was happening in South Dakota and compared what they read in this morning's newspaper with what they were now seeing with their own eyes.

The hundred or so Oglala Sioux behind the barricades in Wounded Knee claimed "lack of respect and sovereign rights" among their many complicated motives. They sought to establish the Independent Nation of the Oglala Sioux. Those lofty ideals seemed remote from the two young Navajos behind the plate glass window. Casuse, the leader, without a doubt, and Nakaidinae, obviously just a follower, were inexplicably silent. Other than continuing to call the mayor a false person, neither had spoken a word, much less made a political demand.

Rumors ran into and over the facts while theory struggled to obtain its proper status as the motive for this whole mess. The crowd spread the stories of Derizotis and McCollum around and learned bits and pieces of how some college kid from Albuquerque had been carjacked there, drove the bad guys to Gallup, and then escaped with his life. Everyone rightly assumed he was halfway back to Albuquerque by now. Truths, and half-truths, about Casuse's very personal vendetta against Garcia surfaced, smoldered, and were passed on. But the crowd's most important questions remained unanswered. What are they doing in there? What do they want? Is this about Casuse and his troubles with the law, or is it about Garcia and his politics? Or could it be that Casuse had to do *something* today just because those Sioux guys in South Dakota did *something* yesterday. Some in the crowd were a little proud of Casuse but didn't say so. Some felt good that there was no more talk. *We are human beings too*, they thought.

The term *copycat* was popular in current fiction and in crime stories in newspapers. Is that what this is? Both sides had guns, and both sides were under intense pressure to have their drumbeats heard. With each passing minute, the need to be heard could be drowned out by the need to regain control. The crowd outside Stearns could see Garcia, Casuse, and Nakaidinae inside.

"Robert," Casuse said, "go and take all the guns off the rack. And load them up. And see they're ready to fire."

Nakaidinae was at first confused as to who would guard Garcia if he did what Casuse said. Nevertheless, he roughly pushed Garcia farther back into the store and began pulling rifles and shotguns from the west wall and lining them up on the glass countertop near the front door. Nakaidinae would later say that he was as surprised as Garcia was to find himself in a gun store with a hundred cops outside, waiting to "shoot to kill." This was something that he wrote songs about, but not something he ever wanted to do.

Garcia tried to shake off the used-dishrag feeling in his knees and the numbness that seemed to have overcome his jaw. He looked around for something, anything that might help him escape. It had been forty minutes since the first rush inside his office. Now his blood pressure was back down, he no longer felt clammy, but the handcuffs behind his back had brought not pain to his wrists but an ache to his shoulders as he forced himself to stand straight up to avoid the pain. He flexed his shoulders and tried to get some movement into his hands, which felt almost numb from the steel bands around his wrists. He still felt a little nauseous, but he felt calm and able to think about his situation.

He'd been in Stearns before many times because he had gone to high school at the same time as Ivan although Ivan had gone to Cathedral High. They met on and off the football field and had become good friends as their fathers had been before them. But as he looked around the store, he had the feeling that he'd never really looked *at* what was in it. There were more guns, knives, ammo, and hunting gear than he had seen in his entire life. He'd never fired a gun of any kind and felt like he was in a museum full of foreign implements of war. In a museum, death by one of the collected weapons was abstract. Here he could smell it. To him, it had a rotten, gamey smell. In time, he realized that it was the combined sweat of three very scared men that permeated the small store. Beyond Casuse's show of bravado, he was starting to understand that Casuse had arrived at a spot he never planned and had no idea how to get out of their common danger. He could do what he said he wanted—kill Garcia—but he would die doing it. Both hunter and captive understood that now. So since Casuse seemed incapable of planning anything or stopping the oncoming gun battle, Garcia looked for a way out.

Garcia had no real understanding as to why or how shotguns differed from rifles. His term as mayor thus far had put him in daily contact with the police department. So he knew, in the sense that any civilian knew, that some handguns were bigger than others were; nonetheless, he always got revolvers mixed up with semiautomatics.

One of the police officers outside, Capt. Frank Gonzales, was a good friend. When Garcia saw him through the plate glass window, it reminded him of a conversation they had just a week ago. The mayor was on one of his "ride alongs," trying to get a handle on the problem of alcohol abuse in Gallup, when Gonzales said, "You know it's really hard for a police officer to hit a moving target. And it's particularly difficult if the target is close to the shooter." The moral of that story, or so it seemed to Garcia now, was that if you were about to be shot anyhow, you might be better off running away. As Garcia looked around the store for an escape route, his casual conversation with Capitan Gonzales, the chief's younger brother, took on a new *albeit* dim promise.

All three men jumped when the phone clanged in the rear of the store. It rang, it rang, and it rang. "Aren't you going to answer that, Larry?" Garcia asked.

"That's not for us," Casuse grunted.

"But it could be."

"No, it's for the store."

"Maybe they're trying to contact us."

"You shut up. I already told you that. You're a *false person*. I don't want anything out of you."

There was a glass case full of bone-handled hunting knives on the east wall. Casuse, apparently angered by the phone call, broke it open and pulled a new vicious-looking knife out of the rack. He ran his finger down the cutting at the edge of the blade to the point where the serrations stopped and the blade arched upward. His eyes matched the glint of the blade off the fluorescent lights.

The phone clanged again. Garcia said, "Why don't you just answer it."

"No, shut up."

"Well, Larry, maybe you should let me call the police then and tell them not to do anything."

Nakaidinae chimed in, "That might be a good idea. Maybe you should let him call them."

But Casuse didn't. He began to prod Garcia around and around the counter as he studied Nakaidinae and his fumbling efforts to load their growing pile of guns on the glass countertop. Nakaidinae's obvious lack of experience with guns was beginning to wear on Casuse. "Don't you know which ammo goes in which gun?"

"I know the difference between a shotgun and a rifle," Nakaidinae said as he picked one of Ivan Stearns's shotguns for himself. He loaded it and pointed it at the mayor. Then, as if to prove to the boss that he could load a revolver, he picked up the captured Sam Browne belt from the floor where he'd dropped it after Casuse told him to bring it with them when they left the mayor's office. Opening the cartridge pouch, moving slowly and deliberately, he took six of the chief's own bullets and reloaded the black .357 Magnum. Then he threw it on the counter with the newly loaded rifles and shotguns.

Hearing, or maybe just sensing something, Casuse held up one hand and put his first finger over his lips. Pointing to the rear of the store, he then cupped one ear and leaned toward the back door. Stearns store backed onto an alley, which was used only for trash pickup and stock delivery to all the stores and bars on the block. Like most of the others, his door was heavily bolted; but unlike any of the others, his was solid steel. It had a large brass bolt lock and an iron crossbar to protect against entry from the rear alley. Garcia and Nakaidinae listened but heard nothing. The bolt and bar were doing their job. Then they heard a low rumble, like a bad muffler on an old truck, but the noise was out front.

Garcia turned and saw a Gallup Police cruiser line up directly in front of and less than six feet across the sidewalk from the front window. As calmly as if he had been showing a tourist around town, Garcia said, "That's unit 99," he said. "It's Sergeant Lorenzo Bustamante's patrol car. That's him inside." Casuse squinted at the car and the officer behind the wheel and then said, "Let's shoot that policeman and show them we mean business."

"Wait, Larry, you'd better think about that. You should think that over and . . ."

"Goddamn you," Casuse erupted and swung his newly loaded 30.30 around at Garcia. Then, inexplicably, he pointed it up at the skylight and fired. "You shut up. I told you already. I mean business here, and everyone better listen to me."

Casuse then turned to Nakaidinae and shouted at him, "Well, how in hell you doing? Do you have all of them loaded yet? Get a weapon and fire it. Fire down the hall to make sure you can do it."

Nakaidinae, the loyal dog soldier, did as he was told. He picked up a .30-60 deer rifle and fired down the hall at the back door. Then he put it down and picked up a .16-gauge shotgun, which he leveled, once again, at Garcia.

"Fire it," Casuse said.

Nakaidinae did although not exactly as he was told. He aimed the barrel up toward the skylight over the center of the store. The blast reverberated inside, jangling everyone's nerves. Garcia's first thought was, *What in hell would they think is going on in here?*

Despite the limp feeling in his knees and the sharp sting of gunpowder in his nose, Garcia tried to think about what assumptions were being made on the street about these first shots. How would these salvos figure into the police battle plan? The mayor realized, but didn't really believe, that the shots might signal the police to storm the place. What actually happened was Chief Gonzales bent his head around the front inset door to see what was happening. He could see all three of them and knew they had not shot Garcia. But Garcia didn't know that.

They might think I'm dead by now, so why not storm the place?

Those outside, while focusing their thoughts on rescuing the mayor, believed those first rounds were aimed *at* them, but Chief Gonzales waived them down and back into a "standby to fire" position. Every set of eyes focused over a set of gun sights, and every trigger finger tensed. More time passed, somewhere between ten and twenty minutes, depending on which reliable outside source you later talked to. As the standoff unfolded, the actual time elapsed became a highly debatable subject. Everyone outside kept looking at their watches. Garcia could not do that because of his handcuffs. For him, time dragged like a muffler on a lowrider.

While Casuse initially appeared erratic, now he was merely bored. He grew tired of marching Garcia around and around the counter. The game was no longer fun. Wearing a new gun belt and holster for his .32, with the bone-handled hunting knife stuck in his belt, he wedged himself in between two glass display counters on the west side of the store. That put him in reach of the rifles and shotguns loaded by Nakaidinae and the chief's freshly reloaded .357, which seemed to boost his courage a little. Then, like a clock that had been rewound, he walked to the back of the store, at a measured pace.

As he did, he snarled at Nakaidinae, "Watch him, watch the mayor."

Casuse, turning his back on his partner and their hostage, acted as though he had all the time in the world. He strolled to the rear of the store. Nakaidinae moved to the right of the front counter and out into the aisle where Garcia leaned on the counter, resting his aching ankle. They were a yardstick apart and about ten feet from the front door. That put them a good thirty feet from Casuse's back as he rechecked the bolt on the rear door.

The inside bolt on the front door was still locked, but the partially broken glass opening loomed invitingly. The mayor's horn rim glasses were fogged from exertion, but he saw the front door as an escape hatch. With

Casuse preoccupied with the back door and Garcia's move out into the main walkway, Nakaidinae's nonchalance turned to nervousness. He let the barrel of his shotgun sag toward the floor and shifted his gaze from Garcia back to Casuse. Garcia, his hands still cuffed behind him, was a leg length away from Nakaidinae. When he saw Nakaidinae squint back at Casuse, Garcia grabbed the moment. He took one long step and kicked Nakaidinae as hard as he could, trying not to lose his balance. He struck a tender spot on the outside of the right knee. Nakaidinae shrieked, stumbled toward the floor; and Garcia jumped forward, gobbled the space between him and the door, and flapjacked, headfirst through what was left of the plate glass door. Just as he reached the door, Garcia heard the thunderous blast of Nakaidinae's shotgun, felt the simultaneous heat and pain of buckshot all over his lower backside, and hit, facedown, on the sidewalk in front of the door.

A woman outside screamed. A state policeman and a burly city cop scrambled away from the doorway. City Manager Paul McCollum, still stationed just twenty-five feet from the door, yelled to the crowd, "Get back, they'll come out shooting."

Garcia, wincing from the shotgun blast to his back and knowing that a gun battle was imminent, played dead. Casuse ran back to the front of the store when he heard Nakaidinae's shotgun erupt. He got there just in time to see the mayor pancake on the cold pavement of the sidewalk *outside* the store. Casuse screamed at the mayor, "Get up or I'll kill you." Garcia continued to play dead. Casuse fired once through the open door toward the crowd and then ducked back behind the doorjamb.

Chief Gonzales took the chance, jumped directly into the line of fire, and dropped his rifle. Garcia winced as Gonzales grabbed his shoulders and yanked him to safety along the brick wall of Lente's Dry Goods Store. Bill Head, Gallup's city attorney, knelt next to Chief Gonzales, a foot from the now completely shattered Stearns plate glass door. The chief pushed Garcia over to Head and screamed, "Get him to the hospital, now." Head pulled Garcia another three feet along the sidewalk and motioned to a deputy sheriff; together they bundled Garcia into a waiting patrol car and rushed him to the hospital.

Casuse was furious at Nakaidinae for losing their prisoner, at Garcia for escaping, and at the world for its lack of respect. So he opened fire. Nakaidinae joined in; and their bullets sprayed cars, the ground, and the open air outside the store. Onlookers ducked, women screamed, and the police, now under direct attack, returned fire.

Within moments, scores of police bullets hit the front door, the plate glass window, the frames around both, the green tile inside the doorway, and the counters inside the store. As the first rounds shattered more glass, tile, and wood, Casuse and Nakaidinae blasted away from inside with all they had. A huge blitz of bullets from inside the store devoured unit 99's windows and Swiss-cheesed both passenger doors. With Garcia outside, and the chief beside the brick wall at the front of the store, the officers were no longer restrained. Gonzales, the officer closest to the front door, fired three quick rounds with his riot shotgun, through the shattered doorframe, at knee level.

Casuse and Nakaidinae continued to fire through the door and the plate glass window, but they were no match for the trained firepower twenty-five feet away. While they managed to shatter the windows and doors of Officer Bustamante's patrol car, not a single officer or pedestrian was hit. Few in the crowd even felt the random whiz of bullets streaming out of the store. But everyone heard the exchange although later opinions would vary widely about who shot first, last, and most.

At the first lull in the barrage, Chief Gonzales ordered the firing of tear gas canisters through the hole in the door. In less than a minute, it did its job, filling the store with blue-gray smoke. The dense acrid smoke signaled a halt to the firing.

The stench of tear gas billowed out onto Route 66, and everyone scrambled to get away from it. They no sooner found cover than heads began to pop back up. Chief Gonzales alternately fired and remained plastered to the brick wall just beside Stearns's front door. As the gas wafted out and the deafening roar of the gun battle halted, Gonzales felt rather than heard his Sam Browne belt land on the sidewalk in front of him. Someone had thrown it out from inside, like a life buoy from a sinking boat. It landed within arm's reach. He leaned down, picked it up, and in full view of the crowd, strapped it back on. Everyone got the message. It's over.

The gold lettering on the Stearns's riddled but still intact plate glass window said, SELL, TRADE & REPAIR GUNS. That was only half the story. The other half was obvious from the number of bullet holes in Officer Bustamante's patrol car. Like much of life, there were two sides to death.

In less than three minutes, a lone young man with a red bandana tied around his head walked through the shattered door and out onto the sidewalk with his hands laced behind his neck. Robert Nakaidinae, apparently unharmed, said in a low muffled voice, "Larry is hurt."

At first no one moved. At the chief's signal, two Gallup policemen grabbed Nakaidinae, cuffed, and jerked him out of the line of fire and into a waiting patrol car. Two other officers, Lt. J. W. Swoboda of the New Mexico State Police and Gallup City Police Officer Dave Cuellar, crept forward into the smoke-filled store. No one outside moved, and there was no sound from inside. In less than a minute, and sputtering from inhaling the settled tear gas, Cuellar called back, "He's had it, he's hit."

Swoboda, just to Cuellar's right, looked down through the smoke and debris and saw Casuse lying on the floor. His head was against the west doorjamb, and his feet were facing the rear of the store. Both saw a gaping wound in Casuse's throat, underneath his chin, and the even larger hole along the right and top of his head, just above the ear. Swoboda later said he could see a slight movement of skin around the wound and a quiver in Casuse's lower lip.

Neither Swoboda nor Cuellar had gas masks. Both tasted the sting in their throats and felt their eyelids close involuntarily. Swoboda motioned to Cuellar to help him drag Casuse's bloody body out through the open door into the fresh air where someone else could check him for vitals. They dragged him about three feet outside the front door and then unceremoniously dropped him, almost on the exact spot where Mayor Garcia had landed just a few minutes earlier.

Chief Gonzales called for an ambulance for Casuse. About fifty feet away, Bill Head propped up the mayor, still handcuffed, in the backseat of the patrol car as they were preparing to move him to the hospital. The mayor and the city attorney got to the hospital, a few blocks from downtown, just as an ambulance started down the hill for Casuse.

Officer Cuellar did one more thing as the smoke cleared. He went back inside and picked up the chief's .357 from the floor where, just moments before, he'd picked up Casuse. He took the gun outside and handed it to his boss. Chief Gonzales opened the cylinder and saw that someone had reloaded his gun. The bullets he'd put in that morning were still on the floor of the mayor's office two blocks away. But now all six chambers held spent cartridges. He checked the Sam Browne belt that had been thrown through the door. Six cartridges were missing from the cartridge carrier. Gonzales could not help but think that the mayor's abductors had used his bullets to try to kill him and his officers. As he inspected his favorite gun, he saw that the pistol grip was chipped, the butt scarred, and the tip of the barrel bloodied.

Garcia's family followed him to the hospital. Casuse's family stayed behind with his body. Nakaidinae seemed to have no family—at least no one stepped forward. He went to jail, alone.

The crowd groaned and gawked. Some mourned. The fascination with terror left a guilty taste; but for the moment, some, particularly the ones in front, seemed to relish the gore, the broken glass, and the body of Larry Casuse. Others, farther back, spoke into microphones and to one another. Even with the smoke gone, there was no explanation, no ransom demand, and no attempt at justifying what had happened. What started apparently as a political protest was now a grizzly crime scene. Nobility melted into criminality.

A paramedic declared Casuse dead at the scene. His family stared at him on the sidewalk like relatives posting a vigil at a patient's bedside. Someone finally covered his body with a blanket. While the autopsy would not make it official until later that night, there seemed little doubt in the crowd about the cause of death. The top of Larry Casuse's head was completely blown off.

CHAPTER FIVE

"Don't Blow on Hot Corn—
You'll Lose Your Teeth before You Are Old"

Clay Ramsey got to his office in Spokane in midafternoon, feeling a little jet-lagged and a bit guilty about his sin of omission with April. The last thing he'd said to her was that he'd take care of the additional research they needed on Alcatraz and Wounded Knee, but he didn't tell her *why*. How could he tell her why he had to do it himself? He certainly was not in the least bit objective. Didn't that make him the worst choice? His chance with Millie began at Alcatraz and popped up again at Wounded Knee. What difference could it make now?

Clay met Millie in San Francisco in the spring of '69. She was taking journalism and creative writing classes at the University of San Francisco; he was following up on a story about young Indian militants in the city. At twenty-four, she was a year younger than he was but seemed older, street-smart, and vibrantly alive in the San Francisco heyday of political activism. Her native beauty was beguiling, but her Navajo views of life were at once baffling and intriguing. Wise beyond her years, she moved easily among her fellow students and just on the edge of the radical fringe.

Clay's initial attraction was largely physical, but he quickly became equally infatuated with her simple examples of living in harmony with the earth and her stories of growing up on the vast Navajo reservation in Arizona. They might have fallen in love had the spring lasted just a little longer. He now knew something he didn't know then—people don't actually *fall* in love. They come to love, just as you come to maturity or purpose. There's no falling, it just becomes part of you overtime.

San Francisco was in its heyday then, and not just because of drugs or free love. It was a thinking place, just as it was a fun place. Thinking back on it, he wondered now why he did not see the perfect consistency between radicalism and thinking. Protesting without thinking was like fucking for chastity, or so they said in San Francisco.

Clay thought back as he read his yellowed investigative notes. The first landing on Alcatraz, March 8, 1964, involved forty Indians who traveled by boat to Alcatraz and claimed the island, in the name of "Native Americans everywhere." That was possible because the federal government decided in 1962 to close the federal prison on Alcatraz Island, citing the high maintenance cost and deteriorating condition. Over the next seven years, the government drastically reduced the cost of maintenance by proportionately ignoring the crumbling and rotting of everything on the island.

Another landing was attempted on Alcatraz Island on November 9, 1969. That one involved mostly young Indians who claimed "ownership" of Alcatraz. It didn't last the day, and while Millie was sympathetic, she wasn't directly involved. The most important landing, on November 20, 1969, was more dramatic, involved Millie directly, and knew most of the occupiers. It was planned as a one-day takeover, but the BIA got plenty worried by midday when signs began to appear all over the 22.5-acre island. The most visible read, "You Are Now on Indian Land." Another one, hastily painted on a large water tower, visible by telescope to hundreds of thousands of people, proclaimed, "Peace and Freedom—Welcome Home of the Free Indian Land."

Partially to get his mind off Millie, Clay reread Tom Findley's *San Francisco Chronicle* article in his Alcatraz file. Findley knew Richard Oakes, a young Indian leader in San Francisco, who organized the November 20 takeover. Oakes was a Mohawk who grew up on the St. Regis Reserve in New York. He dropped out of high school to become one of the famed Mohawk Ironworkers; they built skyscrapers in Manhattan and massive bridges all over New England. By the summer of 1969, he'd gravitated to San Francisco, married a California Indian woman, and enrolled at San Francisco State.

Findley described Oakes as one of the most charismatic bartenders ever to work at Warrens, one of several bars in the Mission District that had become a draw for sixties-era Indian militants in the bay area. He became the principal spokesman for the seventy-eight young Indians, most of them college students, who stormed the rocks, climbed the outer walls, and claimed the former federal prison for their "people." This landing turned out to be the longest period of hostile occupation on American soil in history. In the end, it changed nothing. Alcatraz still belonged to the federal government.

His notes brought back the clear feeling from the sixties and the seventies that the whites didn't want Alcatraz Island, but still wouldn't give it up, largely because the Indians did want it. From its perspective, the Indians didn't own it and wouldn't know what to do with it if they did.

Clay looked up from his notes and the crumbling photographs and let his mind wander back to a long-ago conversation with Millie.

"What did you say his name was?"

Millie squinted through her oval-shaped coal black eyes. "His name was Allen Cottier. He was a Sioux and claimed to be a descendent of Crazy Horse. He led the 1964 Alcatraz takeover, which the papers called a 'landing.' I guess the white-eyes at the newspaper thought a *landing* had a more militant ring than a mere *takeover.* Anyhow, did you read the statement he handed out to the press?"

"I'm not sure. I have a vague memory but . . ."

"Well, it was Cottier who read it, but I doubt he wrote it. Anyway, he and the group offered to buy Alcatraz from the federal government for forty-seven cents per acre. That was the same amount that the state was then offering to pay local Indian tribes for land claims in the prior century."

"Was he alone, I mean, alone at the time he read the statement?"

"No, there were others. One of them was a man named Walter Means. Walter worked at the navy shipyard nearby, at Mare Island, and he brought his young son, Russell, with him to that 1964 landing. You might have heard of him more recently since he is now a leader in the American Indian Movement. AIM is the most militant Indian rights group in America."

And there it was, in his notes, in his memory, and in Millie's musical, singsong voice. *Is the trail from Alcatraz to Wounded Knee to Gallup becoming clearer? If Russell Means was at Alcatraz in '64, maybe the "fuse" really was there.*

By the middle of 1969, the question of what to do with Alcatraz was on the minds of lots of people, not just Indians. Clay looked back down at his notes and laughed at the recollection. Some Northern California politicians wanted a West Coast version of the Statue of Liberty. Bay Area citizens wanted a refuge for abandoned pets. There was even a quickly drowned-out call for a gambling casino.

Clearly, the most hotly debated proposal was by H. Lamar Hunt, the Texas oilman, who proposed to develop a complex of shops, eateries, and apartments on the Rock. Clay could almost see the Birdman of Alcatraz reincarnated as a shop owner. The San Francisco Board of Supervisors actually voted *for* Hunt's idea, which in turn galvanized the Indian groups who wanted the island returned to them as a community center for all Indian people.

Their political timing turned out to be right for a change. Shortly after the October 1969 vote to make Alcatraz a shopping mall, the San Francisco Indian Center accidentally caught fire and was destroyed. The Indians argued against the shopping mall and for a new community center on their *own* land—Alcatraz Island. Many San Franciscans were surprised to learn that there were large groups of Indians in the city at the time. It was an even bigger surprise that they were speaking out on Indian rights issues. Millie was one of them. But San Francisco being what it was, they ultimately axed both proposals. No shopping mall and no Indian community center. The island is today what it was then—a former prison.

Millie paused to let the short tutorial on Indian politics sink in. Then she continued, "The federal government had, in the 1950s, developed a number of programs designed to move Indians from the reservations to the cities."

"Why?" Clay asked.

"Who knows? But it was, needless to say, a departure from earlier policies. FDR's new deal encouraged Indians to stay on the reservation. Truman reversed that. His administration decided to assimilate Indians into American life as rapidly as possible. Indian reservations were supposed to disappear, and the lands they occupied would become the property of surrounding counties or states. That policy was labeled 'termination.'"

"Really? Termination? That was the formal name?"

"Yep, the termination policy included the concept of relocation, through which Indians were encouraged to abandon life on the reservation for the brighter future offered in America's big cities, like San Francisco. Consequently, the Bay Area Indian community became one of the largest in the nation. I know since I am a card-carrying member. Does that scare you?"

"No, as long as you are not carrying a bomb or anything. You're not, are you?"

"Do you want to search me?"

"Absolutely."

"Later, Irishman, let's get back to Richard Oakes. You ought to hear him speak at a rally. He's one of our most outspoken members."

"So how did the so-called termination policy work, I mean, what did the feds do to move Indians off the reservation and onto these wonderful urban peninsulas, like San Francisco?"

"The BIA offered one-way bus tickets, work assistance, free housing, and medical care for a year—but only in the cities, not on the reservations."

Millie made tea while Clay went to the bathroom. These domestic interludes gave both of them a chance to regroup around more probing subjects.

"Why," she asked, "do you care about this?"

"Millie," Clay asked, pausing to make sure his question was taken lightly and didn't offend, "why do you ask? Is it because I'm Irish and have no Indian blood?"

"You don't have to be Indian to understand our problems. I thought that was what your magazine was all about anyway. Is your interest in all this purely intellectual, or is it based on how you feel about the land? Indians feel differently because they really think it is *their* land. The government agrees it's theirs but insists on holding it in *trust* for the Indians. You know, don't you, that Alcatraz was once Indian land. It should be again, now that the prison is closed. The government takes the Indian land, turns it into a prison, closes the prison, but doesn't give it back. Why can't the government be an *Indian giver*? Wait, don't answer that. Tell me this, do you *care*, or are you merely interested?"

"I care because I know mistakes were made, more on my side than yours, but I'm interested in the matter because it's part of what I want to do now that I'm an adult. I want to write about something that matters. This issue, what to do with an abandoned federal prison sitting out there in the middle of one of the most beautiful bays in the world, interests lots of people, me included."

"So if Indians took it back, if they did it without permission, would you write about it or join them?"

"My job is to write. That's hard to do when you are taking something over by force. I'm a journalist. I can observe and comment on what I see. I can even opine. But if I participate, how can I be independent? Does that make any sense to you?"

That was not the answer Millie was looking for. She already knew the obvious—he was a journalist. She was looking for a sign, even a small one, that he might be able to understand her world. Until she got that sign, she had to keep her world and his at a proper distance. On his side, he was infatuated to the point of mental collapse and thought their relationship might go further than it did. But he sensed she was holding back. He assumed, incorrectly, that another man was yards, perhaps years, ahead of him.

To his utter surprise, Millie accepted his invitation to meet him in Coeur D'Alene, Idaho. Clay picked it because of the then still-wild feeling in Coeur D'Alene and the romantic aura cast by the small pre-bed and breakfast hotel. The three-day stay quickened his stirring infatuation into love, although not yet commitment, in a way that he still couldn't explain even to himself. September of 1969 became the high-water mark of his love life.

What happened to us after our magic time at the McKenzie House in Coeur D'Alene in September of 1969? Did we drift apart because I was afraid or because I was neutral? Deep down, I would rather join them than write about them. But at an even deeper level, I was afraid. Did I have what it took to storm the barricades and man the trenches? If all I ever do is write about protests, could she ever be happy with me?

As it turned out, he didn't have to decide. She drifted out to sea, and he clung to the safety of his desk. He wrote about other things. Instead of covering the *real* takeover, the Indian landing on November 20, 1969, he sent another writer from his office. He knew that if he went to San Francisco himself, he'd see Millie somewhere. She would have been on the waterfront, on Market Street, at the Tadich Grill, or at Joe's. But now, with the "fuse" uncovered, he wondered why he'd been so stupid.

That vague feeling that he could write about conflict but had no stomach for the actual fighting was gone. *How in hell did I move on with my so-called life and miss that first powder keg? My gnawing fear of real battle dampened the "fuse" running from Alcatraz, to Wounded Knee, and then back down to Gallup? Didn't I tell April I only wrote about the 1969 Indian landing on Alcatraz Island from the safety of my desk in Spokane? Is that why I didn't tell her that I spent two tortured days in 1973 in Wounded Knee? Why didn't I go to Gallup when everyone else did for the drum march? Millie was my connection to all three powder kegs—Alcatraz, Wounded Knee, and Gallup. My god, I'd never even see her vast Navajo reservation.*

~ ~ ~

Clay waited for April to call back. To kill time, he reviewed old newspaper clips about Wounded Knee and the Sioux reservation at Pine Ridge, South Dakota. Rubbing his hand through his hair, he scanned the dozens of photos of thin dark-haired young men with rifles. Clay's red hair set him apart from them although he was fit, like they were. And he was given to comfortable clothing. His trim physique didn't come from hunting or fishing; he tramped up and down the mountains and through the streams just for the thrill of being there. He loved the deep forest for its serenity; he went there to write, remember, and think. Wrinkles and sun-damaged skin exaggerated his ruddy complexion. At six foot five and just under 220 pounds, he didn't look like the pictures of the guys on either side of the barricades at Wounded Knee.

Poor eyesight necessitated bifocals ten years ago. At least he had that in common with those "in the movement" in the seventies since many of them were obviously similarly afflicted. Being neat and organized was a handy trait for a single middle-aged man with no children. Every man is said to have a defining intellectual trait. In his case, books and writing defined *both* the intellectual *and* physical parts of his life.

Clay began organizing the clippings on his desk, starting with the UPI story dated March 1, 1973, and grinning at the now politically incorrect headline, MILITANT INDIANS TRADE GUNFIRE WITH FEDERAL OFFICERS. The story brought back old, uncomfortable memories. The *siege*, as it was first labeled, involved the taking of eleven hostages in Wounded Knee. The "trading" of gunfire on the first day involved AIM militants firing on automobiles and low-flying aircraft that dared come within rifle range. On the other side, the U.S. Marshal Service brought two armored personnel carriers onto the Pine Ridge Reservation. When they weren't "trading" gunfire, both sides claimed to be interested in obtaining the immediate release of the hostages.

As Clay read, his mind wandered back in time. He tried to place what was before him on his desk inside the long-repressed memory of the day he arrived at Wounded Knee.

CHAPTER SIX

"Don't Kill a Lizard—You'll Get Skinny"

April 17, 1973

Wounded Knee, South Dakota

The driver's side door on the cheap rental car was cranky. When the handle wouldn't work, Clay banged it from inside the vehicle, felt the cold wind against the door, and forced it open. Three hours driving through the South Dakota badlands to get to Wounded Knee Creek was like an Irish road race, only with beat-up pickup trucks.

Just past the muddy little creek, he saw an unimpressive AIM bunker he later learned was called Little Big Horn. His welcome to the scene was officious but casual. "So another reporter from another big city," said the soldier in fatigues with the breath of a policeman who'd been on duty too long.

"Yes, sir, here are my press credentials, Sergeant," Clay said, holding out the Washington State identification press card issued to the *American Warrior*.

"*Warrior?* You don't look like a warrior to me. Besides, those guys on the other side of that line over there"—he pointed to a dirt bunker—"have been here since February 27, that's comin' on near two months now. Aren't you a little late for the fight?"

Clay knew he'd get some static from other journalists who'd been covering the siege story on-site for forty-nine days, not counting today, April 17: but he didn't expect it from the government, particularly the U.S. Marshal Service, one of three law enforcement agencies represented at Wounded Knee, along with the FBI and the BIA Police. "Officer, I didn't come here to fight, I came here to observe. If you've been fighting those warriors over there, maybe I could interview you. We all have our jobs to do."

The agent looked a little worried as if maybe this one was *somebody*, so he gave what passed for an apology in the army. "Sir, sorry, sir. Proceed ahead, you'll find the mess facility over there and the press tent next to it. Good day, sir."

Clay looked around for some sign of normal activity and saw only the effects of a long tour on hostile ground. The jerry-built tents looked out of place on the mushy dirt, held up by stakes and ropes that alternated being too taut or too loose. The on-duty soldiers looked bored and tired; it was hard to tell them from the others who were sitting in small groups, smoking and talking. Guns were everywhere; but no one was firing, not even into the air, contrary to some isolated comments in letters to editors in the Midwest. Clay was struck by the fact that no one seemed to be aiming at anything of either side of the bunker. The press tent and guard station were not exactly in "downtown" Wounded Knee, but he could see it from where he stood, over the top of his car. He parked the rental next to a dirty green armored personnel carrier, an APC in military jargon, caked with mud, pimpled with dents, and displaying a telltale black soot ring above and around the tail pipe. He imagined that whoever was in charge would like to get all these APCs back to the base motor pool where they belonged.

Fifteen or twenty buildings were crammed into the space where the only four roads in town came together. The map showed the old trading post, which was now the "new community meeting center"; the old tourist museum, which was now the "new defense center"; and of course, the old cars which, despite shiny new bullet holes, still functioned.

Clay walked over to the press tent, poured a cup of coffee, and looked at the half-dozen reporters sitting at the two tables, scribbling and talking. And there she was. He burned his knee when he dropped the coffee.

His shout, and the coffee all over the dirt floor, caused all eyes in the room to zero in on him. Clumsiness always draws a crowd. She knew better. She walked over and made it easy for him, "Clay, you look well. Don't worry about the coffee, it tastes like dirt anyhow. This is not the land of late-night coffee and good talk, like San Francisco."

Fumbling with the Styrofoam cup, one knee on the dirt floor, the other soaked with hot coffee, he muttered, "Millie, my god, it's you. I never expected. I mean, Jesus, I mean you look wonderful."

They hugged, perfunctorily at first, then with shared intensity. It had been four years since they'd last touched. Stepping back from the embrace, she said softly, "First day here, am I right?"

"Does it show? What is it, my clothes or my gear?"

Millie looked him up and down slowly and smiled just the way he remembered. Her bright white teeth flared below the dark brown upper lip. Her smile spread upward to her narrow, almost-Asian eyes, and it made them dance. She said, "Nah, it's your beard. You've been shaving every day. None of the other men here bother with big-city rituals. They think looking a little scruffy makes you more acceptable to both the defenders and the attackers. Who you reporting for if I may ask?"

"I'm still writing for and editing the *American Warrior*. I guess I didn't tell you."

"There was a lot you didn't tell me, Clay. Come sit down. We can catch up, and I can tell you what you've missed at the Knee since March 1 when this all started."

"The sergeant at the roadblock said he's been here since February 27. I guess you got here two days after it started?"

"No, he's only half-right. AIM took over part of the town on the night of the twenty-seventh. The news got out the next day, and the soldiers and APCs started rolling in on March 1."

"What keeps you here?"

"Well, actually I've only been here for about three weeks or so—in and out, you know. I'm here because I'm writing a book, well, at least a long documentary on AIM. They have been very active, you know."

"Who for? I mean, who are you writing for?"

Millie leaned back in her canvas-backed chair, shook her head ever so slightly, like she was thinking about how to answer. She looked like a reporter with her brown undershirt, long-sleeved Levi's jacket, and a small spiral notebook in her shirt pocket. But she also looked bright and energetic, not at all like the other reporters who had resumed their individual conversations. As she talked, Clay felt a tenseness that somehow went beyond their personal situation.

"I'm freelancing the book. I have been writing for a living for about two years now. Mostly travel stuff and nature things. This is my first effort at political writing and writing about my people. I'm still political, you probably guessed that. How about you? Are you still writing about those radicals and warrior types we talked about in San Fran?"

"Yes, and even more of it now than then. You might have seen some of our stuff over the last few years."

"Yes, Clay, I have. I've followed your career from a distance, so to speak. I've read a lot of what you've written."

There are a few others, with your writing skills and writing interests, who got here around the same time I did."

"Like me? You mean white-eyes. Isn't that what you called me?"

She laughed and said, "Yeah, that's what my friends all said on the Navajo reservation when I was little. However, that isn't what I meant about others like you. I meant the guys from the weekly magazines showing up after the story is old news."

"Actually it's monthly, the magazine, I mean. That's no excuse, I can see that this story is getting a little stale, but I'm not a reporter for a daily newspaper." Hoping to move on to more neutral territory, he asked, "What's going on?"

"Pretty big day today, this morning, the firing started early, about one-thirty. Most days there is firing, but sometimes it's just to get a little blood stirred up on the other side of the bunker. But today, after the firing settled down, there was an airlift. That happened about dawn, and we've had quite a bit of firing back and forth all day."

"Any casualties, I mean, that you know about?"

"We hear that four or five AIM guys got hit, one of them critically. He was about two hundred yards from one of the BIA bunkers, so the AIM leaders sent out a flag of truce, a little white thing, and said they needed a helicopter to come into the Knee and help him."

"Wow! Does that happen a lot, I mean, a guy going down and the other side sending in a helicopter to help him?"

"Yeah, sometimes. But this time, they said that no helicopter could land inside the Knee, so they agreed to truck him outside the perimeter. Then a helicopter took him to Pine Ridge Hospital. He had massive brain damage from a head shot."

"Who was he? I mean, was he from here?"

"One of the BIA police, who is from here, said the wounded guy was an Indian from Nebraska—he had one dollar and a map of Nebraska in his pocket, but no ID."

"And what do you think, is this a fair fight."

"Sure, as long as you think that it's fair when one side has kids with .30-30 rifles and the other side has well-trained marksman with high-powered rifles fitted with nightscopes."

"How many people are in there? I mean, how many Indians that don't normally live here," Clay said, pointing past the APC and the six-by-six army truck with the muddy brown canvas flaps on the back.

"It's hard to say. Well, hard to count, not hard to say. The AIM guys inside the barricades don't say much 'on the record,' but we hear them off the record, say anywhere from three hundred to five hundred."

"Wow, that's more than I thought. Where are they from?"

"Everywhere, lots from the reservations around here, some from out West, and even a few from Canada. I've talked to several dozen over the last month, off the record of course, and I can tell you they are a different bunch than the ones elected and propped up by the BIA on the Pine Ridge. Some come from big cities, some from farms, some are Rez men, kids, single women—you name it, they are in there. They are mostly Indians, but not entirely. We have some Chicanos from New Mexico and some Navajos too. I even talked to a white guy from Albuquerque. He's a radical everything but very committed to helping win this war. Isn't that rich? You, however, are the first from Seattle."

"I'm in Spokane, not Seattle."

"Right. I misspoke. But Seattle and Spokane are a long way from New Mexico. And both are a long way from here. Anyhow, the ones in there, manning the barricades, they're from everywhere. You want to know something interesting. It's the women in there who are running things—women and dozens of kids who ought to be in junior high. They all are packing iron and lighting fuses."

"And AIM, how many are from AIM?"

"All of them, in one way or another. The leaders, Russell Means and Dennis Banks, are political guys who live and breathe this stuff. Others are here on the first political thing they ever did in their lives. I'd say a majority are Sioux, and most of the Sioux are residents of the Pine Ridge Reservation. They sure in hell don't have any love lost for their so-called tribal leader. His name is Dick Wilson. Dick is a good name for him. He's a real government Indian."

"How long have you been here?"

Millie looked at her watch for some reason and then said, "I got here on March 11, ten days after the first shot. That's all it took for Means and Banks to declare that Wounded Knee was a sovereign nation. They call it the Independent Oglala Sioux Nation. But it's no more independent now than it was then."

"Yes, I read about that, but I'm a little hazy on the purpose."

"That's understandable, seeing as how you weren't at Fort Laramie in 1868."

"No, I guess I wasn't. What's Fort Laramie got to do with it?"

"AIM says their independence declaration is based on the Fort Laramie Treaty of 1868 which, they say, made the Sioux Nation a sovereign power in the eyes of the U.S. government. That treaty says no white man would ever set foot in the Black Hills without permission of the Sioux. It's a stretch, but that's their legal argument. They withdrew the permission for the whites to be here, government or otherwise. Let me give you an example. AIM says the county line is actually a 'border,' you know, like the Canadian *border*. So are you here because of the great airlift this morning? That's the big news of the day."

"It's not why I came, but I did hear something about it on the radio on the way here from Rapid City."

"So you came here through beautiful downtown Scenic and the badlands. You must have come through Porcupine, right?"

"Yes, I did. Pretty crowded there too. I've never seen such widespread poverty in my life."

"Well, welcome to the Pine Ridge Reservation. Home of the once proud but now bowed Oglala Sioux. That's what this is really all about, lifting up their heads and looking at poverty, the feds, and Dick Wilson right in the eye. What time did you leave Rapid City this morning?"

"Just after dawn."

"Dawn was at 5:06 a.m. I know the exact time because of the great airlift. Seven guys in three single-engine planes called Cherokees dropped dozens of duffel bags attached to parachutes in the middle of Wounded Knee at the exact crack of dawn. I don't know . . ."

"Where did they come from, and who are they? Does anybody know for sure?"

"Best guess is those planes came from Rapid City, just like you did. The flight would take less than an hour. Even in those little puddle jumpers, they were flying. Took you a bit longer, eh?"

"Yes, a bit. But please tell about the guys and the duffel bags. Was that what they dropped? The radio made it sound like a mercy flight or something. Why duffel bags?"

"Well, I talked to a guy a little while ago, who talked to a guy—you know how it goes. He says they got food, ammo, medical supplies, a beer or two, and some private mail. I guess they used duffel bags on parachutes because that was the easiest thing to transport. The outfit that handled this was definitely not military, that's for sure, but they must have had some military experience because, except for one plane, they all dropped on schedule, and they all hit on target."

"What about the one that didn't?"

"Dunno," Millie said. "But my guy said that it had two heavy duffels hung up on the plane as it flew out of the drop zone. The way he explained it, the chute lines were hung up on the frame and dragging in the air about a hundred feet below the plane."

"So that makes the guys in the planes heroes inside Wounded Knee and goats outside. Is that how you see it?"

"It beats me. I still can't tell the heroes from the goats. There are Indians on both sides of the barricades you know. The ones over here sympathize with those over there. No one here likes the way the BIA treats the Sioux or the way Dick Wilson and his crowd of managers do things either. Today's surprise airlift into Wounded Knee may have been done for the thrill of it, but I doubt that. Whoever did it had a lot of guts to fly in here at ground level, past the army's heavy guns and the FBI's sniper fire. What's more, those guys apparently did it all for free. These AIM guys don't have a lot of cash. They're in it because they believe it's right."

I can't believe I'm sitting here—God, she is still the most stunning woman I've ever seen. Clay studied Millie's face a little too long. Millie broke his stare. "Clay, you okay?"

"No, I mean, yes, I'm okay. Just a little tired and excited to see you and all, but what I wanted to ask was, do you mean right in the moral sense or the right political result? Are they here because it's exciting to take on the government or because the government is corrupt? Back in Spokane, we hear a lot about freedom, that is, freedom from the federal government. Is that what you've heard here at ground zero?"

"What I've heard is that those AIM guys are every bit as unhappy with tribal leadership, here on the Pine Ridge Rez, as they are with the BIA. Of course, there's more to it than that, but they damn sure don't like the local elected leaders here. They call Dick Wilson's councilmen *goons*. And he's the chief goon."

"By they, are you talking about the AIM dog soldiers or the coup leaders?"

Millie laughed and took the moment to sip on her now-stale coffee. "I never heard anyone here use the term *dog soldiers*. Is that a term of endearment down there in Washington?"

"I'm from Washington State, not Washington, D.C."

"Yes, Clay, but you always wanted to be a warrior, didn't you?"

"I write for the *American Warrior*. It's a magazine, but we try to cover things impartially."

"Me too."

"Do you think this airlift had been planned for a long time? Did your guy on the inside tell you that?"

"I never said he *was* on the inside. But whatever. This was definitely planned. That drop this morning was no accident, and it wasn't planned by a bunch of drunks either—although there are lots of them in town."

"Well, then, it sounds like heroes, not goats. Does your guy, inside or out, know who they were? Do the authorities know that yet?"

"If the feds do, they aren't saying. This blockade is about half military, one-quarter federal marshals, and one-quarter FBI, but the FBI call the shots, and they are real closemouthed until they get before a grand jury. I expect we'll all know soon enough since the beneficiaries of the duffel bags over there will tell us, soon enough. AIM loves to scoop the FBI."

"So the airlift was a successful thing, you'd say?"

"Doesn't matter what I say. Those inside will say it was a great success. Those outside will deny it. You and I will report the dispute, and someday, one of the pilots will write a book about it."

"Millie, what did the feds and all the other guards I saw driving in do when the planes dropped their little parachutes and duffel bags?"

"As far as I can tell, they used the airdrop as an excuse to shoot the hell out of everything. The firefight lasted all morning. You'd have heard it an hour ago."

"A firefight, a real firefight—that's what I missed?"

"Yes, is that what you came to see, fighting?"

"No, I came to see a siege."

"The siege was yesterday. This morning, the truce was broken."

"Which side?"

"The feds say one of their helicopters was fired on as it was investigating the airdrop. AIM says the firing started from two APCs on the hill over there, back of the Gildersleeves' store. Rumors leaking out already say several men were hit, at least one badly. I heard the man's name was Frank Clearwater."

"One of the leaders?"

"No, I think he's Apache. The government quit firing long enough from them to carry him out on a stretcher. They took him by helicopter to Rapid City to a hospital, but I hear he won't make it. He was not the only one shot, there are others that have wounds, but they won't come out."

Clay spent the rest of the day with Millie. They danced around their relationship, or the lack of it, but talked a lot about AIM and the reality of Indian civil rights in the middle of everything else that stirred the political pot in the Nixon/Watergate/Vietnam/African-American era.

"What do you think motivated AIM to pick this godforsaken little town to capture and hold hostage?"

As soon as he said it, he could see Millie's eyes narrow, and those stern little lines on her forehead show up. By disparaging this little reservation town, he gave her the sense that he was just another white-eyes reporter, looking down on the places Indians lived. But she made a quick turnaround and smiled as she answered, "You always were interested, but not engaged, Clay. This is the natural follow-up to November 2, 1972. Did your magazine cover that story?"

"I take it you're referring to the sit-in at the Bureau of Indian Affairs building in D.C.?"

"That is how some people put it, right. Do you realize the real significance of what happened there?"

"Nope, that's why I'm here," Clay answered, knowing it was a half-truth.

"AIM held off one of America's largest and most powerful bureaucracies for some time against the massed forces of the greatest power on earth. On a Friday afternoon, just at closing time in the BIA building on November 3 last year, four days before Nixon's reelection, AIM occupied the BIA building. One of the leaders there, who is now over there behind the bunker, refused to move. Everyone followed his lead. They just sat down and refused to move. Clyde Bellecourt stood and screamed at the top of his lungs, 'We are not moving! This is no longer the BIA building. It is now the American Indian Embassy.'" Millie paused, not only to lower the tension in her voice but also to see how Clay was reacting to her rendition of the most significant AIM protest prior to Wounded Knee. Gathering herself, she continued, "More importantly, for the first time since the Indian massacres in the 1860s and '70s, the news about America's first people got the same front-page coverage as the debacle in Vietnam and the inundating political story of the upcoming presidential election."

"Yes, but it didn't seem, at least out west in Spokane, like the Indian community was exactly overjoyed about what happened."

"You're right. They weren't. American Indians are as divided on the ethics and motives of AIM as the rest of America is. However, this time the sympathies switched somewhat to the AIM side because the government threatened violent eviction, and the AIM guys vowed to die defending their position. The BIA called AIM a ragtag bunch of vandals. That might have been an overstatement. By the time it was over, no one doubted the government drummed up a few obedient Indian officials to condemn the activists as thugs. More importantly, for the first time, responsible leaders, both Indian and white, took notice and paid attention."

Clay's bush eyebrows furrowed, and he queried, "Paid attention? Attention to what?"

"You got me there. After it was over, the mainstream press muddled the facts and obscured the purpose of takeover. Even so, the coverage was widespread and constant, and that, Mr. Ramsey, is a major change. It's like Selma, Alabama, for the civil rights movement or the Watergate Hotel for Richard Nixon. Everything big starts small and usually in some unknown place, like Selma or the Watergate. AIM thought about the politics and started its war in D.C. Now they are here."

"I should remember, but I don't. Exactly how did that takeover of the BIA building in Washington end?"

"Same as it always does, with political promises. President Nixon agreed to establish a special federal interagency task force to review Indian policy. The task force met, prepared a report, and Congress promptly ignored it. Well, not entirely. They passed seven new bills without any input from Indian people, except those employed by the BIA. There were several groups involved, not just AIM, but AIM was the leader. Those groups were collectively called the Trail of Broken Treaties. The BIA takeover gave them another treaty to add to the list."

"So how did they get here?"

"This reservation has always been a storm center for Indian activism. Gallup, New Mexico, my old stomping grounds, is another one. There are AIM members and activists from Gallup, right over there on the other side of the barricades. There are lots of others too." Millie paused, looked down at the floor of the tent, and said, "You remember Alcatraz, don't you?"

Did I? Oh, Millie, I remember every second, and I'm ashamed for walking away. You didn't. I know that now. "You know I do, Millie. And I remember Coeur D'Alene too. Actually, I'd rather talk about that than Pine Ridge."

"In good time, Clay, in good time. What you need to understand if you are going to cover this takeover from the Indian point of view is that every hard-core AIM member is here. Right now. They won't let the government snow them again as they did in D.C. last November. This is a new year and the start of the spring campaign as Custer might have put it."

Both of them sat there, letting the afternoon shadows outside the tent start to creep in, along with the memories that were starting to overcome them. But Clay, always the appeaser, wanted desperately to keep Millie talking, for as long as it took, to get them to the point where he could *really* talk to her. So he returned to neutral ground, political ground, and asked, "I've heard this is a 'tribal fight.' Is that how you see it here?"

"There's some truth in that. The blatant mockery of justice outrages almost everyone here. This is government-sanctioned corruption. Tribal leaders here are petty tyrants. But the Sioux people, many of whom are AIM activists, are determined to make a stand here and now. These people have suffered all their lives because of greedy self-serving bureaucrats, Indian and white alike. They see this as a last chance to live, or maybe to die, with dignity and self-respect."

"Millie, I've actually written a few pieces on those issues, along with Indian sovereign rights. You say you've read my stuff?"

"I have. You're still a blue pencil, Clay—you have great command of language and the printed page. But do you really want to become a red fighter, a warrior, is that why you're here?"

Clay tried to laugh but couldn't quite carry it off. He said, "That's what you called me in San Fran, a blue pencil. I guess you're right. I'm good at nouns and verbs but not guns and blood."

"I didn't mean it so negative, Clay. You're an Irish statesman. Your words are eloquent, and it doesn't matter that you avoid barroom brawls and tribal fights, like this one. Only here, there's a lot more at stake. You can help us by telling the truth in your magazine."

"Us, are you part of this? Are you a secret member of AIM?"

"It's no secret, Clay, I am pretty involved, but my job is to make sure there is some media, even if it's alternative media, that covers what's happening over there in that sorry little hamlet."

"Fair enough. How about the other 'us.' You and me, I mean. Do we have another chance, Millie?"

There it was, Clay just could not wait or give Millie enough time to digest his presence or think through how she felt about it. She got up, held her arm toward him, wrist bent, palm forward, and motioned for him to give her a minute. She'd always used a sort of ritual sign language. Her point was unmistakable. Then she walked over to the other side of the tent, looked out through the flap opening, and stood still, as still as he'd ever seen her. Then she turned and faced him. Her chest heaved a little, she squared her shoulders, brushed back her hair on one side, and moved back to him. He had the good sense, for once, to sit still himself and let her talk.

"Clay, there is a lot about me you don't know. Let me ask you something about chances and about choices. Have you ever been to a large reservation, like mine in Arizona? You know, it spreads over two states and is hundreds of miles across. My little hamlet, Chinle, is bigger than Pine Ridge but still minute by your standards. It's also remote and, by some standards, desolate. Could you imagine yourself there, I mean, living there?"

Clay tried to glean from Millie's eyes whether this was a serious question or a prelude to more talk. Her eyes glistened, but her cheeks and her jaw were unmoving, and her head and neck seemed locked in place. "Honestly, I doubt it. Like you, I'm a product of where I grew up. I love the high mountains, not the high desert of Arizona. Besides, you don't really live there, do you? Aren't you still living on the West Coast and spending summers visiting your family in Chinle?"

Giving Clay a hint that he'd just given the wrong answer, Millie looked away and said in a voice that now sounded distant, "I've been moving around a bit. California, Montana, and my home reservation. My family is everything to me even though I am not there as much as I should be. I've been thinking of choices and changes, though, that's why I asked you. I can't see either of us living on a reservation full-time. It's a place of wonderment for a child but can be one of despair when you are older. You just asked if we could have another chance. Is that what you really want, a chance?"

"Yes," he said, pausing, and then modifying his answer, "I think I do."

Millie just sat. He could not tell whether his answer seemed genuine or incredulous. She just sat, neither took a breath, and both looked away. Then, slowly but deliberately, she busied herself with the tedium of gathering up her book bag, her coat, and, holding her forefinger to her lips, said, "Call me when you make up your mind." She walked out of the tent and out of his life. Again.

~ ~ ~

Later, after a long drive back to Rapid City from Wounded Knee and after a sleepless night in a cheap motel, Clay left South Dakota. He did not realize that April 18, while he was moribund on an airplane headed west, would become a historic day on the Pine Ridge Reservation. A day after the almost historic airdrop to Wounded Knee, a large crowd of local people, some Sioux, some not, did what the FBI, the National Guard, and the local BIA forces had not tried. This small but determined crowd invaded Wounded Knee from the government side of the bunker. They appeared from nowhere and surged forward from the government side over onto the defender's side. This was a federal roadblock. That's what the attackers called it. On the other side, the defenders called it a "blockade." The crowd, variously estimated to be one or two dozen, seemed to materialize out of thin air. All were Indian, and all wanted *in*.

The press reported them as local Sioux who actually lived in and around Wounded Knee. They had not been inside their homes for almost two months now. Now that there were new supplies of food inside the blockade, these people could see no end in sight. For them, it looked like more blockades and roadblocks. They just wanted back *in*.

The last thing the BIA police and the embattled tribal chairman, Dick Wilson, wanted was a bunch of reporters relaying the message to America that the Indians outside wanted to go back inside. That was entirely inconsistent with the government message that the people inside were hostages. The government would have preferred the message to be that those inside wanted to come out. There had been a lot of talk about a compromise, but finally, fourteen Oglala Sioux women and children lost their patience. They rushed the blockade from the rear, pushed through it, and on into the hamlet of Wounded Knee. The federal marshals were surprised, to say the least.

The only Indians on the government side now were ones who *didn't* rush the barricade. Acting under the principle that they probably *wanted* to rush the barricade, the marshals arrested twenty from the crowd who lingered on the federal side and put them in jail in Pine Ridge.

Clay heard about it from the late evening news kiosk when he landed in Seattle later that night. But he'd seen all he wanted to see of protests and lost causes. He still didn't have the stomach to man the barricades. All he could do was go home to Spokane and write about it. Alone, without Millie, again.

God, how many chances does a man get to screw up his life?

CHAPTER SEVEN

"Don't Break Sticks—You'll Have Bad Luck"

Clay fingered the box tenderly and opened it slowly. *Why a tin box? Why not a proper fireproof box safe if these letters are really important? Because I put the first one in this box and it stuck with me, that's why.* The first letter, the one in faded ballpoint on academic bond copy paper was dated October 8, 1973, almost six months since he'd last seen Millie in Wounded Knee. He gingerly lifted the envelope flap as if he were peeking inside a forbidden novel.

Dear Clay,

"Uncertain I am," said the maid to the scribe. "Where, pray tell, do I start?" You are likely as surprised to get this as I am to find myself writing it. It seems too risky to start where we left off six months ago in Wounded Knee, so I'll retreat and start closer to an earlier parting.

When I left Coeur D'Alene and our wonderful three-day enchantment at the McKenzie House back in '69, I was, as you white-eyes say, "betwixt 'n' between." I was betwixt who I was on my beloved Navajo reservation, and the pretty Navajo, educated and engaged out in the big world of politics and change. You, my love, were the ominous "between." You wedged yourself between my nascent cause and my native soul. In one of my dumber life-diminishing decisions, I elected to expand the cause of Indian civil rights by contracting personal involvement with someone on the other side.

Of course, you weren't really on the other side. You were illogically on our side, at least in spirit. A blue-eyed Irishman with a heart as big as Monument Valley is an apt description for you, but my view was a bit clouded by your detached approach to change. I can remember kidding you about your blue-pencil approach to solving the brutal and ignorant trampling of Indian rights by government bandits. You spoke and wrote eloquently in the *American Warrior* but could not quite see yourself astride a charging horse. I knew you were on our side in spirit, but stupidly, I wanted you to grab a rifle as quickly as you did a pen. I know now how implausible that was and how disappointed I would have been if you had given up the written word for the bullet.

When we last met six months ago, you asked about "us." You can't know what the word *us* means to me. You think it's just two adults from different worlds, different planets maybe, trying to mix and match our cultures, like colors and furniture in a house. But there is much more to my *us* than I can explain right now.

What I am working up to is a truce of sorts. I would like to see you again, but my fear of failing is probably as strong as your fear of engaging a radical woman whose life compass is a half-bubble off plumb. How about we just write a few letters, keep our distance, and see whether the word is mightier than the fist?

I'm on the faculty now at Montana State University-Bozeman. They gave me a probationary assistant professor's line in the growing Center for Native American Studies. Our goal is to serve Montana's Indian tribes in a way that helps everyone through research, public service, and teaching. My part, at least for now, will be more on the service side in developing educational, socio-economic, and cultural programs. I will help with liaison services to non-Indian citizens and organizations. Who knows, maybe I can be useful to the *American Warrior* in some small way.

Don't get me wrong, I do want to see you again, but I think we ought to start slow and give ourselves the benefit of a few prairie lengths as a buffer zone for a while.

If you are involved with someone, just send me a little "Dear Pocahontas" letter.

In the struggle,
Millie

~ ~ ~

Clay tried in vain to read between the lines of that first letter. As always, he took her at face value and felt guilty about looking for ghosts in places where she was obviously just being honest—brutally honest, but truthful nonetheless. After balling up a few dozen pieces of typing paper and flipping them over his shoulder, he resorted to pen and ink. Somehow the return to longhand freed his mind as he focused on the flow of ink onto a blank page. Now looking not at the original, which he had hand-carried to the post office the next morning, but at a Xerox copy he'd made, he realized how incipient his opening line was. *I know it struck you as in character, just another example of how removed I was from the action in your life.*

My Dearest Millie,

I'll start where your wonderful surprise letter ends. "In the struggle," while an apt phrase for you, is not the message I was hoping for as I read your letter. I loved you then, and I love you now. But your intuition served you well. I know now that my detachment became a shield between us.

I vividly remember standing with you on the little shake-shingle porch at the McKenzie House four years ago. You were stuffing your beaded bag, and I was stifling a goodbye cry. My intuition often fails me, but the right side of my brain knew that any chance of a life together was dim unless one of us let go of a *shibboleth* or two. At the risk of weeding my words in the middle of a letter, I want to tell you why I picked *shibboleth* to describe what I think kept us apart. It's a Hebrew word, which means "ear of grain" but has taken on a different meaning because of a Bible story. Jephthah's army was victorious in seizing the river Jordan. To maintain his edge, he posted guards at the fords in the river and gave his warriors a catchword, *shibboleth,* to tell friend from foe. He knew that the other side could not pronounce it right, but would say *shibboleth.* The enemy was quickly detected and just as quickly slain. While we were hardly enemies, maybe that's what happened to us. I could not pronounce your life.

I blathered on about diplomatic solutions to Indian civil rights problems, on a leisurely pace, while you acted on a vigorous, if uphill, climb to defeat the government bandits. It was, in retrospect, a problem of pronunciation as severe as that faced by the Ephraimite in the Bible. Of course, they were slain because they mispronounced the catchword. You and I merely parted ways. God, I hated that parting and cannot find words to tell you how glad I am that you are willing to start anew, even if it is from across the prairie.

You once described me as a "good scout," implying that my role as an obliging fellow might not be suited for the front lines. You were correct, although oddly enough, the word *scout* was probably misapplied in all military settings. Some attribute the first use of the word to university students who "scout" about providing the needs of young gentlemen scholars. I have spent many years scouting for the soul of the *American Warrior*, rather than either engaging in my own war or even standing guard as others battled.

I sensed that your role at Alcatraz was probably more than you let on, but admired you for whatever help you gave to their cause. As a reporter, I understood your wariness about telling too much of your own tale. Then, when we met the last time at Wounded Knee, I knew that you were there for more than the telling of the tale. While I am embarrassed about it now, I even thought you might be some sort of secret AIM spy and that your job was to infiltrate the government bandits under the cover of journalism.

Maybe our catchwords separate us as much as anything else does. Your idea that we write to one another could eliminate the clutter of action and the fear of failure. After all, the written word can be more carefully chosen than a verbal response made in the heat of argument or the passion of love. I propose a catchword to match your "in the struggle" closing line. How about "still a barnacle"?

There was a time when everyone firmly believed that the goose, which we still call the barnacle goose, came out of the shell of a tiny gourd growing upon certain trees along the shorelines of all the earth's great oceans. Fable had it that immature birds, so tiny they were virtually invisible, clung to these gourds by their bills. The gourds fell into the sea, where the birds became small shellfish, and attached themselves to anything that floated—logs, canoes, and ships—until the birds were ready for flight. The small shellfish, the barnacle, attached itself to the first thing that floated by. It began life as a gourd, but was incapable of developing into the beautiful bird known as the barnacle goose.

Our words are barnacles of sorts. We can begin anew by exchanging letters. Let's accept the unknown and let what we say compress the prairie between us. With patience, we can wait for the right time for our barnacles to blossom into geese. I don't mean barnacle geese. I have in mind the majestic Canada goose. They mate for life and always fly together.

My tentative words, as we looked at Alcatraz Island, no doubt gave you pause. My academic words likely bored you at the McKenzie House. And the downright foolish words that fell out of my mouth, like marbles out of a torn sack, must have put you over the edge in Wounded Knee. Looking back on it, as I've done a thousand times, I expect you were testing me to see if I might fit into a warrior's life. It was only there, listening to you talk about the women inside the barricades at Wounded Knee, that I realized the obvious—AIM was not just about men calling themselves warriors, AIM was full of women, some with guns, others armed with brains, wit, and commitment, like you.

Your piercing words when we met on the government side of the barricade in Wounded Knee hit me like an oar turned flat against the river's current. I knew you were out of my depth. I wanted to measure the flow, and you wanted to knife through the rocks to the shore. I was attached to a comfortable reality and could not hear the drumbeats you felt within the American Indian Movement. You were beating the drum, not just listening to it.

It does not matter whether we've changed. What matters is whether we can rise to the chance you've given us. I'm sure we want the same reality. We likely both want to unload a bit of fantasy. Speaking only for myself, this is not a time to complete something. We don't have to come full circle or even retrace our steps. This is a time for fragments. Words are fragments and cannot stir things apart. If tasted, nibbled, and savored, our words can serve as binding agents and give us a rainbow bridge, clear across the prairie.

Love from the barnacle,
Clay

~~~

Virgil sat on the small enclosed porch at the rear of April's apartment on Aztec Street in Gallup. April waited inside the kitchen, pretending to fix tea and fuming because Virgil was taking so long. She knew him to be a fast reader and couldn't imagine what was taking so long. She'd printed out both of her e-mails to Clay and asked Virgil to read them more than an hour ago. Then she complicated things by giving him the grand jury transcript; that's when he went outside to the porch.

He got one foot in the door, and she peppered him, "So what do you think? Is this a story or what? Who could have guessed that something like this could happen in this little burg, and . . ."

Virgil slapped the transcript and the e-mails down on the kitchen table and held up his hand. "This little burg is exactly where something like this should have happened if you ask me. Gallup is in the heart of Indian country, and the mayor here was no stranger to the troubles that made this not only possible but also damned likely to happen. And besides . . ."

April stammered, "I didn't mean burg in a bad way, but you know, what do you think of my notes about the abduction of the mayor and the killing of this Casuse guy? Did you know about this when you were a kid? I mean, he was obviously an agitator, but it seems like they could have negotiated a little more before blowing his head off."

Virgil frowned. April had come to know most of Virgil's various frowns. She particularly liked the frown that signaled he was amused. She was always frustrated by the one that came out when he was curious but tried to hide it. This one was the full-brow and squint-eyed version. Multiple small lines crisscrossed his forehead, and others poked out from the corners of his mouth as he clenched his jaws. It was definitely his disagreeable frown.

"April, I read both your e-mails and the grand jury transcript, and I'm wondering if you took the time to do what I did. You seem ready to accuse the local cops of murder or something. How can you murder a guy bent on suicide?"

"Suicide? What are you talking about? Maybe he had a death wish since he barricaded himself in a gun store, but the police killed him, didn't they?"

"Apparently not. Did you read the coroner's testimony to the grand jury?"

"Well no, I was kind of in a hurry, and I put that part off so I could send the e-mails to Clay about the abduction and the shoot-out. Are you serious? Do you really think that Casuse committed suicide?"

"I don't have an opinion one way or the other. The coroner did though. His testimony sounded reasonable, and he was under oath before a grand jury. That means something, don't you think?"

"How could he know? The bullets must have been flying all over the place, and besides, why would he kill himself? That doesn't make sense."

"April, it makes sense to me. Why do martyrs everywhere kill themselves? I don't know, but I'm guessing that the newspapers back in '73 had lots to say about this. Maybe someone ought to look at those. Even without that, look here at the transcript, right here on page 107. The doctor's name was Kettel, Charles Kettel, and he's explaining his findings to the grand jury. Looks like he's using photographs of the body in the morgue taken by a guy named—let's see, here it is—George Hight."

"Well, just tell me the meat of it. I'll read it later, I promise. Tell me the basis for alleging suicide."

"Dr. Kettel found two separate gunshot wounds in Casuse's body. Actually, he found four wounds from two shots. There were two entry wounds and two exit wounds. He was hit on the right side of his chest by one gun, a rifle. Then, in his chin, there is an entirely different wound, this one came from a handgun. The bullet to his chest went out his back, but the one under his chin spiraled straight up and blew off the top of his head."

"What do you mean *in* his chin?"

"I was getting to that. You see it wasn't *in* his chin. The entry wound described in this transcript was just *beneath* his chin. That bullet went up through his skull and came out above his left ear."

"How could he tell where it went in from where it went out?"

"From the size, I guess. He said the hole beneath the chin was one inch in width. A bullet that makes a hole that big is a pretty big bullet. That's what blew off the top of his head. It was a bigger bullet than the one in his side. The one that killed him, the bigger one, was the one that went through his skull. It was either a .38 or a .357."

"So the one in his side was not so bad, is that what he's saying?"

"Not exactly. He said that the one in his side hit some vital organs, and it might have eventually killed him except that the one through the head got him first."

"I don't get it. He has two wounds, but the doctor thinks that the one under his chin killed him. Is that it?"

"Yeah, that about sums it up."

"How can he know the one under the chin was self-inflicted?"

"As I read this transcript, he based the suicide part on two things. The powder burns and the direction the bullet traveled. He found powder burns surrounding the hole under the chin but none on the wound in his side. He testified that the chin wound came from a distance of approximately four inches. That is, the barrel of the gun that made that hole had to be only four inches away from his chin when it was fired."

"What did you mean about the direction of the bullet? I mean, the one beneath his chin."

"Well, as I read Dr. Kettel's testimony—let's see, it's here on page 115 of the transcript—it's the point of entrance in relation to the point of exit of the bullet."

"Okay, I guess, but that doesn't mean it was self-inflicted. It just means that the barrel was close. I mean, couldn't someone else have shot him by putting the gun four inches away from him? You know, like, close range or whatever?"

"April, there are two problems with that. First, the doctor is saying that the direction is important—remember it went in directly underneath the chin, but it came out on the left side of the head. Seems to me that it could only have been done by holding the gun yourself in your right hand and pointing it straight up. Secondly, who could have done that? The mayor was already outside before the police started firing into the store. And this guy Casuse was alive when the mayor jumped through the plate glass door. Several witnesses saw him come to the front door, holler at the mayor, and fire at least one shot at him. That only leaves Casuse and Nakaidinae inside. After the firing stopped, Nakaidinae came out and said Casuse was wounded. The police went inside and immediately dragged the body out. There were no more shots fired after Nakaidinae came out. Casuse was dead when they went inside. That's why the coroner said the wound was self-inflicted. Powder burns, direction of the bullet, *and* no one else inside, except for Nakaidinae."

"But, Virg, isn't this still just an opinion? I know it's an opinion of a doctor, but could he have been wrong?"

"Sure, maybe, but he had the skin samples tested by the FBI. Their lab said the samples were positive for powder burns on the chin but negative on the wound in his side."

"Then there is a real question here. Could Nakaidinae have shot Casuse?"

"Hell, I dunno. But the medical evidence, the timing, and everything else points to Casuse killing himself. He was wounded in the side by a police bullet. We know that because there were no powder burns on that wound. He might have thought he was going to die anyhow, so maybe he just put an extra bullet in his brain. Then he's a martyr for sure, not just a wounded kidnapper with a cause."

"How was the doctor—you said his name was Kettel, right—how sure was Dr. Kettel that the wound in the side was not self-inflicted too? Was that just because there were no powder burns?"

"No, remember that the wound in the side was from a different gun, *and* there were no powder burns. That meant that it was fired from farther away. He couldn't shoot himself in the side without leaving powder burns, and even if he could have, do you think he would have done it with a different gun than the one he used under his chin? Like I said, maybe he wanted to die a martyr rather than a kidnapper."

"Wow, Virg, we need to tell Clay about this right away. I am pretty sure that the book he read about this said that Casuse was killed in the police shoot-out."

"April, that could be literally true but still misleading. He was *killed*, and it happened *during* the police shoot-out. If you stop there, then whoever reads the book would naturally jump to the conclusion that the police killed him. But that's not what bothers me about the story. The thing about this is, if Casuse did kill himself, then he did something taboo for Navajos. Death is something we don't talk much about out on the Rez. And death by suicide, man oh man, that is *bahadzid*. So . . ."

"*Bahadzid*? What does that mean exactly?"

"It means tabooed. We have many taboos. We avoid lightning-struck trees like the plague. Raw meat is taboo. Traditional Navajos never comb their hair at night. And death, well, that's one of our biggest fears."

"Everybody is afraid to die. You Navajos are pretty much the same as the Irish Ryan clan when it comes to the fear of dying."

"No, you don't get it. It's not dying that we are afraid of, it's *death*."

"You're afraid of death, but not dying? The end result's the same, you know."

"Well, I wasn't talking about myself. But for my people, the Diné, we really have no belief in a glorious immortality the way whites do. We sure don't believe in the kind of heaven or hell that you Irish Catholics do. Existence in the Navajo hereafter is somewhat shadowy, full of ghosts and witches. Our elders teach that the afterworld, that's where you go when you die, is a place like the earth, only different. It's located to the north and deep below the earth's surface."

"Wow. That sounds more like superstition than religion. But anyhow, where does suicide fit in with all of this?"

"Death and everything connected with it are taboo and bad. Traditional Navajos out on the Rez won't even look upon the body of a dead animal, except one killed for food. Dead humans are buried as soon as possible. Did you know that family members are more or less restricted to their homes for four days when one of them dies?"

"Four days? Why?"

"My grandfather said that sometime in those four days, his spirit could still be wandering among the living family. Navajos do not want to mix the spirit of a dead person with the spirit of a living person. That might happen if you wander off or if you are not careful what you say. Family members don't talk about the death because they don't want to contaminate themselves with the spirit of a dead person."

"I'm getting it. You Navajos really do have more taboos than the Irish do. We are afraid of ghosts, and you are afraid of spirits. Pretty much the same thing, though, aren't they?"

"Not exactly, we have living spirits and dead spirits. Your ghosts are always dead, aren't they? All our taboos about death come down to fear, fear of ghosts. Ghosts are chindi, that is, they come from the dead."

"Virg, this is fascinating. I knew a little about traditional Navajos, but you are hardly traditional. Are you afraid of ghosts?"

"No, and most younger Navajos aren't either. But many older people are. Remember, only those who die of old age, or are stillborn, *don't* turn into ghosts. We believe—that is, my people believe—that many ghosts return to plague the living."

"Okay, I get that, but I still don't see the suicide part. Is that a different kind of death somehow?"

"Yeah, but I don't remember all of the reasons. It seems like some clan elders believe that, in the afterworld, the suicides are separated and kept apart from other dead people. Remember that only *some* ghosts come back to haunt their families or their clan. There is a belief that suicides, since they are separated off down below, *always* come back. If they are mean enough or disrespectful enough to kill themselves when they were living, just think of how mean they could be when they come back as a ghost. Take my word for it, suicide is not acceptable on the Rez."

"Well then, what could account for Casuse killing himself?"

"I don't know one way or the other. Maybe he was not raised on the Rez. Maybe his family was not very traditional. Maybe lots of things. But the medical evidence is very strong. My guess is that the people—that is, the Diné—rejected the notion out of hand because it's something no one wants to talk about."

"You are probably right, Virg, maybe nobody wanted to talk about it back when it happened. But it is part of the story, and I am sure going to talk to Uncle Clay about it. He is an expert of sorts on Indian warriors. Maybe he knows about this suicide taboo thing."

"Maybe he does. We'll probably never know."

April said, "You know, we might. Maybe Nakaidinae talked about it later on, you know like after the trial or something. I'll make a note of that while I'm researching the rest of the story."

Virgil and April looked at one another as though each was afraid to leave because something was left unsaid. April broke the pause. "Virgil, this story—that is, my part of it—isn't going to get between us, is it? I mean, I want to help my uncle Clay and all, but not if you don't really want me to?"

"No, I think you should do it. It's just that there is a lot of tradition and culture wrapped up in what we do. What happened in 1973 changed everything. Gallup is different now because of the mayor's abduction and Casuse's death. This story might open up some wounds, that's all I am saying."

"That's what I'm sensing, I guess. Will digging into Casuse's life cause us problems?"

"April, I'm not sure what your uncle is after here. As far as Casuse is concerned, it's not his life that's the story here. It's his death. You know there will be two sides to this. Some will say the *bilagáana* police killed him, no matter what some doctor in Gallup found. Others will say he died by his own hand. Hell, even if he did, does that make any difference? Some of my people will be glad to see the story come out again, and some will be sad. Like his family for instance."

"I'm sure that's true. That brings up something else. I got copies of the police witness statements. It looks like most of them jibe with the testimony at the grand jury hearing. But there's one exception."

"What's that?" Virgil said as frown lines started to streak out above his eyebrows.

"A witness by the name of Zunigha gave a little different story of Casuse's death."

"Really? What did he say?"

"Let me find it. It's here in the stack somewhere. Oh, yes, here it is. He was twenty-one at the time and living in Fort Wingate—that's just east of here."

"Yeah, April, I know." Smiling the frown off his face, he said, "I'm the one from here, remember?"

"Yeah, right, you'd know where that is, of course. Anyhow, he was driving by and just happened to come on the scene. He saw Casuse take the mayor into the store although he didn't know it was the mayor at the time. He stayed there, out on the street, the whole time; and afterward, he gave this written, signed statement to the police."

"What did he say about Casuse?"

"He said Casuse fired two shots before anyone fired back at him inside the store. Then, as he remembered it, the mayor was thrown, or ran out the door, and hit the sidewalk right by the front door. He says that Casuse went after him and told the mayor, 'Get up, or I will shoot you.'"

"Really, he was close enough to hear him say that?"

"I don't know how close he was, but that is what he says he heard in his statement. He goes on. Here it is. 'Casuse was shot by one of the officers standing to his left.'"

"To whose left? His or the police officers?"

"Jeeze, Virgil, I don't know. Just let me read you what he says. You can pick the pronouns apart later. Zunigha says, 'They got the mayor out of the way, and there was shooting for a while.' I'll just summarize the rest. They told everyone to get back. Everybody got back. When Casuse came out—that is, when he got shot in the stomach then turned around and walked back in. And then there was shooting back and forth, and they threw the tear gas in. Then Nakaidinae came out with his hands on his head, and there were no more shots after that."

"So he says he saw Casuse get shot by the cops and then Casuse walked back in and then more shots were fired and then there was the tear gas. Did I get that right?"

"Yep."

"There were no more shots after the tear gas, right?"

"He says he doesn't remember any."

"So his recollection is consistent with the grand jury witnesses *and* the coroner."

"Virgil, he doesn't say that. He says the police shot Casuse."

"Yeah, but that is consistent. One wound in the side or the stomach. Let's give that one to the cops. Then he walks back inside the store. The second wound is under his chin. The muzzle of the gun that made that wound was no more than four inches from his skin when the gun was fired, and it blew the top of his head off. There are no cops inside the store after he went back inside. There are no shots fired after the tear gas canister was shot inside the store. So doesn't that mean it happened pretty much like the coroner said it did in his testimony?"

"I'm not convinced. It's just too easy."

"Too easy? Nothing's too easy for a *bilagáana* cop."

"*Bilagáana?* What does that mean, special police or something?"

"No, it means white. White police, in this case."

"Do you think of me as white?"

"No, I think of you as the same as me. But others see me as a Navajo. We are a different race, we're not white."

"That's what I'm getting at. We are the same. I think we are the same race although you are suntanned and I'm not and . . ."

"Red, April, red. That's not suntanned."

"Okay, Chief. But I'm serious here. If this story separated people in Gallup back then, what will it do now? Will it separate us? What might this story do to you?"

"Nothing. If your uncle gets it right, I'll tell everyone I know you. If he screws it up, I'll tell them you tried to tell him but he wouldn't listen."

"Will you help me get it right? I want to bring out the truth, but I could screw it up if you don't tell me when I am doing something *bah-ah-zida*. Is that how you say it?"

"No, that's not how, it's *bahadzid*. Say it slow and kind of curl your tongue around in your mouth when you say it."

"It's not taboo for a Navajo to French-kiss an Irish girl, is it? Maybe you could teach me to say that delicious word by curling your own tongue. Let's try it."

Chapter Eight

"Don't Put Your Shoes on the Wrong Feet—You'll Run Away"

Clay pushed aside the four books on his desk, causing the stack of newspapers at the rear edge to fall to the floor. He'd spent five hours reading up on Wounded Knee; it seemed like five minutes. He knew the story well enough, but reading about it after a thirty-year recess made the distant rumble of drumbeats real again. Like liberal thinkers everywhere, he secretly wished he could have been a part of it but, just as secretly, thanked God he hadn't been. The romance of revolution paled when the reality of jail intervened.

The largest Wounded Knee book was clearly Russell Means's ode to himself, grandly titled *Where White Men Fear to Tread*. Means was the real thing—he had the heart and mind of a warrior, but he also had the publicity instincts of grandiose man. Nonetheless, his evocative title had a simplistic sort of truth. FBI agents everywhere from the Black Hills in the Dakotas to Ruby Ridge in Idaho would likely agree. The middle-sized book was Robert Allen Warrior's *Like a Hurricane*; and the smaller one was *Airlift to Wounded Knee* by Bill Zimmerman. Those three were mostly written from the AIM side. The fourth one, a slim 165-page book, by Stanley Lyman, was a direct first-person account. Lyman was the superintendent of the Pine Ridge Reservation and was believed to be a progressive man much in tune with the Indians he was assigned to supervise. His book was based entirely on daily recordings he made to document the events during the actual siege.

Together, this collection of faded memories, war stories, and get-it-off-my-chest revelations painted a vivid picture of the American Indian Movement in the 1960s and '70s. *Maybe they were gone, but their fighting words survived and made them larger than they were.*

Clay swiveled to his computer table, opened his e-mail program, and began to type.

> April,
>
> You've been pretty quiet down there in Gallup for a week or so. I hope your work is progressing well. I've just spent a bit of time going over Wounded Knee's literary record. Frankly, the direct connection between Wounded Knee and Gallup that I hoped would be in all the books is still eluding me. I've read three good books on the subject this week, and the press coverage from South Dakota and Washington. Gallup is mentioned from time to time because most Indian leaders and shakers either have been to Gallup, or know about its central importance to the Navajos, Hopis, and Zunis. But a direct connection between what Russell Means and Dennis Banks did in South Dakota and what Larry Casuse and Robert Nakaidinae did in Gallup either was missed by the reporters or didn't exist in the first place. On the positive side, the causes and the motivation are nearly identical. But I haven't found anything to confirm they actually talked to one another before their respective forays into the violent aspects of political speech.
>
> The timing of these three books is interesting in itself. The first book (*Airlift to Wounded Knee*) was released in 1976, three years after the takeover. Lyman's book (*Wounded Knee—1973*) was published in 1991, twelve years after his death in 1979. The next in sequence (*Where White Men Fear to Tread*) came out in 1995, and the last (*Like a Hurricane*) in 1996. While all four are somewhat autobiographical, only the Russell Means book was written as an autobiography. The other three are by people on the ground, so to speak, but their literary goal was quite different.
>
> There is a little known secret in the book business, the author never gets to write the content of the dust jacket or the marketing blurbs about the book. That's because this part of the book is usually pure hype. Most authors are dismal sellers. They know the content, but can't "close," if you know what I mean.
>
> The dust jacket on the first book, *Airlift to Wounded Knee*, talks about a one-day story, April 17, 1973. That was seven weeks into

the siege at Wounded Knee. To tell you the truth, I know quite a lot about April 17, 1973, because I was there—in Wounded Knee. That's another story. After this now-famous airlift, everyone remotely involved took a forced trip to the federal courthouse after grand jury indictments were handed up. If you add in the almost four hundred people, mostly AIM members, that were also arrested for actually participating in the siege itself, you get a staggering number of indictments for what many believed was political dissent, *albeit* illegal and violent political dissent. *Airlift* draws a parallel between Wounded Knee and the war in Vietnam. There is nothing in it about Gallup, probably because it tells the story of one day in the siege of Wounded Knee. The authors tie the larger struggle to the Vietnam War.

Lyman's book is handy to have as a fact-checker against the other three, but it's limited to a day-by-day recounting, without much effort to examine either the politics or the consequences.

The 1966 book, *Like a Hurricane*, presents the road map of the American Indian rights movement and attempts to link it to black Americans fighting for civil rights, the counterculture trying to subvert the Vietnam War, and women fighting for their liberation. While somewhat biased, it nevertheless lays out the story of Indian activists who took control of Alcatraz in 1969, the storming of the BIA building on the eve of Nixon's second term in 1972, and the siege of Wounded Knee in 1973. There is a connection of sorts. This book confirms the symbolic value of seizing Alcatraz and directly connects that symbolism to Gallup, New Mexico.

It seems that after Alcatraz was restored to the feds, the young occupiers became celebrities of sorts. The National Indian Youth Council invited them to come to Gallup in 1970. This was an activist Indian Rights group if there ever was one. They protested the Gallup Indian Ceremonial in August of 1970. The organizers of the protest invited many of the young people actually involved in the landing and takeover of Alcatraz to come to Gallup. So in a real way, the road from Alcatraz to Wounded Knee did in fact go through Gallup.

Keep in mind the sequence of the three books. The first, *Airlift*, is a one-day story and connects Indian rights to the Vietnam struggle. The second, Russell Means's autobiography, is about Indian rights but is not tied to Vietnam. The third, *Hurricane*, is broader than the first two and connects Gallup to both Alcatraz and Wounded Knee.

Russell Means' book, the middle in the series, is very important in understanding what happened at Wounded Knee. At least it's the most important one I've found so far. I've heard about a book published *underground* by the actual participants in Wounded Knee. If I can find it, it should clear up some of the mystery and hyperbole in all three of these books.

If we can figure out what really happened in Wounded Knee, then we will have a better handle on what happened in Gallup. Russell Means's book is long by anyone's count. I'm sure they have it in that Octavia Fellin Public Library there in Gallup. To put the book in context, start with the appendix on page 545. It's the text of a speech Russell Means gave in 1980, a rather eloquent statement of his beliefs. He makes the interesting point that he "hates writing." Yet he wrote, along with his coauthor Marvin Wolf, a virtual tome of the Indian rights movement.

Means was not the first to suggest that "writing" epitomizes the European concept of legitimate thinking and that "what is written has an importance that is denied the spoken." Naturally, I disagree. When I read Means' comment, I was reminded of something Ralph Waldo Emerson said, "I have, however, found writers superior to their books, and I cling to my first belief that a strong head will dispose fast enough of these impediments, and give one the satisfaction of reality, the sense of having been met, and a larger horizon."

April, if you have time, take a look at both Means and Emerson. Maybe you will find something that connects with you. In the meantime, keep looking for something that connects Wounded Knee to Gallup.

As I think about some of the things you've mentioned about your young Navajo, Virgil, it occurs to me that he may be the key to figuring this whole thing out. I gather he knows his people and their culture from the ground up even though he was raised in that urban wasteland in the desert known as Phoenix. Let me know.

Keep digging.

Love,
Clay

He clicked Send, powered down his computer, and went around to the far side of the desk to pick up the pile of spilled newspapers from the floor. The headline from a March 1, 1973, Associated Press story caught his eye, WOUNDED KNEE 1973 IS CALLED 'TRIBAL FIGHT.' The AP stringer identified Albuquerque, New Mexico, as his source city. He covered a news conference there called by Charles Trimble, executive director of the National Congress of American Indians. Trimble admitted that he didn't know all the facts, but nevertheless expressed a negative reaction, "It seems to be a tribal fight, a fight against the tribe's sovereignty." The president of the group, Leon Cook, said, "It seems every time we move one step forward, we move two steps back. I don't know what it will solve for the Indian community or for AIM itself."

Another column on the same front page noted that South Dakota's two U.S. senators were flying to the tiny community of Wounded Knee in an effort to end the then two-day-old siege. Sen. James Abourezk and Sen. George McGovern planned to land at nearby Pine Ridge. The AP stringer suggested the hasty trip was an answer to AIM's demand that the U.S. Senate investigate the Bureau of Indian Affairs. AIM posed its demand as the most important condition to freeing the Wounded Knee hostages.

Clay remembered that Senators McGovern and Abourezk had gone to Wounded Knee but couldn't recall what they did there. He leafed through the rest of his newspaper clippings but didn't find any more references. So he returned to the Russell Means book and learned that both senators had actually gone into the Knee, as Means called it, where they visited the eleven people held "hostage" by the AIM occupiers. McGovern asked the Gildersleeves, the Czywcynskis, and Father Manhart if they were "hostages."

Agnes Gildersleeve, wife of the white trading post owner, said, "Of course we're not hostages. These Indians are here, and they have legitimate grievances. You people—it's all your fault. If you people had done something about their problems, they wouldn't be here today. We're here not only to protect our property, but also because we want to help save the Indians, and we know you're about to massacre them."

As a direct result of the early visit by McGovern and Abourezk, negotiations began between AIM leaders and the government. Those negotiations lasted for days. Some people gave the negotiators credit for making sure the 1880s massacre, so eloquently described in Dee Brown's famous book, didn't repeat itself.

As he read through the pile, Clay couldn't help but think about whether those two young activists in New Mexico had given *any* thought to the consequences of *their* hostage taking in Gallup. At least in the Gallup case, there was no doubt about Mayor Garcia being a hostage. If Garcia's abductors had killed him, the news would have spread quickly from Gallup to Wounded Knee. Would the military and the FBI in Wounded Knee have reacted *to that?* Or overreacted? Might they have turned Wounded Knee into the massacre that Mrs. Gildersleeve feared?

The more Clay thought about it, the more he believed that there really was a connection between Wounded Knee and Gallup. *Who would care what he believed? He would have to find hard evidence to prove it. Will April's Virgil give him hard evidence? Is that what it will take?*

~ ~ ~

"Excuse me, I need some help," April said to the clerk in the new state library on Cerrillos Road in Santa Fe. The paint still smelled fresh in the magnificent building not far from the campus of Santa Fe College.

"Sure, what can I help you with?"

"I'm looking for information about a former member of the University of New Mexico Board of Regents. He was confirmed by the state senate here in Santa Fe in 1973. Is this where I can look at minutes and records of his confirmation hearing?"

"We have the governor's papers from territorial days up to the present. Those usually include appointments to boards and commissions. UNM, did you say? What was the name of the regent?"

"The regent I'm looking for is Emmett C. Garcia."

The reference librarian sent her to a desk in the archival section where the rule of the day was preservation of old, sometimes-valuable documents. Every document had to be handled with cotton gloves provided at the desk. If you wanted to make notes, you could only use a pencil. The sign on the desk read, "NO roller balls, ballpoints, markers, pens, or quills. Please."

Three hours reading Governor Bruce King's penal papers, another two reading related newspaper articles, and another final hour reading the minutes from the UNM Board of Regents for 1973 gave April that numb feeling that comes with squinting at blurred pages and taking notes with a number 4 lead pencil. But she could hardly wait to get outside and call Clay on her cell phone.

"Uncle Clay, I'm in Santa Fe, and I've got some really good stuff on our story. First of all . . ."

"April, this is a good time, but aren't you on a cell phone? This could be an expensive call if you're paying roaming charges on top of the long-distance rates."

"No problem. I have a new phone that gives me bunches of free minutes and no hidden charges for roaming. So get your pencil ready."

"Okay, I'll take notes, but you've still got to write up the hard facts and e-mail them to me. We need a record. By the way, did you copy documents, or are you going to brief me from your notes?"

"Yes, of course I did."

"Which, notes or copies?"

"Both, notes for me and copies for you."

"Okay, shoot."

"Well, one of the first things I found was a quarter-page photo from the *Albuquerque Journal*, Saturday, February 24, 1973, captioned NEW UNM REGENTS EMMETT GARCIA AND DR. ALBERT SIMMS—OATH OF OFFICE SIGNED AMID STUDENT PROTESTS. The story accompanying that big photo has another small photo of a fearsome-looking Larry Casuse wearing a red headband and a Levi's jacket. Actually, he wasn't exactly fearsome because he wore thick bookish-looking glasses. Maybe he was a warrior, but he must also have been a scholar because he was a sophomore at the university and the president of a major club on campus."

"Was this protest in Albuquerque? That's where UNM is located if I remember correctly."

"Yes. It was in Albuquerque on the UNM campus at a board of regents meeting. But Casuse was only protesting Garcia, not Dr. Simms, the other newly named regent."

"Well, read the highlights to me and then fax both photos and the newspaper article to me tomorrow."

"Sure. It says the chairman of the board, a man named Calvin Horn, allowed Casuse to protest formally after he interrupted introductions at the start of the meeting. Casuse read a statement to the board. I don't have a copy of the statement yet, but I think I know where I can get a copy. Get this, the paper quotes Casuse, '[My] people will get together and put an end to people like you. You people are not human beings.'"

"Well, that's revolutionary rhetoric for sure. That's dated February 23, did you say?"

"Yep, and six days later, he went to Gallup and abducted Garcia."

"What happened in between the swearing in and the abduction?"

"I don't know for sure."

"I'll tell you one thing for sure. Wounded Knee *happened*. Was there anything in the minutes or records connecting Gallup and Wounded Knee?"

"No, not directly. But my notes are not chronological because I was finding stuff in different places and rooms and boxes. I am sorting through some while we talk because I remember some stuff that happened before this. Wait. Here are the actual typed minutes of that February 23 meeting mentioned in the newspaper. The minutes contain Casuse's actual words to Garcia:

Oath of Office for New Regents: Prior to the administration of the oath of office to Emmett E. Garcia, mayor of Gallup, and Albert G. Simms II, Albuquerque surgeon, Mr. Horn permitted the reading of a statement by Larry Casuse, president of the Kiva Club, protesting the seating of Mr. Garcia. He cited conflicts of interest and lack of concern for the Indian people and concluded, "We're going to find all the human beings in this country—in this state—and we're going to get the human beings together and we're going to put an end to people like Emmett Garcia, and we're going to start with Emmett Garcia. So we don't really care what you people do, because you people aren't human beings."

"April, at least in retrospect, Casuse's language makes it sound like he was planning to kill Garcia for at least a week before he abducted him. Doesn't it say he is going to put an 'end' to him? That's strong language for a formal meeting of regents or trustees of a university."

"Yeah, Uncle Clay, but as you said, this is all in retrospect. I don't know that anyone thought he was serious. If they had, they probably would have done something about it."

"Well, just remember that the Gallup abduction is not an isolated event. Like most political acts, it originated somewhere else. Casuse made that threatening statement in Albuquerque on February 23, AIM took over Wounded Knee on February 28, and the next day, Casuse abducted Garcia in Gallup. Why March 1, and why Garcia? Was it because he was mayor of Gallup, the Indian Capital of the World or because he was a regent of the university, and this was the seventies when a great many students protested almost everything? Or was it because his fellow militants in Wounded Knee pushed him over the edge? It is starting to sound like Casuse was all worked up about Garcia, and then his fellow warriors took action a few days later in

Wounded Knee. Maybe he was feeling the pressure to do something on his own. You keep digging on that end, and I'll look for connections from here."

"Right, and remember you asked me about how serious Virgil was about helping us?"

"Yes, but I didn't mean to make it sound negative. I'm quite impressed with him based on your sense of him."

"Oh, I know that. You'll like him even more when you meet him. The thing about Virgil is that he has lived in both worlds and has a wonderful sense of perspective. He knows a lot about what they call 'the Navajo way.' You ought to hear him talk about political realities and the power of the voting booth over the gun. That's how he put it actually. So he can see not only some of what Casuse saw but also some of what Garcia might have seen too. I told him about the quotes you put in your e-mail from Russell Means and Emerson. He's read some Emerson but hadn't read Means's book yet. He's going to get it in Window Rock."

"Good. He's just what we need. Maybe it will take a philosopher to make the connection between the perpetrator and the victim. On the other hand, it could be apples and bananas. I'm looking for a connection between the perpetrators in Wounded Knee and the perpetrators in Gallup. There were victims in both places and probably on both sides."

"I've talked to Virg a lot. And I listened too. I'll tell him what you said about apples and bananas. He'll get it. Bye."

April drove home to Gallup. It was late, she was tired, but she couldn't wait to start the detailed reading of the newspapers and other documents she copied in Santa Fe. Then she couldn't wait to call Clay again.

"Uncle Clay, I'm sorry to call so late, but this is worth it. I am reading the papers and the stuff about the abduction, and guess what?"

"My guess is that it can wait another five hours until dawn hits up here in God's country. April, fer Chrisakes, I want you to be focused, not obsessed."

"Well, this just won't wait until dawn, either up there in God's country or down here in Indian country. Listen to this. I'll read it to you straight from the paper. Remember, this is just a few days after the abduction in Gallup while the siege at Wounded Knee is still going on. Here's what it says, 'In Albuquerque, meanwhile, a University of New Mexico Indian student organization says Casuse died "for the sake of the animals, the trees, our Mother Earth, and our father the universe." The Kiva Club also called for the release of Nakaidinae and referred to him as "a captive of America's inhumanity and irrational behavior toward Mother Earth." He was only, like Casuse, defending nature by capturing the symbolic Emmett Garcia. Indians believe man is one with nature and is put on earth to protect it while the white man's technological society destroys that relationship. We must undermine all things that represent the forces that are attempting to conquer nature and humanity.' What do you make of that, Uncle Clay?"

"Sounds like the Red Power movement in the seventies. The Sioux and the Cheyenne were using the same rhetoric in Wounded Knee. April, is there something else, or can I get up and make my morning coffee?"

"Yes, there is something else. One of the last things Casuse said about Garcia was that he was 'a *false person* who is symbolic of America's irrational attitude toward Mother Earth and humanity.' Casuse's words and the words used about him after his death are almost identical."

"Yes, that's a good observation on your part, April. The Kiva Club was probably an activist group looking for social change, at least among Indians. Their writing is a combination of revolutionary rhetoric and Emerson philosophy."

"Now, getting back to Garcia, he had two names. His parents named him Emmett, but his friends called him Frank. I don't know why, but it could be important. It's as if he was two different people. He was one person—Frank—to those who really knew him and Emmett to those who didn't. Maybe there is something to this 'false person' claim after all. Emmett was false, at least as far as the Indian activists were concerned. Frank was real, at least to his friends and constituents in Gallup."

"Well, I am not sure about that. You are in Gallup, and I am remote, even from local politics, up here in Spokane. Has your long night's reading given you any better handle on exactly why Casuse was so opposed to him for the regents position? I doubt it was the philosophical notion about loving the earth and the trees and the animals."

April paused as though she hadn't heard the question. "It looks to me like Casuse opposed the appointment because the mayor was a part owner of a liquor store near the Navajo reservation. It was called the Navajo Inn. Casuse said it fostered alcoholism. At least that's what the Kiva Club said Casuse believed."

"April, you weren't around then, but Indians were naturalists and environmentalists long before the Sierra Club got wind of it."

"Listen to this, here is another statement read by a Kiva Club member named Frederick Martinez. He said, 'The city of Gallup—with all its drunkard

Indians, its spit-stained sidewalks, its dirty-smelling bars, and its coldness toward humanity—was Casuse's target when he sought to protect Mother Earth and all its forces from these evils.' So wasn't that worth getting up a little earlier than you planned? Clay, are you there? Uncle Clay?"

"Yeah, sure, I'm here. At least in spirit. That seems a little disjointed. Are you reading from one single newspaper article?"

"Yes, but it wasn't one I got in Santa Fe. It's a staff story from the *Gallup Independent* on March 3, 1973, a recap of sorts. Isn't the *false person* stuff eerie? I mean, it sounds like Casuse talked himself into believing that the mayor wasn't human, so he could be killed without consequences. I'll ask Virgil about this. He was telling me some really cool stuff about Navajo ghosts and witches and taboos. I wonder if he knows about the idea that some people are *false persons* if they are not in harmony with the earth?"

"Well, it seems to me that you have a wonderful source there in your friend Virgil. I take it that you and Virgil are more than just *friends*. Your mother seems to think that Virgil is the *only* reason you're even in Gallup."

"No, he's not the only reason. I'm here to write and to learn. But he can help with that, can't he? I think it would be good for you to talk to Virgil too. He's a gentleman and very thoughtful, and I really like him a lot even though that seems to worry Mom a little."

"April, your love life is between you and your mother. I only asked because you told me before that he was a Navajo who went from the reservation to the university and is now back on the reservation helping his people. The idea of 'one's people' is very strong among Indians all over the country. All the warrior societies were based on allegiance to a clan or tribe or, in the broadest sense, one's people."

"Clay, did you know that's what Navajo actually means?"

"You mean the Diné?"

"So you do know. Virgil has some books that he's going to bring to town this weekend. I'll know more when I talk to you next. In the meantime, I'll dig into the story about the Navajo Inn. Have I told you about that yet?"

"Not much."

"It was a liquor store several miles outside Gallup on the road to the Navajo reservation. Casuse was against Garcia because he was a part owner. I'm making notes on it, and I'll send you an e-mail later today. Now you can go back to sleep, or you can take on the day. It'll do you good."

"You're right. A little more sleep always does me good."

CHAPTER NINE

"Don't Say *Chindi*—One Will Come to You"

Virgil sat comfortably on the floor in April's apartment. Lanky men with bony knees from other cultures always look as if they are about to fall over from a cross-legged position. But Virgil looked at home on the floor. April sat cross-legged on an overstuffed chair. With her angular chin cupped in both hands, she concentrated on Virgil's notion that only the Diné tried to live in *harmony* with the earth.

"Virgil, give me a break here. The Irish culture is tied to the soil too, you know, potatoes and sheep and wool. Our culture is as agrarian as yours is. We love nature and . . ."

"I'm sure you do, but for traditional Navajos, the concepts of nature and the supernatural are tied together. Whites, Irish or not, don't think of them in the same way. My clan's attitude is directly opposed to that of most white Americans. In the Navajo view, nature can only be controlled in small pieces. In our clan, a man might divert the water in a stream to irrigate his crops. But he would never attempt to master the forces of nature by putting up a big dam for erosion control. The Diné look on that sort of thing with suspicion. Man is not and can never be the master of nature."

"Virg, that means that natural disasters should not be avoided or nature harnessed in any way. Is that what you're saying?"

"No, I'm saying that nature is the master of man. I was taught by clan elders that man is a weak creature. He's just one small part of the overall plan that nature has for us."

"Well, we probably feel the same then because God knows the Irish are masters of nothing, not even the bloody soil we dig for warmth."

April loved these philosophical chats with Virgil; but she knew that he was nothing like the typical, understated, and noncommunicative Navajos round Gallup. While he talked and paying only half-attention, she busied herself in the major kitchen, looking for tea and finding only collapsed boxes and crumbs from leftover biscuits. She wondered if that too was the fault of her Irish ancestors. *I'm always out of something*, she thought.

"April, I've learned more about the Irish from you than I ever wanted to know. But seriously, even though Ireland and the Navajo Nation are both poor countries, there is a real difference in how we see nature, particularly in how it affects how we work and what we earn. I mean, Ireland is probably not poor on purpose, is it?"

"What do you mean on purpose? Are you saying that poverty on the Rez is there because Navajos *like* it that way?"

"No, not exactly. But the fact is that many traditional Navajos believe that the gifts of nature are just that—gifts, and a man must be industrious to receive those gifts for his own use. He should never be so selfish as to accumulate nature's riches for the sake of having them. That's an important difference between us. I mean all of us—aboriginal tribes, native indigenous peoples, and the rest of the European world, including the Irish."

"Virg, honey, that's one part crap and one part poetry. We all want things, you know. All of us, you included, want to have things that make our lives better or happier. Riches are not per se bad."

"No, I didn't say that. Some Navajos are greedy. But even then, it's usually on a smaller scale. The real issue is whether we want more than we can use, that is, more than the family can use. Riches, like food, are to be shared with a man's family and, by extension, his clan and related clans. A Navajo chief once said, 'You can't get rich if you treat your relatives right.'"

"Oh god, did you just make that up, or did someone really say that? You accuse *me* of being poetic. Virgil, that's beautiful."

"Yeah, it is poetic, and someone did say it. Or at least they said something like that. I don't remember the exact words, but I remember my grandfather talking about riches and owning things and cheating people. He said someone said it, so that's good enough for me."

"Did he tell you who? Who said it, I mean."

"I dunno. In our world, who said something is not very important. You know, sometimes I think it's only important to whites because they don't trust one another like we do. If a white man says some other white man said something profound or wise, you always want to know who it was. So you can check. And if the person wasn't smart, then you don't listen, so you have to check not only his name but also his smarts as well."

"Maybe your grandfather thought those things and said it was someone else to make sure you listened?"

"Why would he do that? He wasn't trying to impress me. He was trying to teach me something valuable."

"Tell me more about what you think about working. I mean, working for one's daily bread. You know, grubbing for the almighty dollar."

April had finally found some tea although it was not to her liking, black something or another. Virgil put his boots up on her little coffee table and watched her make the tea, careful to let it steep before removing the tea bags and more careful to stir the cream before it could settle on the top. Coming back into the room and into the conversation, she said, "So work is sort of a take-it-or-leave-it proposition, do I have that right? How about you, can you take it or leave it?"

"Nope, I do it for the same reason most Navajos do. I work to get ahead. Of course, I have to make a living, to make money. But I also save as much as I can for the future. But not everyone on the Rez sees it that way. Old people on the Rez think that accumulating things just to have them is stupid. There was a time when no one on the land that is now our home thought that way. White Americans introduced the concept of *possession* to the Navajo. Even today, a Navajo will most often stop working when he feels he has enough and that his relatives are taken care of."

"Are you saying there are no rich Navajos?"

"No. There are several actually. Some great men on the Rez have built up considerable fortunes, even by white standards. But getting rich is not a goal of very many. Maybe that's why we're poor."

"What about all the wonderful jewelry and rugs your people make? Don't they acquire possessions and riches that way?"

"Well, sort of. It takes a lot of skill, and we recognize that part of it. When we see the ability to weave a fine blanket or to work jewelry, we like that. The important thing is how those things make you look. That's actually more important than *owning* them. See, when a Navajo looks good, that is valued more highly than personal wealth. Showing your jewelry and your blankets is not as much a personal matter as it is a family matter. If a man has much jewelry and his wife weaves fine rugs, it doesn't say anything about them personally, but it says a lot about how much money they have in their family."

"Speaking of looking good, you do, you know."

Virgil didn't notice the change in April's voice or the way she leaned forward in the chair, like an invitation. He responded more factually than April had hoped. "Me? I don't look good, I wear the same things every day, and the only rug in my apartment is a leftover from the last tenant."

April's voice dropped a little bit more. She moved down off the overstuffed chair and said, "Well, you look good to me, and it's not because of what you wearing. Actually, you look better when you're wearing nothing at all as they say in the commercials. And rugs are good for more than looking at, they're good to stretch out on too, you know?"

April and Virgil had been talking for hours. It was time to move from family culture to family planning. They stretched out on the floor and moved their bodies together much like they'd been moving their memories. In a short time, they discovered, once again, how much fun it was to let nature's rhythms lead them into a more sensuous harmony than the abstract one so treasured by the Diné.

The next day brought April a sense of renewal. While her eyes focused on the yellowed old newspaper photos on the wide library table, she allowed her mind to drift backward. What was it like, she thought, just a block from here thirty years ago when that historic *march* took place?

~ ~ ~

March 31, 1973

Route 66, Gallup, New Mexico

Not even the hot-blooded rhetoric and the war chants starting to rumble through the crowd coming toward him could warm Gallup's leftover winter streets. A little still frozen mud, lots of wind-strewn debris, and sullen faces painted a dour picture on what otherwise seemed a nice little town. It was a scene reminiscent of other marches, some peaceful, some not. The weekend edition of the *Gallup Independent* had two headlines that bright Saturday morning, March 31, 1973. INDIAN MARCH SET FOR TODAY was the banner above column one on the left side, and NAVAJO EMERGENCY FUNDS ALLOCATED carried the other lead story on the right side of the front page. The first story's strident tone set the stage for the much-feared march on Gallup. The second story's ho-hum, matter-of-fact reporting was apparently written by a reporter oblivious to the fact that both stories were about Gallup's relationship with Window Rock.

Gallup was the focus of two very different worlds as March of 1973 gave way to April Fool's day. Back in Wounded Knee, the siege was still on; and Fool's Crow, one of AIM's leaders, was still behind the barricades. The Gallup mayoral election was just three days off, and everyone thought Frank Garcia would win. But it was no coincidence that the Indian protest march and the final push of the mayoral campaign were scheduled for the same day.

Garcia was Gallup's most popular and its youngest ever mayor. He had roots on the reservation, a ready smile, and a grand plan on how to blend his own ambitions with Gallup's growing influence in statewide economic and political circles. But he was hardly the favorite among the impatient and increasingly militant young members of AIM and UNM's Kiva Club. His political rival for Gallup's first four-year mayoral term, Sam Ray, could smell the opportunity.

The Albuquerque organizers of the march on Gallup and their connection with the organizers of the siege in Wounded Knee were only a rumor at this point. Maybe today would clarify things on that score. The new Kiva Club leader, Larry Emerson, a vice president before Larry Casuse's death, estimated that more than 1,500 Indians and sympathetic non-Indians would march through downtown Gallup. If their estimate proved accurate, it would double the number in Larry Casuse's funeral march, just three weeks before.

Bill Donovan's article in the morning newspaper said the Navajo tribe would "sit this one out." Quoting Art Arviso, executive assistant to Navajo tribal chairman Peter McDonald, the article urged "both sides" not to do anything violent. As the *Gallup Independent* defined it, one side was composed of the young militants at the UNM Kiva Club and their fellow AIM protestors. On the other side, so claimed the paper, were law enforcement, Gallup's business leaders, and its elected government. If that were the case, then why was Sammy Ray, Garcia's principal mayoral opponent, milling in with the protestors?

Notwithstanding the protestations of official Navajo tribal spokesmen, everyone else seemed to know that a lot of people from Window Rock, the Navajo Nation's capital forty miles north of Gallup, would be in town today. They came to make it clear that they supported AIM and the Kiva Club.

"Our protest is not just about Gallup," they said, "but also what's happening 'on other reservations.'"

As one clear-eyed, hard-jawed young Indian put it, "Well, you have the barricades back there in Wounded Knee, and now you see that Gallup has those exact same problems that Indians have to put up with."

Gallup's political and law enforcement establishment braced for the first political rally ever organized *outside* the city. There had been other local protest marches. But this would be the first to protest Indian conditions nationwide, not just local issues like who should be Gallup's mayor or who should be on the UNM Board of Regents. Only a few local citizens turned out to see if the rumors about movie star Marlon Brando and black activist Angela Davis showing up in Gallup were true. Both had said they'd be there to show support for their Indian brothers and sisters. Brando's spokesman said he was somewhere in the Southwest. When pressed, he declined to "rule out" the possibility that the famous actor would show up in Gallup.

The historic Gallup Indian Ceremonial Grounds north of the railroad tracks was a fitting place to begin and end the rally. The brochures and the maps made up each year by the local chamber of commerce always gave the full name the "Gallup Indian Ceremonial Grounds," but the locals just said the ceremonial grounds as if to emphasize the small *c* and eliminate the focus on Indian. These men all had dark faces, high cheekbones, headbands to control long black braids, silver necklaces, and soft handshakes.

The women in the crowd came in all sizes and ages. There were skinny teenagers in Levi's and sweatshirts and old, heavy grandmothers in long squaw skirts and velveteen blouses. Although Navajos made up most of the crowd, there was an obvious smattering of Cheyenne, Chippewa, and Sioux, together with a handful of Anglos, Hispanics, and African-Americans.

The crowd turned quiet when, up at the front of the crowd, a frail man with long white hair stepped up onto the small platform. As the crowd quieted, without any sound or motion from him, he looked up at the sky and held his hands up as if trying to feel for rain. In a high-pitched voice, the little man started a short chant, quieting everyone in the front and sending a chill back through the crowd. Then, seeming to interrupt his own song, he began to speak.

"We mean business when we say we want all human beings to be treated with dignity. The enemy has blood too, and he calls us the enemy. There should be no enmity between us. We pray for the returned POWs and for the people of the reservation. We pray that thou wilt bless our cause."

As the protestors moved out of the huge parking lot in front of the ceremonial grounds and began the march down Maloney Street, hand-painted signs appeared as if by magic, and the quiet talk turned to a low murmur as the crowd moved out of the open area onto Maloney Street and headed west toward the first railroad crossing into the main part of town. By staging the largest march in Gallup's history and by making sure the national print and broadcast media was there to watch, the organizers hoped to attract the attention of the American people to the takeover of Wounded Knee *and* the defense of Casuse and Nakaidinae.

The rough peeling stucco of the exhibit hall, the wooden grandstand, the potholed and badly cracked asphalt parking lot, and the tottering overhead electric lines all spoke to the age and heavy use of the ceremonial grounds. For fifty years, thousands of Indians had gathered here every August to show their wares and their culture. Today stood in stark contrast. Today Gallup would see what many young Indians were demanding—respect us, and the ceremonial will go on; treat us like dirt, we will burn your town down. The more moderate view and the prevailing view on the Navajo reservation was that AIM and its proxies on campuses all over America did not speak for mainstream Indian America. But today, it was hard to tell. This was a united crowd.

Every other crowd that had gathered in this large parking lot had heavy backing from local Anglo and Hispanic residents. Today was very different. The brown and white community did its best to ignore the rally by staying off the streets as the marchers passed.

The doors of the bars and the stores, which heavily relied on the usual weekend Indian migration to Gallup, were mostly closed. Richardson's Pawnshop and Eddie's Bar shut down in the middle of the day. The White House, and the few other bars that dared to open at all, planned on closing promptly at 4:00 p.m. Since it was a Saturday, traditionally the best day for bar business, this was an absolute first for Gallup—closing the bars at four in the afternoon—wow!

A dozen or so Anglos strode with the crowd as they meandered down Maloney, past Sky City, and crossed the railroad tracks on Third Street, just past Bubany Lumber. That was the entry point for Main Street and mainline business. Few whites stood along the parade route, but more than a thousand Indians silently lined the curbs. The street side crowd heard, but did not respond, to the sad-sounding tribal chant and the steady, deep rumble of the drum, which was at once both a harness and a tow for the marchers as they flooded onto Gallup's Main Street.

The massive four-foot-diameter deer hide drum boomed an alternatively calming and then rousing sound. The steady beat maintained by four drummers resonated out and into the crowd and the buildings. It was hard to pinpoint the exact source of the pulsating beat before the front marchers came in sight and everybody got their first look at the massive drum. For everyone on the sidewalk, it was a numbing experience. First, your ears feel tense, then your throat begins to wiggle, and your chin feels the vibration coming up off the pavement. It was as if another drum, a much smaller one, was tapping on the small bones around your head. And inexplicably, the melodic drumbeats had a powerful rhyming effect. A drum, a steadily beaten drum, never breaks its own stride, and that is the ultimate rhyme.

The closer it got, the more ominous the pulsing beat felt. Taking on a life of its own, it undulated down the street ahead of the banners and wove through the hand-lettered signs, which the marchers now carried like spears and shields. The fear that all this struck in the watchers from inside storefronts and second-story windows along Coal and Main streets was patent. Up and down, up and down, the signs and the banners moved in sync with the boom of tightly stretched deer hide over a four-foot-diameter barrel, handcrafted out of naturally bleached cottonwood, with rawhide tie-downs. For a moment, it seemed to many watchers as if the people had melted down into the cement, and only the sound and the signs were alive.

This was no movielike thundering, which by its very absence punctuated the cold air with an effect both serious and yet serene. The echo created by two-foot-long oak—and leather-padded mallets methodically slamming down on the tough, stretched rawhide surface rebounded from surface of the drum and echoed off the cars and pickup trucks lining the street. The effect, while likely unintentional, gave credence to the power of the moment. No onlooker talked as the drum passed, and no drumbeater ever looked back. This was raw power, on autopilot, and no one there ever forgot it.

As the marchers passed the Chief Theater and moved west past the El Morrow, on the south side, it became obvious that the organizers had decided to bypass Stearns Sporting Goods, a block to the north. No one would see the bullet holes in the blue-tile border around the shiny new plate glass window.

The drum, its beaters, and its umbilical marchers passed the Manhattan Café and Mlockers Department Store as seemingly unattached hands bobbed up and down in the crowd. Some were fisted, others clutched posters. One sign, heavily photographed from the curb and captured that night on statewide

TV, displayed only bright red lacquer, slowly dripping down onto an unseen owner's wrist and forearm. After the first forty minutes of the march, the red lacquer looked more like juice than blood, making it seem faulty, not virtuous. But those in a position to get a close look felt a harsh twinge deep in their guts, and many felt weak-kneed. The bony, charcoal-drawn hand was torn and shattered and only loosely attached to the invisible vessel of blood, which grotesquely dripped onto the artificial hand as well as the real hand of whoever was carrying the sign.

Another bobbing poster, as large as the fat lady carrying it, demanded, "Feds, Get Off Indian Lands." A freshly painted bright blue poster, carried by a middle-aged woman in a multicolored Indian robe, said it all. Her message, carried by the national TV cameras to Washington, D.C., said, "We are Humans, not Numbers."

The five men and the lone woman who led the march slowed down as they approached the halfway point and the U-turn necessary to go back across the railroad tracks to the ceremonial grounds. This lead group, which now seemed not so much to lead but rather to hold back the throng behind them, was an odd mix of people. The oldest, a thin but seemingly robust Navajo man, wore a narrow red band across his wrinkled forehead. The deep maroon of the band, knotted at the back of his head to keep his flowing white hair in place, starkly contrasted with the dark blue-black color of his skin. A turquoise and coral necklace hung low on his chest, with white coral *hishi* nestled on an emerald blue velveteen shirt, adorned with a dozen silver buttons. His belt was a heavily patterned and tightly woven string cord, with long brightly colored cord ties at the ends. An imposing black man, marching next to him, contrasted starkly by wearing a dark business suit, muted tie, and double-breasted raincoat. Someone in the crowd told an AP reporter from Albuquerque that the man was a law professor, "from over there in Albuquerque, you know."

The putative professor affected a dark fedora pulled low over his brow to shield him from the wind. Two University of New Mexico students, striding with him, formed the middle of the first row. They looked like twins, with their freshly laundered but unironed jeans, open-necked and long-sleeved shirts, and narrow dark eyes squinting with emotional intensity. The man on the end of the first row seemed a little out of step. He looked around, obviously unfamiliar with his surroundings. Navajos looked nothing like the Pueblo tribes along the Rio Grande. Navajos were more angular as though genetically formed by their history as hunters and gatherers rather than as place-bound Pueblo tribes tending local crops. The exceptionally handsome and sternly erect man wore his jet-black hair completely unbound. His long straight hair hung almost to the top of a wide black belt; and that, along with his buckskin-colored knee-high boots, combined to give him a decided military look. He apparently worked hard to get just the right look, not a typical American military look—more the look of a modern Indian warrior in dress uniform. An uncomfortable-looking choke collar, handcrafted out of elk horn and rawhide, covered his Adam's apple. A well-worn prayer thong hung down to his waist. His beaded midthigh-length plains jacket was unbuttoned, making clear to the world that he cared little about the crisp air or the developing wind. He was the only Plains Indian in the march.

In stark contrast, the only woman in the lead row was fair skinned, bundled up in a brightly colored ski parka over heavy wool slacks and sporting well-oiled, lace-up boots with orange laces. Her coal black eyes were set in narrow lids that darted from one side of the street to the other. Her practical and thoroughly modern attire, her confidant stride, and her compressed lips told her story for all who cared to notice: "Don't look at me, just listen to what I have to say."

The phalanx of newsmen representing most of New Mexico's media, as well as the major national television networks and news magazines, trailed the lead group, staying just out of harm's way. They were on the street, but neither in nor out of the march itself. Flashbulbs flitted in spite of the clear blue sky, and notepads flapped breezily in the wind as ballpoints and stubby pencils recorded the passing emotions of people who had something to say and a special place to say it. All of them, mostly young men, were here to see to it that America's airwaves carried the visual images of Gallup, Wounded Knee, and Washington, D.C., to the rest of America.

The nightly TV newscast from Albuquerque would pick up the reverberating, smoldering drumbeat, and few would mistake its ominous message, "The sound of the drum always precedes the sound of the gun." It was like that for the men who marched with Napoleon, George III, and Robert E. Lee. Now it was AIM's turn. Perhaps it was no coincidence that all of them were fated to lose.

The rhythm of the drum was a sober reminder of the riveting sounds of the gun battle Casuse and Nakaidinae had sparked by kidnapping the mayor. Those who watched the marchers from inside storefront businesses hoped today's words of peace would soothe the wounds of one of the worst-planned and poorly executed political abductions in history. As the marchers eyed the crowd and the crowd warily scanned the protesters, the Indian teenagers in the street made faces at the few Anglo spectators on the curbs. The unintended effect was comic relief to the otherwise solemn march. Mostly, the spectators on both sides of the streets simply watched as if mesmerized by the steady, deep throb of the massive drum.

The one-and-one-half-mile round-trip to the ceremonial grounds took almost two hours. When the marchers got back to the parking lot, everyone moved to a little makeshift speaker's stand and its solitary loudspeaker. Larry Emerson, the principal organizer of the march, was the first to speak. He made it clear he was Casuse's successor and the new leader of the UNM Kiva Club. He spoke quietly but insistently to the hundreds of young Indian students in the crowd, "The Gallup city fathers are listening to you right now. Tell them from now on we want respect. We are tired of being pushed around. We've had it."

Jose Rey Toledo, from the Jemez Pueblo, spoke for and to the activists in the crowd, "I am very proud of all of you for conducting yourselves with pride and dignity. Now convey the message to your elders, and tell them that you have done your part."

Larry Casuse's death both galvanized and cemented the marchers. With Casuse firmly entrenched as a martyr, every speaker mentioned him. Larry Emerson presented a list of demands from the Indian people to the city fathers of Gallup, implying these were Casuse's demands. Peterson Zah, the founder and director of the Navajo tribe's legal aid group, and Chester Yazzie, speaking for Navajo Tribal Chairman Peter McDonald, linked Casuse's death with Garcia's life. So did two outspoken black UNM professors, Fred Ward and Charles Benal. They compared the black man's struggle "for access to Main Street America to Casuse's fight for respect of the Navajo on its own land."

As though their names were woven in an Indian braid, speakers who mentioned Larry Wayne Casuse also mentioned Emmett C. Garcia. Ten of the seventeen demands presented by the Kiva Club were directly aimed at Mayor Garcia. By design, the mayor was out of the city today. By invitation, Councilman Sam Ray, Garcia's rival for mayor, was at the rally to "accept" the Kiva Club's demands. Ray told the crowd that all demands "would be considered by city officials."

The demands chained Garcia to Gallup's long-standing Indian alcoholism problem. No one there needed reminding that the mayor was an owner of the Navajo Inn, but none seemed willingly to differentiate him as only one of *three* owners. No one at the speaker's podium reminded the marchers Garcia was only tangentially connected to the problem because he was not the manager of the Navajo Inn and had no day-to-day involvement in sales or management. At least in this crowd, Garcia was *the* owner of New Mexico's largest package liquor store, and it was located a scant one hundred yards from the vast "dry" Navajo Reservation. You could drive for a hundred miles across the reservation without buying a bottle of wine until you reached the Navajo Inn. That fact alone made Garcia a target.

The activists also demanded that Garcia be removed from the UNM Board of Regents because he lacked the "necessary educational credentials and sophistication." Lastly, the students demanded the city and "new mayor" meet regularly with the Indian community to "review and act upon all grievances and complaints by Indians."

The Albuquerque organizers, wanting to end the rally on a high note, dramatically unfurled a telegram from *inside* the barricades at Wounded Knee. Russell Means, Dennis Banks, Carter Camps, and Clyde Bellecourt proclaimed their solidarity with Larry Casuse, Robert Nakaidinae, and all other Kiva Club warriors and fellow AIM members. Holding the telegram high in the air, as though it were a battle flag, Emerson said, "It is good to know we're not alone." Then he slowly read its message, carefully enunciating each word and pausing for effect after each sentence,

> We here at Wounded Knee realize that our fight is the same fight that Larry Wayne Casuse fought so bravely. His struggle and the life he gave will never be forgotten by the American Indian Movement or the Independent Ogallala Nation of Wounded Knee. We promise you, his family and friends, that we'll never surrender because he didn't. His example will serve as a beacon to guide all of us to victory. The honor with which he died will show every Indian warrior that he doesn't have to live on his knees. We here at Wounded Knee hope to finally realize what Larry fought for. We hope to light the way to freedom for all Indian people. In Larry, we feel the loss of a warrior so badly needed here. The whole Indian nation should mourn the loss of a brave leader. At Wounded Knee, we'll honor him; our spiritual leaders will have special ceremonies for him. In this Indian way, we'll find unity with him and all of you.

The somber words of the speakers floated out to the crowd. The ominous message embedded in the telegram from Wounded Knee was received with thunderous applause. AIM's implicit connection to Casuse, before he kidnapped Garcia, became obvious. Nevertheless, AIM's self-incriminating telegram from Wounded Knee would land in the lap of the New Mexico grand jury as it considered conspiracy charges against Nakaidinae. A Minnesota grand jury would also receive the telegram in evidence as it evaluated conspiracy charges against more than a hundred AIM members.

The telegraphed words rebounded through in the brisk Gallup air. One speaker's concern about the "consequences of the shooting of Garcia and the death of Casuse" expressed relief that at least Casuse would be memorialized at Wounded Knee. In an effort to send Larry's message back from Gallup to Wounded Knee, the speaker encouraged the embattled warriors not to surrender "because he didn't." As it turned out, the embattled warriors in Wounded Knee didn't forget; but on that same day, March 31, 1973, they began to negotiate with the government. On May 7, 1973, AIM's leaders negotiated a stand-down at Wounded Knee. One hundred and forty-six defenders came out, laid down their arms, and were "processed" by U.S. Marshals in Rapid City, South Dakota. All of them were indicted, but none were convicted. Whether or not they surrendered is a debatable historical point, but no one went to jail. Nakaidinae's fate was yet to be determined.

CHAPTER TEN

"Don't Lie about Yourself—Bad Things Will Come True"

Virgil was feeling cramped and a little eyesore in the small cubbyhole as the microfiche reader flashed old newspaper print past him. The Octavia Fellin Library's collection of newspaper articles about Larry Casuse's death also revealed his brushes with the law before his death. Written after his death, the articles reflected more effect than cause. As Virgil scanned the 1973 newspaper file, he suspected there might be earlier articles about Casuse in the 1972 *Gallup Independent* microfiche.

He'd suggested to April that a little digging into Casuse's preabduction life might give them a better sense of what motivated him. Knowing that life off the Rez was never as simple as it looked, Virgil voiced his suspicion, "Is there more to this story than idealism and a longing to help one's people?"

"Virg, what do you mean? It seems clear to me that Casuse was an idealist who died for his cause."

"Did he? You're probably right, but other things played a role too. Is it okay with you if I read some background on Casuse in the library?"

After about an hour, Virgil pulled out his cell phone and dialed April, not really expecting to get her because she was in her own little cubbyhole at Red Rock Publishing's office on East Aztec. He thought he'd just leave a pager number, but she answered on the first ring. "April, it's me. I was just going to leave a digital message for you to page me. Have you been to lunch yet?"

"Going *out* to lunch is what tourist directors do, Virg. Low-paid editorial assistants eat in. That is, unless some tribal hot dog wants to take us out to lunch. Today, like most days, I'm at the desk, crunching soup crackers and munching on smoked albacore. What's up? You didn't call to check on my diet."

"I'm here in the library, and I've read the articles about Casuse's criminal problems. Remember I told you about his accident out on the end of town on the highway to Window Rock?"

"Yeah, sure I remember. What have you learned?"

"Casuse was tried twice here in Gallup before his death on March 1, 1973. I'm not sure of the exact dates, but the trials were held a few months before his death. As best I can tell, it started just after the annual Indian ceremonial here in Gallup in 1972 . . . ."

"Virg, I think the ceremonial was always held in the summer, so that would have made it in July or August of 1972. Was his friend Robert Nakaidinae involved?"

"I don't think so. Nothing I've read mentions anyone else being involved. Apparently, Casuse was driving home to Gallup from Window Rock in the wee hours of the morning when he got into an accident. They say he struck and killed a young Indian girl. The New Mexico State Police investigated the accident and then charged him with driving an automobile while under the influence of alcohol and leaving the scene of an accident. The alcohol charge was later dropped."

"Are you sure about that? You know that raises all sorts of questions. As I get it, part of his big grudge against the mayor was the bar somewhere on that same road, the one that went to Window Rock. Could he have stopped at that bar?"

"Don't know that either. Anyhow, he had a trial on the leaving-the-scene charge and was convicted by a jury. Later, the conviction was set aside because his lawyer failed to bring out several important facts in Casuse's favor."

April quizzed, "What facts?"

"The newspapers don't say. The second trial ended in a hung jury with eleven for conviction and one against. Eleven jurors though he was guilty even after they got the information his lawyer forgot to bring up at the first trial. Actually, the article I got this from was sort of ah, you know, a human-interest story. It went into what his friends said after he died. They said that Casuse took all of the legal problems real hard. He felt moral guilt for the girl's death. The two trials, they say, were emotional ordeals that caused him many sleepless nights. The prospect of having to go through a third trial with the certainty, at least to him, that he would be found guilty may have contributed to what he did to Garcia. At least that's what his friends said after his death."

"So his friends pretty much accepted the coroner's report that he killed himself? Is that the sense of what you get out of the stories in the local newspaper?"

"Well, more or less. They describe him as a dedicated fighter who had the respect of a great number of other Indian kids he met. As a member of IAE's central committee . . ."

"Tell me again what that stands for?"

"IAE was the acronym for Indians Against Exploitation. It was more or less the local chapter of AIM. Casuse was one of five persons who drew up strategy for the organization's opposition to the Gallup Indian Ceremonial."

"Virg, I never really got it straight about why the Indians were opposed to the Indian ceremonial. Do you know?"

Virg looked across the table and fished through the stack of documents they had copied from the library. He found a reference note on a single page, setting the history from 1922 to 1992. "From what I've read, it's a little vague, but it says here that the ceremonial was organized by the business community in Gallup in 1922 to draw visitors to the city. I'll read it to you. 'Local businessmen organized it for the encouragement of Indian arts and crafts and the education of whites to the beauties of Indian life.' It seemed to work just fine for everyone for many years, but the activists in the sixties and seventies thought that the Indians did not get enough respect, and the whites were profiting from the art and culture of the Indians. Of course, I don't know that much about it. It's still a big thing in Gallup and all of New Mexico actually."

"Was Casuse the Indian spokesman in Gallup? Would that have put him in direct contact with the power structure here, including the mayor?"

"I don't think so. But I did see something about a press conference at the time of the 1972 Indian ceremonial. Casuse was there but mostly in the background. The main speaker was a man named John Redhouse. He and a man named Phil Loretto were very vocal about their opposition to the '72 ceremonial. Loretto was quoted in the paper after Casuse's death in '73. I think he was the one who said that Casuse thought out many of the group's policies and demands. They said, this is after the fact of course, that at some of the meetings and confrontations over the ceremonial, Casuse appeared to be under a great strain. Later, after his car wreck out on Highway 666, this became more evident."

"I thought he was the calm and collected type?"

"No, that is not what his friends said later. They told the *Gallup Independent*, after his death, that he was very excitable and high-strung."

"Were they talking about the day he died or just generally before he died?"

"His friends were interviewed after his death about his attitude over the last year or so."

"Yeah, Virg, but did they say anything, his friends I mean, about whether he committed suicide or was killed by the police?"

"Yeah, there was something. Let me look at my notes, yes, now I see it. The *Albuquerque Journal* story on March 3, 1973, says, 'Philip Loretto of the Indians Against Exploitation (IAE) said after the shooting that Casuse was hit by several bullets that were fired into the store as he came out.'"

"Who wrote that story? Is there a byline, or is it just a staff story?"

"It's by Art Bouffard. It goes on. I'll read it to you. 'After the shooting, about thirty Indians met at the Gallup Indian Community Center. Loretto of the Indians Against Exploitation said the Indians were there to *reconstruct* the day's events. Loretto said the group had taped interviews with several eyewitnesses who said they saw Larry Casuse shot by several bullets that were fired into the store as he came out. Loretto said that Casuse came to Gallup with several demands. However, he did not state what they were. Casuse had a run-in with Gallup police and spent some time in jail. He saw many things he didn't like in jail, Loretto said.'"

April was silent. Virgil waited a moment and responded to his own reading, "I never heard of a guy who liked what he saw in jail. Casuse sounds like the real thing. Many of the AIM warriors back in the seventies wound up in jail. Sometimes it was because of their rhetoric or their confrontations with tribal leaders or the BIA. Sometimes it was different, like Casuse."

"What do you mean different?"

"It sounds like Casuse was in jail because he had a car wreck. He may have been drinking. A young Indian girl died. That is not exactly related to his cause for Indian rights."

"Yes, Virg, but what if his cause was that road to Window Rock and the bar out there by the reservation that was owned by the mayor. The road, the bar, Indian drinking, all of it—it was all a part of his cause. Maybe he had firsthand knowledge about drinking and driving on that road after being to that bar. Maybe that's why he wanted to kill the guy who owned it."

"April, speculating with me is just fine, but I don't think you want your uncle to put something like that in his book unless you've got some facts to prove it. I know he's writing a novel, but it has to be historically honest, right?"

"I understand that. I know I'm speculating, but we might find that the problem of Indian drinking was as personal as it was political with Casuse. It looks like he had some personal experience, but that doesn't change anything."

"Okay, April. Do you want to add those two friends, Redhouse and Loretto, to the characters list you're making for your uncle? He will want to know if those names pop up again."

"Right, I have a feeling they will. Virg, where do you think we should go next?"

"There has to be more to the Casuse story and his troubles with the law in Gallup. I have a feeling I'm missing something."

"Virg, I thought of something last night. What do we know Casuse's funeral? I presume he had one, but was it a big deal, or was Gallup focused on the aftermath still, I mean, the survivors—Garcia and Nakaidinae?"

Virgil frowned, trying to remember something he'd seen in the *Gallup Independent* back issues file. "He did have a funeral, and lots of people attended. I saw articles about it, but honestly, I didn't read them closely. I guess I was like everyone else, looking at the 'survivors' as you call them."

"Well, that answers the question. Why don't we reread the stuff about the funeral? Maybe it will tell us more than we know about the survivors. If Casuse died the death of a warrior, maybe there were other warriors at the funeral. Track 'em down, Scout."

~~~

April spent the morning at her desk, trying to organize Red Rocks Publishing Company's 1994 calendar. Since her thoughts were not really on the task, she decided to call her uncle for an update on the project. "Uncle Clay, you sound funny today," April said, hoping that it was the cell phone and not her uncle's recent asthma attack or his visit to the ER that made him sound so weak.

"Are you on that cheap cell phone again? That'd make anyone sound funny. I sound fine to me although my doctor might not agree. He's got me on a new corticosteroid inhaler, and it makes my voice sound funny."

"So you're okay then? I talked to Mom last week, and she said you stopped by the ER on your way home from work for a chat with your local pulmonologist."

"How did your mother know about that? She's got some pipeline, that woman. Maybe I ought to get her in on this little project. But she never was all that political, and this story is shaping up as political as they come."

"Actually that segue ways right into what I'm calling about . . ."

"Segue ways? Is that a word? It qualifies as slang for sure, but I thought it died back in the eighties along with normal conversation."

"Clay, now you are sounding funny, ha-ha. Of course, it's still a word. Words don't just die, you know. It's us young people who keep words alive by throwing them at senior citizens to like check their memories and stuff, you know."

"Right, keep on checking, and you'll check yourself out of a job. Now what have you found about the election in Gallup—the one a month or so after the mayor's abduction. Did he win?"

"Nope, he lost. It was close but nevertheless a loss. I've talked to several people around here. Their memories are dim, to say the least, but everyone seems to think it was a foregone conclusion, what with the abduction and the big march by the Indians and all."

"I thought he was generally well liked? Is it clear that the abduction caused him to lose, or is there more to it than that?"

"Well, he was well liked. What's more, he was doing a good job. The ironic thing is that he was definitely trying to change things for the better as far as the Indians went. He was a leader in trying to get more money from the state to deal with the alcohol abuse problem in Gallup at the time. I mean, can't you see the irony in his zeal to help the Navajo, turning into the reason why he loses an election?"

"What about the establishment, were they behind him?"

"Let me read some stuff to you from the newspapers at the time. This is from the *Gallup Independent* on March 3, 1973. It was the lead editorial—remember, this is two days after the abduction but almost a month *before* the election. It poses the issue pretty well. 'It's a good time for good leadership. No one will ever know why Larry Wayne Casuse, university student and Indian activist, set in motion the course of events, which ended in his violent death this week. But set them in motion he did, purposely and consciously—Casuse and his companion were perpetrators and not victims, principals and not pawns in the drama that unfolded Thursday afternoon. This fact is likely to be obscured by recriminations after such an incident, even though it happened before dozens of witnesses. The community can feel sympathy for the family of the young man who was killed as well as compassion for the mayor and his family during a trying time. But beyond that, we can only puzzle and try to learn from the experience. The state of mind of the two young men is impossible to gauge, but the abduction seemed to be no spur-of-the-moment thing. Casuse seems to have taken pains to draw definite battle lines, making sure that this was no borderline case to be argued and reargued for months to come. Direct threats on the life of the mayor were voiced in front of many witnesses. The immediate retreat to a sporting goods store with its arsenal of guns and ammunition seems to indicate he knew that the day would end in his own death, one way or the other.' Clay, don't you think that fairly well sums it up?"

"Yes, it sums it up from one perspective. April, in most small towns, the local newspaper speaks for the majority of the citizens."

"Wait, Uncle Clay, there's more. The *Gallup Independent* said that 'everyone can work toward color blindness in personal relations and strict interpretation of law that favors neither whites nor any minority group in order to prevent such things as the Public Health Service Hospital siege in Gallup, which ended in a shoot-out six weeks ago. Then that was followed by the takeover of the Bureau of Indian Affairs in Washington, D.C.' So it sounds to me like . . ."

"What was that? Was there a siege there in Gallup too? I must have missed that story. Is there, or I should say, was there a public health hospital in Gallup in 1973? What is the connection between that hospital siege and the mayor's abduction?"

"I don't know, Uncle Clay, but from what I've read, all this stuff is connected. You are the one who said that there must be some connection between what was going in Wounded Knee and what was going on in Gallup at the same time. Didn't you tell me that the takeover in Washington, D.C., led to Wounded Knee? Well, maybe the same thing was going on here in Gallup. Maybe the siege at the local hospital here led up to the kidnapping of the mayor. I gather there wasn't much time between the two events."

"Follow up on that, April. My guess is the Gallup establishment was spooked and voted Garcia out as a way of avoiding more marches and more trouble. I admit I'm a long way from the story, both in distance and in time. I'll rely on you to get to the bottom of it if that can be done after all this time."

"I think it can. You know, this is like a mystery story. The more facts I dig up, the more I think they are connected."

"So he was well liked, and he worked *for* the Indians. How did he lose?"

"Not sure yet. There were definitely politics afoot back then."

"Did that dispute have anything to do with AIM or Casuse?"

"It doesn't look that way. It's a long article, but the sense I get is there was some kind of dispute between the feds and the local officials over who was in charge of housing projects in Gallup. Garcia's position was that the local project should have local leadership. It's more complicated, I'm sure, but that's the nub of it. Garcia quoted the city attorney at the time, a man named William Head, as siding with him on the housing issue."

"Yes, but what did that have to do with the Indians and the abduction?"

"Maybe nothing. Maybe it was just small-town politics. But the articles in the paper are strong. Maybe they got the Indians stirred up. Who knows? Here's another interesting thing. All this happened about the time the Indians set up that big march through Gallup. That was the weekend before the election. And Sam Ray was right there with them."

"First the abduction, then a month later the big march through town, followed by the election two days later when the opponent at the march, Sam Ray, defeats Garcia. Right?"

"What was the vote count? Have you got that?"

"Yes, Ray got 2,077 votes to Garcia's 1,719."

"That could be a landside. That's roughly 20 percent, a lot of votes in a small-town election. If Garcia was the preabduction favorite, somebody turned a lot of votes the other way in a short time.In a rare lead editorial in the *Gallup Independent*, May 5, 1973, the editorial board asked Gallup to account for itself. At the time, the siege at Wounded Knee was still in progress, although four days later, it too would end. Noting that the 'misfit militants who wrecked the BIA Headquarters and made refugees of the peaceful residents of Wounded Knee and are now in Gallup,' we should consider the developments. Garcia is out of office, off the board of regents, no longer chairing the Gallup Interagency Alcoholism Committee, no longer the owner of the Navajo Inn; and Manual Gonzales is no longer chief of police, what else can we expect to happen?

The *Independent* asked the citizens to remember that the Indians said they "would bring Gallup to its knees" and to consider the results. Gallup "chose appeasement, relinquishing rights which should have been nonnegotiable. It observed that Garcia was the biggest victim of all because he had clearly demonstrated the ability to lead, the courage to continue, even after coming near the point of death. Closing on the point of the article, the *Independent* decried the loss of spunk that Gallup used to have, but lost by caving in to AIM's "demands" for reform.

CHAPTER ELEVEN

"Don't Put Salt on Piñons—It Will Make It Snow"

Winter seemed slow in coming to Spokane the week before Christmas in 1980. But on this forlorn Saturday afternoon, the sky grew darker hour by hour; and the cloud deck dropped beneath the status, skimming the tree line from Clay Ramsey's library window. As the cocktail hour neared, Clay stoked the fire for the fourth time today and marveled at the thin blue crust shining on the new fallen snow. The jar of the ringing telephone interrupted his serenity. Clay decided to let the machine do his talking but heard Millie's singsong voice, "Clay, it's me, Millie. Merry Christmas, Irishman. I was sending you another of my elusive letters when the thought struck me that writing the week before Christmas was most un-Christianlike. Since you are out, I'll ring off with a greeting and a . . ."

Breathlessly, Clay interrupted, "Wait, Millie, I'm here. Nobody calls except guys wanting to fix my windshield. How are you, it's really wonderful to hear your voice."

"And yours too, Clay," Millie said, her voice softening the coming storm. "Is this a good time, I didn't catch you working on a Saturday afternoon, did I?"

"No, well, not really working. I'm just reworking a draft of an obit, actually the funeral service, not the obit, of a Nez Pearce chief who died last week over in Idaho."

"And he had a regular funeral, just like anyone else in Idaho, is that it?"

"Sure. The way you put it makes it sound discordant. Don't Navajo families bury their chiefs when they die?"

121

Millie felt uncomfortable but said, "Catholic Navajos or Baptists on the Rez have funerals, but there is really no such thing as an Indian funeral."

"Why is that?"

"Navajos, with the exception of those who have been converted to Christianity, do not come together when a member of the family dies. Death and everything connected with it is repulsive. From the experience in our clan, dead Navajos are buried as quickly as possible, and we don't have a celebration, which is really what a funeral is, you know. In fact, I'm not sure we even have a word for it, in Navajo I mean."

"What's the Navajo word for *death*?"

"I'm not sure. I asked one of my uncles once, and he said something like *bizee hazlii*. But it could be something else. My Navajo gets weaker the longer I stay off the Rez."

"Millie, I can't believe my luck that you called. Your letters are far from elusive. Are you giving some thought to my last letter, you know, where I said we should we should cut the prairie down and feast our eyes on one another again? Although, I'm hardly a feast to look at, you know what I mean."

"Well, it's something we can talk more about, maybe in the spring. I am feeling the need for your touch as well."

"We've been writing for almost four years, and we've only talked on the phone two times in the last thirteen months. I've changed—that is, I'm going to be thirty-five next month, you know. Of course, you are probably still twenty-four even though ten years have passed since Coeur D'Alene. Navajos don't age like the Irish. We get wrinkled, and you get smoother. I need to touch your smoothness, Millie."

"You're a sweet man. I'm ten years older as well. My family, and I'm sure yours as well, has aged slowly. Children are only young once, they grow, but they don't really age, do they? Maybe, well, who knows? Spring break would be a good time. In the meantime, how can I help you with your obit on the Nez Pearce chief?"

Sensing a push back, Clay reluctantly resumed the discussion of death and funerals. "Okay, tell me about the relationship between death and fear. Do Indians think about death as frequently as whites do? It seems like half the people here in Spokane are almost obsessed with death."

"Beliefs about death in our culture are just that, *beliefs*. They're not based on rational thought. But for whites, or I should say Europeans, rational thought is always preferred over instinct or feelings. Our feelings about the land and about nature are mostly economic. Their feelings about those things are mostly intuitive. Indians feel for the land. In fact, you could say we are obsessed with the land."

"What's that have to do with death?"

"In a way, it's the same difference. Indians feel nothing about death. It's just the end, and they let it go at that. Whites think about death all the time. They seem to fear death more than we do. But religion, particularly Christianity, puts a different spin on death. It is feared and loved at the same time because for Christians, it gives them a chance to be better and to go to a better place. At least that's what Christian preachers and pastors say. Indians see death more simply. It's a return to where they started. It's not better. It's not worse. Overall, they don't think much about it. They feel it's over when it's over."

"Must have short funerals then."

"More like *no* funerals. Navajo funerals just don't happen, there's no need for one. But they do grieve for their loved ones, just the same. They gather as clans in chapter houses, but they don't talk about the dead. The Navajo, at least the traditional Navajo, loves the birds, the animals, and the trees."

"You said a funeral was a celebration? That's an odd word for it. What's to celebrate?"

"Clay, you're Irish but not much of a Christian. Celebration is a way of dealing with sadness. You celebrate the passing of someone into heaven, which is where they can sit with God, and peace reigns and all your departed relatives are there to greet you."

"How is that different with Navajos?"

"Traditional Navajos have no belief in a glorious afterlife. You don't live after death, you just go to the afterworld. That is a place similar to the earth, and not at all heavenly. Older Navajos believe the afterworld to be somewhere in the center of the earth from whence Navajos came before they entered this world. So it's more of a circle than a destination. Their gods are not in the afterworld. Their gods are connected to the earth, not to heaven."

"Yes, I've read about Indian views on immortality, and I have to say, they are usually stated in eloquent, almost-poetic terms. Death is often associated with a return to Mother Earth and being at peace with the animals and the birds and so forth."

"That's all true, but it doesn't deal with the reality of death. Most Navajos, except those *really* converted to Christianity, believe that the spirit of the dead travels down a mountain trail after the shell, or body, is deserted and left behind on earth."

"Where does the trail go?"

"Beats me. But I've heard you get there because your dead relatives lead you there."

"Doesn't make much sense to me."

"And Christianity does?"

"Not in a rational sense. But as they say, you have to believe."

"That's part of what I'm talking about." Millie paused as they neared a junction in the conversation.

"Millie, I am feeling quite human at the moment. When can we talk about getting together?"

"Spring break, love. It's coming, even here in Montana."

~~~

Virgil awoke with a start as he often did when yesterday's troubles were still with him today. Window Rock smelled of summer sage and the dust of red clay. He couldn't actually see the famous hole in the giant sandstone that gave the capital of the Navajo Nation its name. Tseghahodzani was the legendary name, he could feel its presence looming large over "window in the rock."

Trailers and hogans shared the town's landscape. The dominant sound in homes and tribal buildings was the cluck of soft-spoken tribal leaders and return-to-the-Rez Navajos like Virgil. He struggled with "the Navajo way" and the Navajo tongue. Both escaped him sometimes.

He let his mind wander over the books on the kitchen table and the notes he'd scribbled until well after midnight last night. His thoughts hovered just out of reach of his emerging consciousness as the sun inched up to the horizon in the East. First light, just peeking over the bluff, turned black to gray. Virgil knew that meant more to his people than it did to fair-skinned Europeans, like April and her uncle Clay.

Johonaaei was the name Navajos gave to the sun. White traders and tourists called Johonaaei the Sun Bearer. Johonaaei moved across the sky on a daily trek and carried the fiery orb. To Virgil's grandparents, the relationship between the sun and the earth was one of compatibility. How could Clay Ramsey, or his niece for that matter, ever understand that? And if not, the Navajo part of his brain told him, if men like Clay didn't see the compatibility, how could they understand the warriors in Wounded Knee *or* Gallup?

The more he thought about what drove those warriors thirty years ago, the more he thought that little had changed over the previous hundred years or so. Maybe that explained the thinking, or even the lack of thinking, of younger men like Larry Casuse. His elders likely told him about the warriors of old, just as Virgil's elders had done. But young men in the seventies had no more warrior training than did young men now. All they had was warrior blood, like him.

Virgil did what he always did when confused or hungry—he called April.

"April, sorry to call so early, but you're up, aren't you?"

"Now or when the *ding-ding* went off with you on the other end?"

"Yeah, right, but the sun's burning a hole in the rock. You know, I've been thinking about what you and your uncle said about the connections between these two events . . ."

"Connections?"

"Yes. Is what happened in Wounded Knee connected to what happened in Gallup? Well, I'm just not sure that this ought to be done. Whose story is this anyway? I mean, in one way it belongs to Gallup, and in another way, it doesn't, you know?"

A half minute passed with only the occasional static of a live telephone call to let them both know that the call was still on. Finally April said, "Virgil, sweet, it is early, and I'm not sure what you are saying. Will this wait till I get some caffeine in me so that I can be obscure with a clear head?"

Twenty minutes later, coffee mug in hand, feet in flip-flops, ear to the flip-upped little cell phone, April said, "Okay, where were you? It was somewhere between you don't believe Clay and you aren't sure Gallup has a story to tell, was that it?"

"April, I probably should wait till I get to town tomorrow. Maybe it will make more sense in person."

"Too late, babe, you've started this little discourse, so let's see where it goes."

"Well, you see, I'm here in Window Rock and you're down there in Gallup, and I'm Navajo and you're Irish. We see the same sun and the same moon, but we see them differently. I'm wondering if we will ever see the connection between Gallup and Wounded Knee the same. You know . . ."

"Virgil, I'm awake now, even alert, given the fact that it's not even six-thirty yet. You still sound wonderfully philosophical, but, honey, you are a fish without a bicycle. Big disconnect. The sun and the moon? Is there some connection I'm missing?"

"Yeah, there might be. You see, the sun is where people in Window Rock think omens come from. We—that is, the Diné—live by those omens. However, white people and everyone else in Gallup only think of omens when you see the moon. So our omens are not only different from your omens, they come from different parts of the sky. It's sort of like night and day. Does that make sense?"

"Well, Virg, they are different, but that doesn't mean the Irish see the sun differently than Navajos do. You mix up the metaphor when you throw in the moon—that's where the night-and-day thing come from."

"No, I think maybe we see the sun differently than you do. We live by the sun's omens, you don't. That's my first philosophical point."

"Virg, hon, where is this going?"

"I was reading last night that when the sun hides his light from the people, it's because he's angry. He is warning that a catastrophe will soon take place. Old people out here on the Rez believe that an eclipse is actually the death of the sun. Only a song by a medicine man, called "Making the Sun Again," can revive the sun. Somewhere on the Rez, during every eclipse, the song is sung. That's why the sun does not actually die during an eclipse."

"They sing during an eclipse, is that it?"

"No, just before. During an eclipse, ceremonies cease, people are awakened, and silence is maintained until the sun *recovers*. It's different with the moon, that is, it's different with you white people."

"Virg, what do you mean different? And even if we are different in how we see the sun and the moon, what's that got to do with Uncle Clay and me or, for that matter, Gallup?"

"I'm not sure, but maybe the Navajo people, and most other Indian people, see sacredness in nature and in things like the sun. That's a reminder to us of how dependent we are on supernatural help and the pleasure of things like the sun. We risk disfavor when we don't follow our elders and their instincts."

"Yes, but what does that mean, Virgil?"

"What I'm trying to say is that maybe we should not be making too many assumptions about what Casuse did in Gallup or what Russell Means did at Wounded Knee based on what a white man would have done under similar circumstances."

"Why not? Do you think that this feeling about the sun or the moon or whatever was relevant somehow in the takeover of the mayor's office in Gallup or the town hall in Wounded Knee is that what you're saying?"

"No, that's not it at all. You're confusing things. I'm just saying that Indian culture places an important value on harmony and on how compatible people are. That's different from how important those things are in the rest of the world. It got me to thinking. What if Casuse in Gallup and Means in Wounded Knee had a different view of life? What if they thought that things important to their people were being ignored or, worse yet, destroyed by leaders in Gallup and Wounded Knee? That might make them willing to take the risks they took. It might also make it really hard for you or your uncle to see exactly why they took the risk at all."

"Now just hold the phone, Virgil Bahe. We aren't stupid or insensitive, at least I'm not. There were many well-intentioned white people back when AIM seized Wounded Knee and Casuse abducted the mayor. Maybe they were not as engaged with the Indian people as they should have been, but some of them really cared, don't you agree?"

"I'm sorry. I didn't mean that you, or Clay, were stupid. I know you are very sensitive, and I'll take your word that Clay is. Think about it this way, in the white world, harmony is viewed like poetry or something. But out here on the Rez, harmony is what life is all about. So maybe Casuse thought he could restore harmony by violence even though he was fundamentally nonviolent. Do you see what I mean?"

"I think so. But still, we all have to be responsible for the harm we cause even if we have good reasons or noble motives. If the motive is to restore harmony, as you put it, then the consequences are the same as if the motive were much less noble, say, for example, it was done just for money. That is the same in town as it is out on the Rez."

"Well, money was not the motive in either Gallup or Wounded Knee, so that's not a good analogy."

"Maybe money was not Casuse's motive, but didn't it seem like others were motivated by money? What about the mayor? Didn't he have the right to protecting his investment in that old bar on the border of the Rez?"

"No, that's not what I meant. I meant that if money is the motive in the eyes of the storywriter, like your uncle Clay, whereas harmony was the motive of the guy that the story is about, like Casuse, then how are you ever going to tell the story? Through whose eyes is the story seen?"

"Virgil, I get it. Let's sit down with Clay and see if we can work it out. Maybe he can tell the story *you* see. Will that do it?"

"April, did you know that the Four Corners region of our reservation up here is covered with thousands of prehistoric sites belonging to the Anasazi?"

"What is this? Change the subject time so you don't have to answer my question?"

"No, I'm answering your question. The eyes of the Diné are the eyes of the Anasazi, the ancient ones. We have hordes of archaeologists every summer digging into those ruins to find the past. All I'm saying is that maybe the past is the past for a reason. Maybe the only eyes that can understand the past are those that saw it happen at the time. I'm trying to answer your question about justifying the writing of the story on the basis of viewing it differently after it is written. No one now can see it the same way as those involved saw it."

"Virgil, you are speaking about Casuse, but what about all the others? What about Garcia? He can see the story now, and he was sure the hell there then. Don't we have to think about his eyes too?"

"Yes, we do. But he's not a long-gone warrior. He's not who Clay wants to revive through his book. Clay's interested in the guys from AIM, not the guys from Gallup, remember?"

Virgil took a deep breath and sat still for as long as he could. April, watching his eyes and the rhythmic lift and fall of his chest, knew he was trying to think of a way to avoid an argument. Neither quite knew how to break the silence. Finally, Virgil said, "You know, there's an old Navajo taboo that kind of fits this situation, not exactly maybe, but pretty close. I might have told you this one, I don't remember, but the young kids say, 'Don't put salt on your piñons 'cause you will make it snow."

"Whew, that's too deep for an Irish girl. Translation, please."

"It seems like Casuse and Garcia were too opposite, like salt and pepper, even though both wanted things to be better. The Navajo taboo about salting piñons is about the difference in culture out on the Rez. Navajo people don't like to alter things, especially in nature. They use salt, it was an important thing on the Rez, but there are some things that should be left natural, like piñons. So the taboo against salting them carried a bad thing—snow too early in the fall before things can get into balance for the winter. I guess it originally started out as a superstition about having an early winter, or a hard winter, or something like that. So it seems like maybe what Garcia was doing in Gallup, at least in Casuse's eyes, was going to bring on hard times, like an early winter. Don't salt your piñons is saying don't do bad things. But I don't know who was salting the piñons, Casuse or Garcia? You could look at it both ways, you know?"

"Well, there you have it. I asked for translation, and I got salted. Or are you just peppering me?"

"It's okay. But abducting Garcia mostly because it seemed like a warrior thing is, to me, pouring salt on piñons. It was a bad thing to do. It could not have made anything better in Gallup."

CHAPTER TWELVE

"Don't Talk to a Person You Don't Know—
It Might Be a Dead Person"

July 3, 1983

Spokane, Washington

As the Fourth of July dawned on America in 1983, Clay Ramsey, an unreconstructed early riser, was editing a story about Reagan's new secretary of the interior when the phone rang.

"Good morning, Mr. Blue Pencil, remember me?"

As soon as he heard her first words, Clay bolted upright in his swivel chair. "Millie, my god, it's you. What is, I mean, why? Never mind. It's been too long. No, never mind that too. It's wonderful to hear your voice, and . . ."

"And yours too, scribe. Happy Fourth of July. It's America's holiday. I just wish it was also America's Indian holiday. But enough with the politics, it took me weeks to nerve up, but I made the call, at five-forty in the morning no less. I knew you'd be up, and one of us had to break the ice, no pun intended. So how are you?"

"I'm fine. You?"

"Sure, you know me. I dream of revolutions, but I live in peace. My soul is at rest if not my heart."

"Your heart? Are you sick? Oh no! Tell me . . ."

"My heart is healthy, lonely maybe, but I'm hoping to cure that. I was wondering if maybe we ought to see one another again. Or are you involved?"

"No, I mean yes. We should see each other. I was answering the last question first. I'm not involved. Never have been, actually. That's one of my faults—but you already know that."

"Yes, that sounds familiar. Let me say something first. Clay, I'm sorry if I sounded a bit huffy in my last letter. I think I was just reliving what happened back at the Knee. God, that *was* ten years ago. A lot happened there, and it wasn't the best time for me to be thinking of myself. But that's a wide prairie and a couple of demonstrations ago. Maybe we could catch up on each other's lives. What do you think?"

"You can't know how much I'd love that. I think about you more than you'd ever know, more than you could know. That's my fault. Maybe I tried a little too hard when I saw you there in Wounded Knee. It doesn't seem like ten years to me. It seems like ten days. Did I make my life sound normal in my letters to you since then? The sad fact is that not much has happened to me. My life is sort of monastic—I write, and I edit, but do I live? If my life were a book, everyone would put it down on page 3 because there's no action to keep the story moving. I write about the lives of others, their real lives, but I live a fictional life. It's passive voice in the flesh. I'm alone, and I don't like it."

"Let's see if we can fix that. I'm still living here in Bozeman, still teaching at Montana State University, but I was down on the home Rez in New Mexico last week, visiting family. That's where I thought of you and our little demilitarized bed and breakfast in Coeur D'Alene. What do you think, want to meet there again and give real life another chance?"

"I'll make it work. Just name the day, and I'll book the McKenzie House. I'll order the Irish scones for breakfast and leave my typewriter at home. While I'm at it, I'll book lots of time to talk. That's what I want the most."

"Me too, Clay. There is something else, Clay. I want to bring you something. Two things, actually. I want to hand-deliver an important letter, and I want you to have a book, the book is important too, but not as important as the letter."

Millie had lowered her voice to whisper level, and Clay could detect a quiver he'd heard before, but not for a long time. *Two things, what does she mean? I don't believe her—she's sick, and that's what's gonna be in the letter—but what's the book?* Millie had always been able to make his chest hurt over the phone. What poets called heartache was not just distant prose in a book for Clay. Her voice was like a little rubber hammer, tapping his body for rebound and reflex. She could raise his pulse, lower his temperature, make his chest feel tight, and his bowels loose. All of that just by voice inflection and, most intensely, by the simple act of whispering. *God, I love her so, don't let me send her away again, please!*

"Two things, a letter and a book? Millie, I guess I can wait for the book even if it is important, but why wait to tell me something in a letter? Today's a good time for news, how about telling me now?"

"It's a long story, a long letter, and I want to get it right. I am going to write the letter tonight and give it to you next week in Coeur D'Alene. I hate myself for making this so mysterious, but I know you will understand. Like I said, it's important, it's my secret, and I want to share it with you in person. Don't worry, it's not bad news. This is something I should have told you years ago, and something I almost told you a dozen times. You will just have to trust me and wait a week. That brings up the other thing, the book. Let me tell you about it because it relates to the letter as well."

"I do trust you, Millie, but I wish you'd at least give me a hint or something. Is this something else I did wrong? I know I was the world's biggest fool and that I did something to keep you away for ten years and . . ."

"Clay Ramsey, you just stop that. You can't know everything, and we've been distant for reasons beyond either one of us. I will try to give you some of it in my letter, and we can talk it through in Coeur D'Alene. But for now, please just trust that I am doing the right thing, finally."

"Finally? What does that mean? Is this something dark, something that kept us apart? I mean, you can't just tell me you have a dark secret and that you'll shine a light on it if I just wait a week. Please, you know I love you. What is this?"

"Loving me is exactly why I have to do this right, Clay. Can't you just trust me for one more week? You'll see it's right, and I can tell you about the book. I will hand you the book, and the letter will be inside the cover. Just read the letter, glance at the book, and then we'll sit by the fire and have a wonderful talk. It's important, Clay, really important."

"All right, you win. Well, I can always use another book, what is it?"

"It's a story that you know a lot about. This book, well, let's just say this is *the* book. I helped write it ten years ago, and I absolutely should have talked to you about it back then. I should have showed it to you when we met in Coeur D'Alene three years ago. In fact, I guess I have to confess that I had it with me then. But things went astray, and I couldn't actually find the courage to bring it up."

"Wait a minute, Millie, things did go astray as you put it, but that was not your fault. I'm the one who owes an apology for that. I tried to do it in my letter right after you left, a day early, remember? No matter how many times I promise myself, I always end up driving you off with some inane comment that spews out at the wrong time."

"Clay, I don't want to start sawing on that old log again, but what you said is exactly why I am bringing this book to you now. I know your heart and your mind. The letter is for your heart, but the book is for your mind. Remember, your point was that AIM, and its followers everywhere, including my own reservation, failed the Indian people. In fact, I think you sharpened your point by calling AIM a *miserable* failure."

"Yeah, that's when you walked over to the closet and started packing."

"Well, I'm over it. I still think you were wrong, but now I want to bring you this book because I think you will see—in the words, the pictures and the whole tone of the thing—that AIM lost the battle in Wounded Knee but won the war."

"Millie, it was a pretty stupid argument in the first place. Some of history's most important events were accidents, but I am not sure I am following you about losing the battle and winning the war."

"Remember I told you there in the press tent at Wounded Knee, the day of the big airlift, about the women inside the barricades and what they were doing?"

"Yeah, but I must have said something stupid that time too because our conversation went south right about then."

"No matter. The book that I am bringing to you is the real story of what happened at Wounded Knee. It is in voice and written—as the painters would say, en plein air. Of course, artists say that in French, and my accent is Navajo, so I won't even try. The real point is this book was written by insiders, people who were there."

"I've seen a couple Wounded Knee books, and I guess they are authentic, what makes this one . . ."

"True? Is that the word you are groping for? This book is true because AIM and its supporters took a great many risks to tell the world what really happened. I took some risks too. I won't spoil it or convince you on the phone. For now, you'll have to take my word for it. These are the true voices of Wounded Knee. When I get to Coeur D'Alene next week, you'll see for yourself. Clay, I'm sorry, someone is knocking at my door, and I've got a class to teach at one-thirty. I'll see you at the McKenzie House next week. Meanwhile, I miss you."

"Me too, Millie."

Clay sat for a long time, rubbing his eyes and blowing his nose. Millie and her book—this was going to be something. Maybe life was going to be good again.

~ ~ ~

Millie sat by the phone, as the sun came up over the little wall outside her kitchen, and cried. She could not make her arms work or her heart slow down, so she wrapped both arms around her chest, trying to hug herself into the courage it would take to write *the* letter. Now that she had promised Clay to bring it to him, she had to do it. A secret kept for thirteen years is hard to give up. She was older now and knew more than she did then. That didn't help. *Each thing we see hides something else*, she told herself. "Clay deserves," she whimpered and then opened the floral notepad, unscrewed the top of her favorite fountain pen, and closed her eyes, hoping the first line would come up behind her eyelids like a vision. She had tried to think of a way to tell Clay for years. Her telephone confession that the secret even existed helped her heart to find a softer rhythm. Now, calmer but still terrified, she still could not think of a starting place. Since squeezing her eyes shut hadn't worked, she decided to start at the end and go backward in time—the fall before describing the wall. Cruel maybe, but hopefully cruel in a kind way.

> My Dearest Clay,
>
> An hour ago, I told you I would bring this letter to you in person. I can only hope you read it with all of the kindness and calm reflection you've shown for thirteen years. There is no other way to tell you other than to just tell you.
>
> We have a son. His name is Blue, he's thirteen now. He looks more like me than you, but he has your heart and a bit of your Irish wit. He is quick to laugh but slow to decide almost everything. What else would you expect for an Irish-Navajo lad just now starting to think about the world? I think he has the best of both worlds ahead of him.

I know you must be floored by this news, finding it startling and renewing and threatening all at once. There are times in our lives when something so unpredictable happens that we need time to let it settle, lest we boil over on the spot. That happened to me thirteen years ago, just as it must be happening to you now.

I began at the end, but that's no excuse for holding off my apology any longer. I am profoundly sorry for keeping this from you. Our son, our beautiful son, is yours as much as he's mine. I never wanted to hurt you or even to keep this terrible but still wonderful secret. All I can hope for now is that you remember our conversations about "the Navajo way" and how important my culture is to me. I feel deeply guilty about deceiving you and will accept your condemnation. It was an act of unforgivable selfishness. It is no defense to tell you I did it for him, for Blue. It is no defense to tell you that Blue is everything I wanted in a son. It is no defense to tell you that he has been loved, guarded, nurtured, and taught. It's no defense because I know that had I brought you into his life thirteen years ago, Blue would have been loved, guarded, nurtured, and taught by you.

This secret has been mine alone. Revealing it is the most painful thing I have ever done. Little pieces of the secret are in the hands of a precious few members of my clan. My sister, Martha, and her husband, Charles, know only that Blue is my son but nothing of his father, or why I insisted on bringing Blue into the world, and then giving him over to them for long periods of time while I traveled about in search of a lost cause. You may find that even more startling than the secret itself.

Why hide his parents, both of us, from him? You must, at this very minute, be asking yourself that terrible question. Even if you could answer it, you can likely never forgive me for it. A one-sided explanation, such as I vainly offer in this letter, will never suffice. But keeping you a secret from your son is a sin for which I cannot ask forgiveness. I have had two great loves in my life—you and Blue. In trying to protect him, I deceived you both. In trying to give him what seemed vital thirteen years ago, I deceived myself. In trying to compensate for my deceit, I cannot redeem myself, but I offer each of you a precious gift. I want you to have each other.

My life has been a constant search for harmony. Pity that I didn't listen more carefully to your voice and so doubted my own. In my desperate search for place and my fear of impermanence, I forgot something essential. Parents who love their children are found in all cultures. I feel now that it was an astounding arrogance for me to think that Blue must grow up Navajo, lest he lose his way in a white world so consumed by material things.

There is so much you know about me that it likely overpowers what you don't know. You don't know how much my sister and I loved our life as little girls and how wise we thought we were at thirteen. Women in our culture often take on leadership roles that Navajo men relinquish in a most honorable way. That is not so in the white world. You don't know how hard traditional Navajo women work to give their young a sense of denial that becomes its own reward. To deny the need for possessions is to accept, even proclaim, an inner happiness.

In our culture, children are always raised by mothers and aunts, who see little difference in their children. Our mother, Martha's and mine, gave much of our care over to our aunt, who saw us as her own. Interfamily adoption is common in the white world as well, but it is done with much formality and only after cautious deliberation. "The Navajo way" is close to the marrow of life, without thought, and unconditionally. I know I am doing little to help you understand what I did. I hope to fill in the thousand blanks next week.

For now, I can only offer the truth as I see it. Blue thinks of me as his aunt, but knows that my love for him is no less than the woman he thinks is his mother. He is now of an age where he can understand, and I am confident that he won't discriminate between Martha and me. His love for Martha and for me is the same—that's part of "the Navajo way."

He thinks that Martha's husband is his father, but when he is told differently, he will think no less of him. Soon, after I see you next week, I will tell him about you and give him time to assimilate that reality. I promise, I won't tell him until I've told you. I owe both of you that. Learning about you will be more difficult for him because he has been raised to believe in the power of living in harmony with the earth. Being thirteen will help. He won't see you as white or as an enemy, as some young Navajos do these days. I have spent much time, mostly in the summer in Chinle, talking to him about the goodness in men. He is a boy without guile and has an accepting way about him.

I am hopeful that you will help me find the right way, and time, to bring you into Blue's life. In a more foolish frame of mind, the one I was in thirteen years ago, I had a low opinion of men who were powerful—always looking for something bigger, better, and different. You did much to change my thinking, but my fear would not go away. I thought that most white men thought only with their heads and must therefore be crazy. You cured me of that as well. I wanted Blue to grow up in a place where men thought with their hearts and didn't get wrinkled from wanting so much.

That has happened. You will find Blue to be a man, although a very young one, who walks quietly, sits comfortably, and can be trusted. He is ready to learn the rest of life's story, and I hope you can find it in your heart to tell it to him. There is an absence in Blue's life because I closed your hand to him. Now, hopefully not too late, I want to see your presence in his life and his hand in yours.

Don't even try to forgive me, but please try to follow my path, elusive as it was.

Love,
Millie

~ ~ ~

Three days later, Millie called and left a message. She would be in Coeur D'Alene on Friday by three o'clock. That gave Clay two more ridiculously long days to wait. While not forgotten, the mystery letter dwindled into the happiness of planning for their reunion. The McKenzie House didn't have their old room available, but the two-bedroom upstairs suite was available. He booked it, ordered fresh-cut flowers for every bowl and vase in the suite, and tried to compose himself. Then, on Friday, he waited for the phone to ring. Millie said she'd call on the road from Bozeman, a six-hour drive from Coeur D'Alene. But since it was only an hour away from his home, he could just wait; she'd call, she always did.

Just before noon, his cell phone rang, and Clay picked up on the first ring. "Millie, are you on the road?"

"Mr. Ramsey, is this Clay Ramsey?"

"Yes, I'm sorry. I was expecting someone else to call."

"Were you expecting a call from Mildred Clark of Bozeman, Montana?"
Hesitatingly, Clay said, "Yes, who is this?"

"This is Officer Kozeliski. I am with the Deer Lodge Police Department."

"Deer Lodge. Isn't that in Montana?"

"Yes, sir, we're right on the Idaho border, a little off I-90 on the road to
Coeur D' Alene. I have to ask you some questions about Mildred Clark. Can
you confirm that I have the right Clay Ramsey?"

"I'm Clay Ramsey, I already told you that. I was expecting her to call.
What's happened? She's on her way here to see me. Is she in trouble?"

"Mr. Ramsey, I am sorry to have to be the one to tell you, but Ms.
Clark is dead. We found her body, well actually, it wasn't us, but her car was
found this morning off the road just south of here on I-90. We got your
name and number in Spokane from a card and a photo she had taped to her
dashboard."

Clay dropped to his knees and held the phone with both hands. It
suddenly felt wet; his hands couldn't seem to hold on tight enough. He could
hear the man talking, but the words were distant as though he was talking to
someone else. "Mr. Ramsey, are you still there, sir? Mr. Ramsey . . ."

"What happened, Officer? I mean, my god, you are telling me she's dead,
is that right?"

"Yes, sir, I'm afraid that's the case. There was a little sticky note on the
photo with two phone numbers. Yours and a hotel in Coeur D'Alene, Idaho.
I gather she was on her way there to meet you, is that right? But we don't
know whether you are family or just a friend."

"No, we weren't related, Officer. I've known her for many years, but it's
been some time since I last saw her."

"So if you don't mind me asking, why was she coming to see you in
Spokane?"

"She was coming here to renew an old friendship."

"Mr. Ramsey, how was that arranged? I mean, how did you know she was
coming if you haven't seen her for, how long did you say it has been?"

"Officer, what did you say your name was?"

"Kozeliski, Brandon Kozeliski. You can confirm that by calling the desk
sergeant and giving him my badge number, 1212."

"Thank you. Officer Kozeliski, why are you asking these questions?
How did Millie die? Have you notified her family? I am happy to answer

anything you want to know, but this is a helluva shock, you know. She called me yesterday—no wait, it was two days ago—from Bozeman to confirm that she would be on her way to Coeur D'Alene this morning. What happened? What caused it?"

"We are not sure about the accident, but it was just her car. No other vehicle was involved. She ran off the road and down a pretty steep canyon on the north side of the interstate. I guess no one will ever know whether she was distracted or fell asleep or what. Our best estimate is that an hour or so passed before someone investigated the tire tracks off the road and the hole in the fence just before the drop-off down into the canyon. You can't see down into the canyon from the road, so her car was more or less invisible until a trucker got curious about the tracks and the hole through the fence. Was there anything you talked about that might help us? Was she upset or preoccupied about anything that you know of?"

"No, Officer, she was in good health and good spirits. I'm sure this was just a freak accident. Have you contacted her family in Arizona?"

"We've already notified her sister. Actually, to tell you the truth, her sister asked us to call you. I gather you don't know the family down there."

"No, I've never met her family."

"Well, we're really just tying up some loose ends. There are a couple of things that you might be able to help us on though. Her friends seem to be pretty political. She was involved in a number of Indian civil rights protests here and around the country a few years ago. You knew that, didn't you?"

"Yes, I did. I work for a magazine, and we covered at least two of the same stories—the landing on Alcatraz Island in '69 and the seizure of Wounded Knee in '73."

"Well, sir, we knew she was involved in Wounded Knee. She was arrested there. I don't remember anything on her record that relates to the Indian landings out on Alcatraz Island. Was she involved in that?"

"She was not involved in the landing or the holding of the prison on Alcatraz Island. She just lived in San Francisco at the time. We talked about it back then, so I know she was not involved. Is that somehow connected?"

"No, there is nothing to suggest that. It's just that her friends seemed to be more on the radical fringe if you know what I mean and . . ."

Radical fringe? Did he just say she was arrested at Wounded Knee? For what? Wait a minute, should I even be talking to this guy? Other AIM guys, and at least one girl, have been murdered, is this what he's getting at?

"No, Officer, I'm not sure what you do mean. Are you suggesting that her death is somehow connected to politics or her friends? Just what are you suggesting?"

"Mr. Ramsey, I didn't mean to upset you. We are not investigating any sort of foul play. As far as we know, this is just an MVA—sorry, a motor vehicle accident. But we have no witnesses, so I was just asking general questions. Let me see if we can wrap this up. Could I ask what your relationship was, sir?"

And so he told the officer what he wanted to hear. He dated Mildred Clark but never got to know her as well as he should have. *He should have gotten to know her well, and he would have, but for Alcatraz. And but for Wounded Knee. And but for his inability to commit to a future with her on her terms.*

Clay's initial numbness carried him through the weekend. He didn't eat but drank a lot of coffee. He showered but didn't shave. He fed both dogs and kept them within arm's reach for two solid days. But he never went outside, they seemed to understand. On Monday, guilt showed up, dressed in a shroud. *How could I have forgotten? What about the letter, what about the book? What about arrangements—what about . . .*

~ ~ ~

"Yes," he said to the perfunctory announcement on the other end of the line that this was the Deer Lodge Police Department and could they be of service. "May I speak to Officer Kozeliski, please?"

"May I ask who's calling?"

"My name is Clay Ramsey. Officer Kozeliski called me on Friday, last Friday. He is the officer investigating a fatal automobile accident involving, well, involving a woman from Bozeman. Is he available?"

"What's the woman's name?"

"Her name? Well, her name is Mildred Clark."

"Are you calling for a copy of an accident report? Because if you are, I can transfer you to the records department."

"No, as I said, I want to speak to Officer Kozeliski. We talked, but there is something I didn't have a chance to ask him. Is he available?"

"I'll ring upstairs. Someone up there will know. Hold the line."

Clay held the line; in fact, he gripped so tightly his hand hurt for almost six minutes. He followed his digital watch as it moved methodically forward as though nothing in the world had changed. Then the phone jarred his left ear. "Yes, Deer Lodge Police Department, how may I help you?"

"I was holding for Officer Kozeliski, is he . . . ?"

"Yeah, sure he's here, hold a sec."

"This is Kozeliski."

"Yes, Officer, this is Clay Ramsey. We spoke last Friday. You called me about Mildred Clark, and I was wondering if you could . . ."

"Yes, Mr. Ramsey, I remember you. The report isn't finished yet, so there's not much more I can tell you. I expect it will be about . . ."

"No, Officer, I'm not calling about the report. Ms. Clark was coming to Coeur D'Alene to meet me. I think we talked about that. What I'm wondering about is whether you found a book or a letter in her car. She said she was bringing a book and a letter to me."

"No letter that I know of. But there was a book on the passenger seat. Well, not actually on it, you know. It was down on the floor by her purse and stuff. Everything was on the floorboard because of the way the car went off the cliff, you know."

"Do you still have the book? She was bringing it to me. If you have it, I will come and claim it."

"No, I don't have anything. Everything in the car was collected by the detail. In fact, I think they just released the personal stuff this morning to the next of kin—wait, I have a note on the pad—yes, her sister from Arizona flew up here and made arrangements to take the body back. They gave her all the stuff in the car. You said you weren't family, right?"

"Right, I'm not, but the book was mine, she was bringing it to me."

"I'm sorry, sir. You'll have to take that up with her kin. Now if the book was yours and she was just returning it to you, then I'm sure you will get it back. But it's between you and them, know what I mean?"

"Well, Officer, I don't actually know her family. Can you give me the sister's address and maybe a telephone number?"

"I can't, but maybe somebody in property can. Do you want to be transferred? It's downstairs."

"Yes, thank you."

Clay got an answering machine from property downstairs and left his name and number. A week went by and no one called, so he wrote to the Deer Lodge Police Department. His letter was given the same priority and response his voice message had generated. Ten days later, he got a call from a sergeant in property, telling him that he could not give out family information except to family. "You know what I mean, right."

He spent hours calling bookstores, trying to describe a book about Wounded Knee without the title, author, or much of a description. He decided that the letter, if it was in the car, was never going to come back to him. *She said it was important, but it was connected to Wounded Knee. That's ancient history, right? I've got to get on with my life.*

So he did. Nineteen eighty-three turned out to be as uneventful as 1982 had been. No one protested about much of anything, and Wounded Knee faded to black.

CHAPTER THIRTEEN

"Don't Stand on High Rocks—
They Will Grow into the Sky with You"

April spent another long day in the Octavia Fellin Library poring over the stories about Garcia and his involvement in the Navajo Inn and his appointment to the UNM Board of Regents. In addition to newspaper articles, she found stacks of official City of Gallup documents; correspondence to government agencies, both in New Mexico and in Texas; and several long substantive reports about housing scandals and alcohol abuse. The stories, each quite different on the surface, stubbornly clung together at a deeper level. After organizing her notes, she composed an e-mail to Clay.

Dear Clay,

As you suspected, the bar connection does shed a little light on an otherwise dark story. Turns out it isn't a bar at all. The Navajo Inn was only a package liquor store. But what a business! It sold beer and wine by the truckload. I mean literally. The Navajo Inn was the largest volume liquor store in the state and one of the biggest in the country. The wholesale distributors sent them tractor-trailer trucks full of Coors beer from Colorado and another one, filled with cheap wine, from California every week.

Garcia's father owned it originally. At some point, he turned it over to Frank, long before he was mayor, or appointed to the board of regents. Apparently, Frank didn't like the liquor business in general and hated running a package store that catered only to

Navajos. So Frank brought in two new partners. They formed a company called ABC Corp. The company owned other stuff too, but the Navajo Inn was their main deal.

About three weeks after the abduction, a bunch of Indian rights groups called a press conference to demand Garcia's resignation from the board of regents. Their main reason was his ownership of the Navajo Inn. They said, "A regent should present a clean public image, be a college graduate, and have experience with education." The groups included the Kiva Club, AIM, IAE, the Gallup Indian Commission, and the Gallup Indian Community Center. They said they had information from a high source that Garcia had made a deal to support the governor's son in his run for Congress in return for his seat on the regents board.

They accused him of what they called "an obvious conflict of interest in owning the Navajo Inn while serving as a regent *and* as the chairman of the agency in Gallup charged with dealing with Indian alcohol abuse. They wanted a new regent to be appointed who was an Indian from Gallup. I will fill you in on more details next time we talk, but someone's at my door right now.

Bye,
April

~ ~ ~

Clay Ramsey's automated "you have mail" computer voice interrupted his review of Frank McNitt's wonderful book on *Navajo Wars*, which chronicled the military campaigns, slave raids, and reprisals on the Navajo reservation for a hundred years or so. He read April's e-mail and sent her a quick response.

Thanks, April, for your short report on the postabduction turmoil over Garcia's appointment to the board of regents. I can see how retaining ownership of that package liquor store would be political dynamite. Where did you pick up this connection? I'm guessing it's your own secret source on all things Navajo. How is Virgil? What happened to the bar? Did Garcia quit the business after he lost the election? And what happened to his position on the UNM Board of Regents? That seems like a more important job than being the mayor of a small town. It is starting to look like the guy had three strikes against. He was a mayor, a regent, *and* a bar owner. If what they wanted was an Indian regent, did they also want an Indian mayor? And by the way, were there any bars in Gallup that were owned by Indians? Get back to me. This is getting interesting.

Now it was April's turn to feel guilty. As it happened, it was Virgil at the door, but he couldn't stay. So she got back on her computer and told Clay the rest of the mayor/regent/bar owner story.

Uncle Clay,

Sorry about the interruption. Virgil says hi, goodbye, and "don't tell your uncle our secrets." So I won't. But I can fill in some of the gaps on the liquor store and the board of regents. At first, at least in late March of '73, Garcia was publicly stating that he would remain on the UNM Board of Regents, but he would sell the Navajo Inn. You would never guess the buyer he suggested—it was the Navajo tribe. Governor Bruce King, who appointed Garcia, said he completely supported the decision to sell the liquor business and stay on the board of regents.

So Garcia bought out one of his three partners. I guess it was Colianni, but I'm not sure. That meant he now, after the abduction I mean, had a two-thirds interest in the business. That gave him a controlling interest and allowed him to sell the whole thing on his terms. Garcia was pretty careful to add, in a letter he wrote, "Selling it would not solve the drinking problem."

Then he announced that the Navajo Inn would be closed for one month effective April 1, 1973. That would have been just three days *before* the election. Of course, we know now that he lost the election. What no one knew at the time was that the upcoming election probably influenced his decision to buy out one of the three partners. He wanted control of the business so he could sell the whole joint. He promised that all the details of the solution would be worked in a month or so. He said he was talking about a permanent solution to the problem.

And get this. Garcia met with representatives of the Kiva Club and three other Indian groups to try to resolve the problem! He told them he was trying to divest himself by either selling his interest or transferring the license. He sounded genuine. He always said he didn't run that place. Now that he had a controlling interest in the company, he was working with the Indian groups who voiced such strong political opposition to him. No one can say the guy didn't try. Then after he lost the election, he kept his word. He formally offered to sell the Navajo Inn to the Navajo tribe. The *Gallup Independent* reported, "The future of the Navajo Inn was now up to the Navajo tribe." Chairman Peter McDonald hired a lawyer, George Vlassis, to negotiate for the tribe. This was in mid-April, two weeks after the election.

But something happened to the deal. I don't know what it was; but on May 14, 1973, Garcia announced that he was reopening the Navajo Inn. Here's my speculation. He lost the election. He resigned from the board of regents. He resigned from the Gallup Commission on Alcohol Rehabilitation; and then, much to everyone's dismay, the negotiations stalled on the tribe buying the bar.

That's when Garcia issued a press release and said, "I believe the liquor business is legal under the constitution of the United States and under the laws of the State of New Mexico. I will not be intimidated by reactionary groups who demand that I close a legal place of business. Any consequences that result in the future are due not to the Indians themselves and will have to be answered by the U.S. government and by the Navajo tribe. I have a right to reopen my business."

Clay, here's another little fact we didn't know. Garcia had, by that time, actually moved from New Mexico. He moved to Arizona and apparently intended to run whatever businesses he had left from Arizona. He put his kids in school over there and everything. This whole thing really did him in. That shotgun blast didn't kill him, but it killed his political and business future in New Mexico. What I can't decide is whether he was the only victim here. We know Casuse was the aggressor and that his actions were morally and legally indefensible, but even if he wasn't a martyr, he was a victim. He gave his life, you know. I'll keep you posted on my digging down here in Gallup.

Love,
April

~ ~ ~

Dawn suddenly appeared dead center on Virgil's front windshield as he drove south out of Window Rock to Gallup on State Highway 264. As always, dawn's arrival energized him. Early morning, he believed, was created as a time to think. More to the point, it was a time to think alone. Like almost everyone born on the Rez, Virgil felt renewed by the rising sun just as he felt relieved when it sat after a long day, struggling to cross the world. Dawn in a country so vast, so barren of people, and so stunning in its solitude demanded that you *think*, not talk, not listen—just *think*. As he dropped down the hill past China Springs and headed toward the Highway 666 cutoff to Gallup, he couldn't help feeling a little sorry for April, who thought dawn was a good time to roll over and go back to sleep.

As Virgil drove the twenty-four miles from his house just inside the Arizona state line, southeast on Highway 666 into New Mexico, he marveled at how beautiful this part of the state was. Headed this way, at this time, the spreading sunrise—over mesas, sand canyons, and strand after strand of juniper brush, piñon trees—made a tableau of isolated parts of the whole. The usual haze that time of year layered an almost purple haze over the sagebrush, its entrapping sand bluffs, and the curve of the blacktop road. This was a sea of desert, he thought. But he had other things to think through and shook his head slightly to bring himself back into focus.

On the seat beside him, he had a fax of an old letter to the editor of the *Gallup Independent*. He could see the block headline of the letter to the editor dated March 3, 1973, CAUSE RATED MORE TALK AND LESS SHOOTING. It seemed oddly prophetic for the breakfast "meeting" that April invited him to last night on the phone.

"A meeting?" he'd responded. "Why do we have to have a *meeting*? Why can't we just have breakfast and talk this over?"

"'Cause this is business, it's serious, and we are going to be grown-up about this," she'd retorted, a little more testily than was called for.

April found the letter in one of the old newspapers in the library. She faxed it to Virgil so he could mull it over before they got together. Actually, when he got it yesterday, he didn't think it was important enough to warrant breakfast, let alone a meeting. April's emphatic "wow, this is awesome" characterization struck him as a typical big-city girl's overstatement.

The letter, written by someone named Sylvia Ann Abeyta, and giving a Gallup address, had a decidedly Rez tone to it. As Virgil drove to town, he was comforted by the thought that this letter could have been written by any one of his several aunts, all of whom had been in and around Gallup back in '73. That didn't change his view that the letter, while thoughtful, was still an emotional overreaction. He couldn't quite shake that thought as he parked and went into the Gallup Donut Hole.

While waiting for April, he read today's letters to the editor in the *Albuquerque Journal.* The big news was that Intel was about to spend a billion dollars in Rio Rancho, Albuquerque's only suburb; most letter writers were either happy or sad that the new plant would be on Albuquerque's west side and not mar the beauty of the Sandias on the east. It was a time of peace, he thought, not like the New Mexico in 1973. Then he reread the twenty-year-old letter to the *Gallup Independent.* As he contrasted the current letters with the old one, it occurred to him that not much else had changed. People still ask unanswerable questions based on knowing only half the facts. Was that "half asked," he thought, deciding the play on words was quite clever.

Precisely at eight, which was early for her, April bounded in. A quick hug, a short sip of strong coffee, and their conversation began to bristle. April's excitement over finding the letter was obvious as she read aloud the first sentence, "We, the concerned citizens, question the handling of Mayor Garcia and subsequent killing of Larry Casuse." April automatically assumed that Ms. Abeyta spoke of *all* of Gallup's concerned citizens at the time. Virgil framed the debate when he said, "Well, she's entitled to her opinion."

"Look, Virgil, she didn't understand how the police could have reacted the way they did, and she even told them how it should have been handled."

"You mean, the way she said they handled things in New York City?"

"Yes. She was talking about a story in New York where police talked several armed men into giving up their hostages."

"Gallup was Gallup, even back then. New York's mayor wasn't a hostage, and the armed men might have been from Greenwich Village, for all we know. Apples and bananas, I'd say."

"All right, I'll take your point that Gallup and New York were different, but she says even the hostages at Wounded Knee were released 'after deliberation' that same day?"

"For openers, she's wrong. The siege at Wounded Knee went on for months and the so-called hostages denied that they were even hostages. There is no doubt that the mayor was a hostage. Remember, he was handcuffed, they held a gun to his head, and then they shot him in the back. Gallup was a whole lot different than Wounded Knee."

April opened her mouth to respond, apparently thought better of it, and said, "Excuse me." As he watched her head for the little girl's room, he shook his head as though trying to reorganize his approach to this issue. *No need to be so dogmatic*, he thought and planned to back off when April got back. He didn't get the chance. She came back in less than a minute, plopped down, and came at him, head-on.

"Virgil, just listen to this lady. She has a lot to say here. 'Several of the persons involved in the writing of this letter to the editor were eyewitnesses to the incident. Their reports, which were not investigated by police or reporters, contradict the UPI statement. Thus, we would like to inform the general citizenry of their account. These persons became aware of something happening with the arrival of at least sixteen police officers. Three were stationed on a roof with either rifles or shotguns, four were in front of the building, four were at the west end of the block, and two were posted at the east end of the block. There were at least two guys, looking like sharpshooters with long guns and big telescope things on them, right near their cars while the chief of police was attempting to direct traffic in the middle of the street . . .'"

Virgil slowly inhaled, held up a donut, and said, "The hole in that story is as big as the hole in this donut. She implies, and you seem to agree, that there were too many cops there. Too many? How could there be too many? They had two pissed-off Indians holding the mayor captive in a store full of guns. Maybe they needed more police, not less."

"But the cops didn't talk, they just blasted away. That's the point of this lady's whole letter. The number wasn't important. See here where she says, 'The incident, according to these eyewitnesses, occurred in the following order. Some shots were fired inside the building, but apparently, no bullets came out. Police then fired into the building. One hostage, apparently a customer or an employee was thrown out or released. During the shooting, it seemed that not many shots came out of the building. Tear gas was then fired inside. The mayor came out of the building. The city manager yelled out what sounded like, "They will probably come out shooting."'"

"April, that's a donut with at least two holes in it. From the grand jury transcript you showed me, as well as all the *other* court documents, it wasn't a 'customer or employee that was thrown out,' it was the mayor himself. He escaped by jumping through a plate glass door. And *all* the shots that were fired before that came from inside the building. The police didn't fire until after those guys shot the mayor in the back as he ran through the plate glass door. And it was only then that the police tear-gassed the joint."

Now it was April's turn to lighten up a little. She took a sip of water then a glug of coffee, nibbled at her toast, and said, "Okay, so she got her facts a little confused. It was a terrifying incident, and probably everyone saw things a little differently. Let's get to her real point, which is, why did they shoot Casuse when he tried to give up? She wanted to know the answer to that one, and incidentally, so would I. Here is how she put it. 'Larry walked to the front of the building, his rifle seemingly not leveled to shoot. An officer shot Larry Casuse with his pistol. Other person surrendered. Police went into Stearns Sporting Goods and pulled Larry out. He was left on the sidewalk. His sister was the only one concerned enough to check his condition. He was left uncovered until at least five minutes passed. The ambulance did not arrive until at least ten minutes had passed.'"

"Look, April, you're right about people looking at the same scene but seeing it differently. Think about it rationally, here comes the guy who's just kidnapped and shot the mayor in the back and now he has a rifle in his hands. She says the rifle was 'seemingly not leveled to shoot.' How do you suppose the cop whose job it was to protect the citizens, including the mayor, would have described that? 'Not seemingly leveled to shoot'? I doubt it. Cops look at guys with guns differently, I'm pretty damn sure of that. It doesn't make any difference whether they are Indians or Hawaiians. It's a pissed-off guy with a gun. They opened fire, what'd you expect?"

"Virgil, maybe you should have been a cop, not a tourist director. But that's not really my point or this lady's. She has legitimate questions that no one answered. Could we just go over her list? 'Since this incident did occur, we would like to ask several questions: (1) How did Larry and the mayor manage to move two blocks without being challenged? (2) Why was not Larry and his confederate given warning and a fair chance to surrender before police started shooting? Is it that the police in this area do not want to give persons a fair chance to talk to justify their actions? (3) Seemingly, Larry allowed the hostages a chance to escape or he released them. Why then was he not given a chance?'"

Virgil held up his hand. "Slow down, we can't do the whole list at once. Let's just take those three. Number 1, 'Larry and the mayor managed to move two blocks' because Larry had a gun in the mayor's back, and Larry's friend had a bomb. Seems reasonable to let 'em walk. Number 2, didn't we read in the grand jury transcript that the cops tried to call the store several times and Casuse wouldn't talk?"

"Yes," April responded, "but this lady couldn't have known that. Her letter was written before March 3 because that's the day they printed it and . . ."

"My point exactly. She's making accusations before she knows the facts."

"Well, her next questions are based on *facts*. She says, '(4) If it was necessary to end the incident, why tear gas not used first? (5) Why were spectators not forced to leave the area for their own protection? (6) Why was an ambulance not immediately on hand? (7) Did the mayor escape or was he released? (8) Why were later newscasts conflicting with eyewitness accounts and the tape on the spot report done by the head of KGAK's news staff, especially concerning the time for the use of tear gas?'"

"Fair's fair," Virgil said. "I answered the first three, you try these. What are your answers now that you know the facts from the sworn testimony?"

"I think they used the tear gas *and* the bullets at the same time. You heard the audiotape. It all happened about the same time. She has a point there. She should have asked why they didn't use *only* tear gas, not why they didn't use it first. I don't know why she's worried about the spectators not being moved away. In fact, that struck me as a good thing. Lots of witnesses that way. And as for the ambulance, I guess it didn't matter. Those ghastly photos on the front page of the paper make it clear that an ambulance would have made no difference for Casuse. Her point about the radio report and the newscasts saying different things seems common though. That happens now every day. Radio's just different, that's all."

"How about her question about whether the mayor escaped or was released? Do you think that's a fair question on her part?"

"Of course I do. How could she know then? How could anyone know? Her question was based on what she saw at the scene, not on what the mayor told the grand jury a week later." Virgil paused, took a sip of his now ice-cold coffee, and scraped the donut crumbs into a napkin, rolled it up, and carefully set it on the little plastic plate. April said nothing, so he reengaged.

"Come on, April, give me a break here. If she was at the scene, she saw what everyone else saw. The mayor came crashing through the plate glass door, handcuffed, and shot in the back with a shotgun blast. Do you suppose one single person on that street thought he was 'being released'? Hell of a way to release a guy. Cuff him, blast him through a plate glass door, and have a nice day, Mr. Mayor. No one could have thought that, not even this lady, although I'll admit some of her other questions are troubling."

"Like what?"

"Well, she also asked why the chief of the police placed himself in a situation in which he could be disarmed. That's a good one. And she asked why they released the name of the deceased before notification of his next of kin. I suppose the first one is just the situation. You know, a small-town police chief is caught in a real bad situation in the mayor's office. Could have happened to anyone. The second one might be just as simple. Casuse's brother and sister were both at the scene. They were his next of kin."

"I suppose you have a glib answer for her next question—number 11, she asked, 'Why did this incident occur in the first place?'"

"Nope, my little princess, you got me there. Why *did* it occur? Was Casuse on a death trip? Was it his own death he wanted or just the mayor's? I don't know, and I doubt that anyone does, except maybe his friend Robert Nakaidinae. He might answer it. Or maybe he was just along for the ride, like the scared kid who got in his car in the parking lot over in Albuquerque at the absolute wrong time. When you or your uncle Clay track down the only two guys who lived through this, Nakaidinae and Mayor Garcia, maybe you'll have an answer."

They both had enough for one day. This so-called research assignment was turning out to be an incubator for how they felt about one another. So April said goodbye to Virgil, watched him drive down the street, and cupped her little blue glass pendant in her hand. As always, it got a little darker. Not wanting to change her future, she took it off and put it in her purse.

CHAPTER FOURTEEN

"Don't Follow in Someone's Footsteps—You'll Get Crippled"

April was relieved that Clay took on the job of finding Nakaidinae and Garcia and left the real job, digging for more facts, to her. She read the local and national media coverage and all of the police files and court records on the case. Clay read all the important books on the subject. Virgil's insight, knowledge of his people, and their culture helped put it all in context. But even with all of this, the critical question, *why*, remained unanswered.

Why did the *incident*, as the letter writer put it, occur in the first place? Sometimes she wondered about people and their choice of words. Was the death of one man and the ruination of another an *incident?* To her, the word implied something innocuous, something ordinary. She looked it up just to make sure. The effort reassured her. *Incident* was not the right word to describe the tragedy in Gallup on March 1, 1973.

Clay didn't have much luck finding Nakaidinae and Garcia, so Virgil said he'd give it a try. Virgil wondered whether anyone else might have some insight into *why* Casuse kidnapped Garcia and died for his effort. How about Nakaidinae's lawyer? She gathered up her notes from the court files and took them with her to the library. Spreading them out on the table in the research room, she compared the official court file against newspaper accounts of Nakaidinae's hesitant steps through New Mexico's legal maze.

He had been taken before McKinley County Magistrate Lido Rainaldi for arraignment on Friday morning, March 2, to face eight criminal charges. He told the magistrate that he was innocent and wanted a lawyer named

Joan Friedland to represent him. Friedland, according to the *Albuquerque Journal*, was an experienced Santa Fe lawyer with something of a reputation for representing the underdog or those in need of a court-appointed lawyer. She didn't do much in the case, apparently only filing a few motions.

Friedland softly opposed the state's effort to move the trial out of Gallup, likely wanting to preserve the record for a later appeal, but not really wanting to have to try the case in Gallup where Garcia, a very popular man, would be a very popular victim. Judge Thomas Donnelly accepted the state's position, which was based on the testimony of Jack Chapman, Garry Hill, and Chester Macorie. All of them supported the district attorney's argument that Gallup was no place for this trial. Ms. Friedland called Nancy Pioche, John Perry, Shirley Montgomery, and John Giovondo to try to convince the judge that a nonbiased jury could be found in Gallup. Judge Donnelly made short work of the matter and moved the trial to Albuquerque, probably feeling that someone else would get shot if he allowed such a volatile trial to be held in a hotheaded place like Gallup.

Next, Friedland moved to quash the indictment on various legal grounds and asked for more time to prepare a defense. She tried to force the prosecutors to give her more information about the government's case. She lost all her motions save one, Judge Donnelly granted her motion to withdraw as counsel. On the date originally set for trial, July 23, 1973, she was somewhat unceremoniously replaced as defense counsel in the case by an Albuquerque lawyer, Thomas E. Horn.

Nakaidinae's new lawyer had less criminal experience, no record of involvement in the Indian rights movement, no political dissent cases, and no obvious connection to Nakaidinae. While he did not take court-appointed cases, he definitely had political connections. These connections likely directed the wholesale changes he made in the Friedland defense plan. According to the motions she filed, Friedland planned to highlight the fact that Casuse had a strong motive to attack Garcia, but Nakaidinae did not. Casuse was from Gallup, Nakaidinae was not. Casuse was part of the radical Indian rights movement, Nakaidinae was not. Casuse acted rationally at the time of the abduction, Nakaidinae did not. Friedland argued in court that her client was temporarily insane and that he had a right to a publicly funded psychiatric exam to prove his claim.

Horn fundamentally altered the Friedland defense plan. He argued, in his first motion in the case, that Nakaidinae was quite sane and did not need a mental exam. Judge Donnelly disagreed and ordered a mental exam for

Nakaidinae even though his own lawyer did not want one. The court-ordered mental examination found Nakaidinae mentally sound and competent to stand trial. Horn wanted the trial moved back to Gallup, but Judge Donnelly denied that out of hand and confirmed a start date for the trial on October 9, 1973, in Albuquerque.

Garcia was a UNM regent, and Casuse was a UNM student. Nakaidinae had no connection to UNM. Casuse was a student leader and president of the Kiva Club on campus. Nakaidinae had no known connection to student activism, AIM, IAE or the Kiva Club. Importantly, Nakaidinae had no known hostility of any kind toward Garcia. Casuse's hostility toward Garcia was quite public. He had appeared before the New Mexico Senate, and the university itself, in opposition to Garcia's appointment as a regent. That fact alone must have been very embarrassing to the university and the governor. And that is where Horn's political connections, and maybe his new defense plan for Nakaidinae, came in.

Horn was a member of a prominent New Mexico family and the nephew of the president of the University of New Mexico Board of Regents, Calvin S. Horn. In short, Friedland's original defense theory painted Nakaidinae *and* Garcia as victims of Casuse's violent abduction. But Horn rejected that theory and fundamentally changed the entire nature of the defense. He did not want to attack the university or the establishment in Gallup. He wanted to portray Nakaidinae as just a dupe, a boy lost in a man's world, and someone who was entitled to the court's soft hand.

Overall it looked, at least as far as the cold record in Gallup was concerned, that the secret of *why* this *incident* ever occurred was safe. The Gallup official court record came to end when the trial was moved to Albuquerque. Maybe part of the answer was buried in whatever court records existed in Albuquerque. Alternatively, the answer might come if Clay, or Virgil, could find Nakaidinae and Garcia.

~~~

Virgil and April stared intermittently at each other and then back again at the notes on her kitchen table. April started it, "But it seems unfair, at least now, twenty-one years later, that they didn't really get a trial."

"Who didn't get a trial?" Virgil asked as he dropped the photocopy of the *Albuquerque Journal* back onto the table and knocked over his cranberry juice onto the *Santa Fe New Mexican*. "The defendant got a trial, the lawyers got a trial, the judge was there and so was the jury. Who exactly are you talking about?"

"You know very well who I'm talking about, Virgil Bahe. Why do you always insist on being so literal about things? The people you call the Diné, the activists, the ones carrying the drum—those are the people I'm talking about. *They* didn't get a trial, that's who."

"Well, they didn't want a trial, they wanted headlines."

"I tell you what, Virgil, let's go through this stack of court files and newspaper articles about the trial. Let's just concentrate on the headlines and see who's right. Are you up to that since you've spilled the cranberry all over the *Gallup Independent?*"

"Sure, although my literal side says the juice is on the *New Mexican,* not the *Independent.* Let's start with the October 2, 1973, headline in the *Gallup Independent.* It says, WRITER FINDS 'DISCONTENT' IN AREA AS TRIALS NEAR. I'd say that was pretty good ink for the activists and the drum, don't you think?"

"Virgil, this headline was in the *Gallup Independent,* but the story itself came from the American Indian Press Service in Fort Defiance, Arizona, and was written by a man named Richard La Course. Funny, I never noticed the byline before. What was the American Indian Press Service anyway?"

"You got me, but the point I think you are making is that the Rez reporter is being mischaracterized by a copy editor in Gallup. Isn't it the newspaper that makes up the headline, not the reporter?"

"I think that's how it works most places. But let's test your theory. Does this headline fairly characterize the story?"

"Maybe, maybe not. What we were talking about was whether AIM and the other activists got the press they really wanted or whether the defendant and the government got what they wanted, which was to skip the trial and go straight to jail, remember?"

"What do you mean, the defendant wanted to skip the trial? Maybe the government wanted to skip it, or maybe the University of New Mexico wanted to avoid the publicity. Garcia and his family probably hated the press coverage. But who says the defendant wanted to skip it?"

"April, Nakaidinae pled guilty in the middle of the trial, remember? When you plead guilty, you skip the trial."

"Got it, Virgil. Moving on with our little debate, this article makes it clear there were two *different* trials coming up in October of 1973. As Mr. La Course put it, these trials created 'a mood of tenseness.' His article talks about the other case, the one in Gallup, involving two other Indians from there. He is also talking about the Nakaidinae case which was set for trial a week later in Albuquerque."

"Yes, that's because he sees the connection between the two different trials even though they involve different people. The first trial he mentions was John Cutnose's trial for the seizure of the Public Health System Hospital in Gallup. Remember, I told you about that case. Cutnose's trial was scheduled for October 29 in Gallup. Had they not moved Nakaidinae's October 9 trial to Albuquerque, Gallup would have had two trials involving AIM activists going on at the same time. And as you can see, the paper is giving AIM some serious ink on both trials. The article says right there in the middle of the page, 'The two young men are rapidly becoming the symbols of the autumn of Navajo discontent.' They say that the trials have brought long-standing discontent to the surface and 'have drawn the interest of the activist American Indian Movement.' That must have warmed many hearts in Wounded Knee. You have to keep in mind that the negotiated stand-down in Wounded Knee was just barely over by October of 1973."

"Yeah, you're right. But I guess I didn't know how strong AIM was in Gallup at the time."

"Nobody seems to know that at the time. But this article says that the first Navajo chapter of AIM was formed in Fort Defiance with about a hundred Navajo members. Fort Defiance was where Nakaidinae lived and Casuse was buried, remember?"

April frowned as she fidgeted with her blue pendant. Shaking her head from side to side, she asked, "When was it formed, does the article say?"

"No. But AIM was forming chapters on most reservations in the early seventies."

Finding what she had been looking for, April said, "Well, Virg, I found it. This article also quotes someone we saw before in the papers, a Larry Emerson, that name strikes a bell."

"Right, he was a student at the University of New Mexico and a friend of Casuse. He was in the Kiva Club with Casuse. Read it to me."

April sipped her tea and read aloud, "'The interest of the City of Gallup and its city officials is to bill Larry Casuse and Robert Nakaidinae as madmen. Larry is now dead, and Robert faces six felony counts in the attempted abduction in March. But the Navajo people believe their efforts were not that at all, but for social and political reasons in Gallup.' Virg, is it possible that they were both right? I mean, La Course and Emerson are friends, and even they admit that Casuse and Nakaidinae did what they did. It's just that AIM believes what they did was not criminal. They see the abduction as resolving social and political problems."

"Well, that makes my point pretty well. Trials are about guilt, criminal guilt, and the narrow issue of who did it. Newspapers want to explore social and political issues. So the newspapers covered what they wanted to cover, and Nakaidinae's trial was squashed because it wasn't politically necessary. That's what it looks like to me."

"Aren't trials necessary to explain why someone does something? It isn't just the facts that are important, isn't the motive important too?"

Virgil moved a little closer to April and softened the debate, "I guess you are right, April, but maybe the motive is more important to the result of the trial—that is, the sentence—as opposed to the verdict. I mean, it's silly to call this an *attempted* abduction as La Course does. This *was* abduction. They did it, they didn't just attempt it."

"All right, look at the next headline. It's dated October 3, 1973, and says, NAKAIDINAE'S LAWYER SEES LESS BIAS HERE. Now avoiding for the moment the obvious grammatical error, what does the headline convey to the reader?"

"To me, it says what the lawyer wants to say. If you read the article, you see it's from the AP wire in Albuquerque even though it's printed in the *Gallup Independent*. So once again, the article comes from one place and the headline from another. The point Horn makes in the article is that jury selection over in Albuquerque systematically excludes Indians from jury duty. But the point the headline writer makes is that there is less bias in Gallup than in Albuquerque. I wonder who wrote the headline."

"Well, Mr. Know-it-all, how does he know that? I mean, how does a lawyer know that Indians are excluded from juries in Albuquerque whereas in Gallup they are not? What is it, the names on the lists, or is it common to list people as Navajo or Chinese or whatever on jury lists?"

Virgil had no ready answer for that, but he had a theory. "Well, Horn told the court that the jury list comes from voter registration cards in Albuquerque. That's 'not representative of the Bernalillo County community and particularly not of the Gallup community,' he argued. I guess he thinks that very few Navajos were on voter registration lists. That's probably the case, at least in Albuquerque. His real point seems to be that Anglos and Mexican-Americans dominate juries in Albuquerque and cannot, as he puts it, 'understand Indian culture or perceive or objectively judge people of a different cultural background.'"

"Well, maybe he's right. How could they really understand Indian culture unless they studied it, like Uncle Clay has, or lived it, like you? How could they objectively judge young men like Casuse and Nakaidinae?"

"April, I guess I disagree, at least a little, but that's not what we're talking about. What is it about Indian culture that they needed to know to determine whether Nakaidinae actually abducted Garcia with a gun to his head in the first place? I mean, culture is important to my people and to me, but if I'd been on the jury and I knew the culture, I would still focus on whether or not he carried the bomb and made the threats to blow the whole damn place up. I would have a hard time deciding the case on political or social grounds. Do you see what I mean?"

"Sure, Virg, I do. Here's a headline that proves both my point and yours, NAKAIDINAE WANTS NO LOS ANGELES HERE. I remember this article. It's important because the reporter actually talked to Nakaidinae in the presence of his lawyer and then summarized Nakaidinae's views."

"If your uncle can't find Nakaidinae, this could be very important. What's it say?"

"Nakaidinae says he was reared in a family of ten children in Fort Defiance, Arizona. Then his family moved to Los Angeles. He came back to the reservation every summer for family visits. He described himself as an 'artist and a painter.' He's going to move back to the reservation 'when all this is over.'"

"By *this*, I take it he meant the upcoming trial?"

"Yeah, sure. They quote him a lot. He said, 'I believe all people should be treated alike. No difference in race, color, or religion. 'The Indian way' will have to pull this world together. They (Indians) will have to do it. Whatever an Indian does will have to be in the interest of reducing the ugliness of the world to save the people.'"

"Pretty noble. Doesn't sound like Los Angeles."

"He goes on, 'I am thinking of the younger ones, the little ones, the children. I don't want them growing up in a world like I did. I don't want to see Gallup become a Los Angeles with all its insensitiveness. Children have to know what the air is like, what stars look like at night, what trees look like, what mountain water looks like.'"

"So is that it? Is that his defense?"

"Virgil, this article doesn't talk about his defense. It talks about him and what he wants for the future."

"Well, I'd say that he sounds like a dreamer and didn't like living on the beach. He wants the open spaces of the Rez. He got his wish."

"What's that?"

"Gallup is sure no Los Angeles. Twenty-one years have passed since he gave that interview. Look around you. Gallup has no smog, lots of trees, and even a few streams. The water is clear, and the nights are magnificent. From all I can tell, it's no more insensitive to its children than anywhere else."

"Point taken. Here's the next article, dated October 5, 1973. It has two headlines. The first one reads, WHAT DID WE DO TO BANKS & MEANS. The second one says, UNM WILL TRAIN NAVAJO TEACHERS. The first one is an AP story from Pierre, South Dakota, and the second one is an AP story from Albuquerque. Funny, both are printed in the *Gallup Independent*. Well, not funny exactly, but this has taught me how much newspapers rely on one another and on the wire services for their stories."

Virgil jumped on this one. "Yes, but are the headlines consistent with the stories? Do the stories prove my thesis that trials are about guilt and innocence whereas newspaper stories about trials are about political or social issues?"

"I guess one is and one is not. The first one, about Russell Means and Dennis Banks, is a story about their trial in Minneapolis."

April was perplexed. "Minneapolis? Why there? Was it connected to Wounded Knee?"

"Yes, it says that charges were filed in federal court in Minneapolis, arising from the siege at Wounded Knee. The trial will be held there. The judge warned Means against using lawyers from the Wounded Knee Legal Defense Committee."

"Against? The judge said Means should not have those lawyers. Why?"

"Well, it says that he said, the judge that is, that he could have them if he wanted, but be aware that if his attorney also represents other defendants in the Wounded Knee case, then he might have problems."

"Like what?"

"Well, they might want him to testify, but not against their other clients. And there could be different defenses for different defendants. But if they are all represented by the same lawyer, then it gets all mussed together."

"Sounds sensible to me. What did Means say?"

"He said, at least according to this paper, that he had 'full confidence in the character and honesty of those who represent him *and* the other defendants.'"

"Well, there's a good example of culture clash. Out on the Rez, it is common for people to band together for a cause. Courtrooms are different. Courtrooms are places where one individual man has to be looked at separately from all others even if there are others on trial at the same time. Seems like Means is mixing up what might be good on the Rez with what might be good in the courtroom. When was his trial scheduled?"

"Not until January or February of the next year, 1974."

"You said there were two articles. What's the other one about?"

"It's consistent with its headline, but the facts are interesting for another reason. The article says that the University of New Mexico has launched a federally funded program designed to equip forty Navajos to fill classroom jobs. Here's the interesting part. Did you know that back then, there were 2,800 teachers on the Navajo reservation, but only 180 of them were Navajos? That's what, 5 or 6 percent? I guess I knew that it was low, but I never thought it was that low. Who is teaching the kids now?"

"I know the numbers are better now, but there are still lots of BIA schools on the reservation, and the BIA is still dominated by Washington, D.C. Not a lot of Navajos in Washington, and not enough of our people go to college, even now when we have junior colleges on the Rez itself."

"The headline for the next article reads, NAKAIDINAE TRIAL SECURITY REMAINS. It's a large banner headline from the *Gallup Independent* of October 5, 1973."

Virgil squinted. "Let me see that one. I must have missed it the first time though. Look here, I guess this is why I did. This article is about the federal court in Albuquerque, not the state court. The defense lawyer, Horn, tried to block the state court trial by asking the federal judge over there to impose strict security in the state courthouse."

"But why?" April asked. "Wasn't the security the same in both courthouses?"

"I doubt it. The feds always have more of everything, including security. That hasn't changed, probably never will. Anyhow, the federal judge balked. He said something nice about how the state courts were competent and could handle security all on their own. What makes this newsworthy is that Nakaidinae's lawyer was saying that there was too *much* security. He argued that the effect of it was to prejudice the potential jurors against Nakaidinae by 'fostering the already prevalent attitude that Indians in general, and this defendant in particular, are savage and violent in nature.'"

"What do you think, Virg? Was there a general feeling then that Indians were violent?"

"I guess I can't say for sure, but my feeling is that just the opposite was true. I mean, the rap on Indians on and off the Rez was that they were nonviolent, even passive, when it came to their rights and stuff. Nakaidinae seems mostly a nonviolent type until you think about what he did. He carjacked an innocent student, threatened to blow up city hall with a bomb, and carried the chief of police's gun down the street when they kidnapped the mayor. Then he shot Garcia in the back with a shotgun. Consider that in the same context as AIM. Its militancy was over the edge. I think Horn's argument might apply to AIM and maybe even his own client, but probably not to Indians in general then or now."

April seemed uncertain but let it pass. "Well, here's the next one. It's a Bonnie Meyer article from the *Gallup Independent*, dated October 8, 1973. She covered the abduction story for her newspaper and went to Albuquerque for the start of the criminal trial. The headline says, PROSECUTION CALLS 23 FOR NAKAIDINAE TRIAL. The article is about the witnesses that the government intended to call against Nakaidinae."

"So the headline fits the article? No social commentary here, just the facts, ma'am, is that it?"

"Virgil, this is serious business here. The DA, Louis DePauli, subpoenaed twenty-three witnesses but said that it was unlikely that all of them would actually testify."

"Well, that tells us they were actually planning on a trial. Wasn't the trial scheduled for the next day, the ninth of October?"

"Yep. It was. Ms. Meyer makes the point that the length of the trial was unclear but makes no mention of the possibility that it won't happen. She reported that the prosecutors said that it would take a week, but the defense attorney said it could be a monthlong trial. They were going to pick the jury the next morning."

"So did they?"

"Did they what?"

"Did they pick the jury the next morning, or did they scrap the whole thing?"

"Here's her follow-up story the next day, October 9, 1973, in the *Independent*. It looks like she wrote it from Albuquerque because she says Nakaidinae 'went on trial this morning in district court for the March 1 abduction of Gallup's mayor.'"

"Well, that's interesting all by itself. They've quit calling it an *attempted* abduction by now—see, it's just a plain old abduction, and it says that after the incident, Larry Casuse was found dead."

"There's a subtle change in reporting. The early articles all said he died in a police shoot-out, this one says he was 'found dead.'"

"Well, they were pretty cautious and said that 'officials said he died of a self-inflicted gunshot wound.' Oh, here's another thing. They quoted the defense attorney as saying the case is prejudiced in Albuquerque because of the 'fortresslike attitude during pretrial proceedings at the courthouse.'"

Virgil wryly noted, "A fortresslike attitude? They are trying an Indian from Fort Defiance who fortified himself inside a gun store after abducting the mayor, and he's *complaining* of a fortresslike attitude? I mean, who built the fort in the first place? That's what you ought to complain about, not the attitude thing."

"Virgil, your gallows humor escapes me. But there is something else here that goes to our argument du jour, which is politics or substance in courtrooms. Apparently, Nakaidinae was examined by an Albuquerque psychiatrist in July of that year, 1973, and found that Nakaidinae was 'apolitical early in life, but changed when he confronted persons who convinced him to become political.'"

"So there you have it. First, he's apolitical, and then he's political. But he must have been political by the time of the kidnapping. He abducted a man at gunpoint for political reasons. This trial was supposed to be about the abduction, not the political justification for it. What happened?"

"Virg, maybe the answer is in Ms. Meyer's next article. The giant headline above the masthead, in block letters all across the front of the paper on October 11, 1973, screams out, NAKAIDINAE CHARGES REDUCED. What happened is they stopped the trial, and his lawyer pled him guilty to reduced charges. So it looks like a political result to a courtroom battle."

"How political? And how did they do it? I mean, did everyone buy off on the deal?"

"I don't know, Virgil, all it says here is that Nakaidinae pled guilty to two reduced charges, and in return, the prosecutor dropped the two bigger charges against him. He was originally charged with kidnapping, but he only pled guilty to false imprisonment. I'm not sure what the difference is except that one seems to be less serious than the other."

"April, look here in the second column. Apparently, Nakaidinae had the same problem you do. He asked the judge to give him a definition of false imprisonment before he pled to the charge. Then after getting it, and being asked by the judge whether he was guilty, he said, 'I guess so.' The judge made him say yes or no, not 'I guess so.' It looks like the prosecutor was happy, but it doesn't say much about the defense lawyer other than he tried to withdraw from the defense that morning. Maybe that says it all from his side of the fence. The prosecutor, DePauli, said that he was 'happy in the manner that the case was disposed of and that the decision was just and equitable to both the state and the defense.'"

"Well, how about the abductees? How about the mayor, was he happy too?"

"Actually, Meyer interviewed him too. Garcia told her, 'I realize, much time and effort, as well as a great deal of cost, were involved in properly bringing the guilty parties to a joint end. It is not so important in this particular case to have had a conviction as it was to have a confession of guilt.'"

"He sounds like a pretty forgiving guy for someone who was kidnapped, shot through a plate glass door, and defeated at the polls because some apolitical Navajo from Los Angeles decided to become political."

"Well, Virg, maybe when we find Garcia, we will get some answers. But for now, there's more, Garcia is quoted in the article as saying, 'Maybe now with better understanding, all the people in our area will pull together for better relations and conditions without violence or the threat of violence.' That is consistent with what he seemed to be doing as mayor with the alcohol issue and the new rehabilitation center. Hopefully, we will find him. I can't wait to hear his side of the story."

"Me too. Finding Garcia is hard because his last name is common. Finding Nakaidinae is hard because it looks like he doesn't want to be found."

"What do you mean doesn't want to be found?"

"I'm hearing that he is still on the Rez, but living a quiet life, and wants nothing to do with your uncle's book project."

"How does he even know about it?"

"Well, Clay asked you to look in the directories around here, and you asked me to look around on the Rez. I asked some guys who seem to know almost everything. They said he doesn't want to talk to me or anyone else about this. 'Leave him alone,' they said."

April closed the chat. "Actually, I've made a couple calls down in my old stompin' grounds around Phoenix, looking for Mayor Garcia. Maybe something will pop up."

CHAPTER FIFTEEN

"Don't Say Your Own Name Too Much—Your Ears Will Dry Up"

"Is this Frank Garcia, the former mayor of Gallup, New Mexico?" Virgil asked. He waited for the expected "no, you've got the wrong Garcia." But this time, he was wrong. Virgil had spent weeks trying to find Garcia. This was a direct hit.

"Yeah, that's me. That was a long time ago. Who's calling?"

Virgil pushed away the long list of other Frank Garcias he'd made from phone books and library notes. "Mr. Garcia, my name is Virgil Bahe. I'm calling from Window Rock, but I used to go to ASU there in Tempe. I'm glad to find you. I wonder if you know how many Garcias are named Frank, and how many Frank Garcias are listed in Arizona phone books."

"I don't know. I never looked. But you must have found me some other way because I don't live in Phoenix, my given name is Emmett, not Frank, and it's not in the phone book anyhow."

"Yes, sir, I know. You live in Tempe, Arizona. Actually, I got your number from someone in your son's office. A guy in Gallup said we could find you if we could find your son, Ernie. I've been looking for you for about three weeks."

"Why? Do I owe you money?"

"No, sir, not hardly. We are hoping you can help us. I am helping my girlfriend, who lives in Gallup. Her uncle, a professional journalist, is writing a book about something that happened back in the seventies. They asked me to see if I could find you."

"What do you want from me, and what does it have to do with me being the mayor of Gallup?"

"It has everything to do with that. Mr. Ramsey, my girlfriend's uncle, is writing a book about the American Indian Movement and what happened in Wounded Knee and what happened to you in Gallup. We've looked at the court records and the big file on your case in the public library in Gallup. We are hoping that you'd talk to us and give us your personal views on what happened."

Virgil paused and waited for Garcia to answer. Thinking that the line had gone dead, he said, "Are you still there, Mr. Garcia?"

"Yes. But nobody has asked for my opinion on any of that for, I don't know, twenty-five years maybe. Are you writing about me or Gallup or the Indians or what?"

"Well, I'm just helping Mr. Ramsey. My girlfriend, April Ryan, and I are doing basic research on the facts of the case. You wouldn't know her because she didn't live in Gallup until this year. But she went to school at ASU same time I did."

"What do they—your girlfriend and her uncle—want?"

"They want to find out what happened."

"What happened is in the court records and the newspapers. You say you've checked all that."

"Yes, sir, we have. And we have talked to people in Gallup and out on the reservation, but it would be very helpful to have your personal views on things."

"Do you mean they want you to find out what *really* happened? Are you interested in the truth?"

"Yes, sir. Clay Ramsey knows a lot about AIM and what they did back then. His book will track the movement of various individuals and groups that were involved in the Indian rights movement. That's why he asked me to see if I could find you."

"So you're calling about Larry Casuse? Is that it?"

"Yes, sir, that's a part of it. I think the book will also cover other places and incidents. However, the Gallup story, your particular story, is the most important part of the larger national story. Do you have time now to talk a little bit? I'd like to explain some things, and then, if it's okay with you, I'd like to fly to Phoenix and interview you."

"Yeah, I've got time. I've got a lot of time these days."

"Mr. Ramsey works for a small magazine in Spokane, Washington, but he's writing this book more or less on his own. I don't think he can pay for your time, but all of us think your story is important."

"I'd be happy to talk to you, and I don't need to be paid for it. All I know is what happened to me."

"Well, Mr. Garcia, that's great. Thanks for helping us. Of course, we both want the same thing—we want the world to know what happened in Gallup in 1973. Mr. Ramsey takes a lot of pride in what he writes."

"What's the name of his magazine?"

"It's called the *American Warrior*. Have you heard of it?"

"No, can't say that I have. Sounds like a political thing. Is it like the NRA for Indians or what?"

"I don't think so. I've only read one or two of them myself. I live in Window Rock and work for the Navajo tribe and . . ."

"I used to live on the Rez myself. Are you a Navajo?"

"Yes, sir."

"Then I have to ask you. When you say 'American warrior,' do you mean Nakaidinae, the guy that shot me? Do you think he and Casuse were warriors?"

"I don't know what he was. I've read a lot of stuff, and my girlfriend has copies of the police reports and stuff, but I'm not sure what Mr. Casuse was."

"I asked you because if you thought he was a warrior, then maybe you think he was also a hero. Do you?"

"No, he wasn't a hero."

"Well, we agree on that. If you thought he was a hero, then I'd have to wonder what you thought I was."

"Mr. Garcia, you were the victim. He took you at gunpoint from your office. As best I can tell, he would have killed you if things had turned out differently."

"Call me Frank. My name is Emmett, but everybody calls me Frank. I don't want you to think I'm starting an argument about this, at least not yet. I need to know if you are, you know, taking sides. Do you know what really happened there in Gallup with me and Casuse?"

"Well, we do, yes, sir. We have researched the story a fair bit already, and we have . . ."

"Yes, but do you know what *really* happened? Or are you satisfied with what the papers said. Those are two different things, I can tell you that for sure."

"We do want to know what happened. I guess I should only speak for myself, but I do want to know the truth. And all of us want to know *why* it happened. We have been asking ourselves that question for several weeks now."

"Well, get on a plane and let me know when you get here. I'll tell you what really happened. I'm not sure why even today, but I can tell you a lot of things I bet you don't know."

Virgil said thanks and called Southwest Airlines. He'd solved a big part of the puzzle just by finding the long-lost mayor. He doodled his travel schedule on the same notepad that contained Frank Garcia's phone number in Tempe. His next call was to April.

"You found Frank Garcia."

"Wow. That's cool. Is he willing to talk? Where is he?"

"Remember Tempe, our old home away from home?"

"Yeah, so?

"So's Garcia. He lives in Tempe, and I just got off the phone with him. He sounds like he's happy to be found and is perfectly willing to give me a detailed interview. He said we would not know what *really* happened until we talked to him."

"Oh man, oh man. That's totally cool. I'm really jazzed. Just think I might have been living next door to him for the last four years. Tempe's so small—course it's surrounded by a big city to the west and two-thousand-tract home developments to the east."

"Well, I will be going to Tempe day after tomorrow."

~ ~ ~

The Rusty Pelican Seafood Restaurant just off I-10 and Broadway Road in Tempe was mostly empty when Virgil came in and asked for Mr. Frank Garcia at the cashier's counter. The perky blonde said, "Sure, he's in the back. Follow me."

As Virgil walked to the back, Frank Garcia pushed out of the booth, stuck out his hand, grinned, and said, "You must be Virgil. How was your trip?"

Frank Garcia looked like a man who'd done a lot in his sixty odd years. Dark, almost swarthy, with a wide smile, and bright inquisitive eyes, he looked prosperous and happy. Heavy glasses, thinning hair, and more than a few pounds overweight rounded out his look—Orson Wells without the beard. This was a man who faced a violent death. Now he sounded like he appreciated how fragile life really was.

They spent the obligatory ten minutes on the basics of their respective jobs and ordering lunch. As it was being served, Garcia said, "So tell me about your project and where I fit in."

"Mr. Ramsey's magazine has been chronicling the role played by men and women who fought for justice for their people. I guess he covered those sorts of stories for thirty years or more. Now he's writing a book, sort of to cap his career or something. He got the idea to write about AIM and what happened to it. When he was researching that story, he found out about what happened in Gallup at pretty much the same time as Wounded Knee. That's how it started."

"I'm curious," Garcia said, "how do you fight for justice by kidnapping people and trying to kill them?"

"Mr. Garcia, I know how that might sound, I mean, the way I said it. I am not taking sides here. I'm here to find out your side. Still, I know the Indians around Gallup were not always treated with respect. Some people think that was part of the reason why you were taken prisoner."

"With me, it's a lot more personal. I was a prisoner, but that wasn't the point. They tried to kill me. It was pure luck that they failed. I didn't think they were looking for justice."

"Maybe they weren't. We are trying to find out why they picked you and why they picked you just two days after the siege started in Wounded Knee. Casuse is dead, and Nakaidinae seems to have gotten lost in the canyons up on the Rez. Mr. Ramsey's magazine mostly focused on those who ended up as defendants. Here he is looking at others, like you, who were victims."

"To be honest with you, Mr. Bahe, I got the sense when we talked on the phone that your boss wanted to write about guys like Casuse and his friends in the Kiva Club or about Russell Means and Dennis Banks and the guys in AIM."

"He has written about them and the other leaders in the Indian rights movement. That's how he came across your name and your story."

"Well, Casuse was not in AIM, I can tell you that. His group was called Indians Against Exploitation although they were a lot like the guys in AIM. They had an axe to grind. What I'm wondering is, where do you think I fit in all of this? I fought a lot of battles, but to be honest, I never thought of myself as a warrior."

"No, I suppose not. We've researched a good part of your story, and we know you fought for what you believed in. Warriors come in all walks of life, you know."

"Well, in my opinion, the guys who kidnapped me weren't warriors. They were just kids. Besides, the real story of what happened to me has never been in print, so I doubt that you've researched it. Do you want to know my story, or do you just want to ask me questions? Either way is fine with me."

"We want to know your story, especially if it has never been told."

"My story has never been told—that's for sure. Are you telling me that if I tell you, then you'll print my side?"

"No, I can't make any promises. I'm just a researcher on this project. Clay Ramsey is the author. But he's a fair man, and he wants to know what really happened. I know you will be in the story somewhere, but no one can promise you how much or how you will fit into the overall book. Did I tell you that he was writing a novel? As I understand it, his book is not a documentary. He calls it a historical novel and wants to get the history part accurate. And there's the legal stuff besides."

"What do you mean 'legal stuff'?"

"I'm no lawyer, and neither is Mr. Ramsey. But he says he can only publish the truth. And even then, there are limitations."

"Like what, for example?"

"Well, he says the book has to avoid unnecessarily invading someone's privacy. He said something about not putting people in a false light. He said that might not be a big deal here."

"Do you know that it was Casuse who said I was false? He called me a *false person.*"

"Yes, sir, I know that. Mr. Ramsey is a brave guy. I don't think he will shy away from something just because it's controversial. I'm sure he won't refuse to write something just because someone's feelings might be hurt. I think the 'false light' thing goes further than that."

"Okay, I'm not sure how much you already know and where you want to start."

"I'd like to hear your story, in your own words, if that's all right with you. And I'd like to take notes. Okay?"

Garcia took off his glasses and juggled around a little in the booth. They'd been there a half hour, sparring and testing one another. Virgil could tell that Garcia really wanted to explain what happened, but could also tell that the memories were not pleasant, to put it mildly. Garcia wiped his brow with a clean white handkerchief, pushed his water glass out to the center of the table, and said, "Sure, take all the notes you want. I didn't have anything to hide in 1973, and I sure as hell don't know. However, what I am about to tell you will be new to you. I hired a private investigator after we moved to Arizona. Actually, it was about a year after. He charged me $1,000. I wanted to know what happened because it never made sense that Larry Casuse would hate me that bad, you know, bad enough to try to kill me just because he loved the earth, and the birds, and all that stuff that the Kiva Club put out after he abducted me."

"Mr. Garcia, is it okay if I interrupt you from time to time? You know, to make sure I'm getting this."

"Yeah, otherwise, you'll just sit there for two hours."

"Fine, first off, did you get a written report from the investigator? That could be real important."

"No, he just told me what he found out."

"All right, sorry to slow you down. What did he find out, and oh, what was his name?"

"I can't remember that right now. I have it in my old checkbook, though, because I paid his bill. He was the first to tell me that Larry Casuse was manipulated into believing that I was going to see to it that he was convicted of killing the young Indian girl in that car wreck the year before. They told him he would be executed, if you can believe that."

"Wow. Okay, you don't have a written report, but do you have anything solid, anything in writing to back this up?"

"Yeah, sure I do. I don't have it right here, but I can get it. All that stuff is in storage. I have boxes and boxes of files, letters, newspaper clippings, tape recordings, and . . ."

"Tape recordings? Of who? What do they say?"

"My investigator taped all the people in Gallup who told us why Larry Casuse was so cranked up. They told us the real story, you know, the one I told you about on the phone."

"Are you saying that Larry Casuse was told to abduct you by someone else, that it wasn't his idea? Was this a conspiracy that included other people?"

"Well, there's a difference between what they wanted him to do and what Larry actually did. I don't think their motive in using him was to hurt me or kill me. They used him to make sure I lost the election. That was their goal. I never believed they wanted me dead, just out of office."

"Why? From what we saw in the newspapers, you were a popular guy, and you were doing a lot for Gallup. You seemed like a guy on the way up, if you know what I mean."

"I was. But some people were in danger of losing their jobs because I knew some heavy stuff about them. It had to do with government funds and the way things had been run for a long time in Gallup. You say you read the newspapers. Did you read about the Zia Project?"

"No, I don't remember that name. April Ryan has done a lot of the basic research on this project. I'm mostly just helping her. She showed me copies of lots of documents and records, but I can't put my finger on that. What was it?"

"It was a federally subsidized housing project in Gallup."

"Wait, I do remember something about that. Seems like she told me, April that is, that you were going to fire somebody in the federal project if you were reelected. Is that it?"

"Well, I couldn't fire someone in the federal government, but I could fire the local director of the project if he didn't conform to the regulations that Gallup set up with the approval of the HUD office in Dallas. The feds over in Dallas were supervising the money spent in Gallup. The truth is that I was a danger to those guys. A danger if I was reelected, that is. I thought they were misusing the money, not stealing it or anything, just spending it foolishly and not being true to the people they were supposed to be helping. I also found out that some of the money was being used for personal stuff. My intent was to disclose everything after the election."

"Why didn't you disclose it before?"

"Because it wouldn't help. I had to wait until June or July or something like that in 1973. It was a matter of when the appointment by the council was due. Before that, it would have done no good. They would've just covered it up anyhow."

"So it sounds to me like they didn't want anyone to abduct you or shoot you or anything like that?"

"No, I don't think they ever thought Casuse was that crazy, unstable, or whatever he was. They thought he could be used to get some bad press on me because of my appointment to the regents and all. They thought that kind of press might get the Indians excited. Then my opposition could use it against me. That's how politics in Gallup was back then, probably it's the same now—I don't know—I've been out of it a long time. Anyway, they thought it might get them a few votes. Elections in Gallup were usually pretty close, you know, so a few votes might be enough to keep their jobs."

"Was it your opponent in the election that was doing this—what was his name, Ray something?"

"His name was Sam Ray. He was not involved in the HUD stuff. He just wanted to be mayor. I'm not sure he even knew anything about this although he was friends with them. But everyone in politics in Gallup is a friend of everyone else. At least that's the way it was back then. God, that was twenty years ago."

"Twenty-one years to be exact, Mr. Garcia," Virgil said. "Could we take a little break here, you know, for too much coffee? I'll be right back if you will excuse me." Virgil was gone a few minutes. When he got back, Garcia was still in the same spot, reading the newspaper, as though today was just like any other day. Virgil tried to pick up where they'd left off. "And you say you have some real proof of this, not just opinions and oral reports?"

"I have official HUD documents, and I have at least one tape recording. The documents are a little vague, I have to tell you that. These guys weren't that stupid, you know, to leave behind documents on what they were doing."

"Does the tape actually connect these guys to Casuse? You know, does it prove a conspiracy?"

"The tape doesn't prove that they actually conspired with Casuse to kidnap me or shoot me. I'm sure that was a shock to them when it happened. What they wanted was to get Casuse to rally the young Indians around Gallup against me. That would create a bunch of bad publicity that could swing the election results to Sammy Ray. He'd already said that he was pretty much in their camp, whether he knew it or not."

"Who knows about this besides you and your investigator?"

"Well, we met with one of them at a café in Gallup, and I recorded it. He didn't know I was doing it of course, but he was completely open about what happened. The investigator was with us, there in the café."

"I don't need names, but was he a resident of Gallup?"

"He was an employee of the Gallup HUD office. He knew about them using Casuse and getting him all cranked up about me."

"Was he in it with them?"

"I don't know. He told us that they met with Casuse several times in Fort Defiance, Gallup, and Santa Fe. They supplied him with numerous photos and even some movie film. In fact, that was done with HUD equipment—I mean, an HUD movie camera. They even gave the Kiva Club the camera. Government property be damned."

"What did they show, the films, I mean?"

"I never saw the film, but he said they shot a lot of drunk Indians around the Navajo Inn in order to stimulate Casuse's hatred of me. In fact, they met with Casuse the day before he came to Gallup to abduct me. Or maybe it was earlier in the week. It's been a long time since I listened to the tape recording."

"Does the tape say that they knew he was coming to Gallup when he did, that is, on March 1, 1973?"

"I can't say they knew exactly what Casuse was planning. All the guy said was that they knew Casuse was planning to confront me in my office."

"Did you ever get anyone else to confirm that?"

"Yeah, about eight or nine years ago, I talked to another Zia Project guy who was dying of cancer at the time. He admitted everything. He even let me record it on tape, right there in front of him. He said he was glad that the truth was out. I showed him the tape recorder before we started."

"And you still have the tape?"

"I have it, but I'm not sure where it is now. It's probably with the first tape and the others on the meetings at the Gallup Indian Community Center."

"Who else could confirm this? I mean, about the Gallup people trying to manipulate Casuse against you?"

"There are at least four others who might have known something about it. Bob Nakaidinae; Calvin Horn; Frank Garcia, who was no relation to me but was a good friend; and John Redhouse."

"What did they do? I've heard some of those names before. Wasn't Calvin Horn a big deal with the regents over in Albuquerque?"

"He sure was. He was the president or chairman of the board, an important man in New Mexico back then."

"How about the others?"

"Well, you know about Bob Nakaidinae. I eventually talked to him. Calvin Horn was there with me when I interviewed Nakaidinae. I always thought Nakaidinae's lawyer must have known this stuff, but I never talked to him directly. Nakaidinae's lawyer was Calvin Horn's nephew, you know. And there was John Redhouse. Redhouse was a friend of Casuse and was in the Kiva Club with him. He admitted all of this to the investigator. I think we have that on tape too."

"Frank, I want to know the details of what Nakaidinae told you during the interview with Calvin Horn, but if you wouldn't mind, tell me what you remember of the abduction itself. Is that still a painful memory?"

"I'll tell you exactly *when* it's painful. It hurts like hell when any little change in the weather affects the buckshot in my back that Nakaidinae put there when he blasted me through the front door of Ivan Stearns's gun shop. That's painful. The memory isn't."

"I'm sure you can feel it. Look, I've been interrupting too much. Why don't you tell it in your own words, and I'll promise not to interrupt so much this time. But you know, to save time, I know the basic details. What I'd love to know is how you felt and what you saw that the newspapers and the grand jury transcript didn't report."

"The grand jury? Was there one? I don't remember that?"

"Yes, there was. You testified before the grand jury and gave them your sworn version of what happened. But it was a sort of question-and-answer thing between you and the prosecutor. His name was DePauli. Louis DePauli. Wasn't that it?"

"Yeah, Eddie DePauli. I think it was Louis E. DePauli, but we called him Eddie. He became a judge after that. I think he's retired now. Still in Gallup though."

"Well, I'm sure they showed you the grand jury testimony you gave just before the trial in Albuquerque."

"I don't think they had a trial. You know, it just went away somehow. I remember writing a letter about it, but I don't remember any trial."

"Yeah, there was a trial, but it only lasted a few days. You were probably going to be their star witness, though, so it's strange that they didn't go over your testimony beforehand."

"You know, I really don't remember there was a grand jury either, but even so, I thought they were secret anyhow. How did you get my testimony?"

"I asked Mr. Ramsey about that. Grand jury transcripts are only sealed until an indictment is returned. After that, it's a public document. Anyone can get one just by going to the courthouse. That's how we got our copy."

"You have one? With me testifying in it? I'd like to see that."

"I'll mail you a copy. We can exchange stuff. We have quite a bit, but I'm sure you have more."

"Well, I've got every newspaper clipping from all over the state on this thing. My staff and my family kept copies."

"So, Mr. Garcia, tell me what happened that day. Let's start with how you found out that Casuse was coming to your office."

"I let him in the office because I thought he was a reporter. I got a phone call at city hall at about 3:00 p.m. that day from someone who said he was a reporter for a Santa Fe newspaper. They said they wanted to discuss the militant situation."

"What militant situation? This was before anything happened in Gallup, right?"

"Yeah, but all the stuff in Wounded Knee had things stirred up in Gallup too. There was a lot of coverage in Santa Fe and Albuquerque about Wounded Knee. Plus, Indian students at UNM had burned me in effigy just before this when I was sworn in as a regent for the University of New Mexico over in Albuquerque. So I thought that the interview would be about all of that, and I wanted the chance to clear the air, so I said to come on down and I could see them in about a half hour."

"Them, was there more than one? Did you get that in the phone call?"

"No, I didn't know that. There was just the one guy on the phone. But anyhow, just a few minutes later, not thirty minutes like I said, the man walked in my office, and I recognized him as Larry Casuse."

"So you'd seen him before?"

"Yeah, at the state senate up in Santa Fe and at the university over in Albuquerque. I also knew he was an agitator at the Indian center there in Gallup."

"Do you think Casuse was the guy on the phone, pretending to be a reporter from Santa Fe?"

"Yeah, I guess so."

"And he mentioned Wounded Knee to you on the phone?"

"Yeah, he did. He said the militant situation too. But I thought it was for real, I didn't know it was Casuse on the phone."

"So then what happened?"

"He pulled a gun, and I grabbed for it. He attempted to shoot three times but didn't realize the gun had to be cocked."

"He just walked in, pulled the gun, and fired—was it all that quick?"

"No, there were some words before, but it all happened pretty fast. He was there to kill me. He made that clear."

"What do you mean? How did he make it clear?"

"Well, after the first three times when he pulled the trigger and nothing happened, then he cocked the gun and fired it."

"At you?"

"Yes, at me. He just missed. He was standing five feet from me, and he missed. He had a little pearl-handled .32. I still have it, you know. They gave it to me after it was all over as a keepsake. Someday I'll show it to you. Anyhow, to get back to the story, I don't know where the bullet went, but I gave up fighting him then because I realized he didn't know how to use the gun. Later I found out that the bullet went straight into the glass top of my desk. There are photos of that in the police file. And you know, I have copies of all those police photos. In fact, I have some original Polaroid, in color no less."

"How long did this take—I mean, the struggle and all?"

"Time stopped, and then it flew, you know. When a man puts a gun right on your forehead and makes you kneel down in front of him and says you're dead because you're a *false person*, well, time just stops, and you forget later how much passed."

"Did you know Casuse?"

"I know he was from Gallup, at least he went to Gallup High School, so he'd know where the biggest bunch of guns was in the whole town. He might have been crazy, but he wasn't stupid."

"What happened inside? I know the newspaper story, but I'd like to know how you felt and whatever you remember that might not have been in the paper."

"Do you know about the phone calls?"

"No, I'm not sure. What phone calls?"

"The telephone rang several times while we were inside Ivan's store. I begged Casuse to answer the phone because I knew the police would negotiate with him. Hell, they would give him anything he wanted. But he was too cranked up. He said he wouldn't talk to them. He just kept telling me to shut up and calling me a *false person*."

"Did he threaten you?"

"Yeah. Several times. He glared at me, called me names, and even talked about shooting a cop out in front."

"Were you scared?"

"I felt like I was going to die. He told me that several times. He fired his gun twice, once up into the skylight and once out the door. He made Nakaidinae shoot too. Nakaidinae was scared to death. Wow, he was as scared as I was. Casuse screamed at him too although not as bad as me. Casuse made him shoot his gun through the back door, like a test or something."

"How did you figure out when to try your escape?"

"I knew I only had one chance of getting out of there alive, and that was through the front door. Casuse gave me the chance when he got tired of waiting and after he made Nakaidinae load up all the guns. He went to the back of the store, and Nakaidinae looked away. I was about six feet or so from the front, and so I just kicked Nakaidinae in the knee as hard as I could, and I headed for the door. Course I didn't know that he'd help me through it by blasting me in the back with his shotgun. Actually, I didn't know it was a shotgun at the time. I didn't know the difference. If I had known, I might not have had the courage to even try."

"Do you think those young men wanted to kill you or to make an example of you?"

"I think Nakaidinae did what he was told by Casuse. Casuse wanted to kill me, and he wanted to ridicule me. And he wasn't afraid to die. Nakaidinae and me—we both were afraid of death, but not Casuse. He was ready. He proved it that day. You know the funny thing about this was that all three of us were young. You keep calling Casuse young, but I was only thirty-four. And we both came from the same place. Did you know that?"

"Same place, do you mean Gallup?"

"No, I mean the Navajo Reservation. I was born on the reservation in the same place Casuse lived. I was born in Mexican Springs. My father wasn't a Navajo, but he could speak Navajo. He was a trader. I lived on the Rez for the first six years of my life. Larry Casuse and I had a lot in common. Instead of asking me about our common heritage, he just tried to kill me. We had our birthplace in common and our connection to the reservation. Both our fathers spoke Navajo. We almost died together too. But for the grace of God and a hell of a lot of luck, I would have died there with him. That's what he really wanted, I think."

"What do you mean?"

"I mean, he thought I would have him executed, so he decided he should kill me first. They made him crazy by telling him I could execute him over the death of that young Indian girl in the accident out on the road to Window Rock. He may have been a college student, but he sure did fall for things. How could he believe that? How could anyone?"

"Maybe we'll never know what he believed except for one thing. He believed in what he was doing."

"So did I. We both believed in the same thing actually. The Navajos had a hard life, and we were both trying to make it better. He used violence, and I used persuasion."

"Well, if you're right about the political stuff, they used his violence, maybe unknowingly, to get you persuaded right out of office."

"You could put it that way. But in the end, Casuse cost me my job, my home, my seat on the regents board, and a backside full of buckshot. All because he didn't want to talk. He just wanted to shoot."

"Did you see the letters to the editor of the newspaper there in Gallup? One of them was particularly strong against the police and accused them of shooting before they talked."

"Well, whoever wrote that wasn't there. Manuel Gonzales tried to talk to Casuse in my office and on the telephone to Stearns's store. I tried to talk to him in both places. I kept saying, 'Larry, put the gun down. We can talk about all of this.' But he was already talked into it, he was ready to die, not talk. That's what happened whether anyone wants to believe it or not."

They sat for another hour and a half, much to the dismay of the waitress. Clay learned a lot about Gallup politics, a little about Garcia's personal history, and almost nothing about Casuse. He decided not to press for other details. Two things impressed him: Garcia's vivid memory of the abduction and the shoot-out and his surprisingly vague memory of all that happened after the shoot-out. The former was consistent with what he read in the police reports and the newspapers. The latter was consistent with reality. A man would sure as hell remember the shape of the barrel of the gun in his face, but he might forget the details of the charges filed against the man with the gun. Besides, Garcia remembered everything important about Casuse. He didn't really focus on Nakaidinae, the accomplice.

On the plane back to Gallup, Virgil scratched out a list of things to follow up on now that he'd heard the mayor's take on all this. He wanted to listen to the KGAK audiotape of the shoot-out.

CHAPTER SIXTEEN

"Don't Shake a Piñon Tree to Get the Nuts—Only Bears Do That"

Clay Ramsey walked though Albuquerque's shiny new Sunport lobby and admired the magnificent Wilson Hurley painting of the Sandia Mountains. New Mexico's nickname—Land of Enchantment—was well deserved. It had canyons aplenty and enchantment galore, not to mention the Sandia Mountains, White Sands, and a real river, the Rio Grande. So a painting of the watermelon-colored mountains in what amounted to the only commercial airport in the state made artistic and political sense.

He caught a cab to the Albuquerque Hilton, which at the moment was buried under the cranes, concrete, and I beams used to completely redo the famous Big I. Intersecting I-40 with I-25 in downtown Albuquerque was a massive three-year highway construction project. Both the hotel and the freeway interchange had been here in 1973.

Was the UNM campus demonstrating against this kind of progress now as it demonstrated then against the Vietnam War, the Nixon administration, and one of its own regents, the Honorable Emmett E. Garcia?

He checked in, had a charred rare filet, and a Caesar salad in the Ranchers Club and called April. "So you're there at nine-thirty on a Friday night? What's the matter, nothing to do on the weekend in Gallup?"

"There's nothing to do in Gallup on weekdays. On weekends, we go to Albuquerque. Which brings me to you and the plan for tomorrow morning. Can Virgil and I come over and spend the day with you? We have lots to cover and he's off, and we could be there by . . ."

"I thought the plan was for me to drive over to see you. I've never been to Gallup, and I thought I ought to see it since it's becoming such a chunk in the book. Why do you want to come here?"

"Well, like you said, it's the weekend. Besides, I want to take you to the wonderful Southwest Collections room at the Zimmerman Library there on the UNM campus. Their collection of oral histories of all kinds of Indians is awesome. You will go bug-eyed over the Navajo part. They have some great stuff there, including some materials on Gallup's historic connection to the Navajo tribe and its world-famous Indian ceremonial. Of course, the old ceremonial grounds have been torn down, the city hall has been remodeled and . . ."

"What about Stearns Sporting Goods? Is that still there?"

"Yeah, and Virgil's uncle says it's still pretty much the same as it was in the fifties, not to mention the seventies. But you've got the pictures, so you know how it looks."

"Yes, I do. Oh, one other thing. I was going through my notes about one of your phone calls to me, the one you made from Santa Fe just after you'd rummaged through the state archives."

"Oh, that one. I was pretty excited, wasn't I?"

"Yes, but we never followed up on something. You said you found a statement by Nakaidinae. Did he say anything about how Casuse died?"

"Partially. It's right here, I'll get it for you."

April looked in her file box and retrieved her copy of the interview. "Nakaidinae was interviewed by a man named Hooten. His full name is not on this statement."

"Whose name, the man who took the interview or Nakaidinae?"

"Sorry. I meant the man asking the questions. His last name is Hooten, looks like he was a Navajo, but it's smudged. He worked for the state, that's all I really know from this statement. Anyhow, this statement was taken in November of 1973. Here's what Nakaidinae said, 'And Casuse went toward the front door, and one of the policeman shot him in the side. He came back into the store where I was, and the police officers dragged Garcia away and began firing into the store. Casuse got hit again in the other side. Casuse fell to his knees. He asked Nakaidinae if he would shoot him, and Nakaidinae said no."

"April, did I hear that right? Nakaidinae says he saw Casuse get hit twice, both times in the side. I mean, once in one side, and once in the other side?"

"Yes, that's what he said . . ."

"Nothing about getting shot under the chin, right?"

"No, Uncle Clay, he does not mention that, but he does say that Casuse asked him to shoot him. That's strange, isn't it?"

"Yes, strange unless Casuse wanted his life to end. If Nakaidinae wouldn't do it, then it looks he did the only other thing he could. That partially explains the wound under his chin. Anyhow, we can talk about this more in the morning. I'll stay over and make the trip to Gallup on Sunday. I'm always happy in a research library. What time will you and Virgil get here?"

~~~

Clay watched April and Virgil walk into the Hilton's lobby through the sliding glass doors at the main entrance. He'd spent the early morning hours reading the *Albuquerque Journal* and the *Santa Fe New Mexican*. He hadn't been surprised to see that most of the stories were about people with Hispanic names. That was consistent with people in the dining room last night, both serving and being served.

"Uncle Clay," April gushed a bit too loudly for his taste, "this is Virgil. Virgil, Clay Ramsey, our editor and defender of all who tread on dangerous ground."

"Virgil, nice to meet you. You look taller than I expected, seeing as how April says she pounds on you all the time. Of course she says that's only to get your attention."

"Mr. Ramsey, good to meet you too. April talks a lot but doesn't have much of a punch."

"How about we get some coffee and then go to the Zimmerman Library? You can tell me about Frank Garcia, and I'll bring you two up-to-date from my end."

After they were served coffee and the dry wheat toast that April ordered, Virgil started, "This guy Garcia is for real. He has a good memory about the day of the abduction, but he gets things mixed up after that. It's been a long time, and I know I wouldn't remember much either after that long. His story is interesting, but you've got a problem if it's true."

"How's that, Virgil?" Clay said because April couldn't talk with a mouth full of toast.

"Because we think the Garcia abduction was part of the Wounded Knee Indian discontent, and militancy, rearing its head up all over the country.

And we know of several connections between Gallup and Wounded Knee. But Garcia has done his own investigation. He thinks that, while Wounded Knee played a role, the real story of what happened to him is tied to local politics. In short, he thinks Casuse was manipulated in Gallup to get him out of office."

"Well, we need to know that if it's what really happened."

"Sure," Virgil said, "but I thought you wanted to write a book that told the big story, one that would interest people all over the country. If the first Indian takeovers in Alcatraz led to what happened in Wounded Knee, which in turn explain what happened in Gallup, that's a national story. But if the Gallup abduction is just another story about small-town politics resulting in a dead Indian, then it's not a national story."

Clay drained his cup and focused on Virgil. "You're right, we want the truth. But we want to make sure Garcia's local politics theory is the truth before we discard Gallup as part of the national trilogy. It could be that local politics played a role in the national story without the locals even realizing the national significance of what was happening."

April wiped her chin and said, "Well, the Indian movement was very strong in Gallup. Maybe there were local politics involved, but I bet that the real story is still the connection to Wounded Knee, just like Clay thought it might be two months ago when we started our research. I mean, we've done a lot. We've read everything there is to read, and we have talked to dozens of people in Gallup and out on the reservation. Now that we have found the former mayor, we can check out his take on things. The first question is why this local political thing didn't pop up when we talked to the other Gallup people, like the former city manager and the former city attorney and the judge. None of them mentioned this. Why is it only coming out now?"

Virgil blew on his coffee, drank a little, and said, "The now part is easy. It's because we just found Garcia, that's why. But why it didn't pop up sooner is more complicated. Garcia says that others know about the connection."

April looked at Clay and said, "That's another reason to be here instead of over in Gallup. You said we needed to track down Calvin Horn, the big-dog regent, and Tom Horn, his nephew, Nakaidinae's defense lawyer. I've done the easy part. Calvin Horn passed away a few years ago. His nephew, Thomas E. Horn, is still a lawyer, but has moved out of state. There is another Thomas Horn in the bar directory, but he has a different middle initial. I think they are all related somehow. I just haven't had a chance to follow up on that yet. Anyhow, the elder statesman of the family, Calvin Horn, was a big deal here back in the sixties and seventies. There is a file a foot thick over at the Zimmerman Library. I haven't seen it yet, but the archivist told me about it on the phone."

"We can work on most of this at the same time. Virgil, April has brought me up-to-date on your interview with Garcia. Is there anything else you learned that I don't know?"

"No, other than to say he was a pretty believable guy. He wasn't bitter about Indians although he is a little skeptical about the connection between Wounded Knee and Gallup."

Clay said, "Yes, I expect he would be. It's amazing that no one in Gallup seemed to make the connection at the time. They feared it but never investigated it. Virgil, there is one other thing. I know you asked Garcia about Casuse's continued reference to Garcia as a *false person*. Did Garcia know why that was so important to Casuse?"

"Mr. Ramsey, I can tell you that Garcia still is bothered by it. He thought of himself as truthful, and he thought he was doing a good job as mayor. He respected all Indians, especially the Navajo. He was born and lived a good long time on their reservation. And his connection to the package goods store near Window Rock was remote. He was a part owner but not a manager. I've been thinking a lot about the *false person* reference, probably more than either of you."

"So, Virg, what's your take on it?"

"Have either of you read much Emerson? Ralph Waldo, I mean?"

"Virg, I took the same humanities course at ASU that you did. We read him, but I can't say I remember much."

Clay seemed amused and said, "You two took humanities together? That must have intrigued your professor."

Virgil ignored him and looked up at the skylight in the ceiling as though it would open his memory. "Actually, I looked up something that I thought he said about this and found a quote. I brought it with me. Here's what Emerson said, 'One would think from the talk of men, that riches and poverty were a great matter; and our civilization mainly respects it. But the Indians say, that they do not think the white man with his brow of care, always toiling, afraid of heat and cold, and keeping within doors, has any advantage of them. The permanent interest of every man is, never to be in a *false position*, but to have the weight of Nature to back him in all that he does.'"

"Virg, that's beautiful. What made you think to look for it?"

"Well, for one thing, they told us at ASU that Emerson was America's first philosopher. America's first people were Indians. So it made sense that he'd think about their ideas and he'd compare them to ideas the colonials brought over here from Europe. In the back of my mind, I remembered something about false persons or something like that. It turns out to be *false positions*. Maybe Casuse heard it the other way, I don't know. He was a sophomore at UNM when this all happened. Maybe he took humanities too."

Clay asked, "Virgil, can I see your book on Emerson?"

"Sure, this is from my box of books to keep from ASU. The underlining there is mine."

Clay read what appeared to be the whole page and said, "Wow. I'd forgotten what a deep thinker Emerson was. I think you may have something here, Virgil. What do you make of the next sentence? Emerson says, 'Riches and poverty are a thick or thin costume; and our life—the life of all of us—identical.'"

April chimed in, "Well, overlooking the fact that he dropped a verb before 'identical,' I think he was saying that being rich or poor is not as important to an Indian as it is to a white. That is what a costume is, right? Something that is not important, but it makes us think we are seeing something different from what's underneath?"

Virgil looked uncomfortable and interrupted, "No, that's not it. Look at the rest of the passage. He talks about transcending continually and tasting the real quality of existence. He was making the point that if you are true to yourself and your people, then riches or poverty doesn't matter. If nature is on your side, you are never in a *false position*. I think that's what he was saying."

Clay, acting the peacemaker, said, "I agree with both of you. You see, Virgil, April is right when she says that the whites see riches as desirable where the Indians see it as mere costume. And you are right when you say that nature has to be on your side. But Emerson said it best there at the bottom of the paragraph. Let me read it to you. 'We differ only in our manifestations, but express the same laws; or in our thoughts, which wear no silks and taste no ice-creams. We see God face to face every hour, and know the savour of nature.'"

April turned to her uncle. "Is there any way to find out if Casuse did read Emerson in college?"

As he thought about the question, Clay's attention was riveted back to the many talks he'd had with Millie and how Indians were the first naturalists. The Indians were philosophers too, just not so much in writing like Emerson.

But his guess was that at least some AIM members had read Emerson—he was their kind of thinker. "If Casuse did study Emerson," Clay said, looking more at Virgil than April, "he likely believed that riches were silks for whites and poverty ice cream for the Indian. He saw Garcia as a man in a false position, which he translated to a *false person*. But that's enough philosophy for now. Let's go to the Zimmerman Library and see what Calvin Horn had to say on the subject."

They parked in the last available metered spot in the Zimmerman lot and walked up the steps to the main floor of the huge adobe building. The Southwest Collections room, where all archival materials were cataloged, was on the solar side of the building in a well-lit area. Two full stories of lightly tinted glass adorned chiseled sugar pine bookshelves. Neatly stacked research materials lined the walls, surrounding the six long hand-carved research tables.

The archivist was typically efficient and predictably quiet. She asked for driver's licenses from all of them, made them sign waiver documents, and in due time, produced three banker's boxes of documents all neatly labeled, REGENT CALVIN S. HORN'S PERSONAL FILES.

Clay, April, and Virgil each took a box, sat at separate tables, and took notes, in pencil of course, on what they found. From time to time, April couldn't contain her enthusiasm and said "cool" or "oh my god," much to the dismay of both Clay and the archivist. Virgil took no notice.

"Let's take a lunch break and compare notes," Clay whispered to his two young researchers.

They found a table in the UNM Union two blocks away. Virgil piled his tray with a 32-ounce Coke, a Big Mac, and fries. April had a salad, and Clay ordered a turkey club and coffee.

As usual, there was no stopping April with either food or information. "Is that place something or what? I mean, what a treasure house of stuff for us. That guy Calvin Horn was some kind of big shot around here, wasn't he? I found letters to and from famous people, piles of stuff he wrote about everything under the sun, and references to lots of boring junk about finances, building costs, and stuff. He was actually both a writer and a publisher. But my box didn't contain all that much about Indians or the goings-on over in Gallup. How about you guys?"

Clay waited for Virgil to respond. When he didn't, Clay volunteered, "Well, I guess I got the lucky box. There's a file in there labeled 'The Abduction of a Regent' that has several interesting things, not the least of which are his notes of the chapter of his book dealing solely with, as you so eloquently put it, the goings-on over in Gallup. Did you two know Calvin Horn wrote a book about this?"

April said, "No." Virgil implied as much by not responding at all.

"Well, the archivist will locate a copy of the book and have it ready for us after lunch. Even without that, I think I may have found what mystery novelists call the smoking gun. The box I was reviewing contains a folder with an audiotape in it. The audiotape is not labeled except for a ribbon with an archival number. But that number is the same as another folder, which contains a transcript of an interview. Guess who was involved in the interview?"

"Who?" April said, looking a little like a talking lettuce head.

"Frank Garcia interviewed Robert Nakaidinae in October of 1973 here in Albuquerque."

Virgil said, "Yeah, I forgot. Mr. Garcia mentioned that when I interviewed him in Tempe. But he didn't tell me that it was tape-recorded or that Calvin Horn had made a transcript."

"Well, the real find is the tape itself. Garcia may have forgotten Calvin Horn was there during the interview. So he may have not known about the tape either."

"Why is that, Uncle Clay? I mean, do you think the transcript is wrong or something? Why do you need the tape if you have the transcript?"

"For one thing, it's nice to be able to check the typist for errors. But more importantly, when you actually hear a conversation on tape, you get the benefit of voice inflection, significant pauses, excitement in the room—you know, all of the stuff a cold transcript leaves out."

"Will they let us listen to it—you know, give us a little room and stuff?"

"Yes, I'm sure we could arrange that, but some archivists are touchy about collected materials. It'll be safer if I can buy a small recorder and just listen to the tape with an earpiece there in the library this afternoon. They ought to sell those things in the university bookstore. Then if it's what I think it is, I'll arrange for a copy of the tape to be made. By the way, Virgil, didn't Frank Garcia tell you that he had a copy of that radio station tape where their reporter was on the scene, at the shoot-out?"

"Yes. He said it's very dramatic. You can hear the actual gunfire, the screams from the crowd, and the bullets hitting concrete walls. Maybe we can compare the two tapes."

"My young friends, this gives our project a historic connection I had not thought about before. You were both too young for Watergate, but it happened in 1973 as well. Watergate unraveled because of some of the same things this investigation is turning up. The political scandal called Watergate was broken open by secret tape recordings, crusading reporters, unrelenting researchers, and somebody with a deep throat. It's ridiculous, but these two 1973 political stories do overlap one another."

"Uncle Clay, we were not reading the papers then, but we did get some of Watergate in college. Is this just the same year, or is there something more to connect our story to Watergate?"

"April, Watergate was that year, the year before, and the year after. The break-in at the Watergate Hotel was in 1972, the investigation was in full force in '73, and Nixon resigned in '74. But no, we don't have two connected stories. The fact that the siege at Wounded Knee took place while the Watergate investigation was going on was purely coincidental."

"Maybe the same is true for Gallup."

"How so, Virgil?"

"Maybe Wounded Knee and Gallup are purely coincidental. You know, maybe they both just happened in the same year."

"So you think Garcia might be right? Maybe the local politicians used Casuse to defeat Garcia without knowing he'd do something really stupid like trying to kill him?"

"I don't know about that. But even if that didn't happen, maybe Casuse was acting out his own principles. Maybe he was trying to help his tribe, not all tribes. Maybe he wasn't trying to mimic Wounded Knee in Gallup. I don't know."

"Virgil, you've got a point. None of us really know. But those boxes in the Zimmerman Library can help get to the bottom of whatever drove Casuse. In addition to the Calvin Horn files, there are archival materials on the various groups and clubs on campus, reports regarding campus demonstrations, and as April has already spotted, some oral histories from Indians all over New Mexico. Those files could tell us whether we have a national story that includes Gallup or a local story that coincides with national news. Virgil, you're closer to this than we are, give us your gut reaction. What was Casuse all about anyway?"

Virgil cleared his throat, studied his empty Coke cup, and began, "Maybe the answer is that Casuse is not the only Indian who went to jail and didn't like it. Maybe he tried to do something about it. I mean, right there in Gallup. There is another event, and it may be related. The so-called Gallup File in the Octavia Fellin Public Library has a small section covering the siege at Tuba City. Do you know about that one?"

Clay looked a bit startled and said, "No, I never heard of it. Where is Tuba City anyway, and who staged the siege?"

"Tuba City is on the Rez over on the Arizona side. A bunch of high school kids took over their high school just a few days *after* Casuse abducted Garcia in Gallup. Maybe we ought to see if the road from Alcatraz ran through Tuba City and then to Gallup before it ended up in Wounded Knee. Anyway, what happened were thirty or forty kids peacefully occupied their high school by sitting in their superintendent's office most of the day. Unlike Casuse, who didn't say much about what he wanted, these kids were explicit. They wanted real change. For example, they asked the superintendent to let the athletes wear their hair long. They didn't feel they should be made to salute the American flag. Oh, and they wanted to be excused from class to attend Indian religious events."

Clay looked perplexed. "As I remember it, long hair in the seventies was the rule of the day, not the exception. Was it different on Indian reservations? I thought all young men wore their hair long back then."

"They did. But not if you wanted to play high school football. It was the same at Gallup High and all the Anglo schools, not just the reservation schools. Jocks had to cut their hair. That was the rule."

"So why should Indians be excepted? I guess I don't get the point they were trying to make."

"Because a lot of Indian students wore their hair long to show that they were proud to be Indian. It wasn't just a thing young people did, it was a thing Indians did. Here's a big difference. Young white kids had long hair, and their parents hated it. But young Indians did it because that's the way their elders wore their hair. They weren't rebelling like white kids against their elders. They were trying to show respect and to show that they were proud, not ashamed to be Indian."

"I guess I missed that. I remember lots of conflict about the American flag though. Many groups in the seventies were rebelling against the fifties' concept that the flag was sacred and you weren't patriotic unless you honored it. Was it the same on the Navajo reservation? Were they protesting it the same way the hippies did in Berkley that same year?"

"I don't know about Berkley, but out on the Rez, the way I hear it now, those kids felt that if the tribe was really a sovereign nation, then the U.S. flag was not the Navajo flag. For Indians, the U.S. flag symbolized bondage. Maybe that wasn't the case for whites, and maybe the white students at Berkley saw other symbols—but whites, unlike Indians, were never in bondage."

"No, but blacks were. and they weren't burning flags and refusing to recite the Pledge of Allegiance," April chimed in.

Clay thought about April's comment for a moment and then turned to Virgil for the answer, "Virgil, is it your sense that these students were reacting to national events or were just looking at their own situation and ignoring the national scene?"

"I think those kids were doing both. They knew what was going on. The Navajo culture was important to them. In that sense, they were a lot like the Oglala Sioux kids on the Pine Ridge Reservation in South Dakota. They wanted teachers who knew Indian culture. They wanted school assemblies that dealt with Indian problems and interests instead of Anglo things, which was the case in all reservation schools back then. I know, I was there, just a little bit later."

"Do you know of any other sit-ins or sieges or whatever that went on back then, that is, at the same time as the Gallup abduction and Wounded Knee? We haven't even talked about that yet."

"Well, yes. There was. I don't know much about it, but there was the takeover at the PHS Hospital in Gallup. I think that occurred before Garcia was abducted, but the trial was later that same year."

"Do you know the details?" Clay asked Virgil.

"I do, Uncle Clay," April said, wedging her way back into the conversation. "I remember reading about that in the Gallup File too, but I didn't connect it at the time. Let me see, I think it was the year before, but it could have been in '73. And the guy in charge, you'd call him the lead warrior, had a funny name, like Cut Face or Big Face or something like that."

"No," Virgil said, "it was Cutnose. But I don't . . ."

"Exactly, it was Cutnose. He and some other AIM guys broke into the hospital to demonstrate against poor health care on the Rez. Then they went underground or something. It's all there in the Gallup File."

"April, that seems like a good thing for you to do. Go back to the file. Virgil, can you help on that?"

"Yeah, but not during the week. I have a job at Window Rock. I can ask around out there. A siege at a public health hospital would be remembered at tribal headquarters. I know some old guys there, I'll ask them."

"Are they as old as me?" Clay said with a grin.

"No, not that old," Virgil said, grinning back, "but they remember the seventies. A lot of things happened back then."

"Well then, let's stop by the bookstore, buy a cheap tape player, and then plod on back to the Zimmerman and see what's on that audiotape."

CHAPTER SEVENTEEN

"Don't Point an Unloaded Gun at Anyone—
The Evil Spirits Can Make It Fire"

October 15, 1973

Albuquerque, New Mexico

Frank Garcia, still recovering from his shotgun blast in March, got out of the car slowly. His brother-in-law, Norman Beardsley, said, "Damn wind, it always blows up here." The Trade Winds Motor Hotel was not aptly named. The wind typically blew hard, cold, and flat at you along Albuquerque's East Central Avenue. The majestic Sandia Mountains loomed high on the east side, there were no palm trees wafting in the breeze, and no one ever that part of town was as balmy. This was a typical October in New Mexico—Indian summer some days and Colorado Rockies winter on others. The Trade Winds Hotel's neon sign, bright to the point of garish, sputtered at night as a sign of the deterioration of East Central Avenue.

Garcia's mood matched the wind as he stuck his chin down and braced himself for the ten-foot walk to the front office. This time, it was Garcia who was a man on a mission. He wanted to know, once and for all, exactly *who* shot him and *who* shot Casuse seven months ago. Nakaidinae might be the only person who could answer his questions.

The politics of this particular October were anything but tranquil. Nakaidinae's trial was over, Nixon's was yet to come; and lots of people, including Nakaidinae and the Watergate burglars, were out on bail. But in Nakaidinae's case, he had a sentencing hearing coming up. All that remained to lessen his legal troubles was to give his promised interview to Garcia.

Robert Nakaidinae was an unlikely and somewhat unwilling hero in the Indian rights movement. Indian activists around the state were incensed by his plea bargain as it deprived them a media outlet for their demands. Collectively, they could see little political gain in Nakaidinae's favorable plea. On the other hand, many in Gallup, and on the UNM campus, were relieved that a public trial had been avoided.

A few Kiva Club members knew of this meeting between the victim and the abductor; they were uniformly opposed. "Why do you want to see him?" Nakaidinae was tired of the question. His answer was unsatisfactory to real warriors. Telling his new friends that his lawyer thought the meeting was important was like telling the bandleader that you were tired of playing the same old tune every day. A waste of breath.

They were equally dismayed by the other reason for the meeting. Garcia, the victim, had offered to write a clemency letter in exchange for a meeting with Nakaidinae, the abductor. The young AIM activists on the UNM campus never saw Garcia as a victim; they consistently labeled him as the false person who forced the reluctant warrior, Nakaidinae, to act on behalf of the oppressed Indian people everywhere. As long as Garcia was a *false person*, what happened to him didn't matter.

Calvin Horn, the epitome of the white establishment, having arranged the meeting, was the first to arrive. Horn had much at stake here. He was the president of the UNM Board of Regents, a widely respected civic leader, and a confidant of the governor. Some thought that he played a role, *albeit* behind the scenes, in the transfer of power from Nakaidinae's first lawyer to his nephew, Nakaidinae's current lawyer. Horn was the principal negotiator in persuading Garcia to do the right thing for himself, his people, his city, and his governor: "Let Nakaidinae plead to a lesser crime—we can only lose by a public trial."

Horn waited patiently in the lobby for Garcia, his former colleague on the UNM Board of Regents. He was confident Garcia would show because he really wanted to meet and talk to Nakaidinae. He was somewhat less confident about Nakaidinae himself since no one really seemed to know much about him. Thankfully, lawyer and client arrived only a few minutes late. Garcia and Nakaidinae eyed one another warily as Calvin Horn and his nephew led the way down the first floor to the rented interview room.

The cramped motel room included a small table, five folding chairs, coffee cups, a pot of almost warm coffee, and a bowl of little white sugar packets. The tape recorder, a boxy reel-to-reel machine of unknown vintage, was set up and ready to flick on. Norman Beardsley, Garcia's brother-in-law and a member of the Navajo tribe, would be taking longhand notes as would Calvin Horn. Horn's notes would find their way into his forthcoming book on the university in turmoil and transition. Beardsley's notes would become part of the box file at Garcia's Pinetop, Arizona, home. Once all five were uncomfortably seated on the steel folding chairs, Garcia took charge, spoke directly into the microphone, and forced a smile at Nakaidinae.

"My name is Emmett Garcia. I was the former mayor of Gallup, New Mexico, and I am speaking with Robert Nakaidinae. I am going to ask him some questions in conjunction with the circumstances surrounding the abduction of myself on March 1, 1973. First, Robert, I'd like you to know that I'm asking these questions out of a personal curiosity, and I'd like to have you state that you fully understand that you're doing this voluntarily and under no harassment. That is, I think, pretty important. Would you state that?"

Nakaidinae seemed either tired or sad. It was hard to tell. His flat expressionless face was bone thin and tightly framed by the white band that bound his long black hair. Without looking directly at Garcia, he whispered softly to his lawyer and his lawyer's uncle, "State that I'm doing this voluntarily?"

Tom Horn spoke into the microphone, "Yes, voluntarily and on your own."

"I am doing this voluntarily and on my own."

"Okay, would you state your name?"

"Robert Nakaidinae."

"Robert, the first question that I would like to know is how you became involved in this thing. What happened? What was your connection with Larry Casuse, and how did you get involved?"

"Well, I met Larry at the Kiva Club as I was hitchhiking through New Mexico. Like my brother was staying in Santo Domingo, and I stayed with him, like I just finished two and a half years of commercial arts school in Los Angeles. And I came back to start my painting career, and I had all my equipment with me, and I was planning to travel around and paint whatever came up. And this is how I came to the Kiva Club because of its Native American Studies. I came with a couple of friends. This is how I got in connection with Larry. I stayed at his place 'cause he had enough room to put the three of us up."

"How long had you known him, Larry Casuse?"

"I met him during the Gallup ceremonial the year before. That's about the first time, you know, the only real contact we had. It was just that one meeting, and I then met him again at the Kiva Club."

"Did you discuss my abduction with Larry prior to the time you actually put the thing into motion, was there a plan behind it?"

"At that time . . . you know . . . a month before was the PHS takeover . . . and a couple of days before March 1 . . . that was the Wounded Knee incident happened and that was about when we first talked about it because . . . like there is a lot of things going on here in the Southwest that wasn't right for Indian people. And we started talking about . . . you know . . . what could be done and he spoke to me about what he tried to do and the different petitions and the different marches he sort of headed . . . and how nothing really came off from that. To me . . . you know . . . I kind of felt what was frustrating him. Nothing ever was being done that he liked . . . the way he wanted it. We just from there . . . you know . . . we talked. Not . . . you know . . . of marching or of demonstrating or petitioning because at that time he was pretty well . . . you know . . . it was behind him now. He already tried all that. There was nothing—to him there was nothing else that could be done. To me . . . you know . . . there's a lot of people . . . even today . . . that do a lot of talking of doing this or doing that . . . and a lot of people—you know . . . a lot of Indian people inside . . . a lot of Chicanos . . . a lot of low-class white people—you know . . . there's a lot of people that talk about doing things in a violent manner. But you know . . . most of that's just talk."

"Well, were you in contact with Larry prior to the time that I went up to Santa Fe to go before the Senate hearing?"

"No."

"Did Larry ever talk to you with the feeling that he thought I was going to do something violent to him? Was he afraid that I was going to do anything at any time?"

"I don't believe so, no."

"You don't think that he was?"

"I don't, you know. There was a lot of talk like we talked about it all night, like couple of days before that, when the Wounded Knee incident happened. They were having that National Council of Tribal Leaders here in Albuquerque, and we went to that. And to us, that was where our elected leaders were, you know, and a lot of them were drinking, and they weren't really doing anything about the problems, except talking about them. They sort of used it as a social gathering, and we saw nothing coming out of it. And if that's our elected leaders, how's their tribe being run?"

"Did, to your knowledge, did Larry ever try to call me in the evening or anything that you know of? Did he ever try to get a hold of me, not so much to talk with me but merely to know where I was?"

"No."

"Do you know of anybody other than the Indian people that were involved with this? Do you know if there were any other groups? I'm not asking you for their names or anything like this, but did anyone else other than the Indian people ever talk to Larry? Did they give him any indication that possibly I was hurting the Indian people or something?"

"At that time, you know, I wasn't really concerned with anything else but Indian problems, and I was mostly associated with Indians at that time. Like I came back from L.A., and I was here about a month and a half that time. I was having car trouble, and I wanted to find out what was going on here in the Southwest, pertaining to Indian problems."

"Well, I was just curious because he mentioned this to me the day of the abduction. I don't know whether you recall it when he told me it wasn't only an Indian problem—that my own people, the Chicanos, were wanting to see me dead, so to speak. And I was wondering why he came out with that, if you had any background at all as to why he had said that."

"I don't remember him ever mentioning any other people, you know."

"Well, to get back to the actual event itself, how did Larry acquire the gun, do you know?"

"I'm not really sure, like he had the gun before I came to meet him."

"How did he get you to go with him that day, that particular day? Was this planned prior to that day or what had happened?"

"I was, you know, like, I was hiking through, and I stayed at his place, and that morning, there was only me and him. We started just walking around. To me, it was that same kind of talk, you know, about changing the government. Until we, he actually pulled the gun on Delbert Rudy I didn't realize until then that he was really going to do it. I was just sort of following him along. He like, he talked about it, you know a lot, like two days before. But we never really set any kind of date or anything like that, we just uh . . ."

"He did it at the spur of the moment?"

"Yeah."

"At that particular time?"

"Yeah."

"Well, how then did you have the bomb, you know, the little homemade bomb that you had?"

"Uh, he gave that to me just outside your office, and he said he put it together that night. I guess he did it sometime during the night."

"Which means that he had actually planned it. Even though it may have seemed spur of the moment to you, he actually—don't you feel that he was actually planning this all the time?"

"Yeah, I could sort of sense that."

"In other words, you felt that he was planning?"

"Yeah. You ran into, at that time I was running into a lot of people that were doing a lot of talking and a lot of preparing and different things, but you know, nobody really did anything about it."

"Of course. You knew that when he picked up Rudy that it was a pretty serious thing at that point, correct?"

"Not really serious, like, at that time, you know, we never, he never, all he spoke about was why we were going over there. And when we did it, all we did it for was the ride. We spoke to Delbert Rudy all the way, he seemed to be okay and everything, you know. To me, it wasn't really serious at that time."

"Well, didn't you know that he was after me, I mean, planned it the night before. I want to know whether he actually had mentioned my name in his conversation in the days previous to the time that he had gone after me?"

"He spoke about you, you know, but he'd speak about a lot of elected leaders—you'd hear him talking about our chairman, the president, the governor . . ."

Given the fact that this was the first time since March 1 that these two men had seen one another, there was a forced feeling of artificial acceptance in the little cramped motel room. Garcia and Nakaidinae acted as though neither had actually been there, talking about themselves in abstract, theoretical terms. They talked about one trying to kill the other as though it had been a staged movie or a college pop-psychological discussion. Even though they talked about carjacking, abduction, Wounded Knee, and remote, unidentified Indian problems, neither man crossed the line from abstraction to reality. Neither gave way to accusation, recrimination, or blame. The forced dispassion was stifling. But it was merely prelude.

"The other questions, of course I have, really relate to the incident inside the store, Robert. Of course, I know what went on during the abduction, and I know what went on getting to the store and while I was in there. But there's a lot of questions that remain unanswered, and these are the things that I'm very concerned in finding out. Number one, we would like to know the actual cause of Larry Casuse's death. You know there has been much speculation that he was shot, that it was suicide, and I would like to have a straight answer from you, being that you're the only one that can answer it. How this man died in the store?"

"He was shot twice, that I know of. He was shot once on this side with a shotgun and on the other side with a .38, and he just sort of started getting weak, and you know, I wanted to surrender at that time and see if we could save him. But he didn't want to be saved, and so, he asked me to shoot him. I didn't want to shoot him. And by then there were a lot of shots coming in, and the tear gas came in so, and he finally passed, and he either passed out then, or you know, he died. So I threw out all the guns around us, except the .32 he had that was the only weapon we, you know, I left him. And everyone else was on the sidewalk. That's when I walked out."

"Well, Robert, do you think he shot himself?"

"No, I don't believe he did."

Garcia had not written a clemency letter, agreed to stop the trial, and come all this way for Nakaidinae's soft expression of opinion about the matter. So he pressed, "Well, how do you account for the shot through his head?"

"The way, the best way I can figure it was like, I left him with the pistol, and it was pretty well near him. But there was a lot of tear gas in there at that time, and when the police went near him, he might have moved, and I'm pretty sure myself that the police did because, like, I read the autopsy report that said there was an inch-and-a-quarter, or an inch-and-a-half hole, that went under his chin and a three-inch hole that came out the back. A .32 doesn't make a hole that size. I thought about it a lot when I was in jail. I thought that he might have done it after reading the autopsy report, you know."

Remarkably, this alternative opinion, based on reading an autopsy report in jail, satisfied Garcia. He dropped the suicide inquiry and changed the subject. "The other question that I had was that, I felt and I mean, I'd like to hear it from you, you know, when I went through that door, I felt that you were the only one that could shoot me. I still believe that way because Larry was standing in the back of the store. There's no way that he could have shot me through all that, all the merchandise and everything. I want to get it all cleared up in my mind. Am I correct in assuming that?"

"I can't say I got the gun and *pointed* at you and shot it. That's not what happened. It was an *accidental* shot. I was mainly just trying to, uh, just trying to, I guess, scare you into stopping at that point. It was a quick break, and uh . . ."

"Well, let me say this. You know, I'm not trying to interrogate you like an attorney. I'm asking you straight to level with me. Exactly what happened in there, Robert? I mean, I can understand your answers if I had you on the witness stand and I was an attorney, but I want to find out what happened there. I'm asking you straight out because in all seriousness, you know, I feel this is being honest with you. In the first place, we could have pushed the thing instead of having you cop a plea. In the second place, I wouldn't have come over and said I'm going to write a letter of clemency if I wasn't sincere in doing this. All I'm asking is that you give me straight answers to these things. I'd like to have them just as straight as you possibly can. Not evading, I mean, if you were, if you intended to shoot me when I went out that door, I mean, I want to know it. I don't think it really has any bearing on the particular case anymore. Your attorney is here. Am I correct on that?"

For the second time that morning, Tom Horn spoke up, "That's right."

Garcia nodded slightly to acknowledge the confirmation. Then he continued, "So I mean, I want to know. By the same token, I feel a real obligation to our police department. They were there trying to save my life under real adverse conditions, and look at the publicity that they got. And then to have Larry Casuse killed and all the speculation as to how he died. All I'm asking is that you clear this up. I don't feel that that's asking too much. I feel that it's over. I think that you're going to get out of it free and clear. I'd just like to have—honestly, without any twisting of the arm, so to speak—have you give me the straight answers on both of those."

Nakaidinae nearly shut down. His long, awkward pause made everyone in the room wonder whether this was the end of the interview. Finally, looking up from the floor and out the window, he said, "No, you know, about, you know, yourself. I didn't *try* to shoot you. I tried to pull the gun away. To my knowledge at that time, you know, I didn't feel like I did shoot you because, you know, when the gun shot by the door, I saw pieces fly right there, and I figured that was where it hit, and you just went out by yourself."

"Well, what you're saying is, it was your shot."

"Yeah, it was my shot. But, you know, I tried to . . ."

Nakaidinae's answer, on the audiotape, is unintelligible, a series of mumbles and throat-catching starts and stops. Garcia tried to make it easier for Nakaidinae. "Well, I don't doubt that, but well, let me say something else. I felt that you were very much uptight and afraid while the whole thing was going on. I'll admit I was probably as afraid of you as I was of Larry Casuse because I didn't know what you were going to do. I felt that he had his faculties pretty much together. He knew what he was going to do. And I really felt that he, you know, that he was going to kill me. I mean, there was no question in my mind. So however, I have to admit that I don't feel that that was done, that it was your idea. I don't feel that, on your own, you would have done it. Otherwise, I wouldn't be sitting here talking to you, but you know, just because I feel that way doesn't mean that I'm right. All I'm asking for is for you to verify that I was shot, and with all true consciousness, you know, do you think that Larry could have shot himself? In other words, he wanted to die, is this correct?"

"Yes."

"He did want to die, huh?"

"Yeah."

"Okay, and to your knowledge, you don't know whether he shot himself or not?"

"No."

"But you think he could have?"

"He could have, yeah."

Tom Horn shifted in his chair, cleared his throat, and looked at his client. "May I say some things that you have told me previously, and everybody understands that it's privileged information, but with your consent, can I tell them some things you've said?"

Nakaidinae hesitated and then said softly, "Sure."

Calvin Horn, seated next to his nephew, focused on the young lawyer, listening intently to what he knew might be dangerous ground for a lawyer. "We've talked about this a lot. I've probably talked about the facts of the case with Robert more than anybody has, and he's always been very consistent on that point. That was the first question I asked. Whether Larry shot himself. Pretty much through the thing he has said, 'I don't know, but leaning toward no.' And then when I got all the police reports and the autopsy report and all of that, and I saw the way the bullet had entered and exited, and the outer burns that the doctor said were on the chin, back then, I knew it did have a certain importance to the case: 'Do you think Larry shot himself?' And Robert's version has been very consistent. You see, he was in front of Larry, between Larry and the front of the store, when that would have happened so that he couldn't have seen it. Whatever shots were fatal and, correct me if I'm wrong on this, they were certainly not fired *after* you started to walk out. I mean, the fatal shots were fired while there was still an exchange of gunfire going on. I've read some reports in the newspapers that indicated that the shots might have come after you had surrendered and walked out, and you don't hold that as an opinion as I understand it."

Garcia interrupted emphatically, "There were no shots fired after he walked out—see, we have the tapes. Maybe you've heard them, where the reporter was on the scene. When you started to walk out, there were no shots fired from that point on. So I mean, he had to have been shot inside that store, prior to the time that you came out. That's the reason that I'm saying, you know, with the condition that he wanted to die, and saying, asking you, 'Will you kill me? Shoot me?' And knowing that he had already been hit, don't you feel that there was a good possibility that this could have happened, that he went ahead and, under duress, shot himself?"

Nakaidinae realized that the exchange between Garcia and his lawyer was over, but seemed reluctant to return to the focus of attention. After a long pause, he said, "Yeah, you know, but the thing that, you know, convinces me is that autopsy report. You know, that's the only thing that stands between, you know, saying that he did it, you know, or he didn't. It's that one report."

His frustration showing, Garcia snapped, "What do you mean?"

"That inch and a half under his chin."

"Well, of course, you know, they pulled him out of the tear gas when they went and pulled him out, I mean, this changed where he was lying, and it changed a lot of factors in that. But, Robert, like I say, I'm being very candid with you, and I'd appreciate the same from you. One of the things that I think is very important to the case is that he did want to die. Another question I want to ask you is, was Larry carrying any material or any books or anything? Did he have any stuff with him, or did you?"

"I had a thick notebook. It had some sketches and some writing."

"Was that *your* notebook?"

"Yeah."

"Okay, well, I'll straighten you out. I've got that notebook. I picked it up after from the police. I didn't know whether it was yours or Larry Casuse's. That's another thing that I wanted to clear up because there are some things in there that indicated violence, in the writing itself, that you are probably aware of, and that's the reason I was asking the question."

"Yeah. I do a lot of songwriting, and you know, I really expand on a lot of writing. There's a lot of—but you know, to me, that's just my writing. I do a lot of writing about me."

"Okay, another thing that I'm curious about is that if there was not a plan of action, you know, that you had, what did you intend to do with me?"

"The way, you know, he was saying it was we were just going to take you around and show you the different things, you know, the different problems in the city and within the state, and that would be about it. We'd bring you back and let you off."

"But didn't he realize that at any time I would have been happy to sit down and go over those same things without this situation?"

"He said, you know, he'd tried to do that already."

"He had never come in and talked to me, ever."

"To my understanding, he was telling me that he did."

"But he didn't. And the other thing I am curious about is how he knew where he was going. To the sporting goods store, you know. He knew exactly where we were going. If it had not been planned, you see what I mean, if he hadn't talked to you about it?"

"He didn't talk to me about it, but you know, he might have. You know, he pretty well had it planned, I guess in his own mind, but you know . . ."

"In other words, he knew what he was doing?"

"Yeah."

"Knew it?"

"Yeah, he pretty well knew what he was going to do, but you know, he never really told me."

"Okay, but how then could he take me around the state when he didn't have an automobile? He planned to go to the store and walked me inside of the store. Another thing that I'm curious about, which you're aware of, is why—if he didn't intend me any harm—why did he actually fire the gun at me three times in my office?"

"That, you know, like, I was standing outside, and I don't really know."

"You know we struggled. You remember that we were struggling?"

"Yeah."

"He actually shot me three times, and the gun didn't go off."

"Like, you know, that I never knew, and you know, there are some things that he did that I never knew, like that incident in there."

"Okay, but now, now I ask you, why would you go along with that?"

"By then, you know, it was, I was in there already. There was no other way out."

"You couldn't talk him out of it on the way down? During the time, did you try to talk to him during the time when you were going from here in Albuquerque to Gallup?"

"Not really. He was pretty well set with what he was going to do, and . . ."

"Couldn't you have told him, well, 'I don't want any part of it, I want out'?"

"Yeah, but you know, he kept saying that, you know, he tried, he tried so many different other . . ."

"See, those are the things that, like I say, that I have questions in my mind as to how this all came about. Were there any other people that he had talked to or tried to get involved that you know of?"

"Uh, there was one other guy. He's from, like, he'd just come down too, and he was staying with Larry. And he backed out before we took off—you know, before we left the UNM parking lot."

"Before you took Rudy?"

"Yeah."

"Is that his name, Rudy or . . ."

"Rudy."

"What was his name?"

"Uh, I'm not sure. I just remember his first name."

"Of course, that's not really that important. The thing about it is, is that at that point, you evidently knew what was going to happen, and the other boy pulled out. You went along with it. I'll admit that Larry and I did have confrontations, actually on two occasions, but never where it was on a personal basis where we could talk to each other. One was on the ceremonial and, of course, the other one was in Santa Fe at the Senate hearing. I think that the whole community of Gallup has been under a lot of tension, and this is another reason that I'm here sitting here talking to you. I think, between the two of us, just being able to sit down and talk about it and being able to air it out and talk to, you know, possibly say, okay, this could have happened. And it was wrong—we both, you know, you admit it's wrong, and I'm willing to say, okay, let's let him off on that basis. And I'll see if we can't pick up the pieces and have the Indian people and the community in Gallup back on the basis where they can work together and not something where there's a confrontation all the time. And that to me is more important than seeing you go to jail. That's the only reason that I'm here. Don't you feel that way?"

"Yeah."

"Well, Robert, do you think there are better ways about going about working these problems out?"

"Yeah. Now, you know, now I know a lot more since the six months has gone by. A lot of Indian people didn't understand what went on and why it went on, and so, myself, I'd like to try to educate them on what's going on actually around the reservation. Like, a lot of them don't know what's going on, you know, even the young kids. There are just so many people that just don't know what's going on, and they've got to be told. To me, by then, I figured everything was exhausted at that point, but I realize that it wasn't, and now I've got to go back and try something else."

"Do you really believe now that the problems that they have been facing can be worked out?"

"Yeah and, you know, it's not just the city to blame, you know, it is within the people themselves that live around there—that's, you know, there's just so many things I've learned."

"You're talking about the Indian people?"

"Yeah, and the city itself."

"Well, I agree with you, and I think that there are problems that have to be worked out, and, Robert, as far as I'm concerned, I'm satisfied now as to what happened, and I'll go ahead and write that letter."

No one said anything for a minute or so. Tom Horn started to talk to his client, "Robert, one of the problems we've had all the way along is he'll be the first to admit he's not much of a conversationalist, but he is a terrific songwriter and poet, and he wrote a song about this incident, and I asked him to bring his guitar. I thought you might like to hear it."

Nakaidinae reached for his guitar. Calvin Horn smiled and asked, "What's the name of it, Robert?" Norman Beardsley quit taking notes. Garcia said, "Yes, I really would."

Robert Nakaidinae sang a sorrowful lyric without much melody. It was about a young man's struggle and the death of a friend. It ended abruptly, where it began, on a sorrowful note.

The lawyer and his uncle looked at one another. Frank and his brother-in-law waited for them to say something. But no one did, so Nakaidinae got up and went outside to the parking lot. The interview was over.

Garcia had his explanation. Nakaidinae had said all he was going to say. The others had not come there to talk in the first place. All that remained now was the final day in court and the sentencing hearing before Judge Donnelly.

The unlikely occasion of a sentencing hearing made the interview of the abductor by his victim possible. With the exception of the pope interviewing the man who had tried to kill him, meetings like this were unheard-of in political violence cases. These two men had met only once before now when Nakaidinae shot Garcia. In this meeting, despite their mutual and constant repetition of "you know," they really *didn't* know.

The first meeting profoundly changed the lives of both in a way that neither could have predicted. The second meeting predictably resulted in the clemency letter that was the quid pro quo for the interview.

But the interview that might have settled any question about Casuse's obvious suicide served only to let it linger. Until Calvin Horn revealed the existence of the interview in his book in 1981, the fact that Garcia interviewed Nakaidinae and the existence of the audiotape and the transcript were almost entirely unknown in Gallup. Garcia and Nakaidinae left the motel room without either knowing why one tried to kill the other or why, having failed, the man with the buckshot in his back was now ready to ask the judge for clemency for the man who pulled the trigger.

CHAPTER EIGHTEEN

"Don't Call the Thunder's Name—The Lightning Will Get You"

April and Virgil sat at her little kitchen table and sorted through two stacks of documents; the first included Nakaidinae's penal documents. Looking at that stack, April said, "Virgil, here's a bundle of letters to the judge in the Nakaidinae case. One of them is from Garcia." The other stack was larger, much larger, and was the stuff of which political scandals are born. These yellowed, rubber-banded insider docs were the ones Garcia had mentioned in his interview with Virgil in Tempe a month earlier. He had, as promised, mailed them to Virgil with a little note—"For the book," it said.

Looking at the first letter from Garcia to Judge Donnelly, Virgil said, "Right. You can tell that Garcia was a literate man, but not much of a typist. The first draft of his clemency letter to the judge in Nakaidinae case was pretty much a mess."

"Yes, I see what you mean. He X'd out sentences and typed the whole thing in uppercase. But the final copy looks just fine. Looks like he had a typist help him. Didn't you say he was living in Arizona by the time this letter was written?"

"Yes, he moved to Pinetop, Arizona, in May, and this letter was written on November 7, 1973, shortly after he interviewed Nakaidinae in Albuquerque. The typist was Garcia's former secretary in the mayor's office in Gallup."

"I will make some more tea if you will read it to me, Virg,"

November 6, 1973

The Honorable Thomas Donnelly
Judge of the District Court
Santa Fe, New Mexico 87501

Dear Judge Donnelly:

As the victim of the March 1, 1973, abduction and former mayor of Gallup, it is my belief the citizens of Gallup, the Indian people of our area, and the people as a whole are tired of marches, confrontations, harassments, violence, and misunderstandings arising out of poor information, distrust, foolishness, and personal ambition. I have, and always will believe, the vast majority of our society is sincere, honest, and well-intentioned in dealing with one another; however, I am not so gullible as to believe there are no cancers, which will contaminate the very foundation we strive to maintain and improve upon. I feel the cures are in communication, compassion, cooperation, understanding, knowledge, and education.

With this in mind, I ask that you grant Robert Nakaidinae clemency.

I am asking this knowing full well the controversy that may follow such a request. Certainly, I do not condone acts of violence of this nature, nor do I believe under normal circumstances they should go unpunished. The issue here is not the guilt of Robert Nakaidinae and Larry Casuse. Nakaidinae has admitted and plead guilty to the crimes they have committed, and Larry Casuse lost his life.

What is important is not the confinement of individuals for a designated period of time, but the realization by the Indian people and the citizens of Gallup that they need to live together in harmony. I believe the Indian people need to express themselves and become involved; however, they must also realize the majority of merchants, public officials, and everyday citizens are honest, law-abiding people.

It is because of my belief in the integrity of the people of Gallup and the surrounding areas that I have taken this action.

My family and I sincerely hope this will lead to a better understanding and help bridge any gap that may have been created by this foolish act.

Respectfully yours,
EMMETT E. GARCIA

EEG/rr

cc: Mr. Thomas Horn, Attorney at Law
Mr. L. E. DePauli, District Attorney

"Wow, April, here's something else interesting. I missed this the first time I looked at this stuff. This is a transmittal letter from Garcia to Nakaidinae's lawyer. Garcia used this to transmit the clemency letter to Albuquerque. This is a little confusing."

"What do you mean?"

"Because on November 7, 1973, Garcia says to Nakaidinae's lawyer, 'I should appreciate very much if you would *not* release the contents of my letter to Judge Donnelly before the hearing on sentencing.'"

"What's confusing about that?"

"Well, Garcia may have been unaware of the obvious inconsistency. This letter could not be of much benefit to Nakaidinae if it was kept from the sentencing judge until *after* the hearing. I mean, the whole purpose of a clemency letter is to get the judge to give clemency. How can he do that if the clemency letter is not given to him before sentencing?"

Virgil pushed back from April's kitchen table. "Wow, April, this stack from the state archives in Santa Fe looks pretty interesting."

"Yeah, it is. I didn't know that governors turn their correspondence over to the state archives when they leave office. Most of the stuff I found about Nakaidinae was in Governor Bruce King's penal papers."

"Penal papers? What's that mean?"

"Archivists catalog and index things into searchable files. Since governors have the power to pardon anyone who has been convicted of a crime, they get lots of correspondence about criminals, usually from friends and family members. So I checked for Robert Nakaidinae and found this stuff."

"Like what?"

"Well, maybe the most interesting thing was Nakaidinae's official admission summary when he was taken into the state penitentiary system."

April dug a manila folder out of the stack and started to read from the admission summary. "This looks pretty official. It gives his prison number and the basic information about his sentence."

"Tell me about that. The newspapers weren't clear on what actually happened at the sentencing hearing. I mean, we know he was sent to prison because the judge rejected the recommendation by the prosecutor and by the victim. Garcia's clemency request was flatly denied. I am unclear, though, on the actual sentence that Judge Donnelly gave to Nakaidinae."

"This document says Nakaidinae was sentenced on November 28, 1973, to a term of two to five years on one count and two to ten years on the other, but Judge Donnelly suspended the sentence on the second count. Something is wrong."

"What do you mean, wrong?"

"You had the official court records copied at the courthouse. They are here somewhere. Right, here it is. Judge Thomas Donnelly sentenced Nakaidinae to the state penitentiary for a period of not less than one year and not more than five years."

"And that was after Garcia met with Nakaidinae in Albuquerque."

"Yes, it says here Judge Thomas A. Donnelly, Eleventh Judicial District, Bernalillo County, New Mexico. Wow, look at this, it gives his prior criminal record. This doesn't look all that serious to me."

"What'd he do?"

"One disorderly conduct charge in Window Rock in 1971 and a traffic ticket in Los Angeles, also in 1971. This says he just finished school in Los Angeles in February of 1973. He was visiting his brother in Bernalillo when he met Casuse at the Kiva Club on the UNM campus in Albuquerque. Apparently, there was a large Indian gathering in Albuquerque at the time."

"Does it say anything about AIM?"

"Virg, I don't remember. When I first saw this, I was focusing on what he said happened in Gallup. Here, you take a look."

Virgil leafed through the four-page summary. "April, there is another connection here. Nakaidinae was interviewed by prison officials after he entered the system. I wonder if he told them the same stuff he told Garcia at the Trade Winds Hotel in Albuquerque. That was just two months earlier. Listen to this, they call him a resident, not a convict. 'Resident's present involvement seems to stem from his association with militant factions of the

American Indian Movement. While he had not been associated with this faction before, the present offense is quite serious."

"Quite serious? That's an understatement. The guy carjacks a student in Albuquerque, kidnaps the mayor in Gallup, and shoots him in the back. That's more than 'quite' serious. What does it say about his version of the shooting?"

"Let's see. On page 2, he talks about what happened inside Stearns Sporting Goods. Nakaidinae says, 'I watched Garcia while Casuse went to get a holster for his pistol. I put a shotgun on the glass counter. I was looking the other way when Garcia kicked me and headed for the door. My gun went off. Garcia went out the window.'"

"Virgil, did he really say that his gun just went off?"

"Yeah, that's as far as he went in this interview with the prison people. We need to go over the rest of this when Clay comes down here. This is interesting stuff."

"Anything else there that we ought to pass along to Clay?"

"Yeah. There are a dozen or so letters here to the governor about Nakaidinae's sentence. Some are before the sentence and some after. Let's put them in chronological order for Clay."

"What's first?"

"April, look at this one, it's dated November 21, 1973. That was six days before Nakaidinae was sentenced. It's from the UNM Kiva Club in Albuquerque."

"Did they ask for clemency like Garcia did?"

"No, they asked for a pardon."

"From the governor?"

"Right, but at that point, there was nothing to pardon. He had not even been sentenced yet. A pardon can't be given until after sentencing. Their position is interesting though. The Kiva Club is telling the governor in this letter that the abduction of the mayor was not 'an isolated incident.'"

"What does that mean?"

"They go on. The letter says, 'This was not an isolated incident, nor was it an attempt to single out the City of Gallup for its discrimination and exploitation of Indian people. But rather, it was part of a larger protest movement to focus attention on America's racism and exploitation of its first citizens."

"Virgil, do they mean AIM?"

"Sounds like it to me. They talk about the big march they had in Gallup on March 31, 1973, and a meeting they had with the new mayor, Sam Ray, in Gallup on July 3, 1973. Here's another letter written two days later to the governor from 'The Diné of the Navajo Nation.' Thirty-two people signed it. They ask the governor to grant Nakaidinae an 'executive pardon from further incarnation in the state penitentiary.'"

"But it's dated November 23, 1973. He wasn't sentenced until November 28, so he wasn't in prison then, was he?"

"No, in fact, he was still out on bail then. The prosecutor was not even asking for a prison sentence because of the plea bargain, and the victim was urging the judge for clemency. This letter is interesting. It's actually the same letter that the Kiva Club sent two days earlier. Different typing and a different name at the bottom, but every word in the letter is identical. Here's the next one, it's dated November 27, 1973, and is signed by Peter MacDonald, chairman of the Navajo Nation."

"That's the same day as the sentencing, right?"

"No, a day before. But Nakaidinae was still out on bond. Chairman MacDonald felt that the one-to-five-year sentence was excessive and asks the governor to consider reprieves, pardons, and clemency. Governor King replied to this one. He thanked MacDonald and said that even though the crime was serious, it would not be in his best interest, or that of the Indian community, to expose Nakaidinae to what he called 'elements of penitentiary life.' Listen to this. Governor King told Chairman MacDonald that he intended to discuss this case with Judge Donnelly 'at the first opportunity.'"

"I didn't know they did that. I mean, do governors talk to judges about sentences in criminal cases? I thought they were separate branches of government."

"They are. This doesn't say he did talk to him, only that he intended to do so. Governor King's letter also says that he has talked to the secretary of corrections, who is 'very sympathetic.' He says they are going to evaluate Nakaidinae for thirty days and then transfer him to the Los Lunas Honor Farm, which is an outdoors minimum-security facility."

"What's the next letter?"

"It's dated December 9, 1973. Look who signed it, Donald Casuse."

"Larry's brother?"

"Yes. He talks about his brother in the letter. He doesn't see his brother as a criminal and is asking for clemency for Robert Nakaidinae. Look at this. He is talking about Garcia's own letter of clemency here. Donald Casuse says, 'I think E. Garcia knew that Robert and Larry meant no harm. It was proven in his letter to the court of Robert Nakaidinae, which I think he wrote to clear his conscience of having an innocent man shot to his death, which makes Robert just as innocent.'"

"It looks like Donald Casuse actually saw Garcia's letter to Judge Donnelly."

"Yes, that's likely since copies were sent to Nakaidinae's lawyer."

"Virg, look at these two. They are letters from teachers in Carson High School in Carson, California. They look like character references."

"Right. They are far too late though. They are dated January 4, 1974. Character references are used by judges before they sentence people. Somebody was sure negligent in getting these letters to the judge before the sentencing. By the time this letter was written, Nakaidinae was already evaluated in the state penitentiary and was transferred down to the minimum-security honor farm in Los Lunas."

"How long did he stay there?"

"One of these letters answers that. Here it is. Governor King said that Nakaidinae was granted parole in June of 1974. He was writing to a supporter and said, 'I do hope he takes advantage of his parole and serves his parole period satisfactorily.'"

"Well, that's what he did. There was nothing in the record after June of 1974."

"No, he apparently moved back to the Rez and has been quiet ever since. My boss at the Office of Tourism says he wants it to stay that way. He is not going to talk to us about Clay's book."

"Virgil, think about it. We have the long interview he gave the reporter in Gallup before the trial. We have the admissions he made to the judge at the sentencing hearing. We have his own words on tape in his interview with Garcia, and we have the statement he made when he went to prison. What more could he tell us now even if he wanted to."

"Nothing."

CHAPTER NINETEEN

"Don't Count Your Sheep Too Much—
Your Flock Will Get Smaller"

Back in his government issue house on the Rez, Virgil studied the old man sitting in the only good chair on Virgil's porch. Virgil wanted to see Wounded Knee through someone else's eyes. He felt that the books and newspaper articles made it seem so senseless. Sam Bahe, his favorite uncle, rocked and took his time. Whatever he had to say about Wounded Knee would be said in his way.

"So, my uncle, you were friends with those who took over Wounded Knee."

The old man looked just past Virgil and answered slowly, "Can't say friends really. But many from here went back there to see if it was real. I knew some who went. A nice lady that lived near Many Farms, she married someone, I forget who, anyhow, she went. So did your aunt. They both told me about the women and the food."

"Aunt Millie? Did she go to Wounded Knee? How come no one ever told me that?"

"'Cause we don't talk about those things, you know why. No sense getting the chindi all excited. I don't like chindi."

"Yes, Uncle. But I need to know now what you know about all of that—about Aunt Millie and about what happened at Wounded Knee. You said they went to see if it was real, what did you mean?"

"Okay. You know, some Indians complain too much—mostly the young ones, but not always. Some just want to take over because they have it bad.

The ones from here who went, they wanted to see for themselves if this was just complaining or if there was really a chance for Indian people to have a better life. We had some jobs here in 1973, not much but some. There's more here now, but I don't know if things are better for the Lakota and the Oglala. Back then they were even poorer than us."

Virgil knew better than to hurry things; and that some elders, like the man on his porch, would only talk about things on their schedule, not his. So he thought it best to wait it out and come back to Aunt Millie later. "Uncle, what did they tell you about the women and the food? I'm not sure why our people would go there for that."

"Why do you want to know these things? You weren't even born then. Your dad, he was a good man, he took you down to Phoenix for the work. Even if he had stayed here, he would not have gone to the Pine Ridge Reservation."

"You have met my girlfriend, April. She and her uncle are making a study of what happened in Wounded Knee. That's why I'm asking you."

"A study? I thought they were asking about that Casuse boy from over at Mexican Springs. He's the one that was killed in Gallup. They arrested the other one that you were talking about. I forget his name. Didn't you tell me that yesterday?"

"Well, yes, I did. But maybe Wounded Knee and Gallup are about the same thing, Uncle. I don't know. As you said, I wasn't even born then. I only know what I heard about Gallup. My folks talked some about it later, but I was not too interested. Now I am."

"You should be interested. Too bad you can't ask your aunt, she was there, did I tell you that? Anyhow, there is a lot to tell about Gallup and the old days. It's not as bad as some thought. There are lots of *bilagáana* that can be trusted there. Most of them have been our friends."

"Did you know about a bar called the Navajo Inn? It was not far from here, just over the state line. That's what someone told me anyhow."

"Yes, I know it. But I didn't go there. Lots did, and some died in the cold after they left there because they were too drunk to get up. But most didn't go there. It got worse at the end."

"Worse? What do you mean, Uncle?"

"At first it was just a place to buy some Tokay wine or maybe some Coors. Later there was a different manager, and some of our people didn't like him."

"Are you talking about the mayor of Gallup?"

"No, I think he was there at first, but later on, it was somebody else. I don't know who."

Virgil's uncle signaled the end of that line of questions, and Virgil switched back to his unanswered question. "Can I ask you what you meant about the women at Wounded Knee?"

"The ones from here that went to the Sioux country said that. They came back and told us that the women were the ones who got the men to stand up to some bad people. Their own tribal leaders were stealing from the people. They said the tribal leaders were selling the Sioux tradition for government handouts. The women were strong, like the old women here. They didn't talk too much, but we listened anyhow. Oh, and the food, I was talking about the food. The thing was they didn't have much to start with, and when the men got their guns out, no more food came in. They got some whiskey, but not much food. So we heard they were very hungry. That's why some went from here to give them some food. Not too much, but some. Just a couple truckloads to help if it could."

"Did anyone from here fight there?"

"I guess so. But you know, fighting is always worse when it's over. Some say they remember more blows than anyone struck. I don't know if they fought or if they just took some food. Virgil, you have a lot of questions about something so long ago and so far away."

Sam Bahe talked a lot, at least for him, about what the people told him when they came back from Wounded Knee. He mixed in stories about Gallup and other places where there were Indian troubles before Virgil was born. But it was mostly just stories about poor reservations. It was cold in both places, and sometimes there was no feed for the cattle and no stove oil at the store. Just as he was starting to sit still for long periods and Virgil thought he was falling asleep, he said, "Did you know I have a book from there?"

"From where, Gallup or Wounded Knee?"

"From the Sioux country. She said it was from inside Wounded Knee where the women were making decisions and the men were shooting their guns."

"Uncle, who said this? Who gave you the book?"

"Well, it was your aunt. You know what happened to her up there, and your mom went somewhere and brought her stuff back. I think she went to her house. Anyhow, the book was there, and your mom gave it to me. It made her sad. But I liked the pictures, and so I kept it in the box, you know, the one in back of the house. Those were some brave warriors, those Sioux. And the ones from here, some of them anyhow, they are in the book. I don't like to talk about this anymore. I've seen it, so now you can have it if you want."

Virgil drove his uncle back to his house on the highway to Ganado, but only eighteen miles from Window Rock. They went inside where after ten minutes of muttering, Sam Bahe found the book, handed it to Virgil, and unceremoniously went to bed. Intending only to take a quick glance at the book, Virgil went into the little kitchen, turned on the bare bulb over the table, and looked at the book. Since it was getting late, he just thought he'd read a few pages and drink a little milk from his uncle's refrigerator. But it was almost four hours later after he read the whole thing that he headed back to Window Rock, without waking his uncle.

The next morning, Virgil took a long, wistful look at the book, now in the light of day and with a sense of real history. Books come in all sizes; but this one, one of the very few of its kind he had ever seen, was printed landscape style as though it were a coffee-table book. But it was too small for that kind of book, measuring barely eight by nine inches. This paperback looked as though it had been printed in someone's basement. The once stiff cover, now well thumbed, looked old and tired, with a garish red color that set off large black letters containing its unambiguous title, *Voices from Wounded Knee—1973*. Along the spine was a motto of sorts, "The People Are Standing Up." The price, $4.95, said it all. Even in 1974, this was a cheap book. But the single dominating feature of the book was a black-and-white photo of a haunting figure, a man with his back to the camera, in a fringe leather coat, his long unbound hair whistling in the wind, and carrying a large-bore rifle pointed to the sky, with a military-style sling.

As Virgil looked it, the starkness of the lone warrior's back was at once captivating but somehow gratuitous. The bareheaded man stood guard against a faraway crest that rose into swells and undulations, standing tall against thinly sprinkled miles of dark grassy foliage. With his feet braced against the wind, the man, just one man, seemed larger than the miles of grassland he seemed to be studying. He grasped the long-barreled rifle as though it were a short spear, with the butt against his hip and the shoulder sling, loose and flapping in the wind. Whoever this man was, he was not posing for the camera—he was waiting, just like Virgil.

Virgil spent the next two nights tossing in bed, worrying about the future and tasting his uncle's wisdom. Clay was asking questions about something that happened to another tribe. *What did any of this have to do with us,* Virgil thought.

~ ~ ~

April rarely visited Window Rock but was glad to go upwind, as Virgil put it, since it really did seem cooler here. The quiet romantic dinner she'd fantasized about turned out, as usual, to be nice but hardly quiet and far more political than romantic.

"Virgil, what's up?" She made the mistake of saying just after he'd ordered the chicken fried steak for himself and the Cobb salad for her.

"Echoes. They are not as clear as I'd hoped, but they are there. I still can't figure how the real reporters and the police detectives missed them."

"Echoes? What echoes? Am I an echo of you, or you of me? That's sweet, but you know . . ."

"No, I was talking about the echoes that bounced back and forth between Gallup and Wounded Knee in 1973. About the connections between the national Indian rights movement and what happened in Gallup. They sound like the same thing to me."

"So what's new? I've always felt they were."

"April, feeling like something's connected is different than *thinking* they are. I'm not talking about emotional connections. I'm talking about actual factual connections, you know, cause and effect. That's an echo—it follows and repeats a distinctive sound. Do you remember what you and your uncle Clay started out to do here? He wanted to write a book that explored what happened to the American Warrior, the one with red war paint who battled the soldiers who were stealing his land and killing his buffalo. Those guys, their grandkids I mean, became AIM, and somewhere along the line, people got shot, mostly Indians but not always."

"Virg, I get that, but I'm missing *your* point."

"Clay is asking whether the landings at Alcatraz, the siege at Wounded Knee, and the abduction in Gallup were directly connected. Maybe it's too subtle, but I think he's asking the wrong question. It's not whether the three places or even the three takeovers are connected. The penetrating question is whether the *takeovers* are echoes of the *people* involved."

"Okay, but whether it's events or people or towns, aren't both you and Clay looking for the same thing? Did what one did cause the other? I see it in terms of the win-loss column. Virg, do you have the answer?"

"Maybe I do. Look at this," Virgil said and slid a dog-eared book across the table to April.

"*Voices from Wounded Knee, 1973.* My goodness, this looks pretty authentic. Where did you get it?"

"From my uncle, actually he is my great-uncle. He got it from his niece, my mother's sister. She left here in a little before we left the Rez and went down to Glendale. I saw her every summer when we came back up to Chinle. She told me a lot when I was little. She made me laugh too. I miss her."

"Miss her?"

"Yes, she's dead."

"Oh, Virg, I'm so sorry. What was her name?"

"We, most of my family anyway, don't use the names of dead people when we talk about them. That might bring a chindi to you. But I'll tell you, her name was Mildred. Mildred Clark. Clark was my mom's last name before she married my dad."

"How did Mildred Clark get this book? Is it authentic, do you think?"

"She was there at Wounded Knee."

"Did she bring the book from there to Window Rock?"

"Maybe, I'm not sure. When my aunt died, it was in her car. She was on a road trip somewhere and had an accident. The cops gave all her stuff back to my mom. This book was there in the car, with her clothes. My great-uncle showed it to me two nights ago when I started asking him about the old days and 'the Navajo way.' He doesn't want it anymore and gave it to me."

"You mean she was one of the fighters there? Was she one of the women that Clay talked about when he went there to cover the story for his magazine?"

"April, I don't know much because she died about ten years ago, just a few years after Wounded Knee. But the thing is, my great-uncle, he knew I was interested in what happened at Wounded Knee, so he remembered this book and gave it to me. I don't have to give it back because he says he is tired of keeping it."

"Is her name in it? Does it talk about her, or did she write it? It doesn't look like the name of the author is anywhere on the cover."

"Her name is in longhand, there on the inside cover. I guess she just signed it. But I don't think her name is in the actual book, but his is."

"Whose?"

"Larry Casuse."

"Casuse's name is in this book! My god, Virg, that's it. Clay has been looking for that direct connection. Wait, am I jumping to conclusions here?"

"No, not jumping. Just concluding. Casuse's name is in this book. They say in this book that he abducted the mayor in Gallup to support what AIM was doing in Wounded Knee."

"God, God Almighty. That's astounding. You've found it, Virg, the direct connection that Clay has been looking for. Show me where it makes the connection, then tell me whether we can trust this book or not."

"April, look right here on page 92. The picture at the bottom was taken in Gallup at that big march that we already knew about. That's the one where they read the telegram from Russell Means and Dennis Banks from Wounded Knee. Read what it says there."

April read aloud, "In New Mexico, Larry Casuse, a Navajo activist, had been trying to bring attention to the mayor of Gallup's treatment of Indian people. Mayor Garcia was the chairman of the state's antialcoholism program, but at the same time owned a tavern on the edge of the Navajo reservation. Shortly after the occupation of Wounded Knee began and partly in a gesture of support, Larry and Robert Nakaidinae forced a confrontation with Garcia, taking him hostage and intending to bring his actions to public attention. In the course of the incident, Larry was shot and killed; Robert was held in jail on $85,000 bond on kidnapping charges. On March 3, one thousand attended Larry's funeral in Gallup."

April's face turned red. "Virgil, this is totally amazing. These facts are the exact same ones we found in the newspapers."

"Yes, most of them. But they got the place of the funeral wrong. It was out on the reservation, not in Gallup. There is one interesting mistake though, they misspelled Nakaidinae's name. They left out the final *a*. I mention that because there are several mistakes in this, mostly in spelling. That makes it look authentic to me. Warriors, not writers, wrote this. One of the mistakes they made is almost Freudian although Navajos are not exactly big believers in Sigmund Freud."

"What's that?"

"Look at page 6. They are talking about the famous Fort Laramie Treaty of 1868, which designated a huge amount of land as the Great Sioux Reservation. They say that the government intended that the Sioux would come into the reservation from the hunting grounds. See that? They misspell *hunting* as *hurting*. Hurting grounds, pretty Freudian, wouldn't you say?"

"Beats me. I never got Freud. I am more into prose, not shrink-wraps. But it is interesting. How was this book made, does it say?"

"Yeah, that's interesting too. Someone set up what was called an 'alternative media collective.' Their job was to collect the facts from the participants inside Wounded Knee and from the U.S. government outside. Their plan was to tell the story of what happened in their own words. It says on page 2, 'We felt our government should not be permitted to secretly conduct an undeclared war.'"

"So how did your aunt fit in? Was she a reporter or what?"

"I'm not sure, but the book says four writers were involved. Two worked with an alternative radio network in Ithaca, New York, called the Rest of the News. The other two on the project came from Chicago and New Mexico. One of these did support work, and the other one covered the siege for a newspaper. They say the newspaper was the *Unicorn News* based in San Francisco."

"Which one was your aunt?"

"I don't know, but she worked as a part-time reporter about that same time out in San Francisco. And of course, she was from New Mexico even if she worked in San Francisco. I guess we will never find out now because of her accident, but it all seems to fit together."

"How could we find out if she did actually write this book?"

"Don't know. As I said, there are lots of spelling errors in this, so I doubt she actually wrote it. My mom says she was a good writer and worked as a teacher somewhere. But she was there. And the book definitely connects Larry Casuse and the abduction of Garcia to the takeover of Wounded Knee. She would have known all about the Gallup story happening while she was there in South Dakota. There is another reference in the book. Look at page 262. That's the entire chronology of Wounded Knee from 1868 to 1973. Look at what they put under the date of March 1, 1973."

April looked around the restaurant and then read aloud but a bit more softly than she had before, "March 1, 1973. Oglala's in Pine Ridge demonstrate in support of the people in WK. Larry Casuse killed in New Mexico. Shooting between marshals and occupiers of WK."

"Virg, does this mean what I think it means? Does it mean that the warriors in Wounded Knee behind the barricades on March 1, 1973, actually talked to Larry Casuse? If that's what it means, they must have talked to him before he died."

"I'm not sure this goes that far. It doesn't say they talked. It implies they did. It is explicit, though, in tying the events there to the events in Gallup. And it clearly connects what Casuse did to Garcia to what AIM was doing at

Wounded Knee. He acted in support of them, and they supported him too. What's the word for that? *Symbiotic*, that's it. Remember the famous telegram from Wounded Knee that was read aloud at the big march in Gallup after Casuse died? This confirms that information was being passed back and forth between Wounded Knee and Gallup. From the perspective of those inside Wounded Knee, Gallup was just another battleground for Indian respect. But even without direct talk, there is a solid connection here in this book. This book didn't influence Casuse because it wasn't published before he died. But we know he was influenced by what AIM did at Wounded Knee. He was showing that influence when he walked into the mayor's office with a gun. He was through talking, just like they were back there."

"When was this written?"

"The siege started on February 28, 1973, and ended on May 5, 1973. Then the feds left the area. After it was over, somebody went back inside the little town of Wounded Knee and dug up the notes, the tapes, and the photographs. Then they published the book in the middle of 1974. I guess it was for sale, you can see the price, four dollars and ninety-five cents, there on the bottom of the cover page."

April and Virgil continued the larger discussion about echoes and people through the soup and well past the salad. The waitress skipped the dinner salad for April, holding out for the Cobb sort-of salad she'd ordered in lieu of a real dinner. Just before the grand entry of the chicken fried steak and just after he poured coffee, Virgil posed his challenge to April. "Do you want to hear my argument, or do you want to still rely on your feelings that they are connected?"

"No, I want to hear you. But my feelings might not change, so don't get your hopes up by relying on the facts too much."

"To start with, you have to consider the character of Casuse and Nakaidinae. Both were young, both had some college, and both were off-the-Rez Indians. Both were literate although Nakaidinae didn't sound like it on the tape we found in the Calvin Horn files in the UNM Zimmerman Library. Both were impassioned about justice, and both had their own troubles with the law. In a way, both were homeless, at least as far as tribal land was concerned. They knew about the reservation, had Navajo blood, even 'hot' Navajo blood, and they needed some way to fit in. But they didn't speak the Navajo tongue all that well, and they were still learning 'the Navajo way' and the whole thing about living in harmony. Lots of things were out of whack for them and most everyone they knew."

"Virgil, you don't have to convince me that Casuse and Nakaidinae were connected. I know that. I thought you were talking about them and AIM or Russell Means or whatever."

"I am. Admittedly, it's not the kind of connection that a lawyer or an accountant would make. I think Casuse and Nakaidinae were directly connected to AIM and its leaders, most particularly Russell Means. The connection is pure cause and effect. They all sang the same song—like it was an echo."

"So are you saying they knew Russell Means or that he told them what to do or what?"

"No, I don't know whether they knew him or not. In fact, I think that the connection between Casuse and Nakaidinae might have been just as loose as the connection between Casuse and AIM or Russell Means. That's what got me to thinking in the first place. When AIM did something bold, Casuse felt compelled to do something bold as well. They acted, he reacted—*boom*."

"Well, I am supposed to be the irrational female here always going on feelings, not proof. What exactly do you mean that Casuse had a *loose* connection with Nakaidinae? I thought they were buddies and that they were in the thing together all the way."

"They acted together, but I think Nakaidinae did what Casuse wanted because he looked up to him and because Casuse was a true believer. I mean *true* in the political way, not the religious way. For his part, I think Casuse looked up to the older warriors in AIM and saw all of them as true believers. So when I say the connection was loose, I mean that maybe they didn't even talk about it. Maybe they just acted on what they thought was principle. It's mostly a timing thing."

"Timing, you mean between Casuse and Nakaidinae? They hadn't been buddies that long, and Casuse and Means were not buddies at all, much less for a long time."

"I think that works *for* me, not against me. Old Indians who live their whole lives on the reservation are pretty much settled in their ways. They forgive a lot, and they understand and accept a lot. But young Indians, particularly those raised off the reservations and who get a little education, are not as patient or as forgiving. What I've read about Means suggests that he was impatient and smart. He was eloquent, and he lived in a different part of the country from Casuse. He was fighting for respect and independence. Significantly, he was not afraid to use violence. No wonder Casuse looked up to him."

"Tell me what you think. Is Nakaidinae as much a timing key as Wounded Knee was?"

"Actually, they are both the same key. It's like one key that fits two different locks. No one at Wounded Knee acted alone, and Casuse would not have acted alone either. The only difference is the size of the group and how many people they abducted. It took AIM's takeover of Wounded Knee *and* Nakaidinae's availability to move Casuse, at least that's what I think. Casuse was definitely on the move, he was ready to do something, something dramatic and very political. But he was unsure of what and even less sure of who was with him. His university friends all showed up after the fact, but none of them was likely to carry a bomb and march down the streets as he paraded Garcia through downtown Gallup. Nakaidinae had a much smaller role in the whole thing. He was younger, more impressionable but probably as motivated by Wounded Knee. We'll never know. We wouldn't even know now if he was here at the table with us tonight. Too much time has passed, and a lot has changed. Time and changed circumstances alter your perception of what you would or would not have done under different circumstances. Notwithstanding, I am pretty convinced that it took both—the implicit call for action from Wounded Knee and the availability of a willing accomplice to carry out the Gallup abduction. Wounded Knee and Nakaidinae are both moving *causes*, and both of them took part in the *effect*, that is, Casuse's abduction of Garcia. The only difference is Nakaidinae survived and Casuse died. AIM cheered from the sidelines and sent a telegram about their warrior brother to his funeral."

"Well, I can see your thinking about Wounded Knee. I agree with your timing because it seems inescapable. But making Nakaidinae a cause of what happened seems very unfair to me. I keep remembering that Casuse died, Garcia was shot and could have died. Nakaidinae might have been responsible for Garcia but not Casuse. I don't think that's fair."

"I didn't mean that. Nakaidinae was a cause, in the sense of making himself available, for Casuse in getting up the courage to make the decision he did *when* he did. But after that, things got way out of hand. Nakaidinae is the guy who pulled the trigger and shot Garcia. He may or may not have intended to kill him, but he did intend to shoot him, at close range, in the back with a shotgun. He is the cause of that. But I don't think he had any idea over at the UNM parking lot in Albuquerque that before the day was over, Casuse would kill himself. I think that was a big surprise to him, just as it was to everyone else who was there that day. That's what you get when you mix limited goals with drastic action."

April frowned and said, "I'm not sure what you mean by limited. The drastic part I get."

"Nakaidinae had no stake in what had happened to Casuse and his upcoming criminal trial over the death of that girl in Gallup. He had no history with the mayor and no drinking problem of his own that we know of. Casuse wanted to march Garcia around the state to make a political point, and Nakaidinae was just naïve enough to join in. But their way of doing it was to match what their warrior brothers did in Wounded Knee the day before. Take a hostage, build a barricade, and hope someone listens to you. They gave almost no thought to the consequences of something going wrong. Something always goes wrong when the goals are so limited, and they make up the means to accomplish them on the spot. So there they were, acting out and not thinking. It's amazing that all three of them weren't killed that day. Garcia and Nakaidinae were the lucky ones—they lived. They both paid a huge price for what happened at Wounded Knee the day before. That's another connection."

"Here's a good idea. You keep that thought while we go to your place where we can feel something far more meaningful."

"You're on."

Chapter Twenty

"Don't Stare at Anyone for a Long Time—You'll Go Blind"

Clay Ramsey squinted at the imposing figure on the dust cover, somehow hoping that it would make the man smaller and the idea bigger. He'd finally finished Russell Means's 554 pages of self-promoting autobiography forty-five minutes ago. It was the last of the stack of Wounded Knee books he'd reread over the last six weeks. *What was it about this one photograph? Why was it different from the hundreds of other photographs in the stack of Indian rights books?*

Clay had put off the rest of his life to prepare for the actual *writing* of the first five pages of his book. His three decades as an editor gave him an edge over most other first-time novelists. He knew that agents, editors, and readers all share one common trait, *instant* judgment. By the time they get to page 5 of a manuscript, they've made up their minds. If they like it, they turn the page. If not, you get the rejection slip, literally or figuratively. Novelists can claim they don't know why they were rejected, but the truth can always be found in the first five pages of any manuscript. The entire book's artistic merit is vetted in those first pages and sometimes in the first five lines.

As he pondered his first five pages, he kept coming back to that troubling photograph. *Should he describe on page 1 what he saw? What words could paint that picture? A man in long braids with his chest thrust forward, stern but friendly.*

Those hollow words didn't sound like the description of a *warrior*. Clay had little doubt that Means was a warrior. But that was painting only the skin, he needed to get down to the marrow. He needed to define Casuse, Means, and all the other AIM warriors inside the battle lines for seventy-one days at Wounded Knee. *What had they really accomplished? Looking back, I can see their search for self-destiny. I can see their lands and their government, but not their future. Was the violence worth it? Are the laws that so restricted America's tribes different now? Is tribal government now in tune with the governed or with Washington and those who hold Indian lands in trust? Isn't it still all about the land and the Indians' reverence of it?*

On one level, there no disputing that a single uprising, among the many, *Wounded Knee* marked the high tide of activism by Indians in the last century. But thirty years have passed. The hope for an Independent Oglala Nation never materialized and with it faded the lofty notion that American Indians and the tribes no longer needed the U.S. government. It seemed clear that Indians wanted the United States to hold their land in trust only until they were ready to determine their own future. *Were they? Did Wounded Knee and Gallup advance or retard that hope?*

On another level, his reading, not to mention his experience, persuaded him that AIM was not then, or ever, the pivotal, core group of men and women that could have brought home the notion of independence. The drumbeats in Alcatraz, Wounded Knee, and Gallup thundered about the past, but did not to resonate to the future. What had AIM stood for? A lot, actually, even if the political success it fought for was never achieved. Clay, long a victim of lists, decided to chart the things that AIM and its efforts in Alcatraz, Wounded Knee, and Gallup *had* accomplished. Later he could dwell on its failures. Or, like America in general, he could ignore them at his leisure.

AIM provided the turning point for Indian activists in America. AIM made radicalism reasonably respectable, once again, in American history. AIM showcased its two charismatic leaders in a spectacular trial for several months in 1974 and won. The ego and stage presence of Russell Means and Dennis Banks, the advocacy of William Kunstler, and the support of hundreds of other warriors turned a federal courtroom in St. Paul into a short-lived center stage for American Indian activism. The trial was one of the first to introduce evidence of federal complicity and incompetence in the handling of Indian affairs, not to mention their money, and their lives.

The federal judge dismissed all charges arising out of Wounded Knee because of government misconduct. Means and Banks walked out free men. They were broke, of course, but free. *That's the American way, right?*

Clay's thoughts turned to Gallup and the results there. Nakaidinae gave up his right to trial, to the dismay of his supporters. He got a long jail sentence, which suited some of his dissenters, and an early release, which surely suited him. But AIM's victory at Wounded Knee eluded IAE and the Kiva Club in Gallup. *Or was it the other way around? The people of Gallup, and its leaders, were never charged, much less convicted, of the kind of malfeasance that was so pervasive by tribal and federal government on the Pine Ridge Reservation. Maybe the results were consistent, after all.*

AIM's high ground was not its activism, nor even its radically violent approach to problem solving. AIM's moment in the sun was the fact that young Indians all over America felt a new pride in simply being Indian. That was true in Gallup as well. Casuse's death, even by his own hand, advanced that pride. Nakaidinae's plea bargain, even to avoid a certain conviction and a longer sentence, gave his acts credence. *It's not who you dance with, it's who you go home with that counts. Some of the warriors died, some lived, some went free, and some went to jail. They are recognized, not for what happened to them but for what they did, good, bad,* and *stupid.*

Clay's challenge, as he saw it, was how to express that in terms that would inspire future readers of his great American Indian Warrior book. Inspiration had to come somewhere in the first five pages. His reader's eyes were not those of Means, Casuse, Nakaidinae, or even Virgil Bahe. How could they ever understand? *How could he write it when he was still a white-eyes?*

The ringing of the phone jarred Clay out of his mental walkabout. The caller ID displayed his boss's name and a Denver prefix. He resisted the temptation to let voice mail hear him out. "Clay Ramsey here. Warren, to what do I owe the pleasure of a midday call?" He hoped the sarcasm would come through.

"Clay, it's nice to hear you answer for a change. I assumed you'd let voice mail hear my not-so-welcome news. But before we dwell on the obvious, let me ask you whether you are still grousing over our reluctance to publish your book?"

"Warren, no, sir. You'll hear no grousing from me. It's not my style. Besides, the final decision is still open. It is, isn't it—open, I mean? That's not why you're calling, is it, to tell me that the decision is finally final, frustrating as that may be to me. I might have to grouse about that."

Clay knew that the decision was probably final. He'd gotten an evasive fax message, but this was the first actual phone call on the subject from his boss. *Fax is much too impersonal for personal communications. Even Warren Suttcliff would tell him personally, wouldn't he?*

"No, it's not absolutely final, not in the sense that here at corporate we've made an arbitrary decision without hearing you out. You asked for time, and we're giving you that. But I have to say, once again, Clay, that this idea to forestall the inevitable by plowing more money into a book that few will want to read cannot possibly help your cause."

My cause? It's not mine, it's theirs. "You know, history is our business even if it has to be current history."

"Clay, there is no such thing as current history. You have lived so long in the past that you've forgotten the excitement of the present. Why do you insist on dwelling on movements and causes and such? There are lots of present stories, modern-day stories, which would fit your writing and editing strengths."

"So you're calling to offer me a job, is that it?"

"Maybe. What would you think about moving? I mean, both literally and creatively. We are talking here at corporate about a new magazine, one that would focus on the present and might well interest you. Do you want to hear about it, or are you still so enamored with warriors of the past that you don't want to hear about today's warriors?"

"Warren, you don't really want me to commit to moving out of the northwest, do you? You want me to give up my plan for a book. Is this an end run?"

"No, it's not, it's entirely legit. We are thinking about a new magazine, one that would focus on what we call the warrior of the twenty-first century, that is, the eco-warrior."

"The eco-warrior? Hell is that? People who fight for global warming or against it? Which side are you gray suits thinking of backing? You already have an attitude, but I can't guess which side of global warming you're on. There are so many political overtones that your side is obscure."

"Well, actually, you've hit it quite well. We think that the issues that deal with water, air, development, and urban sprawl are becoming warlike and that those who fight on either side might want a news magazine that lays everything out. Is that something you'd be interested in?"

So we are back to canning my book by ignoring it, are we? "What do you mean by interested in? As editor in chief, with final say on content and column inches and format and attitude, is that what you mean? If so, yes, I'd be interested, provided that it's a creative move, not a literal one."

"Clay. Clay. You never change, do you? We are working on the attitude thing, but it's still in process. But I don't think we are talking about what you have in mind, what with your view on control and all, I was thinking of you on the writing and editing side, not the business or policy side. Why don't you come to Denver and talk about it? Nothing here is cast in stone on this thing. We are just talking about alternatives that might help us out of the slump that declining readership has put us in vis-à-vis the *America Warrior*."

"Warren, you're right, I don't change, and you don't surprise. Maybe that's why we are like Spam and sushi in the publishing world. You never see those two in the same column or hardly in the same magazine, and you and I never seem to agree on the small things in life, like where I'm going to work and what you're going to publish."

"Come on, Clay, why don't you just think it about for a few days? Then call me, and we can arrange a little time for you here in Denver where we can talk this through. But for now, I really have to run. Things to do, you know."

Yeah, I know. After Clay rung off and cooled down, he knew his hope that the company would publish his book was down for the count. Warren had danced around it. Col. George Cook put it far more directly in 1873, "The American Indian commands respect for his rights only so long as he inspires terror for his rifle."

Had Casuse read about Cook? Had Nakaidinae missed it? Was there a message there for him? Was his pen his rifle? He placed another call to April. *I need to go to New Mexico*, he thought as he waited for April to answer the phone.

~ ~ ~

Clay felt the jarring touchdown of the Southwest flight from LAX to ABQ and wondered again what it was about the wind in Albuquerque that caused so many rough landings. As he stepped into the terminal and smiled at April and Virgil standing there at the gate, he thought they made an imposing if slightly odd couple. Her Irish red curls complemented his straight coal black hair even if his was a bit longer. Her infectious smile seemed to offset his slightly serious look. But it was her energy that set them apart. She always ran; he always walked. Adult Navajos are typically sedate whereas Irish girls often never reach adulthood, much less sedateness.

They had an afternoon coffee in the shop just off the lobby in the Hilton. They made small talk about sisters and such and then arranged to meet in a half hour for an early dinner at Garduños. "What's the plan, Dan" was April's customary greeting these days no matter who or what she was up to. He had spent the last three hours, at thirty thousand feet, ruminating about whether to be merely evasive or outright disingenuous about the chances of actually publishing his book.

April contained herself well enough through the ordering of the meal and the delivery of the two beers for them and coffee for Clay. Then she raised the subject and her voice, "I can't stand it anymore. Clay, what is going on? Are we a go or not?"

"April, your mother's more patient than you, and she's impossible. Let's talk about the Big I a bit and then we can move to cabbages, books, and such."

"The Big I is a disaster. Is that what you are telling us about the book? After all our digging and all your direction?"

"No, bad metaphor, I guess. We are not a *go*, but Warren has not formally killed us yet."

Virgil chimed in, "How formal is death in the publishing world, and who's Warren?"

"Warren is my boss. He lives in Denver, has twelve magazines, ten of which make money for him. The other money loser is even older than the *American Warrior* but was the company's first and is still actually published there in Denver, with all the rest, except for mine. Warren wants me to come to Denver and edit some new rag from there. But that's not a formal kill in our business. It's just a wound that, if left untreated, will become gangrenous and eat away at the profit center until it's amputated like a bad toe. That's a better metaphor."

Virgil, reluctant as he was to interrupt, continued, "I am in the tourism business, and we face the same kind of dilemma. How do we keep the tourists coming to Canyon de Chelly and Monument Valley without losing them to the Grand Canyon? We're fighting for the entertainment dollar. Everyone should actually see all three places, but lots of people are afraid of the Rez. So they stick pretty close to the Grand Canyon even though they often drive a hundred miles through the Rez just to get there."

"Good comparison, Virgil. Here's the only shot we have. If we can write up a truly compelling proposal, we might get one last shot at keeping the old man alive. I don't think they have really made up their minds, but they are close, and we are definitely behind the six-ball."

"The six-ball? I thought it was the black one, the eight-ball, that people got behind on occasion."

"Not if you're Irish. We never make it to the eight-ball—we get into trouble early. The *American Warrior* is over thirty. That's years, not pounds.

She's done—there is no saving her. But if they agree to publish my book, then we go out in style, literarily speaking. So how is the great abduction story coming along from your end?"

Virgil and April looked across the table, giving proper deference to the other. Clay found that refreshing since this program began with him in charge. Now it seems that Virgil and April were, at least, equal partners in the project.

April began, "Clay, Virg and I have worked really hard, so it's a bummer to hear that there is a possibility our work will never see the light of print. Come on, please, have we wasted all this time or not?"

"Time is relative, my dear. You can only waste it if you didn't spend it wisely. True, Warren may not see this as a worthwhile project in an economic sense, but your research and yours too, Virgil, has real value. It's just that being published is hard unless you have an inside track. Did you know that America's publishers rejected over a million finished manuscripts last year alone?"

Virgil looked at April, but she waived him in. "No, Clay, I didn't know that. But you obviously did. How many of those were first-time novelists?"

"Most of them. There were ninety thousand new titles published in the same year. About a quarter of those were by previously unpublished writers. So somebody's getting the job done, might as well be me."

"You think getting published would be easier if your company did it? Is that right?"

"Sure, they know my work, they know me, and they know the subject. I thought it would be a natural. But so far, they have treated the idea like a fungus. Better to avoid it altogether than admit it might be growing somewhere close to you."

April chimed in, "What does that mean, Uncle Clay? Why can't you try for some other publisher?"

"I can. And will if I have to. However, writing query letters to editors or agents is problematic at best. The average editor or agent reads several hundred manuscripts a year and accepts maybe 5 percent or less. That's why I was hoping that Warren would like the idea. For today, I really think we need to think positive and assume that somebody will like the book. If it's as good as the research, then I have a decent shot."

"So, Uncle Clay, how do we start?"

"What we need is a short tagline that lays out the whole theme in one page or less and then a sort of bullet list that generally describes the content of the book, page count, and ending."

Virgil chimed in, "I don't have any bullet points, but I did scribble something out that might be usable for the theme."

Clay was pleased. April looked a bit surprised. "Virgil, I didn't know you had written anything on this. Why didn't you tell me?"

"'Cause I just did it this morning, at your house, waiting for you to dry your hair. It's no big deal anyhow. It's just my scribbling."

Clay interjected, "Scribbling or not, it's a good place to start. Read it to us, Mr. Bahe."

Virgil pulled the piece of lined notepaper from his shirt pocket and began to read,

"The deaths of Indian rights activists and the abrupt end to promising political careers drive the true stories of the warriors, the politicians, and the dog soldiers in America's last conflict with its first people. California was stunned by the takeover at Alcatraz in 1969, and the nation was riveted on the siege at Wounded Knee in 1973. But the road from Alcatraz to Wounded Knee ran straight through Gallup, New Mexico, where one young man died and another lost his way. It was no coincidence that the siege of Wounded Knee and the abduction of the mayor in Gallup both happened on March 1, 1973."

"Virg, honey, that's really good. My god, you *are* a writer. Uncle Clay, what do you think? Is this the theme? Is this what you had in mind?"

Clay stuck out his hand, and Virgil softly placed his single sheet in it as though it might break. Clay sipped his coffee and read Virgil's solitary effort over again. "April is right, Mr. Bahe, you can write. It's a little long for a tagline on the cover, but it can be reworked. There's a lot to go on here once you get past the passive voice. Let's break it down if we can. Tell me, what do you mean by the phrase, 'America's last conflict with its first people'? Isn't the conflict still going? And do you mean that Alcatraz was really the first part?"

Virgil sipped his beer, organized his thoughts, and said, "The debate is still going, the struggle for recognition and respect is still going, but the conflict, or the war that some wanted, is over. I called it a conflict because I thought the word *war* would just inflame things and make it harder to sell to the average Joe. But it is over, no matter what you call it. The movement that those warriors in AIM and IAE stood for is dead. Maybe that's a good thing."

"Virg, what about Alcatraz? We hardly talked about that. Where did you get the idea that it was the start of the movement?"

"From the newspapers and from what I picked up out on the Rez. Those college students from California infected the nation, some good and some bad. But it was the first armed takeover of government property by Indians in modern times. And as I told you in Window Rock, some of my ideas came from my aunt."

Clay said, "I think it was the beginning too. What did you mean about your aunt? I don't think you've ever mentioned her."

"She's dead. And as you probably know, Navajos don't speak the names of their dead unless they have to. So my family didn't talk much about my aunt after she died. I remember her from when I was a kid, but she died when I was seven or eight, something like that. She was a free spirit and didn't live on the Rez when I did. I only saw her in the summers when she came to visit."

Clay shifted in his chair and looked away from Virgil when he asked, "What did you mean about hearing from her on things like Alcatraz and Wounded Knee? They occurred before you were born."

"I didn't mean she actually told me anything about that. But she talked to me about 'the Navajo way' and about living in harmony. She was a very smart woman, probably the first in our family to be college educated. I know now that she was at Alcatraz and Wounded Knee, but that's only because my great-uncle, her dad, told me. She was my mother's sister, so she treated all of us like her own kids. She didn't have any before she died."

"Uncle Clay, wait till you hear how Virg knows for sure that she was at Wounded Knee—tell him, Virg."

"'Cause I have her book."

Clay shuffled his chair back in toward the table and said softly, "What book?"

"This one," Virgil said as he reached for his book bag.

"Look at this, Uncle Clay. It gave me goosey bumpies all over when I saw it last week in Window Rock. It's totally amazing."

Virgil slid the red-bordered paperbound book across the table. Clay picked it up but didn't open it. He just held it like it might disappear. "Go ahead, look it at. There are some pretty amazing photographs in there, but the text is what will really ratchet you up, Uncle Clay."

Clay set the book back down on the table and pushed it two or three inches away from him. Then he took a deep breath and opened the cover to the first blank page. He stared it until April burst out, "Go ahead look inside, Uncle Clay."

Clay closed the book and grasped it to his chest. His voice sounded faint and vaguely ominous. "Virgil. Tell me. Was Millie your aunt?"

"Yes, that's her name on the inside cover—Mildred Clark. It says 'Mildred,' not 'Millie.' Did you know her?"

"Oh god, oh god. Virgil, why didn't you tell me this before? I don't know how to even begin to tell you."

"Tell me what, Clay?"

Tell you? How could I? Tell you about us, about then, about a life lost, two lives actually? Clay, still holding the book to his chest, shook his head from side to side, then with his left hand, reached out and took a sip of water. He sputtered and, feeling some of dribble down his chin, reached for his napkin on his lap as he tried to compose himself. *And her.*

"I knew her, Virgil. We were close a long time ago. She was at Alcatraz. She was at Wounded Knee. So was I. We were close, like I said. But I lost her. Now I know you did too. Would you both excuse me for a moment? I have to go to the men's room."

Their booth was about ten feet from the door to the restrooms. Clay knocked over his chair getting up. "I'll bring this right back," he said as he picked up Virgil's book. Then he walked right past the door to the men's room and out the front door into the parking lot.

Neither spoke for a minute, then April said, "Virg, honey, does this mean what I think it means?"

"What? What do you think?"

"Clay and your aunt. That's what I think. One minute he's fine, and the next he looks like he's been hit in the chest with a cannonball. Did you see his face? God, how could this have never come up?"

"Because there was no connection until I found the book. He must have known about the book, she must have told him if he did know her, that is."

"Virg, he knew her, take my word on it. And he didn't just know her, he loved her."

"That's a stretch, April, maybe he knew her, but nothing he did or said means that they were a couple. What in the world makes you say a thing like that? Feminine intuition? What?"

"Clay Ramsey is a very smart but slightly introverted man. He's never married even though my mom says all the girls chased him. He is definitely not gay. And when he saw your aunt's name on the cover of that book, he almost croaked. So add it up, Chief. Do you think they were just pen pals?"

Virgil didn't answer. It was just as well because they saw Clay come back in the front door, the tattered book still clasped to his chest.

He sat down, put the book on his lap—not on the table, and looked past them at the silk flowers on the ledge behind the booth. His eyes looked like a drunk's, but his voice was that of a priest on the other side of the confessional veil. "Virgil, April, I'm not sure where to start, so just bear with me if you will."

He paused, took a deep breath, and looked squarely at Virgil. "Son, I hope you treasure everything your aunt told you. I do. I hope you cherish her memory as I do. I met her in Alcatraz in 1969. I was covering the landing for my magazine. She was a student at USF. But she was on her way to journalism even then. She and I, well, we spent some time together and then went our separate ways. Later, a year or so, we got together again, but she was way ahead of me in so many ways that I just never caught up with her. She loved life, I wrote about it. That was what kept us from anything more permanent. Instead of tracking her down, I wrote to her. And she wrote to me. But I did love her. I think she knew that, but I probably didn't say it right. Then, then . . ."

"Uncle Clay, did you ever take her home, to meet my mom, I mean? Wait, don't answer that. I don't have any right to ask you such personal things. This is just so sudden, you know?"

"You have every right, April, honey. And so do you, Virgil. I don't mind talking about this, but I don't want to make you uncomfortable. I know you don't like to talk about dead family members, and I respect that."

"Well, actually, it's not because they are dead, it's more like we just don't mention their names. In my aunt's case, we talked about her quite a bit. We just never said her name. So when you asked me her name, it was a little hard for me to answer even though I'm not exactly a traditional Navajo. But I'd like to talk about her if it's all right with you."

"Sure."

And it was. The three of them ordered another drink after the waitress cleared the dinner dishes. Virgil and Clay exchanged a few memories and laughed about Millie. They sat there till closing time, the red book still on Clay's lap. He held it there with one hand, then the other, never losing touch. After fifteen minutes or so, Virgil pushed back his chair and said, "Clay, that book is not really mine. It belonged to my aunt Mildred. Now it's yours. I think she would have wanted you to have it."

"Yes, she did. She told me about it a long time ago. In fact, she was bringing the book on the day that, well, ah, never mind." Fighting the tears by changing the subject, Clay asked, "You say you got it from your great-uncle, right? Did he say whether there was anything else? She was bringing the book to me, along with something else, a letter, a personal letter. Would you uncle have that?"

"No, I don't think so. He just talked about the book and let me go to his house, outside Window Rock. That's where he gave it to me. What was in the letter?"

"I don't know. I never got it. It's been so long now, eleven years. I asked the police for the letter, but they did not have it. I just never knew it would take eleven years for me to find the book. I'm glad to have it. Thank you, Virgil, this is a big day for me. Good night to you both."

As they walked to their rooms, April hugged Virgil. "I love you, you know. Just as much as your aunt loved my uncle. This is pretty incredible."

"Yeah, it's 'the Navajo way.' Live in harmony, you know."

~~~

The next morning, they met in the hotel coffee shop. Clay had the book; and April, as usual, had toast. Clay, adopting an artificial businesslike tone, began, "Well, we need to talk about content and voice before we can work on a book proposal. The first query letter, the one-page tagline, and bullet list has to be striking but not glossy. If an agent likes the concept of the book and sees good writing in the sample, we might be asked for a more formal book proposal. To do that, we need to work a few things out. Virgil, let me follow up on something you said last night. Why do you think the Indian rights movement is *really* dead? From your perspective, is there real peace on the reservation now that we've hit the new millennium?"

Virgil felt relieved that the first topic of the morning was business, not family. "I didn't say that exactly. I meant that the movement the warriors in AIM thought they started was dead. That was a militant movement. All they did was take over buildings and hold somebody hostage to make a point. But before they did that, the college students from UCLA took over Alcatraz. Then the lawyers, the politicians, and the press came in, and it was all over in both places. That's what happened in Wounded Knee and Gallup. Now we have our own lawyers, our own politicians, and with your boss's help, our own press. We can tell the story and beat the drum without firing a shot. That will work. The first way, AIM's way, didn't."

"All right, I see that. Do you both think that the road from Wounded Knee really ran *straight* to Gallup?"

"Well, first off, I don't live there," Virgil offered, "although I could. It's really a neat place. A lot has happened in the last thirty years. The irony is that the Gallup mayor, Frank Garcia, started those changes before he was abducted in '73. I live in Window Rock, at least for now, and that's where the movement is now. It's not militant or very high profile. Besides, it's not just us Navajos, you know."

"Right, but there are tens of thousands in more than a hundred tribes who feel the way you do. My question is whether the road ran *straight* there or just fizzled out in South Dakota."

"I believe it ran straight as an arrow, but April can speak for herself. We've had a talk about it."

"Uncle Clay, Virgil is dead-on right. The road is *straight*. What happened in Gallup would not have happened if there had been no takeover in Wounded Knee the day before."

"What about Alcatraz? I agree that Wounded Knee and Gallup are connected, and that the latter would not have happened without the former. Is that true of Alcatraz as well? Virgil, what do you think?"

Virgil said nothing for a while. Breaking what was becoming an uncomfortable silence, he finally began, "I think the road is pretty straight between Wounded Knee and Gallup, but it's more like a trail in the woods when you add Alcatraz to the mix. The trail from Alcatraz to Wounded Knee is faint in places, and there are some rocks and cliffs that make it difficult to track. But the Indian rights movement got stronger, and the trail became clearer with each landing, takeover, and protest. It was not a mature, well-worn trail because mostly young people were on it. Wounded Knee seemed like an accumulation of a lot of grief and a lot of misery. I don't know as much about Alcatraz."

"I can tell you both more than you'd ever want to know about Alcatraz. I got it straight from Millie. Virgil, tell me if you don't want me to use her name. I think of her by name, so I might slip every once in a while." *I loved all of her, her name included. Why did I waste it? I could have said her name every day, instead, I just wrote it on an envelope.*

"No, Clay, it's all right. We're off the Rez, and no one is here from my clan. What did she tell you about Alcatraz?"

April watched the two and took mental note of the fact that Clay said "Millie" and Virgil said "she." They traded small facts and larger opinions. When she saw a lull in the exchange, she took the occasion to butt in, "Well, guys, I know some of it. I read a little in the library. As I recall, it was mostly UCLA students who lived off the Rez in Los Angeles. They were the first to seize Alcatraz. I got interested in that because Casuse and Nakaidinae, who was also from Los Angeles, were college students and they seized the mayor in Gallup. So it seemed to me that there were some connections there too. Maybe you're right, Virg, it's more like a trail than a road."

"Yes," Clay responded. "But what about later? Were they truly dependent actions? Are you saying that there was an unspoken conspiracy that organized all three takeovers?"

Before Virgil could answer, April chimed in, "No, I think, or at least I *feel*"—April paused and smiled at Virgil—"that the men at Wounded Knee were different and may not have even talked to the men in Gallup in that two- or three-day period when both were getting started. The students, and other activists in San Francisco may never have talked to anyone at either Gallup or Wounded Knee. But even if all three were planned and executed separately, they were definitely connected. Virgil can explain it better. It's really his concept in the first place. He calls it echoes."

Virgil repeated, almost word for word, his thesis about the connections among all three Indian actions. He pointed out the unequivocal connections printed in Millie's book and its authenticity. They all agreed that original authenticity was rare in a documentary. In the end, they reached the same result. *Just like Millie would have wanted us to.*

Clay summed it up for everyone, "All right, I'm persuaded. It is logically inescapable that Casuse was driven on March 1 by something big, bigger than his problem with the Gallup police or its mayor. It makes sense that he acted then because he felt he had to, or he'll lose momentum. Sometimes that kind of compulsion is impossible to resist. Let's move on to the content now that we have the theme in place. I've got some ideas, of course, but let's hear yours first."

"Uncle Clay, I've been thinking about that. Do you remember the letter that I sent to you from the *Gallup Independent*? It was from someone, an Indian girl I think, who was there when the shoot-out occurred. She posed some questions to the people of Gallup in the form of a letter to the editor. My thought was that maybe we ought to think about answering her questions. It's a little late, I know, but they were good questions. I brought them with me. Do you want to see them?"

"Great idea. But what if we use them not as questions per se but as major issues to cover. What's she asking?"

"Well, she wrote a pretty long letter and asked lots of questions. I was struck by the fact that while she was definitely on the Indian side of the debate, she asked some basic questions. I have the copy with me and a list of the questions that I thought we might cover, or answer as it were, in the book."

"Let's start with your list, April. Virgil, have you seen this?"

"Yes, but not for a while. I agree it's a good place to start."

April cleared her throat and said, "Her main point was that Casuse deserved more 'talk and less shooting.' I think we have to answer that. Was there enough talk? Would more have prevented his death? Next, she thought that when the mayor came out the door in the front, Casuse walked to the front right after him. Did that happen? I'm not sure."

Clay said abruptly, "April, those are both interesting questions but not ones that we can or should answer in the book. Our focus needs to be on the larger view. We will have to be careful not to let small details get in the way of the national connection between Alcatraz, Wounded Knee, and Gallup. Actually, there are scores of places where warriors fought the police over issues of respect and local governance."

Virgil smiled at April as he ticked off the hard evidence. "We have the recorded interview between Nakaidinae and Garcia. We have Calvin Horn's books and files. We have Nakaidinae's prison file and his interview with the warden. We have the coroner's report and the FBI lab results. So we know a great deal now that no one in Gallup knew that day. In fact, we know a great deal more now than any single person in Gallup could know, even now. That includes the fifty or so interviews we conducted in the last few months."

"No doubt on that. Are we all in agreement?"

Heads nodded, and April took a sip of water and continued. "Next, we have to deal with the really big question, which I think is really the hook for the book. Is that an alliteration, Uncle Clay? Don't answer. Why did this incident occur in the first place? This lady wrote her letter in good faith and asked the newspaper to treat her questions, all of them actually, with respect. We ought to do that. We ought to respectfully answer the big question of why this occurred at all."

Clay sipped his coffee and said, "The grand jury transcripts in Gallup spell out a motive based on statewide politics. But the mayor's own private view brings in local politics. Then you have the theme that the media covered very casually. Red Power. The media never made the connection to Wounded Knee, but that is reporting as opposed to journalism. Come to think of it, that's good for us. One of them would have written the book. Alternatively, you could argue that Casuse was dismayed over his own personal problems with the cops and with alcohol. The fact of the matter is that there is a fair amount of support for each of those explanations for why this happened."

Which one would have appealed to Millie?

April said, "Uncle Clay, they can't all be right, can they?"

"Let me answer it this way. The larger truth has to be that the abduction in Gallup was actually caused—that is, precipitated—by what happened in Wounded Knee. Wounded Knee was made possible by what happened in Alcatraz. Then we have to present the more focused and local view that what happened in Gallup was molded by local politics. So what is our story here? Is it the larger view or the local view? I suspect that the people of Gallup would agree that local political issues account for *who* was abducted. But those local facts do not explain the actual *day* of the abduction. Those local facts don't square with what happened four years before in Alcatraz or two days before in Wounded Knee."

Virgil studied Clay and said, "Clay, you said at the very beginning that this was war and that it was fought by warriors. There are always underlying causes, which are usually followed by immediate causes. It's the immediate cause that is giving us trouble here."

April said, "Uncle Clay, there is a middle ground. We can describe truthfully what happened locally in each of the three cities and still make the connection between them, like Virgil has outlined. It's like a powder keg in each place, but nothing happens until the first one blows. Virgil used a *trail* as a metaphor because *road* did not seem to work. But instead of a trail or a road between the three cities, maybe what we have is a fuse, a really *long* fuse. Different people set the match to the fuse at three different times, but I think Virgil is right. This is a cause-and-effect thing. The fire in one lit the fuse in the other and so on, you know?"

Yes, that's how Millie would have put it. The effect of one touch can cause someone to step up or back off. Life is caused by how and when we love. And the consequence of life is sometimes death. She would have argued the larger view. The echoes. That's it exactly! The echoes between Alcatraz, Wounded Knee, and Gallup are a lot like the connections among the three of us. We started out from different points, but we are all holding the same fuse now.

CHAPTER TWENTY-ONE

"Don't Whistle Too Loud—You Will Call Up the Wind"

Clay closeted himself for three days, virtually chained to his word processor, hiding from the phone and the world. Now he had it. *It* being the nearly famous kind of two-page memo that Warren Suttcliff claimed were the only ones he'd read. He distrusted letters because they were wasteful and rarely to the point. He didn't like faxes because they were flimsy (at least they used to be). He didn't like e-mail because the writer could disguise length by making the reader scroll down. Warren was a man who knew what he liked; he liked two-page memos. Not two pages or less. He discarded one-and-one-half-page memos just as capriciously as he did three-page ones. So Clay digested, cut, bulletined, bled over his thesaurus, and composed *the* memo that would either get his book published by his employer or relegate it to the slush piles in New York City.

Is this going to kill the book or save it? Dying honorably was something warriors understood. For some of them, it was preferable to life in camp.

Clay gave Warren an economic business plan for the book. He reminded him that the *American Warrior* extensively covered the warriors who made America proud for thirty years. He appealed to Warren's sense of fairness by telling him that the true story of America's last conflict with its first people is driven by death and political tragedy. He theorized that the landing at Alcatraz in 1969 led to the siege of Wounded Knee in 1973 and the abduction of the mayor in Gallup, New Mexico, where one young man died and another lost his way. What began at Alcatraz led inexorably and inevitably to all that followed. He posited that the book would examine the connections among the people and events that made up the Red Power movement in its militancy and its diplomacy. Clay insisted that the leading thematic issue was the Gallup story, the third national story about the emerging Red Power movement. His academic focus would explore important social issues. When will Americans recognize the importance of deep-seated, intangible roots to the soil and the undeniable need to protect and preserve what we have while we can? When will Americans recognize the independence and interdependence of those who were here first and who are still waiting for our respect? When will Americans understand the true value of a diverse nation with differences in religion, language, culture, and perspective? When will those who live on Indian reservations and those who regulate them come together in an understanding of nature, capitalism, and the democratic principles both cultures crave but often abuse?

Warren's answer to Clay's two-pager was, in a word, curt. He told Clay that his idea for a book was not suitable for today's audience and that the decision to close the Spokane office would be communicated in person. Apparently, Warren expected Clay to take the job offer he hinted at in their last telephone conversation. Clay left the following message on Warren's back-line voice mail the next day.

"Hey, Warren, Clay here. It's early in the morning, but this won't keep. It's too late for me, us, and what we've stood for. Your business is yours, and you can keep it, thank you very much. I'll attend to the details of the shutdown and the windup. Look me up sometime. I'll be somewhere west of you and upwind."

~ ~ ~

"April, it's Clay. You're still up. Sorry to call so late, but I figured you'd want to know. God knows you're entitled. I don't quite know how to tell you this but . . ."

"Uncle Clay, I understand, I really do. I guess you are trying to tell me that those bastards in Denver pulled the plug on us. But why? Don't they get it? You're not just another editor of some dot-gone zine that was out of favor before it even got started, you . . ."

"Yeah, yeah. At least the dot-gones, as you call them, were relevant sometime in the last ten years. Corporate thinks that the *American Warrior* actually died a long time ago but has been on life support for a decade or two. So they pulled the plug to stop the financial hemorrhage. I gave them the economic argument that the book would make up the dollar loss of the magazine. I even gave them the natural progression argument. Nothing worked. No more magazine, and no new book. That's life at the corporate level."

"I'm so sorry, Uncle Clay, I know you wanted this one last chance to save something really worth saving. Somehow, we have to find a way to save your idea. You're just not going to give up, are you? What are you gonna do?"

"Well, I'm damn sure not going to move to Denver and edit the *EcoWarrior*, whatever it is. Not that they actually came out and offered me the job, you know. But Warren was working up to it when I cut him short and pissed him off in the process."

"What exactly is the *EcoWarrior*? Catchy name, but I'm not sure of the metaphor."

"I'm not sure either, but my guess is it's something *edgy*, as the bean counter would put it, something designed to sell first, inform a little, and forget about motives or policy issues."

"Well, I assume the *eco* in the name is short for *ecology*. Who exactly do they expect the magazine to appeal to if that is the case?"

"Beats me. I never asked. But what I hear from others still at corporate HQ, they think that the ecology movement and the environmental lobby are like two one-dollar bills, hard to tell apart unless you look closely at the numbers. Actually, it's the kids of the folks who were protested in the 1970s, including the Indian rights movement. Now that I think about it, you and Virgil are probably the very people they think will buy the damn thing or subscribe or hit or whatever you do with the digital version of a magazine, you know, the newly famous *zine*."

"Doesn't sound like my kind of reading. But maybe Virg will be interested. He's really come alive with our research. I'm thinking he's growing into the big picture, at least one bigger than what you see in Window Rock, Arizona."

"So does that mean you no longer have a strong reason to stay in Gallup? Are you gonna take the boy with you when you move on?"

"He's no boy, Uncle Clay. He's his own man in every way. I mean, he was raised off the reservation with Navajo as his first language, but he didn't use it much in Glendale and even less at ASU. Now just when he's comfortable with the language and the simplicity of life on the reservation, we—you and me—got him all stirred up about the big picture."

"What'd I do? You got him into the research, not me?"

"Yeah, but you were the inspiration for finding the long-lost American warrior, the one that fought and died back in the seventies while my Virgil was just a toddler waddling around the reservation. Then he went to Glendale, became a regular sort-of teenager, and earned a college degree. Now he's wondering where he belongs. I mean, he's always known *who* he was, now he's looking inward at *where* he belongs. So it's you every bit as much as me."

"What are you going to do?" *Don't walk away easily, girl, that's what I did with Millie.*

"Well, I don't know. It depends on Virgil in one way, but not entirely. Gallup is just not for me in the long run. I am glad I came, but I am ready for new country."

"Here's an idea, come on up here. The Pacific Northwest is short on Irish women who like books. And bring Virgil, I like being around him. He reminds me of her."

"Maybe I will. But I have to talk to Virg. I presume you want me to tell him about the big decision, or do you want to call him?"

"No, I'd actually rather you did it. I know he will take it fine, but he ought to get bad news from someone who loves him."

"I'll do it. And since you asked, I do love him. I'm not sure what to do about it, but I do. Thanks for asking."

"I didn't ask."

"Sure you did."

As April undressed for bed, she caressed her blue pendant. This little private ritual, the last thing she touched every night, seemed uncomfortably out of place tonight. Usually she put the pendant on the top of her dresser. Tonight, she kept it on and cupped it tightly in bed until she fell asleep, her head swirling with the changes going on about her. Maybe Uncle Clay was right when she was thirteen. Maybe if she held it tight, things would change *her* way.

April waited until morning to call but shouldn't have. Virgil banged on the kitchen window before six. That meant he'd left Window Rock before five. She let him in, yawned at the darkness outside, and gave him the perfunctory hug that preceded coffee on a cold winter morning. "What brings you in from the Rez so early in the winter, Chief?"

"Nothing much. I have a meeting at one of the travel agencies to work out some new arrangements for Monument Valley tours, so I thought I'd stop by. Hear from Clay?"

"Yeah, as you suspected, it's bad. They canned us in Denver. No book, no magazine, no *mas* of anything."

April started the coffee, and they made small talk for a few minutes while the drip dripped. Then Virgil resumed the conversation, "No *mas*? You mean they just killed the regular magazine along with Clay's book project?"

"Yep, but they are thinking of a replacement magazine called the *EcoWarrior* or something like that. Sounds more like an excuse to do what they want than a new *real* magazine."

"How much do you know about it? No, before you tell me that, how is Clay? Hasn't he been there like forever?"

"Pretty much, at least as long as I've known him. God, this is going to be hard on him. He loves his home and the Pacific Northwest. He loved your aunt, and he lost her. Now he loves his book, or at least the idea of the book. He can't move to Denver, and he can't seriously consider being an editor on this new magazine even if they do offer it to him."

"April, where does this leave you?"

"Still here, babe, Gallup doesn't change that quickly, why should I? My job is boring, so my second reason for moving here from sunny Tempe is shot, and . . ."

Virgil got up, started for the stove to refill his coffee, and then stopped. "April, we need to talk about something, it's kinda serious."

"What's *kinda* mean? Oh god, Virg, you aren't sick, are you? I hate that look on your face, what is it?"

"I'm okay, not sick, but I want to make a change, and I want you to give it real serious consideration. I mean, for both of us, not just me. I have been looking around for another job, and I think I've found one and . . ."

"Another job? You mean one with the tribe, another slot, or are you talking another job like *somewhere else*?"

"Yeah, somewhere else. I mean it would still be on the Rez, but not in Window Rock, and it would mean some travel because it's a little more remote so . . ."

April held up her hand and said, "Wait a minute, hold the phone here, let's slow down. What if the book had been approved, and we were starting to outline it right now. Are you saying that this new job would have taken you out of the project or what? I mean, you only learned a few minutes ago that the *American Warrior* was history. What's going on here?"

"It's all connected actually. See, the project, and the research, and all the talk about the end of an era and, well, you know, my aunt and Clay actually knowing one another and all. Well, it's just everything we learned. It got me thinking about my life and all, and yours too, of course . . ."

"Of course? Am I an afterthought?"

"April, don't make this hard. I'm just trying to tell you all of it, but it's getting all jumbled up, and you keep interrupting. So let me finish, please. I researched what Casuse did here and what Gallup was like then, and I see the connections. Then I learned that my aunt was really in it, really in the Red Power movement, and that Clay had a thing for her before I was even born. That's another connection. But the real connection, at least in a temporal way, is that our research is connected to what I want to do now. They wanted a better Gallup, both of them, Casuse and Garcia. But they were at odds. There was so much that they didn't know about one another. So I started thinking, what am I doing to inform my people *and* the people they deal with every day? What am I doing to make those connections real? You know, people like you and Clay and the current mayor here in Gallup, Johnny Pena—he's a real good guy and is respected on the Rez. That got me thinking that promoting tourism on the Rez is pretty limiting. It doesn't do what any of the young men that we researched wanted to do, however poorly they went about it. What they were after was something that would make life better and give Indians and everyone else renewed respect even if they didn't put it that way, you see?"

"I guess so, but what does that mean in real terms for you, Virgil?"

"It means that I made some calls to an outfit in Denver and talked to them about maybe working with them."

"Denver? You mean move there? I thought you just said something about moving somewhere *remote*. Denver is the biggest thing in five hundred miles, except maybe for Phoenix."

"Well, the outfit is up there, Boulder, actually. But I would be moving to the Four Corners region, at least at first, maybe Mexican Hat or Bluff or maybe Cortez. Cortez is not, not quite so remote."

"What's the outfit? I mean, is it a company or what?"

"Actually, it's a nonprofit foundation. It's been around for a while. They are dedicated to Native American rights. They seem like something that Casuse might have really gotten into except that he strayed into militancy rather than diplomacy."

"So have they actually offered you a job?"

"No, not exactly, but we talked three times on the phone, and I'm gonna go up there and talk to them in person next week and . . ."

"At the risk of interrupting again, Virg, dear, what is my role in all of this, and what are you asking them to do?"

"April, I'm thinking about becoming a staff member and policy researcher. They provide legal and technical assistance to lots of different tribes, companies, and even individuals. And as for you, well, I was hoping that you'd think about coming with me. I know you don't want to live on the Rez, but what if I was assigned to Cortez or somewhere like that. It's like Gallup, sort of, only it's in Colorado, but there are some things in common."

"Virg, I came here first to be with you and second to pay my own way in life. Are both done? I hate my job, and now I am getting a funny feeling about you. Are you leaving me? Is that what you are telling me?"

"No, I'm telling you I want you to come with me, but I don't know where yet. Maybe Cortez, maybe Mexican Hat or Bluff. Those three places we talked about on the phone, that is, I talked to the guy in Boulder about those three places."

"If you did this, would you be able to live in Boulder or Denver? Why does it have to be the Four Corners region? I'm not sure what you're telling me."

"This nonprofit is based in Boulder, Colorado, because the University of Colorado supports it. They get office space, clerical help, student interns, and some funding. But the foundation itself has projects in several places across the nation. They provide lawyers, technical people, social workers, assistance, and other stuff, but it's all dedicated to preserving tribal existence and promoting human rights for everyone involved."

"Who's involved? What do you mean?"

"They tell me it means Indians and others who are living either on or off reservations but are somehow connected to tribes. Actually, I think they are primarily about legal issues and Indian civil rights. That's how I found them. I was looking into Clay's question, you know, whatever happened to the American warrior? Well, maybe all those warriors had kids, and their kids now work for nonprofit organizations like this one, and they do research and work to make things better for Indians on and off the reservations, including mine. Anyhow, I asked, what about the Navajos? And they said they are doing some interesting work in the Four Corners region. Would I be interested in coming up to Boulder and finding out more about them and what they are doing. At the same time, we could talk about jobs and stuff and maybe moving. But nothing's really settled. I am just thinking about it, that's all."

"Virgil, that's exciting. I mean, maybe you're right. Maybe this is where all the warriors went, at least their progeny. But is this entirely made up of Indians? What would they think about you dragging along some Irish waif fresh out of college?"

"Actually, we didn't talk much about me or my situation, except to say that I was thinking about changes in my life and about what their work was and, you know."

"Yeah, I know your *situation*. But you didn't mention that I was part of the *situation*, did you?"

"No, like I said, we never got that far. I just wanted some preliminary info so I could talk it over with you."

April took a deep breath, reached for Virgil's hand, and said, "Virgil, we're both young, we both have ideals and dreams to pursue. We love each other, but I can tell you I wouldn't love living on the reservation. From what little I know about the Four Corners region, it's beautiful, but very, very remote. Isn't that a fair description? I mean, let's take it one step further. I am not going to spend my life as clerical person in a two-bit publishing company. What if I found a job somewhere, maybe on some other continent? Would you go with me? I'm not asking, but it's something we need to talk about, don't you think?"

"Yes, we do, of course. Maybe we can do something together. I mean, maybe you could find work that fits in with what is happening politically on Indian reservations. Is that possible? What really do you think you will do if you quit Red Rock Publishing?"

"Hell if I know. My undergraduate degree is pretty useless unless I want to be a writer or an editor or work in a real publishing company. Like you, I have become interested in how others live, but I cannot see living on or near a reservation."

"I guess I knew you would react this way to something as remote as the Four Corners region. But remember what I told you about 'the Navajo way' and how important it was to my ancestors to treat the land with respect? My people were living on the land and giving it the kind of respect that seems to be forgotten today. The traditional Navajo family is something we study nowadays, but there are not too many of them left. The young kids on the reservation, even those raised in somewhat traditional families, are caught up in the culture that surrounds the reservation. The borders are political, not cultural."

April moved and sat as close as she could to Virgil as though he were about to bolt out the door. "So I repeat, if I can't live in Mexican Hat and you can't live far from the Rez, where are we?"

"I dunno. You will probably find this crazy, but I first started thinking about this last Christmas when one of my cousin's kids told me about a book she got for her Christmas present. It was called *Ma'ii and Cousin Horned Toad*. She read it out loud to me although it's a picture book too. In the book, Ma'ii, a coyote, goes to visit his cousin, Horned Toad. The author of the book, a man named Shonto Begay, is one of our rising stars, but he still lives on the Rez even though he's becoming famous. Anyhow, like all coyotes, Ma'ii is always hungry and has the crazy idea that if he eats his cousin, Horned Toad, he will never be hungry again. And like all coyotes, Ma'ii is very cunning and has lots of ideas and plans to trap and eat his cousin. Only none of them work. Horned Toad is safe, and Ma'ii is still hungry."

"Well, there are no coyotes in Gallup, and it sounds like a wonderful children's book. But what does it have to do with moving or changing your life.?"

"'Cause it got me to thinking. It's a story about the antics of a coyote and how they never have enough to eat and how they survive only by their wits. I remember my grandfather telling lots of coyote stories about how deceitful they were, and that's how they survived in a harsh desert climate. But he said, that was no lesson to be learned by man. Anyway, I think Shonto Begay knows about richness and affluence that seems to be everywhere *but* on the reservation. The coyote overindulges whenever he can because he never has enough. Maybe Mr. Begay is comparing coyotes with American culture today."

"What's the comparison? Maybe I'm a little dense this morning, but I'm not sure I get it."

"Well, you have to think about it, or maybe you need to read these stories or hear coyote folklore from an old man on the Rez, like I did. It's about extremes. Rock music is too loud, but Navajo flutes are too soft, at least for young Indians on the reservation today. American culture demands excess in the way young kids dress, from bra straps showing to baggy pants. I started thinking about indoor plumbing and how it relates to coyotes."

"That I have to hear. How in the world does indoor plumbing relate to coyotes?"

"America brought indoor plumbing to the Rez. Now Indians in many parts of the reservation urinate *inside*. You wouldn't know it, of course, but in our folklore, the coyote introduced that practice to bewitch someone. So it used to be a bad thing, and now, because of indoor plumbing, it's a good thing. So I asked myself the question, what does the study of the coyote on the reservation teach us about how young people behave today, about how they dress and stuff?"

"I'm not sure. Maybe your connection to the coyote is more than just a metaphor. What does all this have to do with moving from tourism on the reservation to moving off the reservation in order to make things better?"

"Well, let me tell you another thing about my grandfather. He never slept past the crack of dawn. He didn't when he was young or when he got old. That's because he was taught by medicine men that supernaturals came from the east through the hogan door at the crack of dawn. They came to bless the house. If my grandfather was awake, then the supernaturals saw him as their child and blessed him too. Those blessings included things like livestock, trade goods, and the knowledge of how to live 'the Navajo way.' Now, people sleep long past the crack of dawn. There are older Navajos who say that's because we are no longer willing to greet the supernaturals at the crack of dawn."

"Virgil, you don't really believe that, do you? I mean, those stories are great fun, and some are based in the reality of the times that they reflected. But that was another culture, and yours is different."

"It is, but there is still something to be said for trying to find 'the Navajo way.' I think that the old teachings may help us find a balance, help us to achieve equilibrium."

"Well, you are right about the connection between us. We are both talking about the problems that young people, who may be from one culture, have with the more traditional views of others, either from their culture or from another. The real point is young people have moved further and further away from teachings once accepted so widely on the reservation. It's due, in part, to the influence of other cultures. So the Shonto Begay story and the wisdom of your grandfather not sleeping past the crack of dawn are not so far-fetched after all."

April was becoming impatient with abstraction. "Virgil, we live in times of great conflict everywhere. Values and things like respect for the land seem more obscure to young people now than they ever were. I think some young people are still idealistic. But it's more of a global thing, you know? We had Students Against Sweatshops at ASU, but the same students go out into the desert and throw beer cans and Big Mac wrappers all over the place. Up here, where the reservation is close and where there are more young Indians, the questions are different but still represent values that seem out of sync with those teachings, and maybe coyote folklore, accepted by older Navajos. So there's hope after all. And don't you forget it. It's the women of the reservation who may reinstitute 'the Navajo way' after all."

CHAPTER TWENTY-TWO

"Don't Try to Count the Stars—You Will Have Too Many Children"

April tried to float instead of just simmering. Her conversation with Virgil, so close on the heels of Clay's phone call, tightened her stomach and made her hands feel numb. She vacillated from fear to anger but gave in to anger. So she called Clay's boss in Denver. While getting the number from Southwest Bell, she struggled to get her motives straight in her own mind. She wanted to shout because of what was happening to Clay but listen because of Virgil's bombshell.

"Warren Suttcliff, please, it's April Ryan calling from Gallup."

After explaining that Gallup was in New Mexico, that Suttcliff likely had no clue what she was calling about, and waiting for almost five minutes while Warren figured out who she was, he answered, "April, nice to talk to you. I've heard about you from Clay, you were a big help in researching some of the issues in Clay's book. I'm impressed, what can I . . ."

"Mr. Suttcliff, you can *try* to explain why you think my uncle Clay deserves to get dumped like an old shoe after thirty or more years of work for you. Do you know he's only fifty-eight and has at least twenty years of editing and giving yet to do in this world? I just can't imagine how . . ."

"Ms. Ryan, forgive the interruption, but maybe we could start again and hold off the accusations for a bit. You may not know it, but your uncle has been my friend for many years. I hope what's happened will not change that, but even it if does, the fact remains that Clay Ramsey is, and always will be, a force in our industry. I only wish it could be with my company. We grew up in the business together."

"Then why won't you publish his book?"

"Because he's an editor, and we are a magazine company. And because the *American Warrior* just isn't viable anymore. We would have shut it down five years ago but for Clay Ramsey's belief in it and his importance to me. And by the way, his importance to the company he helped build. But it can't go on. It just can't. Has he given you the readership figures? Do you know about the negative balance sheet and the long-term trend line of the revenue stream? This is a business even though, for men like Clay, we tend to make more personal adjustments, and we stayed the course for him far longer time than we would for any other employee. I understand your feelings. He sent me a few of your e-mails, and he talked a little about you in the context of his book proposal. I'm truly sorry he can't see the world as it is now, and I wish he had taken the lead in the new venture I wanted him on, but I respect his decision. Now can we talk about something a lot more important to both of us?"

April was silent for a moment, trying to take it all in. Was she being conned, or did this guy actually make some sense? He had not said anything she hadn't already heard from Clay about the business side, but Virgil's bombshell made her feel like listening to anything "more important." "What would that be?" she said, taking in a deep breath.

"It would be the *EcoWarrior*. Actually, that is a working title, not a real decision yet. What did Clay tell you about this? I mean, I just need to know where to start it all, or maybe I should just start from the beginning?"

"Yes, the beginning would be good. But I thought that you turned down Uncle Clay's request for a book mostly because of the economics and your sense of its relevance, I didn't know that the *EcoWarrior*, or whatever it is called, is actually tied into the same decision."

"Actually, like the Indian rights movements your uncle knows so much about, the answer is both intertwined and disjointed. Let me start at the beginning. We know here at the corporate offices in Denver that the Indian rights movement of the sixties and seventies was a powerful force for positive change. But it died, at least the newsworthy stuff died, when the young activists moved on to other issues."

"Well, some of them didn't move on, they got killed or went to prison."

"Yes, they did. And Clay wrote about them and got others to do the same. He wrote about heroes and goats on both sides, and he wrote about warriors in other movements as well. He covered the Nixon years, the Vietnam years, the technology warriors, the Wall Street warriors, and lots of others. But he always favored the underdogs. He rooted for the dog soldiers in the battle, hoping thereby to bring respect and fairness to the American Indian. But he had less and less to write about and was pretty disillusioned with the move toward gambling as a panacea for the financial woes of reservations and tribes all over America."

"Gambling? That's a connection we never made."

"Think about it. The Indians used to fight the whites over bars near the reservation, now they invite whites into *their* bars *on* the reservation. The bars are in the casinos. Actually, Clay himself gave me the idea more than five years ago to start a new venture that would be the natural, evolutionary, successor to the *American Warrior*. Sadly, he got so wrapped up in saving his magazine by writing his book that he forgot what he'd said and couldn't, or wouldn't, see where the future lies, either ideologically or financially."

"So where is the future? For Clay and for what he believes in? I'm curious about what you call this natural evolutionary successor to Clay's magazine."

"Let me clarify a couple things. When you read back issues of the *American Warrior*, you see a great deal of both poetry and common sense. Our writers talked about the beauty of the sunrise, the smell of the rain, and the good rich feel of black earth. Just like it must have been when the buffalo herds trampled it, and the plains Indians followed their track but killed only what they needed for food and clothing. While we wrote about the sad end to the herds and those who followed them, we also wrote about the importance of money and power both in the government and in the tribes that were being managed and governed, often unwisely, but maybe with good intentions. The *American Warrior* was, for a long time, the leader in both informing those who cared and irritating those who didn't. But like most good deeds, we weren't left unpunished. As the Indian rights movement shifted from militancy to the courts and as Vietnam and Watergate shifted the country from public respect to private gain, something else shifted—something a few noticed, but many ignored."

"What was that?"

"The land, the air, the water, the rich black earth I was talking about—all of it."

"Shifted? How?"

"Perhaps shifted is not descriptive enough. You see, men like your uncle—and others here at corporate headquarters, hated though we may be—still believe, like the plains Indians, that our nation became great *because* of its land. We still believe in the incredible beauty and fragility of it. However, in growing up, in expanding, in acquiring wealth and position, too many forgot about the land, the water, and the air. The buffalo are gone, but some think they are coming back. Have you been to a high-end restaurant lately and ordered buffalo steak?"

"Nope, I'm against killing animals for food or sport, and I'm not noted for hanging around with those who are."

"Well, you will fit in fine with most of our staff. Come to Denver. I'll take you to Sullivan's Sushi House, and you can order for both of us."

"I guess I see where you are going, but why me? What do I have to do with anything?"

"April, I never got a chance to talk this over with Clay, but I hope you will give at least a little thought to joining us. I know about your education and some of your interests, and somewhere along the line, I got the impression that maybe Gallup is not the city of your choice. Let me be a little more specific. We need young, educated, interesting, and interested people to help us. We need an associate editor to get this new magazine started. We spent years developing a readership of people interested in indigenous people and their struggle to save the land. That readership dwindled. But now we think there is another readership out there with some of the same interest, but maybe with a different focus. The warriors of the sixties and seventies were fighting for their tribes and their lands. They fought the white man because he built bars too close to their land and enticed many of them off their land onto his with the lure of money, jobs, and a reward that had no respect. Now that seems to be changing. The new leaders on tribal lands are building casinos and enticing whites to the reservation based on some of the same lures—money, rewards, and liquor. Only this time, it's *on* the reservation, not just on the border. And tribal government, or so some think, is controlling it."

"What do you mean by 'so some think,' I'm not sure what you're saying."

"You've hit on it actually. The most important question is what is the *impact* of all this? Who's in charge? Who's in control? Is it the tribes and their governments or the slot machine vendors, the land developers, and the casino managers? You're an educated young woman and a writer. Doesn't this fit in with what you already doing? April, doesn't this fit in with what's happening in your life and ours?"

"To be honest, I don't know. A lot has happened in the last few days. Would it be all right if I give it some thought and call you back?"

"Sure, take your time, but remember that time—like land, air, and water—is worth protecting. Don't take too much of it. Call me when you're ready to come up to Denver."

April spent the rest of the day mulling and stewing. She called Clay, he was out. She called Virgil, but he was on his way to Mexican Hat. She called her mother. She was at lunch. So she dug out two academic trade journals on anthropological ecology that had been sent to Red Rock Publishing. As she read, she thought about Alcatraz, Wounded Knee, Gallup, Mexican Hat, and Denver.

Cultural change and cultural complexity were things she'd studied but didn't see up close until Clay's book project. What happened in the last two hundred years to Indians and the land they originally owned here in the West is an encyclopedia cataloging everything good and bad about progress. Greed is bad; ambition is not. Stubbornness is not good, but we praise steadfastness. Air seems infinite but can become unbreathable. Water can be brought to the surface by drilling, which in turn drains the very aquifer that protects it from evaporation. Cities can be built and lakes expanded with dams that serve upstream interests at the expense of downstream habitat. There needs to be equilibrium.

The ancient Greeks believed in the maxim "Nothing in excess." So did the Navajos of old. But our society is very much in a hurry, and wealth seems just a job away. We have Greek immigrants, indigenous Navajos, and impetuous multiracial and multicultural youth. Eighty-five percent of all the people in America live in urban settings. But land—that is, raw land—is rural. There is an inherent conflict between youth, particularly urban youth, and traditional people living in the country, on and off Indian reservations.

Everyone in the city is in a hurry. We're in a hurry to grow up, a hurry to acquire, a hurry to move; but we never seem to have enough time. Culture, like land, needs time. Like land, culture needs caring and renewal. The more April thought, the more she felt. She felt a connection in every bone in her body to the land. Whether standing, kneeling, sitting, or lying on it, she felt alive and part of it. This was something she'd suppressed in a college dorm but rediscovered in Gallup with Virgil on picnics, long walks, and just sitting looking up at the night sky at eight thousand feet of elevation. Gallup was good, but she felt a stirring to go to Denver even if it was another big city. Maybe Uncle Clay would eventually show up. Maybe Virgil can visit often. *Please, God, let him visit* often.

For April, the future was the past, and she wanted those who would read the *Eco Warrior* to understand that. For her, the future was as blue, as deep, and as complicated as her little glass pendant; and she clasped it as tightly as she could.

Early the next morning, April called Warren Suttcliff back. "Mr. Suttcliff, I don't know whether this is right or not. But your idea seems appealing. Actually, it's more appealing today than two days ago. Time, as you said, is worth protecting. My first call was to chew on you, but now I'm thinking about chewing on the *Eco Warrior*. When can I come up?"

Suttcliff said, "Wonderful, I'll buy the dinner and the plane ticket."

She hung up and thought about the first article that she would propose for the *Eco Warrior*. She'd get Clay to write it and Virgil to talk it through. It would be a short travelogue about the road running from Alcatraz to Wounded Knee through Gallup and then turning north to Denver.

~ ~ ~

Clay spent the morning clearing out the office and boxing up thirty years of a cluttered but satisfying life. He welcomed Jimmy, the office delivery boy, when he knocked on the doorjamb and stuck his head in the office. Jimmy was a kid—barely sixteen, but in need of a summer job—and Clay had always been a sucker for kids needing jobs.

"Mr. Ramsey, here's a special delivery for you. Wow, they paid for insurance. It's special delivery. They even made Barbara sign for it at the front desk, and she told me to get to you right away. Is she right, are you leaving the company, Mr. Ramsey?"

"Yes, she's right. Let's see what somebody thinks is important enough to insure."

Clay took the little cardboard box, pulled out the little bone-handled pocketknife that he'd carried since his junior year in high school, and started to slit the box open. Only then did he take notice of the return address—Martha Bahe, P.O. Box 2039, Glendale, Arizona. *This must be from Virgil's mother*, he thought. Opening the box while standing on the front side of his desk, his first look at the contents made him shiver a little. So he moved around to his desk chair and sat down, still holding the box. It held a single-page letter and a blue velveteen-wrapped pouch bound with old rawhide strings. As he read the first few lines, his mouth went dry, and he felt his palms go sweaty.

Dear Mr. Ramsey,

You don't know me, but I'm Virgil's mother. He's told me a lot about you, but I already knew you—I just never knew your last name or where you were. I know you because I am Millie's sister; and I know you through Millie's eyes, her heart, and something precious to both of us. Please read what I have to say before you open the velvet pouch; that is what Millie would have wanted.

I think she was on the way to see you when she died. The officials in Montana gave me all her things, including the book that Virgil gave you and a letter with your first name on it. That's all—just a first name. She had mentioned your name before, but nothing else about you. She loved you, but there was someone more important in her life—you will understand when you read the letter. I would have given this letter to you years ago, but I did not know your last name or how to find you. I'm sorry about that.

When I first got this letter, eleven years ago, I only read the first few lines, then I put it back in the envelope—I was too sad. No one has seen it since; and no one knows about it except you, me, and my sister.

My number is on the box. I know you will call when you read the letter. We can be friends. And we share something precious—you will see in the letter.

Sincerely yours,
Martha Clark Bahe

Clay felt nauseous, and his left calf began to twitch as he tried to center his mind on this moment and avoid the drift to that day, eleven years ago, when he expected to get this letter. Opening the rawhide strings and unfolding the old worn velveteen cloth with hands that were suddenly wooden, he found a beige-colored envelope with her first name in the upper left corner and his in the center. Age had turned beige to sepia, but the writing was gut-wrenchingly familiar. Just two words in her somewhat childish cursive style—her first name in the upper left corner and his in the center, slightly larger. They were written in blue pencil as was the line drawn diagonally across the envelope, connecting her name to his with little blue arrow points drawn into the line. She'd been doing that for years, connecting her name to his with her trademark blue pencil line and the little pointing arrows from her to him. He'd asked her about the symbolism many times, but she ducked each time, saying only that someday he'd see it—like a secret revealed in a Navajo painting. "We are connected," she'd say.

The letter. The secret. My god, what was it that I almost learned the day she died? Something that Millie knew long before that. Shaking his head and reaching for his handkerchief, he lifted the flap and pulled out five half-folded pages of what turned out to be the most painful and pleasurable experience in his life. Pain, they say, adds rest onto pleasure.

He read the first few sentences as though he were biting an apple all the way to the core. Then he slowed down and began to read one sentence at a time. By the time he reached the third paragraph, he was down to one word at a time, parsing the information, the pain, the knowledge, and the secrets into his eager but still unreceptive brain. He spread the pages out on his desk, looked at them individually and collectively, and tried to sort them as though their indelible messages might be clearer in a different order. But try as he might, the only way to clarity was repetition. It took many readings to grasp the whole of it.

Clay thought a day later when he'd recovered from the initial shock and started to think about the new life Millie had just given him. He now knew that pain and pleasure, like light and darkness, succeed each other. The pain he'd felt eleven years ago when the deputy sheriff from Montana called was gone, replaced by the pleasure of her words. *We have a son. His name is Blue, he's thirteen now.*

The apology she offered in the letter had been necessary, for both of them, eleven years ago. *I am profoundly sorry. I never wanted to hurt you or even to keep this terrible but still wonderful secret.* But that no longer mattered now. The secret was so astounding, so fulfilling that its prisoner, profound pain, was unbounded by the letter itself, like the freed rawhide strings lying on his desk. He felt agony, the kind of bone-chilling agony that comes from being deceived; but he needed no recrimination, no payback. He only needed Blue, his son.

As soon as he said it in the dark to himself, his rational brain rebelled. *Yes, but does Blue need you?* Yes, his heart answered; and he searched the letter for the fifth, or was it the tenth time—there it was—"I cannot redeem myself, but I offer each of you a precious gift. I want you to have each other." *Blue and me!*

Millie's letter, beyond her apology and her explanation of the unexplainable, spoke of her culture where children are raised by their mothers and their aunts who "see little difference in their children." She said she wanted to tell Blue, but "not until I've told you." Clay worked those words back and forth in his mind, grinding his teeth and making his neck ache. "Learning about you will be more difficult for him because he has been raised to believe in the power of living in harmony with the earth." *But now he's twenty-two, and God knows what he thinks—not to mention where he is thinking, living, eating, what. My god, I want to train and nurture my soon in Irish ways too, she said he was an Irish-Navajo lad, and he is! His Navajo mother and his Irish father both failed him although neither thought they were. I failed him by my inability to commit to his mother's way, and she by not seeing that my way, the Irish way, could raise children in the way they should go, which is to go in the way they would have their children go. Is it too late?*

Millie's letter said Clay would find Blue, at age thirteen, to be "a young man who walks quietly, sits comfortably, and can be trusted. He is ready to learn the rest of life's story." *But damn it all to hell, is it too late? How many hopes were crushed by Millie's death, how many fears were thrust on him by his father's absence? How many ardent wishes and anxious apprehensions were twisted into the threads that connected Millie to Blue at age thirteen, but kept me a secret, even now, at age twenty-two?*

At the end of it, long after dark and still in his office, with unpacked boxes still staring at him, and after fondling the little velveteen pouch and its precious cargo, he felt overwhelmed. Clay was as befuddled and as exhilarated as a man could ever be. The book, his magazine, his former life, and his loss of Millie—all paled in his mind and oozed out of his heart. His mind could not take hold of the present and could not rest in it, even for a moment. His whole being rushed with irresistible force toward a future as blind, as secret, and as inviting as the ocean or the mountains. In the deepest ocean or the tallest mountain, Clay could see only one color—blue. And it was Blue that would save him.

With that, he dialed Martha Clark Bahe's number and asked to speak to his son.

~ ~ ~

ACKNOWLEDGEMENTS

It took five years to research, investigate, interview, locate documents, cull the gossip from the grist, and create the outer story—the novel you just read. The inner story—what happened in Gallup on March 1, 1973—became a self-centered drive to peel away the facts, one person and one idea at a time. I was already aware from writing *The Gallup 14* that Gallup was an enigma—a small town much loved by those who live there but with a bad rap, not entirely underserved, in other places. Gallup seemed to attract violence, even when its political and social goals were admirable. I hoped to find the literal truth as well as the emotional truth about what really happened that day. A truth that would blossom and bathe my hometown, warts and all, in the soft hazes of time well spent.

The outer story, why Gallup became one of AIM's last battlegrounds, was much harder to unearth. How two good men, Frank Garcia and Larry Casuse, came to a flash point that neither could have imagined before March 1, 1973, is as much a matter of opinion as it is of history.

The inner story was exceptionally well documented, but revealed little beyond the obvious. Abducting the mayor, trying to kill him but failing, and then marching him down the street to an inevitable dead end at Stearns Sporting Goods was an exercise in utter futility. It was so poorly planned and so ridiculously executed that no one can explain why more bespectacled young men didn't die that day. The outer story needed invented characters whose personal conflicts mirrored those historical characters that populate the inner story. I found all the invented characters unknowingly blending into the scores of real Gallup citizens, who bore eyewitness to the life-and-death struggle inside Stearns's store. While none of them knew it, they were the fiction models for Clay Ramsey, Millie Clark, Virgil Bahe, and April Wade. You will never know how much you told me about a town we all loved.

I could not have written this book without Frankie's unfailing good humor, generous offerings of time, records, and insight. We often disagreed about why these events befell him and occasionally debated the significance of outside influences on his abduction, shooting, and loss of political favor in Gallup. But his love for the town, the Navajo reservation that he grew up on, and the people who lived in both always came through and always uplifted my story. He was never bitter and always mindful of opposing views. As a unique observer of what made Gallup great as well as what made it unsavory, at least in a political sense, he passed the test of time as well as high public service.

Each day and each year spent wading through dusty records and fading memories necessitated the generous cooperation of scores of people. Some did not relish the attention; others seemed glad to be asked. A great many helped me find the truth and are too numerous to name. But the following bear special thanks: Ursula Casuse, Frank Colainni, Alan Cooper, Judge Eddie DePauli, Judge Tom Donnelly, Pete Derizotis, Octavia Fellin, Jeanette Vidal Gartner, Frank Gonzales, Manuel Gonzales, Don Green, Bill Head, Harold and Nancy Husband, Mattie Jo Irwin, Steve Kennedy, Judy Kozeliski, Ed Lente, Billy Martinez, Paul McCollum, Bob and Sally Noe, John Pena, Sam Ray, Judge Joe Rich, Jack Starkovich, Ivan Stearns, Jay Vidal, Bryan Wall, Fred White, Franklin Zecca, and last but certainly not least, Peterson Zah, whose personal insight into Gallup's troubled days was invaluable.

Many writers and editors helped me shape the book; but the errors, glitches, and goblins are all mine. I sincerely appreciate the detailed edits by Judge Craig Blakey, Dave Knop, Becky Mong, Kay Kavanagh, and Bob Rosebrough, who also enlightened me with his own recollections and research as a fellow lawyer, writer, and former mayor of Gallup. The wonderful staff at the Octavia Fellin Public Library in Gallup, the New Mexico State Library and Archives in Santa Fe, and the Zimmerman Library at the University of New Mexico spent countless hours helping me document this story as did the court clerks at the McKinley County District Court in Gallup and the Bernalillo County District Court in Albuquerque. And lest I offend, I must acknowledge the Gallup High School Class of 1957 for their unfailing good grace in letting me blather on about this story over the years and especially during our class reunions from the nineties through the aughts.

As is the case with all my books, my wife read every word, repeatedly, through seemingly endless drafts and gave me equal measures of encouragement and constructive criticism. Kathleen Stuart is my editorial saint.